Rumours of Magic

Book one, of no
in the Chro

by:
L R Attridge

MAPLE
PUBLISHERS

Rumours of Magic

Author: L R Attridge

Copyright © 2024 L R Attridge

The right of L R Attridge to be identified as author of this work has been asserted by the author in accordance with section 77 and 78 of the Copyright, Designs and Patents Act 1988.

First Published in 2024

ISBN 978-1-83538-141-0 (Paperback)
     978-1-83538-142-7 (E-Book)

Book Cover Design and Book Layout by:
     White Magic Studios
     www.whitemagicstudios.co.uk

Published by:
     Maple Publishers
     Fairbourne Drive, Atterbury,
     Milton Keynes,
     MK10 9RG, UK
     www.maplepublishers.com

A CIP catalogue record for this title is available from the British Library.

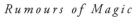

The tale of a wizard who died before his time,
and a wizard who wanted it all, but deserved nothing.

Acknowledgements

Thanks to my best and only brother, Colin Attridge, for volunteering to read my book in the first place and encouraging me to find a publisher, and for his constructive feedback on the original version.

And for Sue, Thank you for being there.

The Land of Kermells Tong

The Northern Ocean

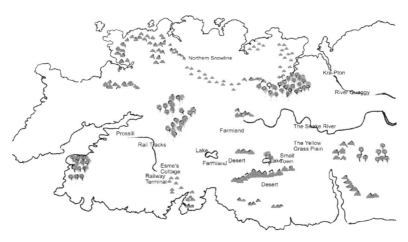

The Southern Ocean

1

No matter where you hail from in this vast and extraordinary universe, we all share, there is one thing you have in common with every other being everywhere. Death. Sorry to raise this just as you've settled down to read, but it just so happens that this story begins with Death.

Oh, and a house – or rather the memory of a house.

It's an extremely old house. There are no records of when it was built. It's not local to anyone. There are no neighbouring properties. It's not on any bus or rail routes. You can't drive there either. It's on no street anywhere, so you won't find it on a map or sat-nav. If it had a postcode or zip code it would be a string of zeros. The house is not so much on the edge of town, it's more on the edge of our minds, along with all our other fading memories. Though no less real for that. It's an ancestral memory rather than one of our own, so it never completely fades. Eventually, however, and without exception, it *will* become a memory of our own.

The house is big, dark and forbidding. There is no WELCOME on the doormat, and it would be thought cynical if there were. But in the centre of the mat, faded by millennia rather than wear, is a device resembling a pair of linked horseshoes, which on closer inspection – not that anyone would – is a depiction of an hourglass.

The skull and crossbones motif over the house's shadowy portal might give you a clue as to who lives here. And, no, it's not a notorious pirate. No-one as lightweight as that. This is the residence of the Soul Reaper Himself, and the crossed bones under the skull are in fact crossed scythes. The door knocker is a claw-like skeletal hand, which is ancient but shows little sign of wear, because almost everybody arriving here is anticipated and ushered through without ceremony. Unscheduled callers are extremely rare. But they happen.

***

There was a knock on the door. A dull thud like a lead ball hitting a stone floor. From His study at the back of the house, Death looked up from the ledger He was updating and peered down the long, panelled hallway to the front door. He looked up at the ancient clock on his study wall. A pointless exercise really, as it had no minute hand and the hour hand was stuck eternally at the eleventh hour. And it was not as if he was expecting someone who might be early or late. All Death's visitors were in a sense late, of course. He took a sip of tea, which trickled down through His hollow ribcage, and then he placed the cup back in its saucer on His desk. He stood up and stalked slowly to the door, His unshod bony feet clacking on the stone flags.

There was another thud at the door.

ALL RIGHT, I'M COMING, He called, wearily. His voice echoed mournfully through the house. He'd had a bad day, having mislaid His scythe earlier and been awkwardly late gathering some impatient souls. And now on top of that, today of all days, He gets a once-in-a-millennium caller. YES? He asked, in His best hollow tone.

'Er... want to buy some lucky white heather, Guv?' The caller was a recently deceased traveller, who hadn't quite grasped the concept of being dead yet. He took a long step back when he realised whose door he'd knocked on. He was a short, eager man, who in life would have been rosy-cheeked, but in death was pale-and-puffy cheeked.

Death considered the question. Did He need lucky white heather? White didn't score highly on His list of favourite colours, which tended to err on the dark side. Unless it was on a lily, or a shroud, of course – they were alright. But as for lucky? I DON'T THINK SO, said Death. And it struck Him that the man had a whole armful of the allegedly lucky flowers and looked like one of the least lucky people He'd ever seen. And He saw plenty in His line of work.

The traveller dejectedly lowered his heather, and turned to walk away. Death shrugged His skeletal shoulders with a loud chiropractic click, and left the heavy, studded oak door to creak itself shut slowly and loudly. He was on His way back to His desk when the traveller called out.

"'Old on a minute, Guv! I've got something that's right up your street.'

Death returned and stepped outside. He looked left and right. There was only a caravan with a large, pale grey horse standing patiently between the shafts, and as far as Death could see, everything was as it should be – black. And not a street in sight for anything to be up.

Then He heard the sounds of boxes, pots and pans being thrown about, as the traveller rummaged in the back of his caravan. Moments later, 'I've found 'em!' he shouted triumphantly, and dragged a heavy wooden chest onto the tailboard.

The Grim Reaper stalked to the man's side, curious. The traveller unlocked the chest and threw back the lid. 'Are they not the finest Life-

Timers you've ever seen?' he announced, staring into Death's empty eye-sockets. 'Everyone guaranteed to last a lifetime.' And he grinned, toothily.

Death peered in and stroked His jawbone thoughtfully. WAIT, He said. He clattered back to His study. He walked past His desk into the immense Vault of Lives beyond it. Every man, woman and child; every troll, dwarf and dragon; every beast, bird and fish – every living thing that walked, crawled, slithered, flew or swam on planet Crett, – had a Life-Timer somewhere in the Vault. Except for wizards and witches, that was, whose Timers were in His study.

HMM... He thought, looking at the banks of hourglasses of all colours, designs and sizes that lined the aisles. In the flickering torchlight that barely lit the vast area under the high vaulted ceiling, He found and pulled down the Great Ledger of the Unborn, and thumbed through it until He found what He was looking for. It was as He suspected. He was getting low on Timers designated for wizards. He slammed the book shut, setting the nearest shelves of Timers rattling, and returned to the front door.

HOW MUCH? He asked, and then wondered why. After all, what could the man possibly want money for where he was going?

The traveller grinned, hardly believing his luck. 'Five golds – *each* – and another thirty years of life.'

I'D WANT MORE THAN LIFE-TIMERS FOR A BARGAIN LIKE THAT.

After a few silent moments of stalemate, Death remembered the traveller's horse. It looked a fine animal, and it had been a while since He'd had such a luxury. His work would be easier with that. I WILL TAKE THE HORSE ALSO.

The traveller promptly agreed. 'Well,' he said, rubbing his hands together, 'where's the gold?'

AROUND THE BACK, said Death, jerking a skeletal thumb in the direction of a side gate. He immediately began counting the Life-Timers He'd been sold. Fifty-six. Then mentally He began calculating the cost. FIVE TIMES SIX IS... ER... THIRTY. THAT'S NOUGHT, CARRY THREE... UM... Before He was anywhere near working it out, the traveller was out of sight. It didn't take a lot of brains to be Death. In fact, His skull was almost as empty as a Troll's promise.

At the back of the house, bags of coins were stacked against a high stone wall. The man's eyes widened and his jaw dropped at the sight of it all. Each sack was marked with its contents. He picked up one marked 100 Gold, heaved it onto his shoulder, hobbled back to his caravan, and went back for another.

DO NOT TAKE MORE THAN YOU BARGAINED FOR, TRAVELLER! Death warned him when He saw the man heading back and looking decidedly shifty.

The traveller waved cheerily as he disappeared around the house. On this third and final visit, he considered the Grim Reaper's warning. His head said *'Don't take any more than you should'* but his heart said, *'Death surely won't miss a few golds when He's got this lot.'* He glanced around guiltily. Then, instead of removing 20 coins to bring the total down to the 280 he was due, he heaved the full sack onto his shoulder and staggered crab-like back to his caravan. He hoisted it on board and trotted hastily to the front seat.

In a vain attempt to cheat Death, he grabbed the reins and slapped the horse. The caravan shuddered, but instead of surging forwards, it plunged steeply and unexpectedly downwards. Without the horse. From where he sat, Death's house seemed to soar upwards. But whichever way he looked at it, the traveller was on his way to join his ancestors around the Great Campfire in the Beyond. Three sacks of gold drifted slowly to the piles at the back of the house.

The bemused horse stood pawing the space beneath its hooves, wondering what was next. Death patted his muzzle and led him around to the stable, making a mental note to check His ledgers to see if he was due an appointment with a stable lad in the near future.

In His study, He stood the new Life-Timers on His broad ebony desk. These were earmarked for wizards, and would go on the shelves behind His desk rather than in the Vault of Lives. He stroked each one with a practiced, ritualised movement prior to putting it in place. At His touch, the sand inside hissed softly through each Timer's waist. Names, cloudy at first, formed on the Timers' cases. Potential wizards were being born, and mystical representations of the lives before them were being etched into the glasses of the Timers by the unseen hands of The Powers That Be. Not that their futures were predestined, but without some roads before them there could be no journeys.

2

The planets Earth and Crett are near neighbours. They are both in the spiral galaxy known on Earth as the Milky Way. They are also in the same solar system. Which isn't remarkable, because planets have to be somewhere, and some are going to be near others. But what is remarkable about Earth and Crett is that the people on both worlds believe they live on the third planet from their sun. And they are both right, because their two planets are in precisely the same orbit.

Crett circles the sun six months behind Earth and six months ahead of it. So, the two worlds are always obscured from each other on opposite sides of the sun, and Crettlings and Earthlings are likely to remain forever unaware one another. And if one day they do discover one another, they will both realise how lucky they had been until then.

The evolution of life on Crett, following the Huge Thump they believe set the universe in motion, was, according to their evolutionary biologists, shaped by some appallingly unnatural selection, and characterised chiefly by the survival of the genuinely baffled. And as a world always behind and in front of Earth, it is both curiously bygone and familiar.

Sharing the Goldilocks zone with Earth, Crett has a similar ecology. Seen from near space, it has its share of green forests, brown deserts and vast blue seas. If you're familiar with Earth, then you'd feel at home on Crett. Though there have been developments among Crett's flora and fauna that might surprise you. Some of its inhabitants might surprise you, too, especially the trolls, dwarves and demons – and especially on a dark night. Though, to be fair, on a dark night you'd want to avoid some of Crett's human population, too. Which is something else that would make you feel at home if you are familiar with Earth.

It's been said of the people of Crett that they can try the patience of a brick. Not all of them, of course, but enough to make the generalisation valid. A high proportion of its peoples dwell directly below the northern snowline in a region called Kermells Tong, the capital city of which is the sprawling metropolis of Kra-Pton. Nobody remembers why it was called this, but it probably was, and from a great height.

Kra-Pton's proud boast is the University of Havrapsor, an ancient seat of learning housed in a rambling building of cloisters, courtyards, archways and towers, some of which defy architectural and engineering logic.

Kra-Pton's shame is the rancid River Quaggy, which doesn't flow unless it has rained heavily for days, and is more of an open sewer than a river.

Crett has been slow to move on from an Arthurian age. But now it was leapfrogging several ages and moving into its first industrial revolution. It was not so much a time of sword and sorcery, but more a time of magic and machinery, though with plenty of swords still around.

Havrapsor University is a repository of mostly magical knowledge. Wizards live and work there, passing on spells and skills to successive generations. But of late, the place has been in decline. The university had once been every academician's dream palace of learning. It had been renowned and respectable. Its staff and students were an example to all, and it had been responsible for some of the brightest minds on Crett. But times were changing.

By the sheer momentum of what it had once been, the university retained a measure of its former glory. But there was now laxity among students and staff alike. And as with all such institutions, much depends on the quality of the leadership. At Havrapsor the most senior wizard was the Archchancellor, the quality of whose leadership had seriously deteriorated in recent years. As, indeed, had the man himself. These two things were connected, as we shall see. We shall also see that matters would get far worse before they got better.

✳✳✳

Many grains of sand dug from the unsafe Beach of Time have now passed through the narrow waists of the Life-Timers that Death obtained on that day the traveller called, and the life stories etched into the glasses are now following their destinies, more or less.

3

Death heard an alarm screeching from the shelves of Life-Timers behind the desk. These belonged to wizards and witches, who required his personal attendance at their passing over, so Death kept them close by, and had them alarmed. Not that He anticipated problems. He just liked a bit of magical gadgetry. He located the errant Timer and plucked it off the shelf to read the name:

Wimlett Tregrus.

DAMN! He cursed. IT'S STOPPED.

Some grains of sand were wedged in the waist, stopping the flow. This was unheard of. Death supposed it meant that Wimlett must be dead. But all the while there was sand at the top of the Timer, he still had some unlived life, so technically he could not be dead.

There was only one thing for it. He banged the Timer on His desk.

Wimlett Tregrus was more than just a wizard. He was the Archchancellor of Havrapsor University. Which might not have been the top job in the Land of Kermells Tong, but it was potentially the most powerful. He had access to some extremely potent magic, and had the ability to use it.

His position made him the keeper of Eldrum's Drum, a powerful ancient artefact that was one of the symbols of his office. In appearance, the Drum was very like one you might see at the head of a parade. In reality, it was a trans-dimensional storehouse of spells. Over the centuries since the university's foundation, the Drum had accumulated a wealth of rare and sometimes unstable magic. It was customary for each Archchancellor to lodge their personal and most powerful spells in the Drum on the day they died. Not that there was anything significant about the timing: it was typically because they'd meant to do it sooner, but rarely got around to it until it was almost too late.

**

Death slammed Archchancellor Wimlett's Life-Timer onto His desk for a second time. Old wizard Wimlett felt queasy and disoriented when He did this. But he felt no immediate urge to put his magical and personal affairs in order. Consigning his spells to the Drum could wait, he was sure.

He was getting on in years but he was fairly certain he wasn't about to die. He had another more pressing problem.

Living.

<hr>

4

Another grey dawn seeped over the dullish green, ice-capped mountains of Kermells Tong, just as it had yesterday, and, if everything went well, would again tomorrow. The sun, at first looking like a lightly poached egg, rose from behind a tall peak and slowly turned into a bright, golden ball.

All around the city of Kra-Pton the creatures and characters of the night were slinking home. Muggings and robberies would cease until the sun dipped again. The officers of the Watch – the city's law enforcement body – began their day searching the alleys and gutters for missing comrades and other victims of the crimes that took place in the night city.

The sun climbed lethargically, its harsh light hitting the city's roads, contrasting them sharply with the shadowy side streets and alleyways. Its warmth dried the pavements and dirt roads, and the night mists that always clung to everything, began to evaporate into the air in curling wisps.

Inside the weathered stone walls of Havrapsor University, those who were young and active rushed about drawing curtains and closing shutters to keep the sunlight from penetrating the gloomy, mysterious halls, and causing damage to the ancient upholstery and carpets. It was a task repeated periodically throughout the day as the sun moved around the building.

The resident academics were happy enough with closed curtains. They preferred the softer light of candles, especially on the mornings they returned after a heavy night sampling the juices of some of the more exotic vegetables being distilled down at the Piggin Wissall. This was the nearest tavern to the university. Early most mornings, somewhere between the university and the Piggin Wissall, a few wizards could be seen heading back. They'd be keeping to the shadows because the university had thoughtlessly been built east of the tavern, and the slanting sunlight hurt their eyes.

Sometimes, some of the younger wizards would be limping home, rubbing their elbows and silently cursing the magic carpets rolled up under their arms. But these walking wounded were the lucky ones. Every now and then a young wizard would be killed while flying home with his carpet on autopilot, having dozed off in mid-flight without having issued the all-important command mentioned on page 3 of the User Guide:

Warning: Avoid tall upright hazards, such as buildings and trees. These can seriously damage your carpet and/or you.

Also please note that if you have purchased an older or cheaper model (Anything older or cheaper than a Magicarp Swoop 7) it may not be fitted with topographical awareness in the autopilot, and you will need to add the vocal command 'Avoid obstacles' when giving the 'Autopilot on' command. Good luck.

Most if not all of the students had carpets from the threadbare range, considerably older and cheaper than a Magicarp Swoop 7. This was also true of many of the university's staff.

Archchancellor Wimlett frequented the Piggin Wissall, as did most of the wizarding fraternity. And being a fair-minded Archchancellor, he made sure he was always the last to leave the tavern. That way, none of the other wizards was ever caught being late. He preferred to walk home rather than risk a carpet. Usually there was a greater risk from walking the night streets than flying over them. But the gangs that prowled the locality at night knew better than to provoke a defensive magical outburst from the inebriated Archchancellor. Even brawling with trolls was preferable to that.

5

Death steepled His fingers and stared eyelessly across His desk. FANCY ANOTHER? He asked.

'I'll get them,' replied His colleague. 'Same again?'

YES, said Death. MAKE IT A DOUBLE. OH, AND BRING ONE OF THOSE ORANGES WITH THE BITS OF CHEESE ON STICKS STUCK IN IT. AND MORE PEANUTS. I LIKE PEANUTS.

Naphrat the Gaunt, Death's equally skeletal right-hand helper, clattered back to the desk and unloaded his tray.

THE REASON I'VE ASKED YOU OVER, NAPHRAT, IS, WELL... I HAVE SOMETHING IMPORTANT TO TELL YOU. I'M GOING TO TAKE A BREAK. TO BE HONEST, I'VE HAD ENOUGH, He said, carefully prising a cube of cheese on a stick out of an orange. He'd pricked a finger on one of these pointy sticks before. It hurt. And who'd have thought they were sharp enough to prick bone?

As Naphrat took his seat and sipped his drink, he contemplated this strange news. It didn't bode well, that much was clear. 'What exactly do you mean, Master?' he asked cautiously.

I REALLY DO NEED A BREAK, said Death. IT'S BEEN AN ETERNITY SINCE I HAD ONE.

Naphrat weighed His words. He was struggling with the idea. *Death take a break? How long? Where?* And more crucially, *who would take over?* 'But Master, nobody reaps like you.'

MY MIND'S MADE UP, Death said, gazing out of His study window into the distant scenic blackness beyond, that He liked to admire.

'I suppose I could take over for a while,' Naphrat suggested, tentatively, hardly believing what he could hear himself saying. But thinking it would be preferable to having to work for someone new. 'I wouldn't mind... you know, just for a *short* time.'

Naphrat had acquired a lot of experience over the years, but he was still just a lowly helper. He wasn't thinking that Death would actually let him take the reins. Or, if he did – and perish the thought, that He would take him up on his rash offer – He wouldn't leave him doing it for any longer than was absolutely necessary.

Naphrat had unwittingly achieved exactly what Death was fishing for. The Grim Reaper preferred others to help out voluntarily rather than be asked. Then if things went wrong there was absolutely no doubt where the blame rested. And it was so much pleasanter chastising others when they knew they deserved it.

I'M GLAD YOU THINK YOU CAN HANDLE IT, NAPH. THANK YOU. Death leaned back in His chair, contentedly clasping His hands across His lower ribcage and nodding His skull appreciatively. His helper sat opposite looking a little dazed.

Four days later, Naphrat was sitting at the big ebony desk in Death's study reading a postcard.

DEAR NAPH,
I THINK THIS MUST BE THE HAPPINESS
THAT THE LIVING TALK ABOUT.
REGARDS
D.

A couple of days later, Naphrat received another card, bearing unbelievably bad news. He read it slowly, and then read it again.

HELLO, NAPH. I'VE DECIDED TO STAY.
I'VE BOUGHT A TAVERN.
THE JOB'S YOURS.
LOOK AFTER THE HORSE.
D.

Death rarely joked, especially about His work. And Naphrat was less than amused. He felt he'd been lumbered, cornered into doing something he was not sure he was capable of. He was feeling a little scared, too.

But after an hour or so's thought, he reasoned that, well, someone had to do it. And who else was there? Where do you find another Death at short notice? He stared down the long hallway towards the front door where Death had departed less than a week ago. *We can't have lost souls wandering about not knowing where to go,* he thought. *Yes, it's a worthwhile job. And it can't be that difficult or I wouldn't be the one left to do it.* That settled it. He leaned back, Death-like, in the big chair. *Should I call myself Death now?* He wondered, savouring the idea briefly. *Better not push my luck,* he decided. He'd worked with Death long enough to know that His decisions, unlike His reapings, were revocable.

He spun Death's chair around and surveyed the rows of Life-Timers that lined the wall behind. Could he handle all this? He hardly dared to think about the hundreds of thousands of Timers that filled the Vault behind the study – the entire population of Crett. Suddenly he felt cold. Colder than normal, that was.

The chill came not from contemplating the Vault; it came from an alarm that was blaring close by. He was new to this – what should he do? *Damn it!* A Timer was malfunctioning. It was on the racks behind the desk. He could see which one because it pulsed.

He stretched out a calcareous finger and hooked it down. It had stopped but there was still sand at the top. How could that happen? He turned it around and read the name. 'Hmm... a high wizard,' he murmured, and banged it on the desk a couple of times to dislodge the grains in the Timer's waist.

***

This periodical thumping of the Timer was beginning to have a serious effect on wizard Wimlett's life now that it was happening more regularly. Sometimes his future was arriving in the wrong order, and occasionally, after a really violent shake, episodes from his past were happening all over again, when a grain of sand that had already gone through went around again. He wouldn't have minded so much if it were just the better episodes. His timeline was getting more jumbled and juddering by the week.

He was spilling his drinks now, too, which was seriously annoying, as drink wasn't cheap. However, he still managed to get drunk. But the roller-coaster of his timeline was very tiring, and would have been for a man half his age. He couldn't manage the all-night sessions so often now. This saddened the old mage, as he liked to get pleasantly drunk over a longish period. He would take a night out now and then, if he felt up to it, but would come back earlier. He would speed up his inebriation with a little applied magic, increasing the potency of his drinks and his susceptibility to them.

Compressing his inebriation was less enjoyable, though. And he knew that other wizards were spending a lot of time and the university's resources trying to work out what spell he was using. It could save them a fortune. Whatever Wimlett had discovered, it was working out a lot less expensive than anything they'd come up with so far.

The old Archchancellor knew full well things were going from bad to worse at the university. He was losing his grip, but he was no fool. He began to suspect that bad magic was responsible, because he was unable to get either his own life or the life of the university back on track. His personal confusion was affecting the entire establishment. Such were the hitherto unknown repercussions of a seriously faulty Life-Timer.

6

Wimlett had cut quite a dash in his younger days. He had been a wizard to admire in both appearance and academic achievements. He'd managed to embody all that was traditional in magic circles, while pushing the boundaries. It was inevitable that he should rise to the Archchancellorship at Havrapsor. When he walked the cloisters and corridors of the university the deferential nods from students and masters alike were genuinely felt, never mere formality.

His regal blue robe was always creaseless, of a smarter cut than other wizards', and it hung well on his tall, lean frame. The burgundy sash at his waist was always perfect in length and fastening. Outside, he was never seen without his broad-brimmed, conical hat – in matching regal blue with a gold band around it and gold moons and stars decorating it. His curly-toed slippers were always in good repair, and more importantly, never heard to scuff the floors as he walked. Wimlett wasn't critical by nature, but scuffing floors was something he disliked in other wizards, along with tapping their staff on the ground as they walked. He viewed such practices as slovenly and said that they let the place down. As a younger man, he always carried his staff at a proper angle, never tapping or swinging it, and in a grip that revealed his ornate ring and seal of office.

He had the open face and affable manner of a man to be trusted. In those days he had a neatly trimmed beard, too, which was a departure from the straggly and overgrown bushes that were common then. It was copied by many. In homage to one of his predecessors, he waxed his moustache into a handlebar. Which was not copied so much. His eyes were deep-set, sky blue, and could be unnervingly penetrating. Unlike many things about him, those eyes never lost their lustre as he aged.

But Wimlett's nose was unquestionably his finest and most distinguishing feature. It was large and slightly hooked, aquiline, and supremely wizardly. Though with age it grew into more the kind that a witch might envy.

There was once a lot to admire about Professor Wimlett Tregrus, Archchancellor of Havrapsor University. But not so much nowadays. Now in his seventies, his hair and beard had turned white and wispy, the handlebar moustache was waxed not nearly so neatly, and his face was creased and leathery. If it were not for the attentions of the university's launderers his aging robes would be similarly creased. Like many an older man, he felt comfortable in his old clothes and had no desire to replace them.

To his dismay, he was likely to scuff the ground with his curly-toed slippers, and he felt it wouldn't be long before he was tapping the ground with his staff, using it as a walking aid as he shuffled around campus. Worse still, whenever he became animated or drunk, lightning strikes from latent spells would flash haphazardly from his fingertips.

But Wimlett remained in many respects the wise and genial wizard he'd always been. He still had the respect of many of his peers. Though that pool was shrinking as he became less and less competent, and more often disoriented by the defective Life-Timer in Death's study. Unrest was growing in the hallowed halls. Some senior staff were beginning to feel it was time for a change at the top. And chief among them was an ambitious and scheming wizard named Dennis. He was doing all he could to exploit the situation.

It played right into Dennis's hands when Wimlett's magical powers began firing off accidentally, frequently and dangerously. It started mildly and even amusingly, but it soon ceased to be a joke. Especially among the customers at the Piggin Wissall. Whenever Wimlett had too much magically enhanced alcohol, disaster would strike. At one time, if you were to approach any of the toads, newts or ducks around the pond on the green opposite the tavern, most would croak or quack, but some would complain bitterly, 'I'm a wizard!'

Annoyingly for Dennis, but fortunately for some unintentional toads, newts and ducks, the effects of Wimlett's rogue magic slowly diminished to the point where they wore off after a couple of hours. Some wizards speculated that the Archchancellor's staff, which was a powerful artefact like the Drum, was responsible for this, intervening with some damage control for its owner. Things noticeably improved whenever Wimlett took his staff to help steady himself.

Dennis, to get back to him, was one of the senior staff at the university. He'd wheedled his way into the upper ranks by being ruthlessly smarmy. It helped, too, that his smarminess masked an almost total indifference to the feelings of others. He'd long had ambitions to be Archchancellor, hence his chronic dislike for Wimlett. In his mid-forties, Dennis was young for a senior wizard, and by his own assertion, quite handsome. His thin moustache and thick hair were blonde and neatly trimmed. His cloak was a little flashier than most others, as was his manner. He was frequently referred to as 'someone you wouldn't buy a second-hand cart from'. Compared with Wimlett at the same age, he was his polar opposite.

Dennis never frequented the Piggin Wissall, affecting to disdain the place, but spent most of his spare time in the back rooms of the university's Library Tower, studying the rare collections of spell books, and secretly plotting Wimlett's downfall. His tenacity paid off, and many useful and even harmful spells were now locked in his mind, and could be cast with a wave of his hand, or a snap of his fingers. He was not a wizard to be messed with. And soon, he thought, he would achieve his ambition of becoming Archchancellor. Though his ambition went far beyond ousting Wimlett and running a mere university.

Wimlett wouldn't last much longer. Dennis would see to that. But he was too clever and crafty to try to overthrow Wimlett on his own. Wimlett might have been losing it, but he was still a powerful wizard. He possessed Eldrum's Drum and the staff of office. Dennis had to tread carefully. Much as he disliked socialising, he knew his best course of action would be to involve others in his plans. To *use* others, more like. He hoped to reap the rewards, while getting others blamed for whatever happened to Wimlett in the process.

Dennis had noted a few wizards who might follow him. He'd heard rumblings of discontent in the Great Hall, and knew some bore Wimlett longstanding grudges, and he'd encouraged them. He'd learned that even the most agreeable of people could be made to seem disagreeable over time and with the right kind of gossip. So, on a day when he felt he'd left things simmering long enough, he invited some of the malcontents to his rooms to discuss the situation.

7

Later that same night, a small group of wizards crept stealthily along a narrow stone-walled passageway on the first floor of the residential wing of Havrapsor University.

'Which loom did he say?' asked Cho Kin, squinting, trying to read the room numbers in the flickering torchlight. Cho was a wiry wizard from the Eastern Kingdoms who was at Havrapsor on a student exchange programme. He addressed his question to Rumpitt-cum-Slowly, a senior lecturer, the oldest and tallest member of the group. Rumpitt had an almost permanent frown and a tendency to whinge, which meant that Cho, who was generally upbeat, didn't get on too well with him. They rubbed each other up the wrong way. And knowing how much it irritated Rumpitt, Cho took great delight in mispronouncing words whenever he was around him.

'Loom?' repeated Rumpitt. 'I haven't ever seen a loom up here.'

'I think he means room,' said Pelgrum, another senior staff member, a short wizard, but very round, probably as tall lying down as he was standing up. He added, 'And I think he's winding you up.'

'Wouldn't you think he'd been here long enough now to speak properly?' Rumpitt argued, ignoring Pelgrum.

'Two months isn't that long really, Rumpitt,' said Pelgrum, in Cho's defence.

'Fink you long, there,' Cho interrupted, mischievously. 'Flee month's plobabry nearer.'

Rumpitt looked up at the ceiling and rolled his eyes. 'Anyone bring a phrase book?'

'I make sense, don't I, Pelglum?' Cho pleaded, knowing he had an ally in the round man.

'Of course you do, Cho. He's just being awkward. Though he doesn't hear very well, as you know.' He tried to be the peacemaker, but was thinking all the while that they were as bad as each other.

'Leave me out of the conversation in future,' snapped Rumpitt. 'And if he calls me Lumpitt again, there's going to be trouble. Okay?'

'Yeah?' retorted Cho, archly.

'Yeah!' said Rumpitt, needlessly standing on tiptoe.

'Yeah...' Cho repeated. 'Let's see what kind of trouble you got.' He took up a stance that showed he knew nothing about martial arts, and let out some supposedly threatening shouts while weaving his flattened palms at various angles in front of him.

The conspirators hadn't realised it, but they had arrived at their destination. Stumbled upon it, more like.

Dennis wrenched open his door to see what all the noise was. He studied each of them briefly. 'It's about time,' he sneered. 'I've been waiting ages for you people.'

'Er... sorry, Dennis,' said Pelgrum, lamely. 'We forgot which rooms you said.'

'*My* rooms,' said Dennis. 'How difficult was that? Now come in and be quiet, or you'll rouse the curiosity of the neighbours.'

Rumpitt's hearing was intermittent, and he wasn't using his hearing trumpet because he couldn't always be bothered. 'Er, I'll get them, shall I?' he asked.

'What? Who?' said Dennis, impatiently.

'The neighbours,' replied Rumpitt, loudly. 'No point starting till we're all here.'

'Have I missed something?' asked Dennis, turning to Pelgrum.

Pelgrum looked around. 'I don't think so, Dennis.'

Dennis looked back at Rumpitt. 'Where's his hearing aid?'

Pelgrum reached cautiously into Rumpitt's robe – not a thing one should do lightly to any wizard – and pulled out a rather ornate horn, ivory with gold inlaid swirls, which he thrust into Rumpitt's hand. 'Here, put this in.'

Rumpitt twiddled with the end and put it to his ear.

'Better?'

'Pardon?'

Pelgrum snatched it back, removed the cap from the narrow end, and then gently guided the older wizard's hand back to his ear with it. 'Why do you keep turning it off like that?'

'Can't stand Cho's voice!' he snapped. 'So, if he doesn't shut up... it goes off again. All right?'

Dennis sighed. 'Close the door, Pelgrum. If we don't get started soon, it'll be dawn.'

'Anywhere?' asked Rumpitt, pointing at the few chairs in the room.

Dennis ignored him. They all found seats in a musical-chairs manner, after which Dennis stood glaring, waiting for them to settle.

There was a knock on the door. The last of the conspirators had arrived. Dennis huffed, shook his head, and went to let him in.

It was Maddlin, another small man, who, unusually for a teaching wizard, was clean shaven. He was also quite bald on top, had a small pug nose and flat ears, and according to his students his head resembled a pale football. He appeared to be wearing spectacles, but had dark rings around his eyes from many sleepless nights. He worried a lot. And there was always a lot to worry about if you had a nose for it, even a small one. He was known for being a great listener, and not saying much – which was not a good combination in a lecturer. His usual tactic was to initiate a discussion and leave the students to it while he caught up on sleep.

The rest of the group knew he wouldn't be contributing much. Dennis wondered aloud why he'd even bothered to join them, and why he looked even more bleary-eyed than usual.

Pelgrum got up and whispered in Dennis's ear. 'He never did sleep well, poor chap. But it's been worse since he had his bad experience with Wimlett down at the Piggin Wissall a week ago. He spent a couple of hours as a toad. That wore off only just in time for him to be turned into a duck.'

Dennis didn't really want to know, and wished he hadn't asked, but at least he now remembered why Maddlin was there.

'Oi!' called Rumpitt. 'Are we having this meeting or not? Only I did come here specially. I do have other places to go.'

'Oh, yeah, rike what?' taunted Cho. 'You got nowhere else to go, old man.'

'Old man?' Rumpitt repeated, rising from his chair, his face reddening.

Dennis cleared his throat loudly and meaningfully, and glared at them, daring either of them to say another word.

Rumpitt sat down again. Cho smiled to himself, although not inscrutably.

Dennis went into his bedroom and returned with a chair. He banged it down heavily in front of himself the reverse way around, and sat down with his legs astride it. There was a knock on the floor from the room below, and a voice shouted something obscene about the noise level 'up there at this time of night.' He ignored it, and stared stony-faced at his guests. At length, he stood up. 'Now you're all here *at last...*' he said, getting that off his chest, 'I've asked you here tonight to talk about the Archchancellor...'

'Why? What have you heard?' said Rumpitt in a hushed voice, peering about him. The others craned forward.

'Nothing!' snapped Dennis. 'Will you let me finish?' He looked from face to face. 'The Archchancellor. What are we going to do about him? Because *something* needs to be done. And the sooner the better.' He paused, waiting for at least one of them to reply now that they had a legitimate opportunity to speak. Instead, they looked from one to another for a long moment, and then...

'Do you mean what I think you mean?' said Maddlin, surprising everyone.

Dennis smirked, thinly. The others noted this look, and they all thought in unison that they wouldn't buy a second-hand cart from him.

'What do you think he means?' said Pelgrum, turning to Maddlin.

'Yeah,' said Rumpitt. 'What do you think he means?'

Cho took a deep breath. 'I think I know what you think he means,' he began.

'You think you do?' said Maddlin, rubbing his bare chin, and beginning to wonder if he knew himself what he thought he meant.

Coming to the boil, Dennis sprang to his feet and cut in, 'I know what I think! I think I'm losing the will to live! If only we were on the fourth floor I think I could cheerfully throw myself out of the window right now! Or better still, you lot.'

'Did he just suggest we throw Archchancellor Wimlett out of a window?' protested Maddlin, diffidently. 'We can't do that. It's... it's... well, it's not, you know...'

The others hung on his words, waiting for him to complete his thought.

'... wizardly.'

'Please pay attention,' sighed Dennis. 'I've asked you all here tonight...' his voice trailed off.

'I was paying attention, wasn't I, Cho?' Maddlin whispered, none too quietly.

'I'm sure *I* was,' griped Rumpitt.

'Shut up, shut up!' stormed Dennis. 'Please.'

They all froze. He was more threatening when trying to be polite.

He watched them for a moment, daring any of them to start up again. The silence remained intact. He mused briefly that, if it wasn't so expensive, or unsporting, he'd hire an assassin to do what he had in mind. Then, after he'd removed Wimlett, he could deal with this lot.

'Now! Are you quite ready? As I said, I have asked you here to discuss the Archchancellor. We need to do something about him...'

'Yeah... he turned me into a labbitt, once,' said Cho, nodding vigorously.

'A labbitt?' sneered Rumpitt. 'What the hell's a labbitt?'

'You know...' said Pelgrum. 'Little furry bugger, long ears, jumps about a bit. Nice in a pie.' The little round man patted his stomach.

'He a menace. Got to go,' snapped Cho, smacking his fist into the palm of his hand, rousing Maddlin, who was starting to drift off.

'Absolutely,' Maddlin managed before is eyelids drooped.

'Yeah. I never did like the man that much,' Rumpitt chimed in. 'Always far too tolerant and pleasant for a man in his position. You can't trust a man who smiles that much. Has to be up to something. Give me a man with a good honest scowl any day.'

Dennis took a long breath and sighed deeply. 'Do I take it then, that we are all agreed? Wimlett has become a liability to this noble institution, and he should be asked to stand down? Forced to, if necessary.'

He let his words sink in. A couple of heads nodded slowly.

'Well?' he prompted.

'He can't just do that,' said Maddlin, for some reason raising a hand. He lowered it to stifle a yawn.

For someone who didn't say much, he was being irritatingly vocal tonight, thought Dennis.

Maddlin explained himself. 'Wimlett was elected. By university rules he can't be unelected without a majority vote from the senior staff. Or... or...'

They all hung on.

'Or it's got to come from him. He's got to say something like... I don't want to do this anymore.' He gave this a moment's thought, then added, whether whimsically or not, no-one could be sure, 'Or... we could poison him, I suppose.'

'Well, I can't see him just giving it up,' said Rumpitt. 'Nobody's ever done that.'

'We could try to embarrass him into it?' suggested Pelgrum. 'That would be a much more wizardly thing to do.'

'That a good idea,' agreed Cho. 'We *shame* him into going.'

'I know someone who would break both his legs, for the right price,' muttered Maddlin, still riding his tangential train of thought, his pale round face giving nothing away.

Before interrupting their brainstorming session, Dennis made a mental note to find out, if he really meant it, who it was, and how much. 'No,' he said, 'I think embarrassment is best. I like that idea. I like it a lot. Any thoughts on how we might do it?'

'No.'

'No.'

'No.'

'Er... no,' said Maddlin eventually. 'He's never done a disreputable thing in all the years I've known him.'

'There must be some way we can catch him out,' said Dennis, almost salivating at the thought. 'We'll have to watch him. See what he gets up to. Then pounce when he's not expecting it.' A smirk hung on his face as he imagined a thoroughly discredited and shamed Wimlett, head hung low, slouching off into obscurity.

'Er... excuse me.'

'Yes?' said Dennis, returning Pelgrum's quizzical look. 'You've thought of something?'

'If Wimlett does stand down, who will then be Archchancellor?'

Dennis straightened himself up, and smoothed down the folds in his robe. 'Why... me, of course.' And he grinned, almost charmingly.

'Oh.'

'Is that a problem?' he asked, fixing them with a look that didn't leave them in any doubt as to how this awkward silence should be resolved.

'Not especially,' said Maddlin, unsurely.

Rumpitt just shook his head.

Pelgrum and Cho whispered their agreement, choking on it a little.

'Good,' said Dennis. 'That's settled then. Now, off you go. We'll meet here again tomorrow evening. That should give us time to think about how we might go about this. And we can sort out the details before we make our move. So, same time, same place.'

The wizards muttered their assent and got up. They'd had enough for one evening, anyway. As they filed out of the room, Dennis gave each of them a weak half smile, a grudging 'thanks for coming' and an almost imperceptible nod. Then he called after them, 'And don't be late this time!'

The door clicked shut and they shuffled down the passageway, mouthing obscenities as they went, and making gestures towards the door that weren't wizardly.

8

When, on occasions, Wimlett grew tired of the company of wizards, he would hitch Muffin, his faithful donkey, to his little two wheeled cart – a somewhat rickety mode of transport, but it suited Wimlett's needs – and he would take a slow drive to the Flying Unicorn, a tavern a couple of miles out of town.

This wouldn't have been a wise thing for any normal individual to do of a late evening, but Wimlett, being Archchancellor – a *wizard* among wizards, as it were – was not considered normal. Though not in an unkind way; it was simply a matter of fact. The other patrons were usually pleased to see him. As was the landlord, even though Wimlett spent less money these days and unaccountably became drunk in less time. *Magic of some sort*, he guessed, ruefully. He'd asked around to see if there was such a thing as a magic blocker or disrupter he could hide somewhere in the bar. But those in the know would shake their head and suck in air loudly through their teeth. 'Could be dangerous,' they'd say.

In the main, the clientele at the Flying Unicorn was a mix of trolls and dwarves. The relationship between the two species was often strained. Usually because a troll accidentally trod on a dwarf. Not a rare event with dwarfs so small and trolls so big and clumsy. Following such an event, the landlord would admit them only on alternate nights for a few weeks until both parties cooled down.

Wimlett preferred to drink with the dwarves. They made him feel tall again, because he'd developed a bit of a stoop. And they were always such happy little fellows, singing their mining songs, usually about gold, quaffing their ale and occasionally fighting. He liked them because they were always happy to include him in their merriment and leave him out of their fighting. Though even their fighting was done in good humour when among themselves.

By contrast, the trolls were quiet and sombre. They would watch in a brooding silence as Wimlett drank himself under the table. He would then lay there singing wizarding songs at the top of his voice until the trolls could bear it no longer and threw him out.

Generally, around midnight, when the landlord had plucked up the courage to call time. The trolls would drain their jugs and file out in an orderly manner, and with a somewhat rolling gait. And if Wimlett was sleeping it off on the pavement outside, one of them would gather him up and dump him back in his cart. It was said of trolls, that they hadn't climbed the evolutionary ladder, but had unluckily walked under it. But they sometimes confounded their critics with an altruistic deed or two – usually after a few drinks, which tended to soften them rather than make them aggressive. Having put Wimlett in the cart, the troll would pat Muffin's rump to get him moving. The donkey would then turn around and take a slow walk home. Once there, he would wait outside the Archchancellor's smallish, stipendiary house until one of the wizards chanced by and carried him inside.

Dennis had noticed this pattern. He saw, too, how he could use it to bring about Wimlett's downfall.

⚜

9

The second meeting of the conspirators was due to start. Dennis heard them arguing outside his door and yanked it open. 'Come in and sit down,' he said, hurrying them along. 'I have a plan.' He glanced around outside after the last member of the quartet had gone in and closed the door quietly.

Cho, Pelgrum and Maddlin found their seats straight away, but Rumpitt went straight to the fire, lifted his robe and toasted the backs of his legs. 'Brrr... it's chilly out there tonight.'

'What are you doing?' said Dennis, already unsure his temper would stand another meeting.

Rumpitt pretended not to hear. He needed a few more seconds' precious warmth. That done, he looked up and acted as though he'd just realised Dennis was talking to him. 'Oh... me? I was just warming the hole of my body,' he said, to his own amusement.

'Sit down,' snapped Dennis, 'while I tell you what we're going to do. Then, you can go and stand in front of your own fire.'

'It's all right for you, Dennis,' returned Rumpitt. 'But when this meeting's over, I still have to go out there, through the cold night. It might be raining by then. Or snowing. Or blowing a gale. Or worse.' And when these plaintively delivered concerns were met with an impatient silence, he stepped in with the other foot. 'What about coming over to my place for a change?'

'Yes...' agreed Cho, readily, thinking how grumpy Rumpitt would be if they did all troop over to his rooms for a meeting.

Rumpitt only smiled.

'What about *my* rooms?' muttered Pelgrum. 'Eh? What's wrong with my rooms?'

'I don't think so,' said Rumpitt, letting him down ungently. 'You have the smallest rooms on the block, and with you in there, there wouldn't be room for the rest of us.'

The little round man grunted something.

'You not tork to 'im rike that!' snapped Cho, springing to his defence and rising from his chair to take up his less than convincing karate stance.

Rumpitt stood up and raised his staff, waiting for the smaller man to bow his head. *Then, I'll have you, you little bugger*, he thought.

'Shut up, **shut up**, SHUT UP!' screamed Dennis. There was a muffled complaint from the room below, and the occupant banged on his ceiling with a broom handle. Dennis stamped a tattoo on the floor in reply, stormed across to the front door and screamed abuse down the stairway. Rumpitt was thinking that Dennis didn't seem so bothered about attracting the attention of the neighbours tonight, but decided not to say so.

Dennis came inside and slammed the door. 'Now listen, you people,' he said, icily. 'We are here to plan Wimlett's downfall. And, in order to get the magical upper hand, I suggest we also work out how to get his Drum of office away from him. His staff, too, if possible. We need him weaker.' He paused for a moment, glaring from face to face. 'So... if you all want to keep your jobs when I'm Archchancellor, you'd better start paying proper attention to the matter in hand. Or else.' He paused again to let the threat sink in. But pausing in this company was never a good idea.

'Or else *what*?' asked Maddlin, not by way of a counter threat, but seeking clarification. His students had kept him awake half the afternoon with thoughtless questions about their coursework, and he was already drifting.

Dennis raised his hands abruptly and red fire shot from his fingertips, incinerating the small table next to Maddlin. 'Or else that!' Dennis spat out the words.

Maddlin's yelp was followed by a moment of stunned silence from the others.

'Bit bloody silly, isn't it?' Rumpitt muttered. 'Setting fire to a harmless table.'

'It was going to be *him*!' shouted Dennis, waving a finger at Maddlin – they all ducked instinctively – 'but I changed my mind!'

'You can't do that,' said Pelgrum. 'Wizards don't go around using hostile magic against one another. Not outside a formally regulated and supervised duel. It's far too dangerous.'

'Why ever not?' asked Dennis, who was rumoured to have flouted that rule on a number of occasions. 'He was asking for it!'

'I didn't hear 'im,' said Rumpitt, rashly trying to be clever.

'That's cos you fink you're deaf,' said Cho in impeccably irritating mock Eastern.

'What?'

'That's cos you... oh, velly funny.'

'It's just not wizardly,' stated Pelgrum, trying to be firm, but sounding sulky instead. 'That's why not.'

Dennis counted to ten. *What an absolute shower*, he thought. *No wonder Wimlett always has the upper hand around here.* 'Either listen or go home. Now.'

The wizards fell silent. Dennis moved another small table in front of them and stood behind it, fixing them with a menacing stare until he was sure he had their attention. Then he began.

'I have asked... *now what*?' A hand was up.

'Do you think I could open a window, er, just a tad?' asked Pelgrum, timidly indicating the size of the tad with his finger and thumb. 'Er... just to let some of the smoke out, that is.' His eyes were smarting and he was blinking frantically, which helped make his point.

Dennis eyed the smouldering table. 'Right. Stay there. I'll see to it.' He motioned with his hands and muttered something arcane. The window obligingly slid down a little, allowing a cold draught into the room. Rumpitt surreptitiously slid his chair nearer the fire. Dennis caught sight of the movement.

But before he could say anything, Rumpitt asked, 'Well? What's this plan of yours, Dennis? We might as well hear it now we're here.'

Dennis smiled thinly, sat down astride his reversed chair, and rested his forearms on the chair-back. 'It's quite simple, really...'

⸺◈◁▷◈⸺

10

The plan was put into action three nights later – on the very next evening, in fact, that Wimlett's old donkey and cart were spotted trundling out of the university gates with him holding the limp reigns. Muffin knew exactly where they were going.

True to form, Wimlett was ejected from the Flying Unicorn about four hours later. He exited through the same window as usual. Creatures of habit, trolls. The landlord now left that window open whenever Wimlett called. The old mage's protective magic had opened the window for him a couple of times, but the landlord didn't like to rely on it.

Wimlett lay in the gutter and waited for a kindly troll to find him at closing time.

Sure enough, about an hour later a couple of trolls rolled out of the bar. One was about to tread on him, but Wimlett managed to call out to attract their attention. The trolls, drunk as they were, knew the drill. They lifted him effortlessly into his cart, turned the donkey around and sent him off home.

***

'Here he comes, now,' hissed Dennis.

The other three wizards, and student Cho, slunk quietly out of sight and waited in the shadows by Wimlett's modest house on the campus.

Not confident of the strength and practical skills of his co-conspirators for what he had in mind, Dennis had hired two guards from the local garrison to help out. Stan Twill and Billy Turner stood at Dennis's shoulder as Wimlett's donkey ambled up to the front door and stopped. Muffin was used to seeing a few people around when he brought his master home, and was vaguely surprised and disappointed when he saw no-one. But he wasn't alone for long.

The university rarely slept. Even in the small hours there was usually some activity in the grounds. Tonight, though, this corner of the campus had been sealed off by some magically created and strategically placed diversion signs. The conspirators had been busy. And although they'd overlooked the fact that Muffin would also get diverted, it wasn't a problem because the old donkey blundered obliviously through their handiwork.

When Dennis gave them the nod, the two guards stepped up and gently eased Wimlett out of the cart. They propped him against the house, where he promptly collapsed in a heap on the pavement. Ignoring him, the guards proceeded to take the wheels off the cart.

'Stop!' hissed Dennis. 'Haven't you forgotten something?'

The two men looked cluelessly at the cart, then back at Dennis. 'Er... permission to start, boss?' ventured Billy, when nothing else came to mind.

Dennis held out a nose-bag full of carrots. 'What about these?'

'Yeah, they look real nice, boss. But me and Stan 'ere, we've already eaten, see?'

Dennis indicated the donkey.

'Oh, yeah. Distract the animal,' Billy mumbled. He took the bag and passed it to Stan, who had a way with animals. Before Stan joined the Kra-Pton garrison, he'd been a vet of sorts. He gave it up when he found it didn't pay so well. Often, the animal he'd saved was given to him as payment. Or he'd receive a bill for failing to save it. He took the nose-bag, slipped it gently over Muffin's ears and gave him a reassuring pat. The old donkey snorted his appreciation.

The guards turned their attention back to the cart and in minutes they'd removed the wheels.

'What now, boss?' asked Billy.

'Take the cart inside and put the wheels back on it,' said Dennis, rubbing his hands together, more from the glee of what they were doing than from the chill of the night air. 'Our big surprise for the Archchancellor, remember?' He grinned broadly, his teeth flashing in the light from the lamppost across the street.

Stan hesitated. 'That's not gonna be easy, boss.'

'Turn it on its side, man. It should go through the doorway quite easily then.'

'Wiv respect, boss. I 'ad that figured out for myself,' said Stan.

'Then what's the problem?' asked Dennis, testily.

'It's the weight and awkwardness of the thing, boss.' Stan studied the cart and Billy stood by nodding sagely. 'Ah...' he said, at last. 'It's all right, boss. I've seen the problem.' He turned to Billy. 'Give me a hand to unhitch the donkey, will you?'

Billy smirked and walked to the other side. Ten minutes later the cart had been moved and reassembled in Wimlett's living room. Stan coaxed Muffin into the house and hitched him between the shafts, and the two guards stood back and admired their efforts. *This is sure gonna surprise 'im when 'e wakes up*, thought Billy. *And he's sure gonna have a job getting it back out on the street again. Still...* he chuckled to himself, *that's not my problem.*

Dennis magnanimously gave each of the guards a coin for their trouble. A very small coin, in fact. The two men saluted mutely and marched briskly onto the street. When they judged themselves out of earshot, Stan muttered, 'What a tight sod,' and Billy agreed wholeheartedly. They shoved the coins into their pockets and headed back to the garrison bar where the ale was cheap.

Had they turned around, they would have seen Dennis's co-conspirators arriving.

***

'I'd love to be here when he wakes up,' said Rumpitt, surveying the unreal scene in Wimlett's rooms. 'Finding himself in his cart in here. That should wipe the cheeriness off his face.'

'Who?' said Maddlin, as the other three peered simultaneously into the empty cart.

'Why, Wim... where is he?' muttered Pelgrum. 'Shouldn't he be in here?'

As one man, they hurried to the door, and began jostling to get out.

'STOP!' ordered Dennis, cringing at the sound of his own voice blaring across the night campus. 'Now, stand still. All of you.'

They stopped instantly and disengaged themselves from one another.

'Now, form a line, and don't all rush to be first, it's not dinner time.'

Knowing Dennis's mood swings, and the nasty things he did to harmless tables, they still managed to annoy him by being too gentlemanly: 'After you.' 'No, after you.' He raised his hands towards them, and they stopped the moment they saw him. Meekly, they moved in single file through the doorway. Dennis lowered his hands and followed on. 'Not that way, idiots,' he called, trying to keep his voice down, as they wheeled in the wrong direction. 'He's here,' he said, pointing at the slouched and sleeping man.

'Oh, yes, so he is,' said Pelgrum. 'What shall we do now?'

Dennis sighed. 'Take him inside, and put him back in the cart where he belongs.'

'Oh, yes,' said Pelgrum again, unsure. He wasn't built for this sort of thing.

'I help,' said Cho.

Rumpitt pulled a face and looked at Maddlin. 'I suppose we'd better help as well, then.' He stepped forward and grabbed Wimlett's feet. 'Right,' he said, presuming to take charge, 'on the count of three...' There was a short pause. 'Three!' Rumpitt yanked Wimlett's feet up dragging him forwards from his sitting position and onto his back, hitting the man's head on the stone paving in the process.

'What happened to one and two?' asked Pelgrum. 'And what exactly did you have in mind, when you got to three?'

Maddlin yawned, and Cho was about to chip in but was cut off.

'Where were you all?' said Rumpitt, huffily. 'Do I have to do this on my own? Let's try it again, shall we? Get a hold of the top end.'

'Hokay,' Cho intervened. 'I count this time.'

'Oh, for goodness sake,' said Rumpitt, looking skywards.

'Look,' said Dennis through clenched teeth, 'you're all getting in one another's way. Just stand him up against the wall. Cho's the youngest and strongest...' He paused to study the wiry easterner, not too sure of what he was saying. 'Let Wimlett fall across Cho's shoulder, and he can carry him inside and drop him in the cart.'

'Sounds good to me,' said Rumpitt, hoping to see Cho crumple under Wimlett's dead weight.

Cho staggered bow-legged through the narrow doorway, catching Wimlett's head on the door frame, but without waking him, and dumped him in the cart. Fortunately, the old wizard landed on a thick folded blanket that he kept there for cold evening rides. Muffin turned his head and saw the commotion was only wizards. He made a donkey noise which was roughly 'Huh,' and carried on munching the carrots.

'Right, you lot. Outside,' snapped Dennis. 'If this doesn't make the old fool the laughing stock of the faculty when they find him in the morning, then I'm a troll's uncle. We'll meet in my rooms in two days to catch up.' As an afterthought, he added, 'And don't be late!'

Wimlett shifted slightly, then settled back into sleep.

'Yeah, let's call it a night,' said Rumpitt, setting off for his rooms.

'It's a night,' said Maddlin, obligingly.

11

The whispering of the Life-Timers on the shelves behind the big ebony desk changed subtly, not quite triggering an alarm. The alarm attached to the Timer responsible for the change was holding back to see if it would sort itself out. That Timer had been known to restart spontaneously.

Naphrat, working at the desk, sensed something was amiss and looked up from the Great Ledger of Souls.

'Did something just stop?' he wondered aloud, and a little surprised, too, because he was not expecting any deaths among the wizards and witches on the shelves behind him. He looked down at the page, his hollow eye-sockets following a practiced and Death-like finger as it travelled down the list.

'No-one's due for months.' He looked behind him at the rows of Timers, stood up, and ran a spindly finger along the bottom row, reading the names to himself. The Timers tinkled melodically, each producing a different note. He'd once considered lining them up in scales so he could play them, but dismissed the idea as inappropriate. Then... 'Oh, no. You again. I might have guessed.' He plucked the Timer from the shelf and banged it on the desk. The sand began to flow again.

12

Wimlett awoke with a start, feeling groggy. He pushed his squashed hat back from his eyes and looked at the smoke-yellowed ceiling directly overhead. *Coal fires will do that,* he pondered absently. *Especially when you don't get the chimney swept.* 'Where's the sky?' he asked, as if expecting the ceiling to explain itself. Slowly, the rest of his surroundings came into focus, and he saw that he was indeed inside his house.

This was more than a regular hangover. His head hurt more, and when he reached up he found two bumps sensitive to the touch. He didn't recall getting into a fight. So, what had happened? He sniffed the air. The smell reminded him of a stable. He got up unsteadily and climbed out of the cart. *The cart?*

How did I manage to do that!? He winced, and berated himself for thinking so loudly in such a fragile head.

Muffin eyed him briefly and lowered his head to reach the last carrot nestled in the bottom of the nose-bag. Wimlett scratched his own head, avoiding the bumps, while mentally sizing up the cart and the doorway. *How could a donkey pull a cart that must be, what... five feet wide, through a doorway that can only be three feet wide?* He stepped back, taking in the whole picture – 'Cart... room... door... donkey...'

He tried to piece it all together. A bit worse for drink, he must have arrived home and fallen back into the cart while trying to get out of it. He must have flung his arms out to save himself and triggered an old spell. It had magically transported him indoors with the donkey and cart.

'Yeah, that must be it,' he decided, pleased with himself, and unthinkingly snapping his fingers with a loud ominous click.

There was a flash from his fingers. He dropped to the floor reflexively and covered his head with his arms. A dazzling electrical ball of blue flame ricocheted around the room a couple of times, amazingly missing everything. But on its third circuit it caught the tip of Muffin's tail. It travelled the length of his back, and earthed itself on all four of his iron shoes. The old donkey's ears flattened, his eyes bulged and his nostrils flared. The room filled with smoke and the smell of singed hair. Wimlett got up and began fanning it away but stopped the moment he realised he might summon more unwanted magic.

As the smoke cleared, Wimlett saw daylight where his front door should be. The door was missing. It wasn't even in the street when he stuck his head out and looked both ways. Muffin and the cart had gone, too – except for the wheels, which were clattering to a standstill like spun coins on their last rotations, one each side of the door frame.

The only evidence that Muffin had ever been in the room was a mound of dung in the middle of his carpet. Wimlett eyed it critically. 'Took him by surprise, poor Muffin,' he muttered feelingly. He was going to miss the old fellow. 'Oh, well. At least the cleaner's due later today,' he consoled himself.

He sighed deeply and thrust his hands into the pockets of his robe. His shoulders drooped. Life would go on, he supposed, but he was feeling miserable. He'd lost his faithful old donkey. His cart had gone. His head hurt. And he needed to contact the university's works department to get them to come and fit a new door.

It was at times like this that he heard the call of the Piggin Wissall. He kicked one of the cart-wheels as he left. From habit he turned round to lock his front door and found nothing to put a key in. He silently cursed because he couldn't just walk off and leave the place open. He was about to search his aching head for a protective spell but then a couple of students wandered by, looking curiously at the damage, so he commandeered them to stand guard while he was gone.

⋯⋯❖⋯⋯

13

Late winter was imperceptibly becoming early spring in the northern hemisphere of Crett. At Havrapsor University this was the time of year when a new intake of students was sourced and vetted. Along with the perennial rivalries over funding, clean tables in the dining hall, non-contact sports, and so on, the faculties were vying for this year's intake of fresh students. The pickings were never great. Even the few who were admitted were whittled down further by the end of the first term to the few who might conceivably make the grade. The sons of wizards were given automatic admission. They were naturally inclined to wizardry. But they were a rare commodity because wizards were almost always celibate.

Also given immediate entry were the seventh sons of seventh sons. These were usually pre-gifted with magical abilities, but seldom with the knowledge of how to apply them, having grown up in non-magical households. They could be disruptive, so their parents were usually glad to be rid of them, and it meant one less mouth to feed.

Because of the patriarchal culture at Havrapsor, girls were not considered for entry. Even the rare daughter of a wizard was not admitted. Worse still, this bias meant that the extremely rare, almost unheard of, seventh daughter of seventh daughter would be lost to the world of magic, too, and spend her life only vaguely aware of her unique gifts. She would grow up to become a young lady who felt remarkably lucky to find herself, for reasons unknown, ruling over a country, a continent, or an empire.

The first thing the new intake learned was that the previous intake was that bit smarter than they were. And the intake before that, smarter still, and so on up the ladder to the Archchancellor, who was reckoned to be the smartest wizard of all. His was the office to which many aspired, but few would ever attain.

It was a hazardous climb. Wizards were not by and large well disposed towards one another, and the route to the top could be perilous. A lot of fingers were trodden on, and backs stabbed. Except, that was, among those in the highest echelon, the senior staff, where fairer play was the norm. The post of Archchancellor was filled from among these master magicians. He was elected by the vote of his peers, preferably with the blessing of the outgoing incumbent if he was still alive and, apparently, the gods.

A hierarchal pyramid was in place, from the Archchancellor at the top, down through levels of increasingly more people with increasingly less power, to the entry-year students at the bottom. It was the most basic and naturally occurring of all power structures. At the moment the top man was Wimlett. Perhaps not the strongest by some yardsticks, but he had his strengths. He certainly looked the part, had a thorough though failing grasp of magic, and he was popular at all levels. But his strength lay in more than his personal attributes, because like all Archchancellors before him, Wimlett inherited considerable power when he took possession of Eldrum's Drum and the staff of office.

Something else in his favour, which endeared him greatly to his peers, was that a man like Wimlett would do less harm than someone like Dennis. The superior magical strength that came with the office had to be kept out of the wrong hands.

***

Two days after Wimlett's interrupted journey home, there was another clandestine evening meeting in Dennis's rooms. The conspirators were subdued this time. They filed in sullenly, and found their seats with barely a word.

'Well, that didn't work out too well, did it?' moaned Rumpitt, eventually. 'Nobody found it in the least embarrassing. Certainly not Wimlett. Everyone's been commiserating with him over the loss of his old donkey ever since. His popularity's gone up, if anything.'

'I didn't notice any of you coming up with any better ideas,' retorted Dennis. 'And it looks like we're going to need some.'

'How about stealing the Drum?' suggested Maddlin. 'That would certainly shift the balance of power in our favour.' The little, ball-headed man looked pleased with himself. The idea had been mooted by Dennis at a previous meeting, but not taken seriously. Maddlin had been dozing at the time.

The room went silent. The Drum of Eldrum was possibly the most powerful magical artefact on the planet. They mulled the idea over. Could they do it? What would happen if they did? What would Wimlett do? How would he explain its disappearance? The Drum's loss would be an embarrassment that Wimlett would find hard to come up from smelling of roses. And it would reduce his powers. But on the down side, they couldn't make use of the Drum without it being obvious that they were the ones who'd taken it? Which would be seriously embarrassing *for them*. Also they had to consider the fact that in the wrong hands the Drum might become seriously unhelpful, disrupting their own magic. Though Denis felt he could probably handle that.

'No,' said Dennis, when all these points had been aired. 'I don't think so.'

'Okay,' said Rumpitt. 'Let's get someone else to steal it for us.'

'It's a thought,' said Dennis. 'But the Drum still finishes up on our doorstep.'

'Umm... supposing it rains,' offered Maddlin, trying to keep up.

'Pardon me?' said Rumpitt.

'Well supposing it rains,' Maddlin repeated. 'It'll get wet.'

Dennis looked at the others. 'What's he going on about, now?'

Maddlin yawned deeply from a sleepless day in class, rubbed his eyes and looked down at his boots. 'Just wondering, that's all.'

'Let's do a little brainstorming, shall we?' said Dennis, moving the meeting along. He didn't want them wasting any more time. They needed to focus. But the occasional sounds of footfalls and voices, coming up from the street below the window, of people walking past in ones and twos, going out for the evening, probably for a drink, were starting to distract his visitors.

***

In his small house across the courtyard, Wimlett awoke with a start. It was evening. Which didn't make sense at first. He must have slept right through the previous night and then on through the day. He must have needed it. He'd been through a lot lately. He lay on his back for a while, gathering his thoughts, not sure whether to have breakfast, lunch or supper. What he *was* sure of, though, was that something had changed. He couldn't put his finger on it. He felt somehow different.

In a very large house on no street anywhere, Naphrat was holding a Life-Timer. A minute ago, he'd banged it down hard on Death's big ebony desk. For good measure, he'd given it a really hard second thump, too, and shaken it like a maraca for a few moments. Now he was peering closely through the glass. 'That's started it again!' he confirmed. But something was troubling him.

When sand flows through Life-Timers from top to bottom it takes on a faintly darker hue. Only a practiced eye would notice it. Going by the slight discolouration in the sand at the top of the Timer he held, Naphrat guessed that a good number of the grains that had already passed through had been jolted back up. The implications were troubling him.

There was nothing he could do about it. He couldn't break it open, separate the grains, and refill it. He knew only too well what happened when a Timer was broken while in service. It rarely happened, and when it did it resulted in someone like him. It was usually an accident, but Death had done it sometimes deliberately in order to create a helper. The Powers That Be frowned on it, though. He looked again at the Timer's mixed grains and shrugged. It probably didn't matter, he decided. They'd trickle back down again soon enough. It would sort itself out.

Wimlett sat up and eased his legs over the edge of the bed as he normally did to start his day. Only this time he felt different. He didn't have to sit and wait for the energy to get moving. He sprang up from the bed. His body felt so alive. His mind was brighter, too. He caught sight of himself in the mirror and turned to see who was standing behind him. Nobody. The young wizard staring back was *him*.

He was in the bloom of youth. He was a seventy-five-year-old man in a twenty-five-year-old body. How was that possible? As far as he knew, it wasn't. And if anyone *should* know, it was him. He didn't see any point in looking into it, though, because he doubted the condition would last. It was probably due to the rogue magic afflicting him.

On the other hand, it could be down to something new they were distilling down at the Piggin Wissall. There had been some bizarre side effects from newly-introduced ales in the past. The landlord's cavalier method of testing new brews was to serve them up and see what happened.

Wimlett dressed, transforming his robe into something more presentable. He was going for a walk. He pulled a cloak around his shoulders, tweaked his hat back into shape and put it on. The night was young and so was he. And so was his door, he noticed. He picked up his staff but then replaced it in a corner by the fireplace. Yesterday he would have taken it to lean on, but today he didn't need it. He pulled his hat down at a jaunty angle, just as he used to, then squared his shoulders and headed for the Piggin Wissall at a brisk pace.

⋯◄▻⋯

14

'Have you thought of anything useful, yet?' asked Dennis. A few lame suggestions had been dismissed and the meeting was becoming progressively more fruitless. It was probably time to wind it up. And he wasn't the only one to think so.

'Yes,' Cho piped up, 'what about a drink?'

'Good idea,' agreed Rumpitt. 'Mine's a large G 'n' T, Dennis.'

'I don't keep any drink in my rooms,' said Dennis, hastily sliding between his guests and the sideboard where he kept some 'medicinal' brandy, and some even less 'medicinal' old malt whisky. He kept these for himself. Certainly not for visitors. 'And I certainly wouldn't have anything to spare.'

'No, I didn't think so,' said Pelgrum, quietly.

'Come to think of it, I don't fancy drinking in here,' said Rumpitt, casting a disapproving eye around Dennis's rather basic room. The décor seemed to have exhausted all possible shades of dull brown. 'I need some atmosphere.'

'What do you have in mind?' asked Dennis, warily.

'Well, I don't know about the rest of you, but I reckon if we leave now, there'll still be time for a couple of halves down the Piggin Wissall,' said Rumpitt, standing up a little quicker than usual, and having to steady himself.

Cho was about to deliver a barb about his age, but held back. Things had been different between them this evening. They'd been seeing eye to eye. The others had noticed an edgy, undeclared truce. And now the pair were in full agreement about a trip to the tavern. 'Right!' said Cho, noticeably avoiding baiting Rumpitt with 'Light' this time. 'I'm with you.' He beat Rumpitt to the door and opened it for him.

Maddlin and Pelgrum looked at each other and shook their heads as Rumpitt and Cho disappeared into the passageway with their arms around each other's shoulders.

Pelgrum turned to Dennis, who was watching open mouthed. 'Cho did him a favour this morning, moving some weighty equipment.' He shook his head again. 'It'll end in tears, I know it.'

15

Once at the Piggin Whistle, Wimlett shouldered his way through the crowd to the bar. He was determined to find the wine or ale, or whatever it was he might have drunk the previous night.

First, he looked for the landlord to ask him if he was trying out any new brews on customers. But the man wasn't about. He'd probably have denied it anyway. Wimlett scanned the array of bottles on the glass shelves behind the barmaid. He knew roughly where the new stuff was usually kept, so he concentrated on that section.

'Can I get you something, sir?' The barmaid smiled pleasantly.

Wimlett considered this for a moment, then considered the low cut of her dress for a little longer. 'Umm...' was all he could think of for openers. The girl waited patiently while he found his concentration and looked again along the rows of bottles.

'Yes...' he said, and an idea came to him. 'I'll have the same as I had last night, please.'

She gave him a puzzled look. She'd never seen him before. 'Maybe the other girl served you.'

Wimlett hesitated. *Of course, she wouldn't recognise me from last night,* he thought. *Nor will anybody else in here, for that matter.* Though some of his older colleagues might just about remember him if they saw him.

'Oh... er... let me see, then. What shall I have first?' He looked at the bottles again. 'I'll have that blue one on the end. That tall one next to it.' He pointed to a bottle containing yellow liquid, and continued, 'That green one on the shelf below, and one of those red ones on the bottom. Umm... that should do for starters.'

She was impressed. She picked up a tray and arranged the bottles so it was evenly balanced, and then took what she deemed a suitable glass from the rack above her head and placed it in the middle of the tray. Wimlett lifted a handful of coins from his pocket and rattled them onto the counter. 'What's your name?' he asked.

'Triona...' she replied, pausing for a beat or two before adding a deferential '...sir.' She explained that she hated being called Trionasir, which often happened if she didn't pause in the middle.

'Keep the change, Triona...sir,' said Wimlett, with a smile, and she responded with a pretend-cross face. There seemed to be a spark between them. *Not that it could come to anything*, he thought ruefully, guessing he'd probably be his old self in a few hours. Unless he could find out what did this to him... He took the tray and carefully picked his way through the crowd to a corner where the only empty table was.

It wasn't long before he drained his final glass. Though what he hoped to accomplish by checking them all out, he wasn't sure. Did he really want to stay back in his twenties? And, thinking about it, if it really was one of these drinks that made him less than half his age, did he really want to wake up half his present age tomorrow morning? A twelve-year-old?

As the last of the froth rushed towards his nose, he spotted Rumpitt and Cho coming into the bar. *This could be awkward.* He'd known Rumpitt since they were students together. He didn't want to be recognised looking so young, especially as he had no explanation for it. Rumpitt would probably accuse him of concocting a vanity potion, like some third-rate witch. The chances of Rumpitt remembering him from fifty years ago were pretty slim, but he still paused the glass in front of his face until they'd gone past him into the small side bar. *Hurry up*, he thought. When they'd gone, he slammed his glass down on the table and rushed for the back door. Nature called.

Shortly, he was back in the bar-room feeling comfortable, standing at the counter selecting more bottles. He'd decided to risk a return to childhood, if it meant the chance of dating the barmaid as a twenty-something. He'd experiment. If he found the culprit, maybe he could work out the dosage to enable him to swap from old to young, as and when required. *A double life.* But some annoying ethical questions frightened the idea away. He was frustratingly hampered by the age-old problem of being one of the good guys. After a minute, and another furtive ogle of the barmaid, he decided on his drinks.

He wouldn't overthink this. He'd continue looking for the cause. Though how he'd identify exactly which drink it was, having had all these bottles, might prove difficult. He was relying on his magical sensitivities to alert him. So far, they hadn't. He headed back to his corner with the loaded tray, almost tripping over a drunk dragging himself back to the counter. Wimlett gave him some verbal abuse, and discovered how liberating it was to be swearing like a twenty-something again. He parked himself back on the chair where he'd left his cloak so as not to lose his table.

He made good progress, and was soon halfway through his eleventh bottle of the evening. The liquid in his glass was deep purple. He'd been mixing reds and blues. There were small puddles of mixed colours on the table in front of him and it crossed his mind that the contents of his stomach must look something like that. He guided his glass back to the table and added a small measure of something green and sticky. It floated on top for a moment before sinking lazily to the bottom and rising again. In another time and place he might have invented the lava lamp. He watched the blob rise, and, as he did so, the alcohol in his system reached a tipping point and his mind went blank. He pitched forward and struck his forehead on the table. He then slid slowly from sight, hitting the back of his head on the chair as he went down.

While Wimlett lay unconscious, a troll entered the tavern. His name was Basalt, and today was his birthday. This wasn't the first tavern he'd visited, so he was feeling a bit rocky. The resident troll at the Piggin Wissall – more of a troll-and-a-half, really – was named Chunk. He was employed as a bouncer, and that was exactly what he did to unruly revellers. He took his job very literally. Also, he had a policy of not allowing other trolls into the tavern this late in the evening, because by this time they were usually already drunk and surly. And the bar was too tightly packed with soft human bodies to have a rock-solid troll lumbering about. A sign on the door made all this clear, but it was wasted on a drunken troll. Which meant Chunk's priority was to get Basalt back out onto the street.

The ensuing fight achieved everything that Chunk was there to prevent. It went on for almost half an hour, with neither troll gaining the upper hand. It ended only when Chunk crashed through a table and found a sword underneath that a tipsy soldier must have forgotten to pick up when he left earlier. Chunk grabbed it and made a wild swing at Basalt.

The sword slipped from Chunk's massive fingers and skidded across the sawdust-strewn floor. It slid under some occupied tables and thudded into something, provoking a stream of thunderous abuse from one of the drinkers that was directed at both trolls. The brawling stopped instantly. Silence hung nervously in the air, probably waiting for the opportunity to make a dash for the nearest exit.

Nobody had ever heard such a colourful torrent of words. At least, not all in the same breath, and delivered with such power and passion. They were uttered by an old seafaring man, who'd garnered an impressive vocabulary on his travels. The sword had taken a slice off the bottom of one of his boots and impaled itself low in a leg of his table with such force that it jerked his drink into his lap.

Chunk blinked and took in the situation. Basalt looked apologetic, even though it wasn't him who'd let go of the sword. The trolls called a truce, thinking maybe a draw was a fair result after all. Silence saw its chance and made for the door. Muted conversations started up again around the bar and a shaky calm returned. But not so many of the bar's patrons were in a fit state to chatter as there were earlier. Some were dazed, and some lay inert among splintered tables and chairs.

Rumpitt and Cho had watched the fight from the relative safety of the doorway into the small, side bar. They'd stayed alert in case the action tumbled in their direction. When the fighting stopped, Cho stepped in to see if anyone needed help, but Rumpitt put a restraining hand on his shoulder. 'Best not to interfere,' he whispered. 'No one's been badly hurt as far as I can see, except for some cuts and bruises. The furniture got the worst of it.' Little did he know the true extent of the damage.

'Yeah. You're probably right,' said Cho.

Rumpitt took a last look at the mess and both men returned to their table. 'Looks like we'll be drinking elsewhere for a while.'

They missed the final piece of the action. Basalt stooped and pulled the sword from the table leg. He tipped the table in the process, but the old seafarer was by the bar, drying his trousers with a towel. The troll was toying with the idea of taking a decisive swipe at the bouncer while his guard was down. But looking around at the havoc they'd caused between them, he sobered a little and decided it was time to stop. He threw the sword away. Two people in its path swerved out of the way, but a third instinctively caught it – which would have been fine had it been a long ball into the crowd at a game. This time, the catcher wasn't pleased with himself for long.

Chunk saw what happened. He winced, and held out a hand to Basalt in a gesture of friendship. Basalt eyed it warily, then nodded, smiled and took it. Putting his other hand on Chunk's shoulder, he steered him to what was left of the bar and ordered two large grog and turnips. After all, for another ten minutes, it was still his birthday.

16

The lounge bar of the Piggin Wissall was wrecked. As the survivors went home or back to their rooms at the university, news of the devastation spread quickly. It had been so bad that even Dennis was perturbed to hear of it. In no time at all, gawkers gathered to see the damage. And when the landlord opened his wallet, he found some of them willing to help clear up the mess.

A couple of bodies were found in the debris and dispatched to the morgue. And when the splintered furniture was being taken out to a scrap cart that had been called, the helpers thought they'd found a third. Wimlett was discovered senseless under the remains of his table in the corner, very drunk but not very dead. Nobody knew who he was. He didn't have a shred of identification on him. A couple of regulars thought he looked vaguely familiar. But Wimlett hadn't been seen looking like this for a very long time.

'What shall we do with him?' asked Triona, with concern.

'You found 'im...' snapped the landlord. 'You deal with him.' Everyone's nerves were a bit shredded.

Triona looked down at the sleeping wizard. 'You know, mister,' she said, studying his inert features, 'your nose is on the large side, but you're quite handsome in the right light. You ain't dressed too shabbily for a student either.' So, rather than have him dumped in the gutter – as was the custom with drunks who couldn't shift themselves – she asked Chunk to carry him up to her room. The troll was eager to make amends for his part in the devastation. He was glumly aware, too, how much it would affect his pay. He obligingly scooped up the young Wimlett and plodded up the complaining stairs with him. When he'd manoeuvred himself through the doorway, he gently laid him on the sofa to sleep it off.

***

The city was sleeping. Most of it. It was the brief, pre-dawn interlude when the night prowlers were heading home and the early risers were lying in bed wondering how much longer would still count as early. In this hushed interval, when the world seemed to stand still, a dark-clad figure slipped silently over Triona's balcony.

He crossed the narrow balcony and went in through the bedroom door that was left open. In the half light, he could just make out the figure of a sleeping man on the sofa. That was unusual. He crept past him and stopped by the bed where Triona was sleeping.

The prowler was Dennis. He studied Triona closely. After what he'd heard about the big fight in the bar earlier, he was relieved to confirm that she was alright.

Once a fortnight, Dennis spent the early hours with her. He always arrived a little before dawn, and left shortly after sun-up, while she slept on. Her work at the bar meant late nights and mornings. He arranged his visits for the days he wasn't due in class till later. And in case anyone called at his rooms unexpectedly, he always left a note on the door saying he'd gone fishing or was doing research out of town. He thought of his explanations more as euphemisms than excuses. He always left some money on Triona's dressing table before he left. Not that she was that sort of girl – well, not entirely – but because he'd grown annoyingly fond of her. And knew she didn't earn much at the Piggin Wissall. It was an odd relationship, which neither of them had ever examined too closely. There had never been any need to. Until now, that was.

Dennis was uneasy. His attention went again to the sleeper on the sofa, and with mounting curiosity, and with a pang of jealousy, he crept stealthily back to see who was competing with him for the girl's affections. He slowly drew back the blanket...

'You!' he hissed, recognising the younger Wimlett. Not many would have, but for years Dennis had had an old picture of Wimlett on his dartboard, until both the dartboard and the picture had fallen apart. Not that he played darts. He used the board to perfect his aim with spells, toning them down so that he didn't blow the door off his room. 'But how...?' He dropped the blanket and stepped back. Wimlett stirred, and settled again.

It was unlike Dennis to be so completely thrown. He was unsure what to do next. He told himself to stay cool and think straight. But it wasn't working. Two contrary emotions had triggered together – in a single moment, a deeper affection for Triona and a deeper hatred for Wimlett had both crystallised.

He stared at the sleeping wizard for a full minute, his blood boiling, and a howl of rage not far from his lips. His mind was whirling, but he waited. He breathed slowly and deeply. Little by little he re-established some self-control. When he had calmed himself sufficiently, he looked from Wimlett on the sofa to Triona on the bed and smirked. He knew exactly what he would do. And this was going to shame and discredit the old mage totally.

Dennis had immediately discounted a full-on murderous assault on him. Wimlett's magical defences would have reacted automatically, and with devastating effect. He had defences of his own, but Triona might get hurt in the collision of forces. He couldn't count on this younger version of Wimlett being any less powerful than the older one. And anyway – he had something subtler and more sinister in mind.

Dennis shut his eyes tightly and extended his hands over the sleeping wizard. Magic crackled from his fingertips and Wimlett began to rise. He guided him through the air and deftly brought him to rest next to Triona. It pained him to see them together, but it had to be done for what he had in mind. After draping one of Wimlett's arms across the girl, and congratulating himself on the attention he'd paid in Wimlett's own kinetic magic lectures, Dennis crept silently back out onto the balcony and closed the door.

Triona's room was over the front of the tavern and to one side. Once out on the balcony, Dennis turned and placed both hands on the wall, and began chanting softly. He was putting a spell on the building. When that was done, and still seemingly in a trance, he turned to the city and extended his arms to the sky. 'When this city awakes...' he whispered into the air, 'every person here last night will remember it was Wimlett, the Archchancellor, who was responsible for what happened here.' He lowered his arms, and as an afterthought, raised them again, adding, 'And that goes for the trolls, too.'

17

Wimlett awoke before Triona and slid quietly from the bed. He noticed his reflection in a mirror and wasn't surprised to see himself old again. His brief youth clearly had nothing to do with the drinks at the bar. It had been some rare and rogue magic, he assumed. Magic like that was seldom permanent.

He glanced back at the sleeping girl and allowed himself a moment of smug satisfaction. He put on his curly-toed slippers and crept downstairs and out through the side door.

There were very few people on the street this sunny morning. It took him a moment to get his bearings, and another to notice the damage to the Piggin Wissall. Hugely curious, he peered through a gap between the boards covering the front windows and saw some of the damage. 'Wow, I really missed something last night!' He shook his head in disbelief, which hurt a little, and then he walked unsteadily back to his house.

Later that day, he found out more about the damage that *he'd* apparently caused. Mainly from overhearing bits of conversations and snide remarks from a group of wizards that had formed a clique around Rumpitt-cum-Slowly. Wimlett felt betrayed. He and Rumpitt had been friends over the years. Though admittedly not so much since he'd become Archchancellor. Friendships don't always survive when one is elevated over another, he knew, but it still saddened him.

Wimlett couldn't remember a thing about what he was supposed to have done down at the tavern. Maybe he'd been restless while he was unconscious. Maybe he'd been flailing his arms about and firing off more rogue magic. It was likely. And it was worrying. They might not let him back in there again! There was no getting away from the fact that the damage could all be down to him. It was consistent, too, with him feeling not very rested when he awoke that morning, as if he'd been up to something strenuous in the night.

18

Nine months later.

Naphrat, the Grim Reaper's helper – recently promoted to Head Reaper but not holding his breath, mostly because he had none to hold – appeared in Wimlett's rooms. The place felt cold, so the Dark Angel went and stood by the fire, forgetting for the moment that he was the source of the chill.

Wimlett was dozing by the fire in his over-stuffed armchair toasting his toes, and for some reason he felt the urge to open an eye. On seeing a darkly-clad figure looming in front of him, he promptly opened the other one and sat to attention.

'Dennis?' he said, squinting through sleep-clouded eyes. 'Is that you?'

'No,' replied Naphrat, in a cadaverous voice that was never Dennis's.

Wimlett realised who it was. 'So soon?' he said, looking absently at the clock on the mantel. 'Is it that time already?'

Naphrat looked at the clock, too. 'What, a quarter past eight?' he said, hollowly.

'No,' said Wimlett. '*My* time.'

Naphrat produced a Life-Timer from his robe, and eyed it critically. There was still sand dropping through the narrow waist. Though Wimlett couldn't help noticing there wasn't much left at the top. 'No, not yet,' said Naphrat, and tucked the Life-Timer away quickly.

Dying didn't frighten Wimlett, but hearing Naphrat say 'not yet' was very welcome. Much better than a summons to get his affairs in order. He'd grown quite fond of this world, even though it didn't always seem to like him. Not everyone was allowed time to put their affairs in order, but for a wizard in his position, the Reaper would make sure that any lose ends were tied, especially that he'd remember to deposit his spells in the Drum.

'So why are you here?' asked Wimlett.

'I have something to tell you.'

Wimlett raised an eyebrow, a nervous prompt for the Dark Angel to continue.

'Firstly, don't ever mistake me for Dennis again. That's really insulting.' His skeletal frame actually shivered at the thought.

'And secondly?'

Naphrat composed himself.

'You are about to become a father,' he stated, flatly, and, after a dramatic pause, added, 'as no-one else will tell you, I felt, *in the circumstances*, obliged to tell you myself.'

'Really?' Wimlett wasn't sure which was the most absurd part of this, the news itself or the fact that Naphrat was delivering it. *And why did he say 'in the circumstances' in such a loaded way?* He leaned back in his chair, allowing the news to percolate down. There could be no question as to what this related to. All he could think to say after a long silence was, 'Not in your usual remit is it, delivering birth announcements? – When's the birthday?'

'A few days... you'll know when.' Naphrat hesitated. 'After all, you are a wizard.'

Wimlett got out of his chair and stood eyeball to eye-socket with the Reaper. 'Yes, you're right. I am a wizard. Not a bloody clairvoyant! Now, when exactly is this going to happen?'

Naphrat took a step back. Nobody spoke to him like that – not since Death had been away. 'Clairvoyant, Magician, Wizard, Whatever... It's all the same to me.' He squared his shoulders. They clicked loudly. 'Two days' time... at the Piggin Wissall. As you might have guessed.' He cocked his head on one side. 'Alright?' It was more of a conclusion than a question. That was it. His duty had been discharged. He threw his cloak around his shoulders theatrically, turned on his heel and stepped out through the wall. A horse whinnied outside. Moments later Naphrat was gone, leaving only the impossible sound of hooves beating on thin air fading into the distance.

Wimlett stood quietly for a full minute. He was going to be a father. The thought kept circulating. He never saw this coming. His fear of being banned from the tavern all those months ago had been well founded, so he never did get to see, or hear about Triona's condition. Dennis, too, was unaware of it. He gave up calling on Triona after finding her balcony door locked a couple of times, and getting no answer from his insistent tapping. He didn't know why, but he knew it was somehow Wimlett's fault.

Wimlett's reputation had been seriously damaged by the events of that fateful night, and now it had left him – and Triona with a bigger problem. He remained in office only through the respect and goodwill he'd built up over a long and mostly successful career. All the tutt-tutting over his having fathered a child could be the final blow to his credibility and career.

But who would know he was the father? His younger self was unrecognisable to everyone in the tavern, including Triona herself. Naphrat knew, of course, but he was different. He didn't gossip. No-one else knew.

He knew nothing of Dennis's presence on the night. But that didn't matter because Dennis had been so deeply troubled by the event that he'd used a blanking spell on himself to block out parts of it.

And why on Crett had Naphrat taken it upon himself to tell him. How weird was that! Yet he was grateful to the Reaper. It didn't take him long to work it out, though, that *'in the circumstance'* meant that a child born to a magician of Wimlett's stature should not be allowed to grow up not knowing who he is.

Wimlett dismissed the idea of remaining anonymous. The burden of being one of the good guys weighed heavily again. Naphrat was right about owning up. He would face it squarely, whatever the consequences. He slumped back into his armchair, put his feet up on the stool near the fire, and sat mulling over what the future held for him, for Triona, and for the child.

***

Naphrat's visit had stirred some forebodings in Wimlett – the old, robed skeleton with the big scythe had that effect on people. Thoughts of putting his affairs in order clung to him since the encounter. And now that he was going to be a parent, he felt the need even more strongly. He had to think about the child. A *PARENT*. The word grew large in his mind. He said it aloud. Parent signified so much – responsibility, care and affection. His reluctance to engage fully with the situation was dissolving. Something was taking its place that he couldn't quite figure out yet. But it was accompanied by resolve.

Put pen to paper. That's what I must do.

He would list his few possessions, and who should get them. He would write a letter to be opened posthumously by his successor as Archchancellor. He would even lodge his spells in the Drum. In fact, he'd start with that.

But first he had to write them out.

There were good reasons for this. He had to make sure none were missed. The wording had to be correct for reciting them to the Drum. And he had to keep a copy outside the Drum for ready reference. The Drum could be temperamental, so access for retrieval might not always be easy.

Paper! He had none in his rooms. His stationery was in his office in the main building. And he wanted to get this done now. The spells part of it anyway. He could do the rest at the office. But the only paper to hand was in a book on loan from the university library. Long overdue. That would have to do. And the more he thought about using the book, the more he warmed to the idea. He could write on the blank pages and in the margins. And the book would serve as a safe hiding place for what he was about to write. He dare not leave such information lying about at home or in his office.

He needed a place no one would think to look – *Someone like Dennis*, he thought, uncharitably, though correctly – and yet somewhere he could find it readily if he needed to. The book was perfect. Returning it to the library with his notes would serve his purpose perfectly. His was the only date stamp in it. *No-one would ever take a book like this out again. I'll just leave it on the counter when the librarian's not about*, he thought, smiling to himself. *Now, where did I put it?*

By the time he'd rummaged everywhere, the room looked as if he'd been burgled. Then he remembered it was wedged under a leg of his sideboard to stop it rocking. He eyed the old book's worn leather cover and read what remained of the gold-lettered title. He thought the cover far too elegant for the contents. He grinned to himself. 'It's a good thing you were the right thickness,' he told it. 'You're not a subject I would have chosen to read up on.' He wiped the dust off with his sleeve, and placed it on the table.

With the aplomb and sense of occasion of a pianist about to give a recital, he sat down at the table, pushed his sleeves back, squared his shoulders, fixed his eyes on the first blank page in the book, and began to write his best spells in his tiniest and neatest handwriting. Many a margin was scrawled in, too. After triple checking them, he recited the spells for the Drum. Which was easy once the Drum realised it was to absorb them and not action them.

That evening, he returned the book to the library. He left it at the front desk and crept away. Paske, the librarian, spotted him from where he stood among the shelves, but said nothing. After all, Wimlett was Archchancellor, and he could hardly reprimand his boss.

When the old mage had left, Paske sifted through his record cards, changed a few dates and took the book to a remote high shelf in a dim and cobwebbed alcove. The librarian couldn't help wondering why Wimlett had chosen that particular book. It wasn't his style at all. Or anyone's really. Then, as he lifted it to the shelf, he felt the square indentation on its back cover, made by something heavy. 'Ah...' he murmured.

19

Two days later, ignoring his ban on entering the place, and having explained himself to the midwife, Wimlett stood in an upstairs front room of the Piggin Wissall watching his baby being born. When it was over, and all the rapid, shallow breathing had subsided, and Triona was sleeping soundly after all the exertions, the midwife told him he could pick the baby up. A little girl. He glowed with pride. *This is the real magic*, he thought, as he leaned forward to lift and cradle the tiny bundle.

The next thing he knew, he was watching, stupefied, from a few feet above the scene, as his body slumped down onto the bed, and his falling staff came to rest in his baby daughter's hand. Her tiny fingers closed tightly around it, and it glowed for a moment.

Wimlett's ghost floated down from near the ceiling. He righted himself and stood aside as the midwife and her two helpers screamed at the sight of his corpse draped across the bed. They fled the scene, horrified. Triona shifted, mumbled something and returned to sleep. The baby looked up and smiled contentedly. Wimlett smiled back, only to realise that she wasn't smiling at him at all, but at something behind him.

He turned to see what had grabbed her attention. 'I didn't hear you come in,' he said.

'No-one ever does,' said Naphrat, in a voice that seemed to echo down the centuries.

'It's a bit inconvenient you showing up right now,' complained Wimlett. 'You could have given me a few minutes with her, surely? – If only to say, 'Hi, I'm your father' or something. Great timing, I must say!'

'Look, consider yourself lucky. I would've been here sooner, but some silly bugger started a war over in Jarwhalley. What a battle… bodies everywhere… caught me on the hop, I can tell you.'

Naphrat avoided apologising, because it meant feeling sorry. On work matters, he tried to have only thoughts, not feelings. Not that he was incapable of feelings; he was just wary of them. It was best not to be emotional in his line of work. He tried to distance himself, for fear of becoming morose.

Naphrat liked to be early, especially at the death of a wizard or a witch. He liked to give them some warning that their number was coming up.

He liked a little chat, too, before he ushered them into wherever they believed they were going. He usually did this while waiting for Death to arrive, because the Master's personal presence was deemed necessary for wizards and witches. But that couldn't happen as things were now. Wimlett was the first wizard to die on Naphrat's watch, so he was going to have to make do with second best.

Wizards, witches and cats could see Naphrat, as they could Death Himself whenever He showed up. Cats were sometimes renewing their acquaintance with them eight or nine times.

'Is that mine?' asked Wimlett, staring at the Life-Timer Naphrat was holding.

'Hmm? Yes,' replied the Dark Angel, and held it up to the light. 'The sands of your Time appear to have run out,' he said, matter-of-factly, tilting the glass to one side. Then, 'Shit!' he muttered to himself, 'There's still some at the top.' He glanced quickly back at Wimlett, his neck clicking loudly.

This was embarrassing. The ghostly mage drifted closer and peered over Naphrat's shoulder.

'You mean...' Wimlett began in an incredulous tone, 'that I died before my time?' He was feeling increasingly more aggrieved. It was bad enough that it had happened when it did, but the fact that it shouldn't have happened was doubly galling.

Naphrat fumbled the Life-Timer back inside his robe. 'Well,' he faltered. 'In answer to your question, I think *yes*, just about sums it up.' He gave the Timer a surreptitious shake, sending a few more grains in the wrong direction. He began to attempt an explanation, but for the life of him, in a manner of speaking, he couldn't think how or why it had happened. 'I've had a bit of trouble with this one,' he said, pointing at the pocket of his robe. 'The Master got some cheap ones off a traveller a while back. They've all been okay except for this one... which keeps stopping.' He paused while trying to line up his thoughts again. He'd never had to explain anything about deathly goings-on to a mere ex-mortal before. 'So I've had to give it a bit of encouragement now and then. A whack or a shake... you know.'

Wimlett was seething. But he forced himself to calm down sufficiently to consider his predicament. Or rather Naphrat's predicament. *This accounts for my problems in recent years. Every time Naphrat shook or banged the Life-Timer to restart it, he shook some sand back to the top, making my history repeat itself in fits and starts. It probably explains the rogue magic, too.*

'That's about it,' said Naphrat, hearing his thoughts and trying to make light of it. Then as Wimlett was still staring hard at him and making this really awkward, he tried another tack. 'Look,' he said, suddenly all business-like, 'I haven't got all day – there's going to be an earthquake in Naggies Hop in a couple of hours, and I've got to go and stalk the streets.'

'Well,' said the late wizard, trying to maintain his cool, but venting some of his anger in sarcasm, 'I think it's a bit much. You know, me dying before my time. Not to mention all the other hassle that job-lot Timer-thing has caused me. I think you owe me something. Big time – no pun intended. What about Death?' he demanded, looking around him. 'And shouldn't He be here, anyway?'

Naphrat peered at the Life-Timer again, and experimentally gave it a gentle flick. Nothing budged. 'Death's away right now. I couldn't get hold of Him if I wanted to.'

'Well?' said Wimlett. 'What happens now?'

Naphrat's gaze shifted from the Timer to Wimlett a couple of times. In the process, he found himself being drawn inexorably into sympathy for him. He fought it back, but to no avail. He didn't quite know what to say. *I wish the Master were here*, he thought. 'What do you want to happen?' he asked, almost in desperation. 'Maybe we can work something out.'

'What are the options?' asked Wimlett, sitting himself on the edge of the bed, though he had minimal weight to take off his feet.

'I could put you forward for early reincarnation; I suppose. You could be a dog next time... or even a rabbit?' he tried, making a poor attempt at selling the idea.

Wimlett sat in silence.

'That's a lot of fun, or so I've heard,' Naphrat heard himself say and winced. 'Or what about something ethereal? A ghost, maybe? You're practically one now, so it wouldn't be difficult. A bit boring, perhaps, but the hours are good, and the chain rattling isn't compulsory... Well? What do you say?'

Wimlett thought about the offer. He thought he was already a ghost, but he wasn't about to argue the point with Naphrat. 'I'd like to see my daughter grow up and go to the university,' he said at last. 'She is the daughter of a wizard, after all, and so she should.' He knew what he was suggesting was against the university's rules. *His* rules, he remembered. Though, in his defence, he had inherited them. And he had a vague recollection of reading somewhere that things had not always been this way. Perhaps now was a good time to change things, to accept women into the ways of magic. Those who qualified. After all, his little girl was the daughter of an Archchancellor. A rarity indeed!

'The only one *ever*,' Naphrat chimed into his thoughts. And although Naphrat's skull face was expressionless, Wimlett thought he caught the flicker of a smile. The Reaper began nodding. 'I suppose you could help make that happen, old chap, if you were around... even as a ghost. And assuming she needs your help.'

Old chap? Wimlett thought. *Just who does he think he is?* 'I want... er... what's my daughter's name?' he stammered.

'Eydith,' Naphrat obliged. 'With a 'y'.'

'Bloody silly name,' he muttered.

'Don't blame me,' said Naphrat, 'I told her that, but she said her mother insisted.'

'You've spoken to Eydith?' said Wimlett, amazed.

'Our minds have met. She *is* the daughter of an arch-wizard, you know.' At the backs of his hollow eye sockets, some stars twinkled momentarily, betraying an unexpected touch of something mellow and good-humoured lurking back there.

Wimlett reconnected with his train of thought. 'Yes, I want Eydith to go to Havrapsor. That won't be easy. She'll need help, I know, so I want to be around, if only as a ghost. What about you? Can you do anything to help her get in when she's old enough?' It was a long shot, but worth trying.

'It'll be up to whoever's Archchancellor at the time, not me,' Naphrat said, sounding almost regretful. 'But, as you say, she is the daughter of a wizard – the highest. If it's her destiny, she will. But I will say this...' he paused for dramatic effect while mustering his gravest prophetic tone: 'She will make some powerful enemies, but some true friends.'

Wimlett let that pass. 'Can I ask for just one more thing?

Naphrat thought he'd already offered the old mage plenty. 'Let me hear it first.'

'I thought you could hear my thoughts.'

'Not always. And not when I'm thinking myself. I'm louder than you.'

'I'd like to stay in touch. With you. And not just about Eydith's affairs. But because I'm guessing it can get lonely being a ghost. From my knowledge of them, they don't socialise a lot. And I don't know who else I can talk to.'

'I don't see why not.' Naphrat sounded oddly pleased, almost as if he might have suggested it himself. Perhaps it was a bit lonely being a Soul Reaper, too, sometimes. He shook the emotion off quickly. 'But I must make it clear that I can't help Eydith in any way, and neither can you – *unless* she decides she needs our help. Desperately. And asks for it. We can't interfere unbidden.' He stood in silence, waiting for Wimlett's reaction.

'Agreed,' said Wimlett, at last.

'I will give you twenty years as a spirit in this world – what do you say to that?' And before Wimlett could argue, he added, 'It's more than the Master would've given you.'

'Okay, agreed.' Wimlett stood up. 'Where is He, anyway?'

Naphrat brushed the question aside, and turning to go, snapped, 'Good! That's all settled. Come...'

'Where are we going? I thought I wasn't passing over.'

'You're not. We're going back to my place for drinks.'

'What about that earthquake?' Wimlett reminded him.

'Oh, bugger that. It'll be too panicky down there for an hour or two. I'll go when it's calmed down a bit.'

Wimlett glanced over his shoulder at his daughter. She raised a tiny hand and opened and closed her pudgy fingers, as if waving them goodbye. His imagination, surely? She still clung to his staff with her other hand, he noticed.

The pair left the room just as the midwife arrived back with help. In the yard below, Naphrat took the nosebag off his horse and swung easily into the saddle. With a wave of his arm, he wafted the ghostly Wimlett up behind him.

20

'Wimlett's dead,' Rumpitt announced, as he planted himself in one of Dennis's big, brown armchairs.

'What? Really? When?' asked Dennis, in rapid fire, smothering his elation with an acceptable, sombre frown.

'This morning.'

'And you wait until now to tell me?' Dennis snapped.

'This morning, tomorrow, next week. What's the difference? It won't bring him back,' said Pelgrum.

'I don't want him back, stupid. I want his job.' Dennis threw his cloak around his shoulders, and stormed to the door. 'Come with me!' he ordered.

Rumpitt eased himself out of the chair. 'Where are we going?'

'To the Archchancellor's house. To find the staff and Drum.'

Rumpitt raised an eyebrow but followed him out of the room. Pelgrum and the others wanted nothing to do with this for now, so Rumpitt left them to their own devices. The two senior wizards ambled across the campus to Wimlett's house, giving the impression that they were on innocent business and engaged in idle chatter. They were discussing what form an election might take. Whether it should be a contest of wizardly prowess, or... unsubtle difference... a duel of magic.

Rumpitt said, 'Most of the seniors will want whoever has the most wizardly merit and knowledge. For me it'll be someone without a fixed bloody cheery expression on his face. I like to see the old fireworks of a duel, but I don't think there's anybody capable of it these days.' Then, catching the affront on Dennis's face, rapidly added, 'Apart from you, that is.'

Dennis smirked. He was noted for some occasional fireworks. He'd provoked and survived a number of duels of power, and it was doubtful whether anyone would go up against him now. 'Yes, I think you're right, but there might be some hothead who fancies his chances.'

'Hothead?' Rumpitt repeated to himself. 'Suicidal idiot more like.'

They reached the little house. Rumpitt pushed the door open, and stood back to allow Dennis in first. Inside it was gloomy.

Dennis produced a flame on his finger and lit the remains of a candle that was stuck to the worn plank table. As his eyes became accustomed to the low light, he started to look around. The Drum was easy enough to spot, but the staff wasn't obvious. 'Can you see it?' he said, having no success himself, and keeping his voice down so as not to draw the attention of passers-by – and forgetting Rumpitt was half deaf.

'No,' replied Rumpitt, when he'd repeated himself. 'But it must be here somewhere. He can't take it with him, can he? Perhaps it's with the Drum,' he suggested, following Dennis into the study.

'Not that I can see,' Dennis muttered, checking around and behind the instrument.

The magic Drum began to glow. It turned rapidly from its usual aged ivory colour, to an angry shade of red.

Rumpitt took a step back. 'Do you think it'll explode?'

'No,' said Dennis. 'I don't think so.' But he took a step back as well, just to be on the safe side.

The Drum cooled slightly.

'There. You see. It's all right now,' said Dennis.

'Do you think it knows you're not Archchancellor yet?' whispered Rumpitt.

Dennis scowled at the comment. 'Perhaps. But when I am, it won't matter if it knows or not. It will be mine, and it will do whatever I want.'

Rumpitt doubted that, seeing the redness flicker again in the Drum, as if in response. He looked around the room. There was a rickety desk in one corner. He drifted over to it, and casually opened the top drawer.

'Find anything?' asked Dennis, suddenly appearing at Rumpitt's shoulder.

Rumpitt had. He'd found an interesting-looking envelope which he quickly slid under the desk pad. 'No... nothing,' he lied.

When Dennis turned away, Rumpitt pulled the letter out again. It was addressed... *The Next Archchancellor*. He slipped it into his pocket and pretended to carry on looking around.

'Well,' said Dennis, after another five minutes, 'I think we'd better go. We'll come back another day, when I'm Archchancellor. And perhaps the Drum will see fit to assist us in locating the staff.' The Drum flared, briefly.

When the coast was clear, the two wizards walked out into a dull, cloudy late afternoon and quietly closed the door. They went back to the main dining hall, where they went their separate ways.

When he was alone in his rooms, Rumpitt put some water in his kettle and hung it on the trivet over his fire. He muttered a fire-raising spell and waved his hands at the remains of a few charred logs, which obligingly burst into flame. He took the letter out of his pocket and re-read the addressee. '*The Next Archchancellor*,' he whispered, as he sank slowly into his armchair and waited for the kettle to boil. Steam finally began to belch from the spout. The old wizard leaned forward and began to steam the letter open.

At last, he was able to remove the contents. 'Well, well, well. The crafty old goat,' he said, grinning. 'He's guessed Dennis might become Archchancellor. What a rotten trick. Clever though.' Rumpitt read it again, relishing the bit about the Drum not functioning properly without the staff. 'Dennis will not be pleased when he finds out about that. Not one bit,' he muttered, refolding the letter and replacing it in the envelope. He was looking forward to seeing Dennis's face when he found out. But first he'd have to get the letter back to the house where Dennis would find it. He looked out of the window. It was still too light.

When it was dark, Rumpitt donned his black cloak and strode across the campus to the Archchancellor's house as quietly, and as quickly as he could.

After standing inside for a few moments to get his breath back and help calm himself, he took a tentative step into the darkness. He took another slow step, then another, trying to recall the layout of the room, until he found a window. He pulled the curtain aside to let in some street light. There he paused. And froze. There was a rustling noise coming from the study, and a faint red glow coming from under the door. He pictured an angry Drum, glowing hot, and waiting to pounce, on the other side. No, that was silly, he thought, and gingerly pushed the door...

A black-clad shape by the desk spun round, 'Wha...' hissed Dennis, startled by Rumpitt's entrance.

'Oh, it's you,' said Rumpitt. 'I saw a light as I was passing,' he lied quickly, 'and I came to investigate.'

'Light? What light?' said Dennis, tetchily. 'Damn!' he cursed, and stomped off into the bedroom. He came back with a blanket which he draped over the Drum.

While Dennis was out of the study, Rumpitt slid the letter into the top drawer of the desk.

'I've looked in there,' Dennis whispered.

'What?' Rumpitt was startled. 'Oh, the desk. Did you find anything?'

'No,' Dennis replied. 'Well, that's not strictly true. There was an old apple core and a black banana. I think we need to check his office.'

'Some seniors were in there this morning looking for a will, and anything else of interest. It would be common knowledge if they had the staff.' Rumpitt pulled the drawer open, made a big show of fishing around deep inside and picked up the envelope. 'There's something here, I think, wedged up against the side of the drawer,' he said, trying to sound suitably surprised.

'A letter? I didn't see that before.' Dennis snatched it from Rumpitt's hand. 'Where's that candle?'

'Out there,' said the older wizard, making for the living room. Dennis followed eagerly, holding a small flame ready on an outstretched finger.

'Close that curtain,' Dennis hissed. 'We don't want everyone to know we're here.'

While he did that, Dennis held the envelope to the light. 'It's addressed to me,' he whispered.

Rumpitt looked over his shoulder, 'It says, *The next Archchancellor*, Dennis.'

'Only a formality,' Dennis assured him, as he ran a finger under the flap, tearing it open. Dennis read it quickly, after which he went quiet, and sat down in the armchair by the fireplace.

'Something wrong?' Rumpitt asked, casually.

Dennis looked up into Rumpitt's face. 'Bastard,' he whispered.

'I've been called worse,' said Rumpitt.

'Not you,' said Dennis. 'Wimlett!'

'What's he done?'

Dennis spat the words out. 'He's cursed the Drum. It won't work properly without the staff. And he's hidden it.'

The Drum glowed. RED.

'Was there anything else?' Rumpitt knew there was. 'I thought I saw something on the back of the letter.'

Dennis scowled and turned the paper over. He read it aloud through gritted teeth. 'Once you have the staff and the Drum, you will be the most powerful magician in the land. Use this power wisely and well. Or not at all.' Then a P.S. warned, 'And *never* use your own magic too close to the Drum if you don't have the staff with you. Without the calming and restraining presence of the staff, the Drum will distort your magic. It will not work how you intend. It may even work against you.'

'Damn!'

21

Soon after Eydith was born, Triona took her far away from Kra-Pton to the Land of Corin, where she would grow up in more friendly magical surroundings. Here witches ruled, and taught the children. There were a few wizards, but they kept themselves to themselves. They were obsessed with creating new labour- and time-saving devices, which gave them time to create more devices, which in turn gave them more time to... and oddly they seemed busier than ever.

Although the Land of Corin was run by the witches, it was ruled by a king. The covens were a little jealous of one another and each refused to let a witch from another coven have the rule over them. But the king was popular, there was order, and for the most part, the people were happy.

Triona had decided that as soon as Eydith reached seventeen, she would tell her about her father. So, shortly after her seventeenth birthday, she sat her down and had the talk.

'You mean I'm the daughter of a wizard?'

'Yes, Eydith, I thought I should tell you before you read it in my mind,' said Triona.

Eydith stared wide eyed at her mother. Had she been found out, she wondered? 'I would never do that, Mother,' she said, feigning innocence. Though it was almost true because she hadn't got the hang of it yet, and most of what she picked up was pretty scrambled.

Triona got up and went to the cupboard where she kept the brooms and mops. She selected a very straight pole, almost as tall as Eydith. She held it out, and tried hard to think of something fitting to say before handing it over. But all she could think of was, 'This was your father's staff. He passed it to you on the day you were born.'

'My father's staff?' said Eydith, her eyes widening in awe. But a dark thought crossed her mind. 'But... a witch told me that a wizard only passes his staff on when he dies.'

'He died,' said Triona, softly and flatly. 'When you were born.'

Eydith ran her fingers along the blackened staff. 'It looks very strange, Mother. Not a bit how I imagined a wizard's staff would be.'

'I wouldn't know,' said Triona. 'But one of the nurses said it changed its appearance and became like that as it fell into your hand.'

22

At Havrapsor University, back when Eydith was far away and still a baby, Dennis devoted himself to coaxing, cajoling, threatening, and manipulating his fellow senior wizards into supporting him. He cleared himself a crooked path to the Archchancellorship, succeeding in spite of the assistance of Rumpitt and Pelgrum. Which, to their credit, was half hearted.

That was over sixteen years ago. He began his reign with a period of benignity in order to dupe the senior wizards into continuing their support until he was firmly established in power. They soon saw their error. Now he ruled through fear, not respect, and the university's reputation across the land of Kermells Tong was at a lower ebb than it had been even in the last days of Wimlett's rule.

Dennis had spent the years since his election searching for the staff of office. He had even offered a reward to anyone who could bring it to him.

He had the Drum removed from Wimlett's little house, and it was now chained to a large iron ring screwed into a wall in his new palatial rooms in the East Wing of the University. He'd had his predecessor's house utterly demolished. The letter he found there was incinerated one day in a fit of anger by a fireball from his fingertips.

As Archchancellor, Dennis's rule was as fierce and firm as Wimlett's had been fair and friendly. And the Piggin Wissall was totally out of bounds to lecturers and students alike. Except for himself, of course, when he was out searching for Wimlett's staff.

23

A few weeks after her seventeenth birthday, armed with the knowledge of her wizardly heredity, Eydith set out on a journey that would change her life. It brought her to the great gates that kept her and the rest of the unwizardly world on the outside of Havrapsor University.

Regardless of what her mother had thought appropriate clothing for such a visit, she was wearing a knee length black dress, belted loosely at the waist. Her boots were mid-calf length, with flat heels, and being a tallish girl, five feet nine inches, she was glad that the fashion for higher heels was over. Around her shoulders she wore a short dark-green cloak with a loose-fitting hood with braided edges, sewn by her mother. She liked to describe her hair as dark blonde. It was coppery, and looked good, she knew, against the green of her cloak.

Eydith didn't know it, of course, but she was lucky to have inherited her mother's snub nose. As an aspiring wizard she might have relished having the family feature; but as a self-conscious young woman she would no doubt have been more pleased with the selection her genes made for her. Her eyes were deep and blue like her father's and capable of his same penetrating gaze. Though it was less intimidating when not coming at you down a long, craggy nose.

She looked around the massive wooden frame of the gates for a bell-rope, or a knocker – anything, in fact, that she could use to draw attention to the fact that she was there and wanted to go in. Her fists didn't produce much of a knock. But the staff in her hand looked as though it might make some noise.

She raised it and brought it round in a wide swinging arc. It was not one of her best ideas. Already, this powerful wizard's staff was displeased to be in the hands of someone it considered a mere child. It liked even less the idea of being used as a knocker. Especially on these big, magical gates that it had helped to build many years before. The gates sensed the staff coming and flinched.

The staff halted itself a fraction before making contact, knowing where it was. Home.

Unexpectedly, the great iron bolts slid back of their own volition, and the gates flew open as if they'd been hit by an invisible tidal wave. Carried by the momentum of the staff, which completed her swing the moment the gates opened, Eydith stumbled headlong into the quadrangle. What she said next was most unladylike. She struggled to her feet, and dusted herself down. There was a dull pain in her knee, which on examination revealed a tiny cut, oozing the tiniest spot of blood.

Most wizards have an aversion to the sight of blood, and Eydith, as a proto-wizard, was no exception. Her knees buckled and she briefly passed out.

At the sound of the gates flinging themselves open, a number of wizards had appeared in doorways. They saw Eydith crumple, and hung back to see what would happen next. All except one, who was of a mind to investigate. His name was Linkwood. He scurried across the quadrangle and knelt beside her. Not to be outdone by this show of courage, others began to come forward.

'Bring some water!' urged Linkwood.

'Get a stretcher!' yelled another. 'Bring bandages!' yelled another. 'And smelling salts!'

The panic was becoming deafening, with wizards and students shouting and hurrying off in all directions to look for non-existent first-aid items. Health and Safety had not arrived in Kra-Pton. Especially not at the University where it was once tried and then forbidden on the grounds it might invalidate a lot of what they did magically.

From his rooms in the East Wing, overlooking the quad, Dennis heard the commotion below. He strode to the window to see what the fuss was. There was a young *woman* down there, and water was being brought by the bucketful in answer to Linkwood's request. The young wizard was cradling Eydith's head in one hand and brushing her hair away from her face with the other.

When the water arrived, Linkwood reached out, expecting a cup to be put in his hand, but instead felt the weight of a two-gallon bucket. 'You've got to be kidding,' he groaned, and thinking quickly, shrunk the bucket to cup-like proportions.

Two more wizards appeared carrying a stretcher between them. Goodness knows where they found it. Probably conjured it from an old illustration they'd found, and the chances of it staying in the material world for long were slim. Whilst another, skilled in the art of mending cuts and grazes – and who was incidentally, acutely colour-blind – was attending to the bloody scratch on Eydith's knee.

Dennis stood quietly at his open window, watching. But unable to contain himself, he opened the door and stepped out onto the balcony. 'Keep the damn noise down will you!' he yelled.

Eydith's eyes opened suddenly as though someone had switched her on. The world in which she found herself was filled with noise. People were rushing about, and getting in each other's way. Some trying to help. Some just curious. But there was one who was trying to drown her in a miniature bucket of water. She choked, and pushed it away.

She was also aware of someone complaining about the noise. With Linkwood's help, she sat herself up, and managed another sip of the water. After that, she placed the tiny bucket on the ground beside her, and... 'Are you all deaf!?' she yelled at the top of her voice.

Everyone stopped. The ensuing silence was, in its way, as deafening as the noise.

'Thank you,' said Dennis, now that some kind of normality had been restored. From his higher viewpoint, he appeared to be looking down his nose at Eydith. His face was fixed in a quizzical frown. 'What's the meaning of this intrusion, *girl*?'

Eydith didn't see his lips move. The question went directly to her brain, ignoring her ears, and spread like cold syrup across her psyche. She didn't answer until she was standing firmly on her own two feet. Something was tugging at her mind. She bent down without taking her eyes off Dennis, and picked up the staff. Unheard by all, it coughed and wheezed, and thought, *Oh, no, not by the throat again.* It's hard to describe how an ancient piece of wood sounds when it speaks. Something like a crusty but venerable old man with a long white beard, and, sometimes, as Eydith would later discover, a short red temper.

Eydith tilted her head to face Dennis. 'I've come here to learn,' she announced, a little more confidently than she felt. 'I want to be a wizard!'

She heard chuckles around her, and could see hands covering sniggering grins.

Dennis smiled his characteristically superior thin smile. 'You can't be a wizard, *girl*. Only seventh *sons* of seventh *sons*, and the *sons* of wizards, can be wizards,' he told her, emphasising the male dominance of the University, and making it quite clear that the University gates were closed to females. Then his face brightened a little. 'Now – Linkwood, isn't it? – show the young lady out.'

Dennis spun round and disappeared back into his rooms.

A gentle hand touched Eydith's sleeve. 'I think you've upset him,' said Linkwood, with a passing grin – an attempt at humour to cover his self-consciousness at talking to an attractive girl. He shook his head and his pointy blue hat shed some sequins. He could clearly do with a new hat. 'I think you'd better leave,' he said, sympathetically.

'I don't want to cause you any trouble... er, Linkwood? You've been kind. So I'll go,' her friendly words were delivered in a tone that showed how angry she was. She stormed back through the open gates into the dusty street. Linkwood caught up with her.

'Where are you going?' he asked, keeping pace. 'Have you got somewhere to stay?'

'Nowhere,' she replied, irritably. Probably to both questions.

'Will you stop a minute? I know somewhere not far from here.'

She stopped in her tracks. 'Okay. Where?'

'Come back to the university.'

'I can't go back there without *him* knowing.' She pointed the staff at the university as she said this and Linkwood ducked.

'Whoa! Careful where you're pointing that thing. It nearly had our gates off, so I don't like to think what it might do to me.'

She looked at the staff in her hand. 'Oh, yes. It kind of did, didn't it?' She lowered it out of harm's way. 'Perhaps I should aim it at *him* next time.'

'I wouldn't advise that. Dennis's magic is more than a match for your old staff, I'm sure.' He looked closely at it for the first time. 'Interesting, though, how you made it do that.'

'Very,' she said, as impressed with it as he was. 'But it still doesn't get me inside without *him* knowing.'

Linkwood put a conspiratorial finger to his lips, and whispered, 'The cooks' entrance. Just follow this wall to the end, and turn left twice. Keep going and you'll come to a low door in the wall. Wait there and I'll let you in.' He paused before heading of, 'Oh, and call me Link. Everyone does. Well, everyone except Dennis, that is. When he remembers who I am.'

Eydith considered her options. Not that she had many. It was getting dark. She had nowhere else to go, except home. And she couldn't face that, having left with such high hopes and expectations. She'd promised her mother that somehow she'd make it as a wizard. And unless she accepted help from good people like Link, she might never get past the barriers created by awful people like Dennis.

Link took her silence for a yes. The young wizard turned and went back inside, leaving the gates to close themselves.

She decided the best thing to do was meet Link, at least for tonight. Tomorrow was another day. She hurried around the building and down a narrow alley. She found the low door, and waited. Link's route through the building was more convoluted, and running through the corridors was prohibited, so he took longer.

She heard him on the other side of the door. He swung it back with a faint squeak. As he stuck his head through, the last of the sequins fluttered down off his hat. When he opened the door wider, light from a torch burning inside flooded the alley. Momentarily, the shadows around her appeared to be alive, and she ducked hastily under the low portal. Link closed the door firmly behind her.

He beckoned her to follow and they emerged into the kitchens. Pots and pans hung from the ceiling. Cupboards, sinks and ovens lined the walls. Tables and chopping blocks filled the floor space. The place was warm and everything looked recently wiped.

'Where are all the people?' she whispered.

'Probably in the dining hall this time of day,' replied Link. 'I expect you're hungry, too. I'll find you somewhere to hide your bag, then I'll get us something.' He led Eydith to what looked like just another kitchen cupboard door. But the cupboard was bare, and he signalled her to get inside with him. She hung back, wondering what he might be up to. He signalled her more insistently to follow. When they were inside, in the semi-darkness, he pushed a panel at the back, which opened into a small octagonal room, where all the walls were in fact, doors. He chose one, seemingly at random and ushered her through. 'I won't be long,' he said, 'make yourself comfy.' He plucked a torch from a wall bracket and lit it as he started to walk off.

'Suppose someone comes?'

'Er... Don't open the door unless they knock like this.' He did a rat-a-tat...tat, and was gone.

Eydith was now alone in a dark room, waiting for her eyes to accustom themselves. Was there a chair in here? As if someone was reading her thoughts, the room became lighter. There was no obvious source for the light. Who'd done that?

'Who's there?' she asked, timidly. Then, getting a grip, 'Who's there?' she demanded. Reassured by the lack of response, she looked around and saw a table and a couple of chairs. In the corner was a bed of sorts, and on the floor was a tatty rug. She walked over to the bed and gave it a tentative push with the heel of her palm. It felt reasonably soft.

The staff shivered in her grasp as she tried to let go of it and lean it against the wall. Her fingers were locked tight around it. And then a voice that seemed to speak from some ancient and elemental place spoke to her mind. 'Don't put me down just yet. I haven't made up my mind if you're staying or not.'

'Who said that?' she said, glancing rapidly around the tiny room.

'I did,' the staff replied, still speaking directly into her mind. 'I am called Sprag.'

Although the voice was in her head, she was drawn to the staff as it spoke. 'You can speak? In my head? And hear my thoughts? How long have you been doing this?'

'For you – ever since your father gave me to you.' It paused, remembering the moment. 'Well, not exactly gave. He dropped me as he fell dying, and you grabbed me. I switched off soon after, though. The thought of a baby waving me about like a cot toy was unthinkable. I switched on a few weeks ago when I was handed to you again. Since then, I've been getting used to the idea of… things.' It didn't elaborate, but she sensed it was about it being in the hands of a girl.

The staff's voice was austere but not threatening. Eydith settled remarkably quickly with the idea of the staff having a persona. It was now Sprag. She'd heard that wizard's staffs sometimes had an affinity with their owners – though *owners* seemed hardly the right word – but she had no idea that this affinity meant person to person, mind to mind. She sat on the edge of the bed. 'My father…' she whispered, 'tell me about him.' A warm sensation came over her mind as she felt Sprag thinking fondly of the old wizard.

'He was called Wimlett,' Sprag began.

'I know,' said Eydith.

'Don't interrupt,' said Sprag, sharply. 'And you don't need anything but your mind to speak to me,' it explained, sounding mildly exasperated.

She went quiet.

The staff continued. 'He was an old wizard called Wimlett. He was Archchancellor of this university, you may know…' It felt her mind nodding, but it carried on, regardless. 'The role became too much for him, and he began drinking a lot. I sensed at the time, however, that there were forces at work that even I did not know of. Wimlett went out a lot at nights. And as a result of this unknown force acting on him, he travelled in time, too, as I recall, but not too far, short hops back and forth. He found it very disorientating. And wearing. And then…' he paused, meaningfully, '… then he went womanising.'

Womanising?

'Yes, but only the once, I think. I can't be sure, because he didn't always take me with him at nights. And his mind was often too foggy to read when he came home.'

Wizards are mostly celibate... her thought trailed off as she felt Sprag's presence assert itself.

'But not always,' said the staff 'Which is obviously why you are here.'

She felt awkward and moved past that thought quickly. It would doubtless ambush her later. Right then her thoughts were racing. *And what about him – my father – dying like that? Was it natural? Or suspicious? You must surely have some idea.*

'I read his memories when he slept,' Sprag continued. 'They were fragmented. But they didn't match the stories that were going around. Things like him being drunk and bragging that there was nothing he couldn't do. That's when Dennis...'

Dennis? Eydith thought, *what's he got to do with it?*

'I heard that Dennis put a spell on Wimlett to discredit him – that sort of thing,'

No, she thought, frowning.

'Just listen, will you?' said Sprag, irritably. Eydith shut up.

'Where was I? Ah yes: when the inn local to the university was severely damaged by two brawling trolls, Dennis discovered your father asleep upstairs on the sofa in your mother's room, where she'd taken him to sleep the night off. Dennis saw his opportunity to discredit your father, and moved him by magic, to your mother's bed, where he would hopefully be discovered in a compromising situation and lose the Archchancellorship for bringing the office into disrepute. Dennis had a soft spot for your mother, you see – which was why he showed up in her room – and he became enraged with jealousy when he found your father there. He already hated your father for being Archchancellor, and this was too much for him. By moving him to your mother's bed he hoped, too, that the result would be an offspring. Which it was. And very few people know of that. Dennis resisted the urge to slay him with magic right there and then – knowing he'd probably come off worse the instant Wimlett was roused...' The staff paused, as if contemplating the scenario.

Yes? She leaned mentally closer.

'Yes,' said Sprag. 'Wimlett was mild-mannered, but could do pretty well anything. Anything but get the sex of his offspring right. It was then that Dennis put a spell over the whole city, ensuring that every man or woman, and every troll, would believe that Wimlett caused the devastation to the Piggin Wissall by rogue magic.'

Well, how do **you** *know, then?*

'I'm not a man, woman or troll.'

Oh.

'That spell brought disgrace on Wimlett. And all because Dennis wanted him out of the way. Dennis was even responsible for getting the drunk troll to the inn that night to start the fight,' said Sprag.

Eydith was seething. *That's terrible. Poor father. There has to be something I can do to make this right... er... Sprag?*

'All you can do is wait,' said Sprag, sagely. 'Believe me, you will find a way to avenge your father, and to be accepted into the University. Because I will help you, and so will Wimlett, if you ask him.'

My father. She frowned. *He's dead. You did say* dead, *didn't you?*

'He no longer lives,' Sprag tried to explain. 'Not in the way that you would define living. He's in a state between alive and dead. He has befriended Naphrat, Death's helper. Together they keep a general eye on Dennis.

What, like a spy? said Eydith. She was not keeping up with this too well.

'Spy?' said Sprag. 'No, not exactly. He and Naphrat try to make sure Dennis doesn't get out of hand. Potentially, he has the power to rule all Kra-Pton, and maybe beyond, but he can't harness it because he lacks a vital magical element.'

Sprag chose not to mention this was itself. He went on, 'Naphrat is doing what he can behind the scenes to make sure it doesn't happen, sending Dennis on pointless searches sometimes. And he needs your father's help to keep him informed. Wimlett keeps a fatherly eye on you, too.'

The staff went silent, as if it had finished, then said, 'But Naphrat and Wimlett increasingly need help from people in the real world. People with both a magical *and* a physical presence who can oppose Dennis more directly.' The staff paused again, to announce what it had been leading up to: 'Which is why I believe you are here now.'

This was all going to take some processing for Eydith.

Sprag picked up on this. 'I know you'll have lots of questions. But, for now, I just want to ask you to do one thing for me.'

'Okay,' she said weakly.

'Do you want Wimlett's and Naphrat's help?'

'Of course I do. You know I do.'

'Then ask for it. Say it now, out loud.'

'If you say so.' She got up, looked around self-consciously, and said, 'Father. Naphrat. I need your help. *Please.*'

24

Eydith heard Link returning, and put all thoughts of Sprag out of her mind. Link knocked, using a prearranged rat-a-tat...tat. She let him in and noticed he didn't seem to be carrying any food.

He went over to the table, and from inside his robe produced a table-cloth. He shook it out in front of him and it billowed out over the table, drifting into place like a parachute. He snapped his fingers and orange sparks spat across the table. When the smoke cleared, Eydith saw a small banquet set out before them.

'How did you do that?' she wondered.

'Oh, it was nothing really,' he blushed, slightly.

'No, it wouldn't be for a Seventh Level wizard,' said a disembodied voice inside Eydith's head. Then the voice added, 'Even you could do it with the right words.' It was a new voice. A more human voice. It wasn't the staff talking. *Can you hear me, Sprag?* She thought.

'Of course, mistress. What do you want?'

She liked the 'mistress'. *There's another voice in my head? Who is it?*

There was mental silence for a minute or two. She was aware only of Sprag probing around in her head. Then... 'There's nobody in here but me and you, mistress,' replied the staff. 'Unless your father's here. I thought I sensed him when we came into the room.'

'*Father?*' she thought, experimentally. But the voice didn't answer.

She brought her attention back to the room where Link was seated ready to eat. 'Why did you go to the dining hall when you could've done all this in the first place?'

'I didn't know what we were having today, so I went to check a menu.'

'What...?' She let the next question go. She sat down and eyed the spread hungrily. 'Just one thing, though. What about knives and forks?'

Link snapped his fingers, and there was cutlery.

As Sprag had suspected, Wimlett was in the room. But he was hanging back for now. He was standing behind Eydith as she tucked into her roast chicken dinner. He was watching Link across the table scoffing chicken vindaloo with an extra helping of curry sauce. *Glad I won't be sleeping near you tonight*, Wimlett thought.

'When can I learn to do magic like you,' asked Eydith, just as Link had overfilled his mouth with chips dripping with curry sauce.

He wasn't expecting her to speak while they were eating. It wasn't customary among wizards in the university's dining areas. So, to clear the large mouthful he'd taken, he chewed faster. His cheeks were getting redder and redder. On the inside they were becoming like magma chambers of a volcano. After a couple of snorts through his nostrils, curry sauce finally erupted from his mouth in a colourful explosion.

Eydith saw it coming and ducked away.

Wimlett wasn't so quick. And he was right in the line of fire. 'Oh, shit,' he moaned – as it went straight through him.

Link was now spluttering and gasping. And Eydith was panicking. Not least because of the apparition behind him. *Who's that tall, pale figure in the black robe?*

'Oh dear, *him*' she heard Sprag say. 'That's Naphrat the Gaunt.'

What's he doing here? She said, her voice rising in panic. She'd been about to rush around to Link, but stopped at the sight of Naphrat.

'I don't know, mistress,' replied Sprag. 'But I think the correct question is, whom has he come for.' They watched helplessly as Link looked about to gasp his last.

'No!' cried Eydith in desperation. 'Don't take him now! Please!'

It occurred to Sprag that something odd was going on. The Grim Reaper's aide wouldn't normally be here doing this. There was no need for him to personally conduct the passing over of a mere Seventh Level wizard. Linkwood's soul would be garnered with others on the Reaper's rounds. And Sprag was right. Something was going on.

Naphrat shot what seemed like a quick, friendly grin at Wimlett, and raised his scythe.

Eydith could only watch, open-mouthed and appalled.

As the young wizard was about to expire, Naphrat swung the scythe and gave him a resounding thump on the back with the blunt end, dislodging the chip that was blocking Link's airways (in another time and place it might have become known as the Naphrat manoeuvre). Link spluttered and filled his lungs with precious air. The Assistant Reaper checked a Life-Timer in his robe, and nodded, satisfied. Tiny lights at the back of his eye sockets twinkled for an instant at a job well done.

Naphrat knew that he, Wimlett and Eydith would need all the help they could get against Dennis. They could ill afford to lose even Linkwood. So, Naphrat had managed to destine the young man to help them – having first cleared it with The Powers That Be, of course.

The Assistant Reaper's work done, he left the room as inconspicuously as he'd arrived. It was an unusual errand, and a pleasant change for him to be extending a life. Back in Death's study, the name Linkwood dropped a long way down the Lists in the Ledgers.

⸺⊷⟨❖⟩⊶⸺

25

While they were cleaning up, Eydith occupied her mind trying to work out how she might find a legitimate way to remain at the University. She didn't want to stay cooped up in that little room for more than a couple of weeks, if possible. And she couldn't expect Link to look out for her much beyond that, either.

Sprag had told her that she *would* find a way to become accepted into the University. And that the other voice in her head – which may have been her father – had told her she *could* do magic like Link. All she needed was the right words. So, where would she find them?

Sprag provided the answer. The library.

She asked Link to take her there. She knew he could hardly refuse, because he thought he owed her a huge favour. He thought it was her who'd dislodged the food from his throat. He found it hard to believe she could pack such a punch, but she wasn't going to enlighten him. Not yet, anyway.

'I want to see the old books,' she said. 'The ones with the most powerful spells… you know, from a long time ago. Serious magic.'

'Okay,' he said slowly and cautiously, 'I have access to those. Anything else?' he added, a little playfully, trying not to grin at her nerve.

'Yes,' she pushed on, undaunted, 'I need to learn, and quickly. In fact, I'd like to start right now.'

Link went silent, trying to avoid the pleading look on her face. But he couldn't. 'We'll have to choose the right time,' he started to explain. 'The books you want are not allowed out of the library. I can't borrow them. You'll have to study them in one of the reading rooms. But first you'll need some basics. And you'll need to work your way up by degrees to the sort of books you want to study. I can help you with the basics, of course, but once you've mastered them, you'll have to learn by yourself. There's a point at which magic becomes personal.' He paused, letting her digest what he was telling her.

She nodded. 'Thanks'

'Do you want to take the full eight-year course?' he asked, guessing that she hadn't properly thought this through. 'Only I don't think I can hide you for that long.'

'Eight years? Is it really that long?' she said, screwing her eyes tight shut at the frustration of it all, and huffing loudly.

The voice of Sprag entered her mind. 'No need to worry, mistress,' it said, 'I know all the spells. I was there when your father was learning. I can help you assimilate them.'

'Okay,' she said, mentally. Brightening, she looked up at Link. 'When can we go there, then?' she asked, starting to feel something truly exciting was about to begin.

'You're deadly serious, aren't you?' Link looked her in the eye, and didn't doubt it for a moment. 'Let me check the best times.'

***

A few days later, Link heard on the grapevine that Dennis was going fishing. This is what Dennis always said when he was going on another expedition in search of Wimlett's staff. He couldn't stand fish. And why sit on a riverbank for hours hoping for a fish to bite, when he could simply summon one from the water? But he needed a cover story, because it was an embarrassment to him that after so long he still didn't have the staff.

Leads as to the staff's whereabouts had become scarcer over the years. So, when a rumour reached Dennis on one of his recent prowls around the inns of Kra-Pton, he knew he'd have to follow it up. Rumours of magic that he couldn't account for beyond the confines of the university were of special interest. Most of what he picked up on the grapevine was unexceptional, everyday magic, but this new rumour concerning magical activity around the city of Prossill was worth following up.

Prossill was further than he'd ventured so far in his quest, and would mean being away from the university for some weeks. But something about the story that had reached him was compelling. It centred on a woman and a baby who'd shown up in Prossill about seventeen years ago – the very time the staff went missing from Kra-Pton!

Link promised Eydith he would take her to the library when Dennis had left. He knew the Archchancellor was usually away for several days on his so-called fishing trips.

'How will you know for sure when he's gone?' Eydith asked. 'Does he make a big show of leaving?'

'On the contrary,' Link replied. 'He usually sneaks out at night, with his two special guards.'

'*Special?*' said Eydith, raising one eyebrow.

'Well, he thinks they are. The pair he used to have, Billy and Stan, got too old for traipsing around with him. And too fed up with his moods, too,' said Link. 'Now he's got a couple of new lads. Probably the only ones left in the garrison with the patience to go with him. The Sergeant owes Dennis a few favours, so he lets him borrow some help and protection occasionally. Not that he needs either, but he likes bossing people about. And he doesn't like to demean himself with manual labour of any kind. He usually gets them to load his stuff and the Drum on his wagon shortly before he leaves, so we'll wait until then.'

Eydith knew very little of the Drum, so this was an opportune moment to ask Link about it.

The Drum's past was more hearsay than history. And so far it hadn't come up to expectations, in Link's eyes, not for a magical artefact of such supposed significance. 'It supposedly contains the greatest spells of all the Archchancellors, going right back to the very first one – a man called Eldrum the second,' he said, trying to recollect what he'd heard in his first term.

What Link could not tell her was that the Drum was a powerful channeller of magic. For its owner, it could intensify his magic, and nullify or disrupt the magic of others. Dennis knew this. He also knew that its powers were limited without the staff. Wimlett had seen to that. Wimlett had also endowed the Drum with a personality of sorts. He used to talk to it, rather like gardeners talks to their flowers. He treated the Drum as though it were a person, and it responded. It even developed a mischievous streak, which delighted Wimlett, even though it worked against him sometimes, when it might douse a candle or hide his meal. Wimlett would hear a chuckle from the Drum and threaten to kick it.

Now the Drum was chained to a large iron ring screwed into a wall in Dennis's study. It tried to roll away at first, but found it couldn't break the magically impervious iron chain. It resolved to wait until the end of Dennis's term of office, or his death, whichever came first, like a captive animal. But it was smugly happy, knowing that it contained, unavailable to him, more magic than Dennis could know in twenty lifetimes. And he couldn't access any of it without the staff. Which, knowing Sprag as it did, the Drum was pretty sure would never happen.

But the Drum did get freed from the chain sometimes. On Dennis's occasional jaunts following up on rumours of magic, he always took the Drum, reasoning that if it was in the vicinity of the staff, it might betray its whereabouts in some way. For these trips, the Drum would be manhandled into either a large sack or under a canvass sheet and put in the back of a cart. And this was about to happen.

26

On the eve of Dennis's 'fishing trip', Link rushed back to Eydith's room to tell her that he'd seen Dennis's guards loading a cart. He'd seen the Drum, too, because no matter how many covers the two guards draped over it, the electric-blue light of its shape still managed to shine through, as it mischievously advertised its presence to all.

Link returned to the quad to see what was going on. From his vantage point in the shadowed cloisters, he watched the cart with Dennis and the guards on board roll slowly and quietly out through the gates and into the night. The Drum tired of lighting itself up – and of attracting moths – so now the cart and its occupants were just dark shapes in the darkness. When they had completely disappeared over Yonder Hill (as the hill behind the university was called), the quiet of the night was suddenly interrupted by soft cheers that seemed to emanate from the fabric of the building itself.

'Dennis has gone,' said Link, poking his head round Eydith's door and smiling. 'Are you ready?'

She nodded and picked up the staff, ready to follow him into the unknown. The library.

Link led the way through many corridors and passages, avoiding anyone who might show some interest in them, like a senior wizard taking a late stroll. Eydith could hide her face in the hood of her cape, and lower her voice half an octave, but there was no way of disguising her legs, loath as he was to do so, without a longer cape. He suggested she crouched lower if anyone looked in their direction. But after doing this a few times she was beginning to feel a bit ape-like.

At the next vacant room, he pushed her inside and slammed the door. 'Put your staff down,' he told her.

'What?' asked Eydith, unsure.

'Put the staff *down*,' he insisted, 'I'm going to change that dress you're wearing into something more practical. I'll be directing magic at you, and I don't want your staff deflecting it, or worse still, throwing something back at me.'

She grudgingly laid Sprag on the floor. '

'I'm only going to change your clothes into something a bit more masculine, you know, so you don't stand out so much.'

How rude, she thought, then realised what he meant. Sprag, listening in, held itself in check.

She was pleased with the clothes Link gave her. They were very practical. A loose jacket that hung long at the back, with a collar she could raise to hide her hair, and tights, and a pair of boots that came just above her knees. It occurred to her to ask why, if he could do this, he wore a cheap old hat from which all the sequins had fallen off. But she thought better of it.

He opened the door and checked the hallway. All was clear, as it usually was this time of night, so they continued down to the library. To reduce the chances of meeting people, Link took her on a less frequented route. But it had its drawbacks.

As they progressed deeper into the bowels of the university, Eydith tried not to think about the darkness and cobwebs hanging from the ceiling. There was a cold draught, too, and she could see her breath. *Surely there must be a nicer way than this*, she thought. She didn't like having to grope her way along passageways where the walls were damp and spidery. She followed Link closer now, afraid to let him out of her sight. But soon there was a welcome light ahead. When they turned a corner, she saw a large, black, rivet-studded door, with a flaming torch set into the walls on either side of it.

'We're here,' said Link, reading the sign that said, YOU ARE HERE. 'I'll go in and see if there's anyone about.' And he disappeared inside.

Eydith stood alone in the flickering light, holding Sprag in both hands, ready to defend herself. Nothing happened, apart from the occasional blast of cold air. It was beginning to feel like too long, when suddenly Link was back. 'It's all right. There's only Paske in there,' he said, quietly. 'And I think it's safe enough for him to know about you.'

'Who's Paske?'

'The librarian. He knows where everything is. Just tell him what you want. Come on, I'll introduce you.' He trotted back inside and half dragged the drowsy Paske out from behind his desk. The nightshift was not conducive to wakefulness or helpfulness. But when faced with Eydith, the librarian revived somewhat flushed, and bowed his head.

'Hello, Paske,' she said, with a winning smile. 'I'm told you can help me. I'm looking for the books covering the most potent spells. They're probably the very old ones... and hopefully not in the basement of this... er... basement.'

Paske arched his eyebrows. 'Potent spells, indeed? You will be careful?' Link vouched for her. With his hands behind his back, and swaying to some rhythm only he could hear, Paske nodded in the general direction, and muttered, 'Down there, on the left. Just passed the Romance section.'

Confused and conflicted, Paske watched her go. *What's a girl doing in here*? Should he report her to Dennis? Yes, of course he should. And he'd be in trouble if he didn't. But another side of him thought, *who would know*? He hated Dennis. And what's more he quite liked young Linkwood. So maybe he'd smother his passion for the rules and live dangerously. He did allow himself the occasional lapse, after all. He nodded privately. He'd convinced himself.

Eydith wandered along the aisles until she came to the section she was looking for. She glanced up at the shelves, and ran a finger along the spines of the books, reading the titles as she went. This was a difficult enough exercise in itself, but made harder by the books not wanting to be read, and moving their title letters into some odd-looking anagrams. 'Can you hear me, Sprag?' she whispered.

'Of course I can, mistress,' it snapped.

All right, all right, don't take that attitude with me, she thought, tightening her grip on it.

'Okay, okay. Don't choke me,' it complained.

'I don't honestly know whether I'm holding you by the throat or the foot.'

'Watch, and I will show you which way up I am.' The staff started to writhe disconcertingly in her hands, and took on a green glow, which put that part of the library in an eerie light, but she continued to hold it firmly with both hands. Sprag was twisting and turning within its almost metallic sheath, changing from its usual flag-pole straightness into a gnarled and knotted branch. She wasn't sure if she liked the new look, but she resisted the urge to think so. Moments later, it became still, and glowed with an orange aura, which enveloped Eydith as well, fusing with her aura. Finally, when its metamorphosis was complete, it rested inactive in her hands.

She would have to get used to this new look, but it was certainly more like a wizard's staff now. She held it up and looked more closely. Runes were writhing in the depths of its sheen, and, encouragingly, she was beginning to understand some of them. She sensed Sprag in her mind again, hanging around as if it owned the place. She wondered whether, if she concentrated hard enough, she would see its true being. But fearing she'd regret it, she stopped herself. But she did realise why she wanted to do it. She couldn't keep referring to Sprag as '*it*'. The voice in her head sounded male. At the very moment she thought this, she felt Sprag subtly, wordlessly pressuring her to be referred to as *he* and *him*.

'I should have told you sooner. And changed sooner,' Sprag said, pleased to be in his original form again. 'Now... it's time for you to learn.'

He told her which books to look for first. As Link had said, this had to be done incrementally. Though she seemed to be taking a we'll-see-about-that approach.

She collected an armful from the shelves, and ferried them to a reading room. She dutifully turned each page as and when instructed by Link, but when she was sure he wasn't watching, she would touch a page with the staff. Immediately, the writhing letters became still, and she was able to read the spells. With Sprag's help, she needed to read them only once and they were lodged in her mind.

After three hours, Sprag pointed out that, even though she'd done a lot, she was still only in the first-year books, and that it would be unwise to try to learn too much at once. 'There's another day tomorrow,' he said.

Link noticed she'd been reading what looked like a recent addition to the library. The gold page marker was shiny and new, and its red leather-bound cover was still stiff and unscratched. Paske usually tipped him off about new acquisitions, but hadn't mentioned this one. As he was in hailing distance, Link called him over.

'We've had nothing new lately,' the librarian assured him, 'And not for a long time in this section. It must have been misplaced.' He squinted at the title. 'The last time I saw this it looked a thousand years old,' he whispered. 'Now it looks new. What is that child doing?'

'Have you found anything that interests you?' Paske asked her.

'Oh, yes... This one's amazing. I didn't know you could do a fraction of the things it says in here.'

'Did you know it's one of the oldest books down here?' he asked, warily.

'No, I found it in the first-year section. Though it does seem a bit advanced. Exactly the sort of thing I'm looking for, though,' was her matter-of-fact reply.

'What's it doing over here? And what did you do to make it look new?' Paske wanted to know.

'Nothing,' said Eydith, honestly. 'I just picked it up off the shelf.'

Sprag was saying nothing.

'Try another,' Paske suggested, taking a quick trip from the room to pick a book from the advanced magic shelves, curious to see what would happen. 'Only five-hundred years old, this one.' It tried to back away. But he passed it to Eydith, who accidentally brushed it against Sprag. She felt the spells within tingle, as though they recognised him. They did. He'd helped write them. The book suddenly looked as new as the day it was bound. Link swallowed hard, and knew he was in the presence of powerful magic.

27

By sunrise the following morning, Dennis had put some distance between himself and Kra-Pton. He and his two guards would soon reach the plains that stretched from the Snake River to the desert at the foot of the Cludells, a mountain range that was home to trolls. Dennis's immediate concern, however, was barbarians.

Dennis hoped to avoid the barbarians that roamed the area. Not that he feared them especially – he usually managed to bribe or threaten them in order to obtain safe passage – but he didn't want to waste time with them.

His two guards, recently assigned to him by the Sergeant of the barracks, were called Jook and Psoddoph. Dennis's initial reaction was: What were your mothers thinking?

The two men, both in their early twenties, disdained full battle armour for such light duty, and wore leather jerkins over chain mail vests. Though they had brought lethal-looking spiked helmets, should they need them to protect their heads and faces. Also, in the event of a skirmish, they had with them three of the very latest, automatic, rapid, multi-firing crossbows. These were untried and needed testing, so the guards were half hoping to run into some barbarians.

The two men were similar in height and build. They both wore their hair short and sported short black beards, outlining the square jaw-line common to guards. But they differed broadly in temperament. Psoddoph was brighter, and the more cautious. He was a problem spotter and solver. He could read, too, and was helping Jook with it when they had time to spare, and when Jook could be bothered. Jook was better at enjoying life, and was inclined to be impulsive. He also liked a cigarette now and then, which didn't appeal to Psoddoph, but he didn't make an issue of it. They hit it off most of the time, and were happy enough to be assigned together.

Jook sniffed the air. 'What's that awful smell?' he said, pulling a face and covering his nose.

'It must be the Snake River,' replied Dennis, 'we must be getting close now.'

'I never smelt anything like it in me life,' said Jook.

As they drew nearer the river, all three covered their noses and mouths with makeshift masks. But the smell was penetrating.

The river was little more than a stream at the ford where the road met it. But judging by its colour and consistency, and the pungent fumes rising from it, Dennis thought it would be advisable to use the crossing boards, in case it dissolved the iron rims of the cart-wheels.

'Did you see that?' cried Psoddoph, suddenly, pointing to his left. Two other pairs of eyes followed his finger, and saw the cloud of dust that was heading towards the distant horizon.

'Yeah...' replied Jook. 'It looks like a cart with no wheels being pulled by a donkey with its arse on fire.'

'Thank goodness,' sighed Dennis, with more than a hint of relief. 'That's how it looked to me, as well.' It had a familiar look to it, too, though he didn't mention that.

While Dennis was at the back of the cart showing Psoddoph where the crossing boards were stowed, Jook saw the opportunity to hop to the front and take the reins. He didn't like to say so, but he didn't want Dennis in charge of the horses when it came to guiding the cart across the river. He wasn't too impressed with Dennis's driving skills. And younger men always reckon they're better at such things. Dennis seemed okay with this and once the boards were laid, he stood back with Psoddoph to watch

The crossing went well, but as Jook urged the horses up the sloping bank on the far side, one of the wheels hit a rock and the cart jarred to a halt. From the back of the cart, there was the ominous twang of a crossbow firing, then another, and another, as the pre-loaded crossbows automatically discharged themselves. The bolts sprayed out from the cart like a muted firework display, minus the colours. Jook scrambled down, lay flat and covered his head with his hands.

Psoddoph had the presence of mind to grapple Dennis to the ground on hearing the first twangs. The Archchancellor's outrage petered out the moment he caught on, and he stopped his foul-mouthed tirade in mid-sentence.

After a few more twangs, all became quiet, and the three men nervously got to their feet, ready to duck at the slightest hint of the sound of a bowstring stretching, or a click from a crossbow mechanism. It all *seemed* calm enough. Jook checked the cart, and warily pulled back the canvas covering the Drum. He stood back and scratched his head. Then, sad faced, he turned to Dennis and solemnly announced, 'The Drum's dead, I think.'

The other two came closer and peered in. The Drum had caught an entire salvo of arrows and looked like a large sleeping porcupine.

'Oh, no,' Dennis groaned. 'This is terrible. What am I going to do now?' he whimpered, steadying himself with one hand on the cart and clutching his brow with the other. He seemed to be sobbing.

The two guards looked at one another at a loss. In the end, Psoddoph stepped up. 'There, there, now,' he said, putting a comforting arm around Dennis's shoulder. 'Don't take on so, boss. Me and Jook will fix it for you. Good as new, we will.'

'Can you do that? *Really?*' said Dennis, between sobs.

Psoddoph nodded.

'Promise?' said Dennis, looking deep into the guard's eyes. Then he snapped, 'Cos if you don't... you're in *serious* trouble. Both of you!'

The guards urged the horses up the embankment and got the cart onto level ground. When Dennis had calmed down, he got on the cart while Jook and Psoddoph went round picking up all the bolts they could find and reloading them into their magazines. Only this time, they didn't attach them to the crossbows.

They pressed on. While Dennis drove, the other two sat gingerly pulling the bolts from the Drum. What they needed now was a lot of something to patch it with. Little did they know that the Drum could repair itself in an instant, but it was enjoying all the attention, so it let them get on with it. Under one of their seats they found some old goatskins, some thread and a rusty needle. They cut the skins into squares and stitched them over the holes in the Drum as best they could. Some hours and a few miles later, it looked like a patchwork quilt. Dennis was not amused. It was far from 'good as new'.

The two guards covered it over it and turned their attention to the crossbows. Dennis decided that the cart would be better defended if they placed them, fully loaded, one on each side, and one at the rear of the cart. Jook and Psoddoph could then ward off attackers while he drove the horses.

'Yeah,' murmured Psoddoph, slowly, while silently wondering how Dennis expected him to aim, fire and reload, while he was driving like a bloody maniac along some potholed dirt road, or ploughed field. Jook was having the same thought.

***

As the day wore on, the travellers began crossing the grassy plains of the Tong. At this time of year, the grass was about six feet tall. The black-topped road out of Kra-Pton was long and winding as it followed the boundaries of the freehold farms, and it was never possible to see further up the road than the next bend.

Dennis wasn't pushing the horses too hard, as it was almost midday. Also, the road was winding even more, and the corners were coming up more regularly. He allowed the horses to pull at their own slow pace, which was making him drowsy.

Suddenly, he was jolted from his reverie as the two animals stopped dead in their tracks. Psoddoph, who was watching the rear, fell back into Jook, who dropped his cigarette and nearly burned himself.

'Can't you be more careful?'

'Do you have to smoke those things on duty?'

'On duty?' queried Jook. But before they could start an argument on what constituted being on duty, Dennis turned on them.

'Shut up you two and man the crossbows,' said Dennis, urgently. 'We've got company.'

Five barbarians, of various shapes and sizes blocked the road, riding slowly towards them. Dennis was used to the usual ruffian-cum-hero barbarians with loads of fur round their boots; overly large, leather lunch boxes: big sword and small brain. But he'd never seen female barbarians – though logically they had to exist – and there in front of him were four of them. The fifth, a male, as previously described, was bringing up the rear of the group.

Dennis steered the horses to one side in the unlikely event that the approaching party only wanted to pass him, and he brought the cart to a stop as they neared. But the barbarians kept coming as if they hadn't noticed him, or were choosing not to. Not noticing him was something Dennis could tolerate, but ignoring him ... well, that was different.

The leader, or at least the girl in front, had noticed the cart. Though not in a very focused way, that might inspire her to stop or swerve. Dennis, on his part, had taken her in fully. He noticed the two small triangles of leather and fur on her chest, for one thing. He noticed the far away expression in her eyes, for another. That came from smoking too many exotic herbs and drinking too much young ale: a combination which made the communication from brain to mouth intermittent and dangerously slow.

She drifted sideways towards the cart, and when her horse was about a half a yard from Dennis's horses, she pulled back on her reins and yelled for those close behind her to 'Thtop!'

The girl behind her realised all too late what was happening. And the leader's horse, which had been slow reacting to the yank on its reins, was nudged further forward and jammed between Dennis's two horses. Now, nobody was going anywhere.

An argument broke out among the women. Dennis didn't recognise the language, and looked to Psoddoph for help. The guard shrugged. The women argued on animatedly, waving their arms and shouting, probably obscenities, with scant regard for the men present. Dennis sat and watched, and he found that if he ignored the obvious obscenities, he could make some sense of what was going on.

He didn't like what he was hearing, and, acting on impulse, tried to get his horses to back up. The leading woman felt the animals buck.

'Thtop!' she yelled again, and then looked slightly bewildered at what she'd said. Everything *had* stopped, and was likely to remain that way for a while yet.

'Thith ith a thtick-up,' she said, un-shouldering a bow and pointing an arrow at Dennis. The point began making a loose figure of eight in the air in front of him. Dennis began to relax a little, he considered the chances of being hit, even at this close range, were pretty slim. He stood up.

'Who are you? And what do you want?' he demanded, attempting to take control of the situation.

At this, two of the younger women behind her raised *their* bows and slotted arrows into the strings. The front woman re-sighted her arrow. The wizard instinctively half covered his face, and backed down slightly.

'Thith ith the clan of Herman ze barbarian,' she lisped, 'and ve vill not let you parth until you 'ave given uth all your money.' Her eyeballs seemed to move independently while she tried to remember the rest of her script, then she caught up. '...And all your shiny stuff. Isn't zat right, Herman!'

Herman the barbarian was asleep in his saddle.

'Hannah!' the leader called.

'Yes, Mama?'

The leader sighed. 'Not in front of thtrangers. You *know* I don't like you calling me Mama, in front of thtrangers.'

'Sorry, *Helga*.'

'Zat's better. Now vake your father. *Herman*, I mean.'

Hannah wheeled her horse around and trotted back. She gave Herman a gentle nudge. When that proved ineffective, she shook him more vigorously. This made him fall out of his saddle and hit the road. But, thanks to some thick fur clothing, he landed with only a muffled thud. Hannah sprang from her horse and rushed to his side, where she proceeded to kick him as hard and as often as she could. Accompanying each blow with some foreign obscenity.

'Hannah! Thtop zat. Can't you thee he ist thleeping?' shouted Helga.

'Of course, Mama. It ist ze safest vay!' Hannah snapped.

As Herman began to stir, the girl left him alone and remounted her horse. He rubbed his eyes and saw the cart. He yawned, lurched to his feet, and staggered to his horse. 'Vere ist mien stick?' he asked everyone.

'You haff it in your 'and, you ass,' Hannah replied, on behalf of all those present.

'You vill not speak to your far... er, Herman, like zat,' snapped Helga.

Hannah shrugged. She snatched the gnarled old walking stick from his hand and thwacked him on the shoulder with it. She felt so much better after that, and thrust it back into his hand. Herman then made a great show of straightening his right leg. This done, he put the stick against it and launched himself toward the cart with an exaggerated limp.

'Vot ist goingk on, voman?' he asked Helga.

'Can you not thee? My horth ith thtuck in ze cart, ze wrong vay round. You *thtupid* barbarian.'

'Of course, my dear. But ve vill deal viz zat later. Now, vot are all zees people doingk in our vay?'

'Ve are robbing zem, Herman,' Helga tried to explain, 'but zay don't theem to get it.'

He beckoned one of the girls forward. She looked marginally brighter than the others. 'Do you know ze language ov zees men?' he asked.

'Yes, Farzer, zay are from Kra-Pton.'

Good. Vell, Hilda, you vill speak viz zem...' he stifled a yawn, 'sayingk zat zay are being robbed. You know ze zort ov zing... throw down ze loot, and all zat jazz.'

'Shall I tell zem about ze trouble as vell, Farzer?'

'Trouble? Vot trouble?'

'Ze big trouble, you know. Ze bit where you say you vill kill zem, and all zat stuff viz ze arrows and ze sword.' She looked around to see who *had* the sword today.

'Oh... er,' Herman looked at Jook and Psoddoph, considering his chances. 'Yes, tell zem zat,' he added, tentatively.

Hilda lowered her bow, dug her heels into her horse's flanks and urged it forward. She stopped about a yard from the cart, looked at Dennis and smiled. The Archchancellor ignored it, but Jook and Psoddoph weren't going to pass up an opportunity to smile back at a pretty girl... even if she was a scantily clad barbarian, with long golden hair. She brushed back some loose strands that had fallen across her face.

'Herman the barbarian bids you good day, fellow travellers, and requests... er, no he doesn't...' she corrected herself, '... he orders you... yes, that's right, orders you to throw down all your valuables and everything. Uzzervize he vill severely kill you all.'

Having set out the situation, she smiled pleasantly and raised her bow again.

'Ain't you going to do something, boss?' hissed Jook.

'Like what?' said Dennis, from the corner of his mouth.

'Well... you know... a fireball, or something would be nice.'

'Are you mad?' Dennis snapped. 'One wave of my hand and: zonk, zonk, zonk!'

Jook grinned. '*Zonk, zonk, zonk*? What the 'ell's that?'

'I was making the sound of us each receiving a bloody great arrow in the chest,' said Dennis.

'For now... just do as she says.'

Jook and Psoddoph threw down what money they had in their pockets, and the two youngest girls scrabbled in the dust for it. The others looked on, chuckling.

While the group was distracted, Dennis motioned with his eyes, and the two guards moved in front of the canvas that covered the Drum in an effort to hide it from Herman.

Right on cue, Herman asked, 'Vot ist under ze sheet?' He was yawning as he limped around the back of the cart, and still flinching exaggeratedly from the pains in his ribs and legs.

Hilda brushed her long golden hair aside again, and spoke to Jook. 'He wants to know what's under the canvas, my good man.'

'Oh, it's only an old Drum,' said Jook.

Hilda lowered her bow, 'Zay say it ist just an old Drum, Herman,' she called back.

The tired barbarian lifted the corner of the canvas and peered underneath. 'So I see,' he mumbled, quietly, 'Tell zem I vont it down here, now.'

Hilda translated Herman's message, and the two guards lifted the Drum over the side of the cart and lowered it to the ground.

Herman yawned and started to walk. He was doing fine until he realised he hadn't got his stick, and then he keeled over. Just before Hannah was about to kick him again, Herman's youngest daughter, Eva, noticed he was still awake. She snatched up the stick and gave him a sharp, stinging rap on the arm, before passing it back and helping him to his feet.

'Now, vot voz I sayingk? Oh, yes. Ze Drum, mien got!' he exclaimed, then yawned. 'Vot a load ov ol' rubbish! Ist zis all you haff?'

Dennis looked at Hilda and shrugged. The girl herself shrugged, translating his question.

He continued, plaintively, 'Yes that's it, I'm afraid. Even our food is all gone.' Noticing a flicker of sympathy in Hilda's eyes, he sniffed, as if stifling a sob, milking the moment for all it might be worth.

Herman sighed. 'Vell, ve don't vont zis poxy Drum zat's for sure. Haff you seen ze state ov ziss, girls?'

The Drum was getting heartily fed up with the rude comments, but it held back. It was considering a quick makeover, but a change of ownership to barbarians wasn't exactly an upgrade.

'Put it back on ze cart.' Herman sighed heavily, again. 'And you two girls can give zem back zere money... how much voz zere, by ze vay?' They held out their hands and showed him the measly collection of small change. Herman sighed yet again, 'Ah, vell, give it back any vay, I don't vont zem spreadingk tales about how Herman ze barbarian robs ze poor people.' His chin dropped to his chest, and he limped back to his horse. Once there, he shook his head wearily, reached into his saddle bag, and took out a brown paper package, which he tossed to Psoddoph. 'Take zis,' he said, as it arced through the air, 'you need it more zan I do.'

Ten minutes later, after much heated debate and a lot of arm waving, the combined company of Kra-Ptonians and barbarians finally managed to untangle Helga's horse from the carthorses. A cheer went up, and after much handshaking and many expressions of thanks, and the two guards being very impressed with the hugging and cheek kissing, they bade one other a fond farewell... till next time?

Dennis waited until the barbarians were out of sight before he tapped his horses into forward motion again, and half an hour further into the afternoon, Jook asked no one in particular, 'Has anyone got anything to eat?'

'There's the parcel Herman gave us,' Psoddoph suggested, remembering. He found it under his seat.

'Be careful with that, you two,' said Dennis, having had an alarming thought, and slowing the cart to a stop.

Psoddoph eyed the parcel this way and that, and then peeled back the wrapping. Out of the corner of his eye he saw the others had assumed a defensive crouching position, heads tucked under folded arms – also as illustrated in the handbook of the Magicarp Swoop 7 for when disaster seems imminent.

They held their breath as Psoddoph turned back the last corner, and the package revealed its deadly contents... 'Anyone fancy a cold, chip butty?'

⊶⋘⟨⟩⋙⊷

28

Late the next evening, when the coast was clear, Eydith went back to the Library with Link.

She gathered some books and spread them on the table in the reading room. Sprag selected one and opened it where she'd left off.

Link accepted that he wasn't needed now. The staff was helping her far more than he could. He stood back and watched in wonder as the transfer of magical knowledge began. A minute later he jumped when someone tapped his shoulder. It was Paske.

'Is there really any point to this?' the librarian whispered. 'She's never going to be allowed to use what she's doing. And there's going to be trouble when she's found out.'

Before he could say anything, Eydith, having caught every word, jumped up and glared at the man. 'I am the daughter of a wizard,' she announced, firmly, hands on hips, eye contact unwavering. 'I have a right to be here and learn the ways of the wizards. I need this knowledge to develop and apply the magical gifts that no-one can deny I have. And if because of your outdated lore, the Archchancellor will not allow me to enter *this* university, as is my birthright, I will earn that right as a mage-ess in some other place. Then, I will come back and avenge my father for the appalling way he was treated by Dennis.' She stuck her chin out defiantly, and waited for Paske to reply.

Link looked at Paske and waited for a comeback. When it didn't come, he broke the awkward silence by asking, 'Can she say that?'

'What?' said Paske.

'Mage-ess.'

'No, I don't think so.' He pulled Link to one side and whispered, 'What she should've said, was *lady wizard*, but we all know they don't exist, don't we? I think it might be best if we got a few of the lads down here and threw her out, before Dennis gets back, don't you?'

'What?' Link was taken aback. 'We can't do that,' he whispered, hoarsely.

'Why not?' said Paske. 'Who'd know?'

'Well, I would for one. And what do you think that staff of hers is going to do while she's being manhandled out?' Before Paske could reply, he added, 'I'll tell you. It won't lie there and watch, that's a dead cert. It minds her better than a troll guard would. And another thing… I like having her around.'

'You need be careful of this librarian, mistress,' said Sprag, in Eydith's mind. The staff had been listening too, and amplifying the conversation for her.

What shall we do? She thought back.

'Wait and see,' said Sprag. 'He's not strong enough to harm you. And any assistance he might summon will be asleep in a dorm now.'

Link smiled, silently congratulating himself for standing up to Paske for her. Although they'd whispered, he had a strong suspicion she'd heard. 'It's very late,' he told her. 'We should be getting back. But if you want to stay longer, I don't mind.'

'No, I think I've had enough for tonight,' she said.

At the door, Link turned the opposite way from the way they'd come in. 'I know a better way back – one that it isn't so damp, spidery and creepy.'

'Well, thank goodness for that.'

29

A few hours later, and quite a few miles away, Dennis was staring at the swaying rumps of the horses, his head lolling back occasionally, trying to stay awake. In the back of the cart, Jook and Psoddoph were on hands and knees with their heads hung over the sides of the cart.

'I wonder how long he'd had those chip butties for,' Jook said, groaning. He stared biliously at the road moving below him.

Psoddoph ignored him. He was busy bringing his share back up... 'Huey!'

30

Eydith followed Link along an alternative zigzagging passageway that led away from the library. It was said of the university's ancient architects and builders that they had a passion for passageways. And as the original plans were lost centuries ago, no-one knew where they all were or where they all went. Occasionally a student would make it his special project to find and map them all, but they were never seen again.

Torches lining the walls flickered brightly as they passed. 'Why ever did you take me down all those creepy tunnels, when we could've come this way in the first place?' she asked, with a hint of exasperation.

'I thought you should know about them,' Link replied, over his shoulder. 'So you didn't go wandering down there on your own.'

'I would *never* go down there on my own.'

No, thought Link, *I probably wouldn't either.*

Back in the little out-of-the-way room that Eydith was using as her temporary student digs, she leant Sprag against the wall by the old stone fireplace. There were logs in the bucket in the hearth, and some sticks already in the grate. The jug at the side of the hearth had water in it, so Link poured some into a pot and hung it on the trivet. 'Well?' he said. 'Will you do it, or shall I?'

'Do what?' she replied.

'Light the fire,' said Link, grinning.

'I'll do it.' *Can you hear me Sprag*? she thought, loudly.

'Mistress?'

Help me, she thought.

'Do as I show you,' said Sprag.

She saw colours entirely new to her and heard unrecognisable sounds – they were swimming together in her head. When she closed her eyes, the sights and sounds seemed to solidify. The vision coalesced into words.

'Now straighten your arm, and point to the sticks,' Sprag instructed. 'Say the words, and, in your mind's eye, see the fire ignite.'

She recited them to herself, slowly and deliberately, replicating every syllable. The instant she imagined a flame in the hearth, a tongue of fire crackled from her fingertips, and the sticks burst into flame.

Link smiled approvingly, and placed a couple of logs onto the fire. Meanwhile, Eydith was blowing on her fingers, the ends of which were still alight. She blew harder, but the flames wouldn't go out.

'I did it, Link!' she yelled, still blowing on her fingers and looking hastily around for somewhere to douse them. *The water jug, of course!* She plunged her hand in and a cloud of steam rose. She took it out slowly, half expecting it to burst back into flame. When it didn't, she eyed her fingers, critically, thinking that there ought at least to be blisters. But there was no damage and no pain. In fact, everything was as it should be.

Link grinned, 'It was all in your mind.'

'What? I was on *fire*! Didn't you see it?'

'The flame was all in your mind,' he insisted.

'How come you saw it as well, then?'

Link tried to explain. 'It's sort of an aftershock. Happens the first couple of times. And then – once it doesn't bother you, that is – it doesn't happen anymore. You just don't think about it.'

'Hmm,' she said, 'You might have warned me.'

'To be honest, I'd forgotten about it myself till just then.' he said, tossing one more log into the fire. A shower of sparks spiralled up the chimney, reflecting like tiny sparkling gems on the polished ebony of Sprag's twisty exterior.

Eydith ran a finger down the staff's smooth surface. The writhing runes that covered it stopped moving as her finger passed over them, and written spells surfaced, like so much antique graffiti. The spells mirrored those in her mind, and as she changed her thoughts, the runes changed with her, showing her what words to say for whichever spell she lighted upon. She wanted hot water in the little iron pot. The runes appeared. She read them mentally. The flames intensified, and in moments, steam was bursting from the bubbles.

Link noticed the staff sparkling and watched, fascinated, trying to read the runes himself. But they writhed like snakes, and he couldn't make sense of them. This was way above a Seventh Level wizard.

Wimlett was back. He gingerly, and literally, stuck his head through the door before entering the room, to see who was home, and make sure there was nothing messy or volatile being eaten. He didn't want to witness a repeat performance of the previous night. He liked to visit Eydith more frequently now. He'd kept an eye on her over the years, but his interest was spiralling now that she was at the university. She had directly asked for his and Naphrat's help, too, so he could show himself any time soon. Naphrat was holding back, saying they should leave her to it, and merely observe for a while, but Wimlett was losing patience with that.

31

The light was fading on the Tong plain. Flocks of starlings were flying back to Kra-Pton, making impressive swirling patterns in the sky while trying desperately not to bump into one another, and the first stars of the evening were appearing.

Dennis idly flicked the reins at the horses, not because he wanted them to go any faster, he just couldn't think of anything else to do. Jook and Psoddoph were over their digestive problems, and were looking for signs of civilisation on the far horizon. The near horizon, too, come to that. It didn't really matter, as long as what they found was human, and friendly.

32

Wimlett floated by the wall next to Sprag. Eydith sat watching pictures in the fire. Link sat opposite her, his eyes half closed, wondering what it was he'd just had for dinner. He'd let Eydith conjure up some dinner tonight, using some of the magic she'd learnt that day. In fact, it wasn't that bad. It was just that he couldn't place what it was.

'If you've got nothing else to do tomorrow, can we go to the library again?' Eydith asked.

Link looked up at the ceiling, mentally reading an appointments book. As a Seventh Level wizard, he was still required to attend a lecture or two, and to take the occasional class himself, but tomorrow looked free.

Wimlett idly ran a feather-light finger down his old staff.

'I don't have anything special lined up,' said Link. 'But we need to be wary of Paske. I get on well with him, but he's a bit of a rules man, and he's probably having a crisis of conscience about you being here.' He took a long sip of the wine he'd conjured to wash down whatever it was he'd eaten. The wine was blackberry tonight, by way of a change from his usual dandelion and burdock. And as he drank it he made a mental note not to keep producing what they needed magically. There were limits to the co-operation of magic when it came to basic everyday things.

'He seems afraid of me,' said Eydith. 'He retreats into himself whenever I'm near.'

'You're a girl,' said Link. 'He's not used to being around females – especially in his personal domain, the library. You're bound to unnerve him a bit. To see him really afraid you have to be around when Dennis pays him a visit. Paske fears him more than anyone. Hates him, too. It's almost comical to see him when Dennis strolls in. And I think Dennis gets a kick out of scaring him.'

'Is *everyone* frightened of Dennis?' Eydith asked.

'Only as a powerful wizard with a bad temper,' said Link, examining his empty glass. 'Not so much as a man though,' he ruminated, absently. 'I think deep down Dennis may be as insecure as most other people.

'If he has a 'deep down', that is,' she said.

'I'm not afraid of him,' said Wimlett, his voice on the very edge of audible. 'Never was. And he certainly can't hurt me now.' But nobody heard except Sprag, who waited to see if his old custodian would announce himself formally this time, instead of hovering on the edge of things.

'I said…' Wimlett repeated, 'he doesn't frighten me.'

Still nothing.

The old mage thought about this lack of attention for a moment, then muttered, 'How rude. I'm being ignored, aren't I?'

'They can't hear you,' said Sprag.

'And why not, do you think?' said Wimlett, addressing the voice he couldn't place, and becoming annoyed.

'I would be inclined to believe it's because you're dead,' said Sprag, 'or has it escaped your notice?'

'Blast!' said Wimlett, banging his fist through the table soundlessly. 'And who are you? Who spoke?' he wanted to know, looking around the small room, but seeing no-one to whom the voice could belong.

'I did,' said Sprag, slowly, drawing his attention with some subtle glowing.

'You can hear me, staff?'

'My name is Sprag.'

'Alright, staff – Sprag.'

'How come you never said anything to me when I was alive?'

'I tried,' said Sprag. 'How I tried! But you wouldn't listen. You always put my voice in your head down to too much wine. If you had listened, you would not be in this mess. Between us we could have contacted Death or Naphrat and sorted out that business with the faulty Life-Timer. We could have worked something out.'

Wimlett was dumbfounded. Aghast. Ashamed. How could he have been so stupid? *Okay, the drinking*, he admitted. But that was only an excuse, and not a credible reason or answer.

'But you could've gotten through to me, surely? After all, we were together long enough.'

'I repeatedly tried. But it was impossible.' And then by way of mitigation, Sprag went on, 'I began to see my powerlessness – and yours, too – as evidence of something bigger at work. Destiny, perhaps.'

'The Powers That Be,' added Wimlett, thankful to glean a sheaf of self-respect from this harvest of condemnation. 'And we may never know why.

'Oh, I think we might,' said Sprag, rather cryptically.

'One day, eh?'

'But, anyway,' Sprag said, moving the conversation on, 'you did all right... mostly.'

Wimlett shrugged, possibly in agreement.

'Most of the time, in your final years, you only used me to lean on,' Sprag ruminated, as Wimlett went quiet. 'Not as a symbol of office, or even to complement your powers. But I gave you power.'

'Gave me power?' Wimlett retorted, indignantly.

'Yes, I did,' intoned Sprag. 'And stopped you from doing serious harm to other people. And to yourself, on some occasions.'

'I don't recall any of that,' Wimlett challenged.

'You wouldn't,' said the staff, unintentionally a little too harsh for Wimlett's liking. 'When your magic fired off randomly, I reversed the effects on others whenever I could, returning them to normal,' Sprag recalled with no relish.

'What about the spells I created? The clever ones... the ones only you and me know about.'

'Mostly my doing, though some of yours, too, I'll allow you that. Now I serve Eydith, and she has that same power to create. With my help.'

Wimlett was a ghost without a leg to stand on, but he rallied well. 'I can be of help, now, you know – now that she's asked.'

Sprag sighed, almost audibly.

Wimlett continued. 'She's on a mission, staff...'

'Sprag,' corrected Sprag.

'Naphrat wouldn't have let that Linkwood out of his clutches, if the boy wasn't important to her and her mission, would he?'

'No, I'm sure he would not,' replied Sprag. 'How exactly do you intend to help?'

'Naph and I aren't sure yet. Things are coming to a head, that's for sure, but we're still watching to see how the situation develops.'

'Can you hear voices, Link?' asked Eydith.

'What sort of voices? Wheezy breathy, kind of voices – muffled, like someone in the distance talking through cotton wool?' Link suggested.

'Yes, I suppose it did sound a bit like that,' she agreed.

'No, I didn't hear anything,' he said, grinning. Then he said, 'OUCH!' as her pointy-toed boot impacted with his shin. 'I deserved that,' he granted. 'No, really, I did hear something.'

Eydith took a sip of wine, and screwed her nose up. *I hope he doesn't conjure this one up again,* she thought. *Yuck. Are you there, Sprag?*

'Mistress?'

Are you talking to someone?

'Yes,' he replied. 'Your father.'

Oh… how is he? Is he well?

'Well… no, mistress, he's dead.'

Don't start with the clever remarks, I'm having enough trouble with Link.

'Sorry, mistress. I was merely being factual. I suppose he's all right. In the circumstances.

'He says he's ready to help. Now that you've requested it. But he and Naphrat – and myself, of course – haven't yet decided how best to help. So he will hold back for now. He can speak to you through me, if necessary.'

Give him my regards, she thought.

'I will… she sends her…'

'I heard,' said Wimlett. And he found himself wondering about the absurdity of Eydith having a guardian angel who was in fact the Dark Angel. *How did that work, exactly?* No doubt he'd find out in due course.

Link swirled the last few drops of his second glass of wine around the bottom of his glass, and drank it down. He snapped his fingers, and two more logs cart-wheeled into the fire. Eydith was impressed. He poured himself another wine. 'Have you given those voices any more thought?' he asked, quietly, and without looking up.

Are you there, Sprag?

'Yes, mistress,' came the sleepy reply.

Is it okay to tell Link you can talk?

'I can see no good reason not to, mistress. I'm as certain as I can be that he's on our side.'

Me, too.

She heard what sounded like a match being struck. *What was that?* she wondered.

'Just clearing my throat, mistress.'

Wimlett chimed in, 'Tell her about the power of the Drum.'

'Anything else?' said Sprag, and he started to speak...

'I heard,' said Eydith aloud, forgetting to think it. But it didn't matter now.

'Heard what?' asked Link.

'I was talking to my staff.'

'I guessed as much.' Link knew it could happen between a magician and their staff. But only extremely rarely. How many more surprises did this girl have for him?

33

'I can see lights,' said Psoddoph.

'Where?' asked the other two in unison.

'Over there,' Psoddoph pointed, 'just beyond that ridge.'

'Looks like a town,' said Jook.

Dennis recognised it. 'That was just a village a few years ago. Still is a village on the maps. I do wish people would update the maps of Kermells Tong.'

Psoddoph scratched his head. They didn't have a map with them. So how would it help if they didn't have one that had been updated?

Ten minutes later they were in the town, driving slowly between rows of brightly painted houses. The lights from the windows lit the streets well.

They needed somewhere to stay for the night. Dennis reined in the horses at the roadside. The two guards jumped down from the cart to stretch their legs while he strutted off to find somewhere to stable the horses.

Minutes later, he was back. 'There are stables a hundred yards down the road on the left. Take the cart down there while I find a hotel. Meet me back here when you're done.' He started to go, but paused. 'And make sure you bring the Drum back with you.'

34

'Have you seen Dennis?' asked Jook, joining Psoddoph on the street outside the hotel the next morning. He squinted in the low early sunlight and yawned almost wide enough to take his jaw off its hinges.

'Not yet,' Psoddoph replied. 'He might be down the stables.'

As if on cue, Dennis appeared, leading the horses.

'Morning, Dennis,' they said together, cheerily.

Dennis cringed. He hated being on familiar terms with his minions, and only tolerated it now because they were travelling incognito and he didn't want to draw attention to himself by being too much of his usual overbearing and arrogant self. *We're just three guys on the road together, one regular guy and two soldier guys*, he said to himself, adding, *Yuk!*

'What do you want for breakfast?' asked Jook, turning to go back into the hotel.

'Nothing,' said Dennis. 'We can have something later.'

'We need to eat, boss. You never know when you're going to get the chance again, this far from home,' said Jook.

'Without a map,' Psoddoph interrupted.

'So, we're not going anywhere till we've 'ad some breakfast.'

Dennis clenched and unclenched a fist, huffily tied the horses to the hitching rail and stormed off down the street. After a dozen paces, he glanced over his shoulder to make sure they'd gone inside. *That staff might be here*, he thought. *After all, it was only a rumour that the staff was in Prossill, and we're in that general direction – maybe I should check this place out, while I'm here.*

He crept stealthily down the street, mentally sniffing for magic or magical artefacts, listening at doors and peering through windows, until he picked the wrong house. The one with the yappy dog tied up by the front door. Dennis didn't have to worry about him, though. It was the big one sprinting round the side of the house, dragging its kennel that he really needed to worry about. Dennis fled, and reluctantly called a halt to his search. It was just that he was so eager to get on and do something. He had a strong feeling that this trip was going to produce results. But he was now wary of getting chewed by one of the neighbourhood dogs. It had all happened too quickly for him to bring his magic into play. Though he was wary of doing that, too. He had to restrain the magic for now. *We're just three guys*, he reminded himself, cringing again, and modifying it to, *We're just a moderately important guy accompanied by two idiot soldiers.*

35

Eydith was wide awake. A brand-new day. She picked up Sprag and thought about breakfast. *Porridge would be nice*, she thought, and waved a hand while saying the words that came to mind. And there it was, steaming-hot on the table, just the way she liked it. She was getting good at this. Though Sprag did interfere to insert a dish at the beginning of the spell.

'Is my father here, Sprag?' she whispered.

'Yes, mistress.'

'Is he awake?'

'No, mistress, not yet.'

'Where is he, exactly?'

'Halfway up the wall behind you. He's on his back, and gently drifting across to the next wall.'

Eydith was curious. 'Why doesn't he stay in one place?'

'Well,' said Sprag, 'he's about the same weight as the air around him and he tends to move with it. He can control it while he's awake, but when he's asleep, he drifts. The air currents, slight as they are in here, take him around the room. He'll probably do about five circuits a night in a room this size.'

'What happens when he wakes up and finds he's not where he started?'

'Very amusingly, he usually says, "Where am I?" and starts flailing like a drowning man until his feet are on the ground again.'

There was a rapid *rat-a-tat... tat*, on the door. The agreed knock. Eydith slid the bolt back and Link came in. 'Good morning, everyone,' he said, cheerfully pushing his hat back from his eyes. He heard only Eydith's reply. And he was completely oblivious of the effect that the sudden draught from the door had on the sleeping Wimlett.

Wimlett was heading into a corner of the room many times quicker than his usual drifting speed. Had not the turbulence woken him just before he met the wall, he would have drifted on through. As it was, he saw it too late and butted it silently. 'Ouch! Where am I?' Then he rubbed his head, felt a phantom lump, and again said, 'Ouch!'

One of the many inexplicable things about Wimlett's life, or rather death, was that he was immaterial and yet he could bump his head. It shouldn't happen. But he was developing a theory about it. Now was not the time to ponder it, though. Finding he was floating halfway up a wall, he panicked. He couldn't abide flying, even a few feet in the air like this. He didn't mind how high he was, as long as his feet were on something attached to the ground, like a building or a mountain. He'd tried to convince himself he had nothing to fear, because ghosts can't be harmed, but the logic was no match for the fear. And until he could work out why he still *did* come to harm sometimes, that fear would stay with him.

At the moment the only one enjoying the invisible air show was Sprag, who had the presence of mind to break his mental link with Eydith before Wimlett's language became unsuitable for the ears of a young lady. Which it did.

'I hope that makes you feel better,' said Sprag, when Wimlett was finally down and had concluded the episode with another flourish of expletives.

'It does, actually,' said Wimlett. 'Swearing saves violence. If I swear, I don't smash anything or hurt anyone, including myself. So, now I swear, and everyone wins.'

Sprag was interested to know how he managed to smash things and hurt himself when he was a ghost.

'I've no idea. Even Naphrat is baffled.'

'Well... if you've calmed down enough now, perhaps you can speak to your daughter.'

'Yes,' said Wimlett. 'Good idea. Now's as good a time as any. It's about time we properly met.'

Sprag opened his mind to Eydith's and scratched on hers to announce himself.

Sprag? I thought you'd gone back to sleep.

'No, mistress, I was protecting you from your father's outrageous language. However, he has calmed down now and wishes to speak with you. You can talk through me.'

'Hello, Father,' she said, looking around the room.

'I'm over here,' said Wimlett. 'You'll get the hang of it, I'm sure.' After that, he found himself a little tongue-tied looking for the right words to continue the conversation. 'I can hardly believe we're doing this after all this time,' he started. 'You've grown into a young lady your mother must be proud of. Because I certainly am.' Then he broke off, not wanting to embarrass either of them.

Eydith said, 'She tells me I get a lot of who I am from you.'

'I'm not so sure about that. But it's good of her to say so.'

'It's what's brought me here, Father,' she said. 'Things I have to do because of who I am. Because of you, really.'

The conversation went on like this, in a stilted but heartfelt way, for a minute or two, until Wimlett pulled himself together. 'We have so much to talk about, Eydith,' he said, warmly. 'And we'll have a lot of time to do it. But for now, as you say, there are some serious matters – the matters that brought you here – and we have to focus on them first.'

She couldn't agree more.

'I went to the Piggin Wissall last night,' he told her. 'I met Naphrat going in – which was handy – though for some reason the place emptied soon after we arrived,' he said, seemingly oblivious to the impression the pair of them must have made. 'Then Naph called it a night, and I drifted off and found a bar to haunt on the other side of Snake River. And guess what?'

'What?' Eydith prompted.

'I saw Dennis.'

'What was he doing there?'

'He's looking for the staff,' said Wimlett. 'It's a good thing he doesn't know you've got it. I'll go after him again tonight and see what else I can find out. I didn't see the Drum. But no doubt he has it with him.'

'He left here with it a few days ago,' Eydith confirmed, and related what she'd heard to Link.

'Right,' he said, 'Best thing we can do for now is get on with your magical education. Let's get down to the library before there are too many wizards about.'

She finished her porridge first, then picked up Sprag.

'Are you coming, Father?' she said, looking around the room.

'He's already gone, mistress,' said Sprag.

Link cautiously opened the door to check the hallway was clear. It was, so he took Eydith by the hand and led her down to the library. Not that she needed him to hold her hand, but neither of them was complaining.

36

Link cast his eyes around the library. 'There's no-one here,' he whispered.

'That's odd,' said Eydith. 'Surely Paske should be here, at least?'

'He is, mistress,' said Sprag. 'Somewhere.'

'Sprag says Paske is here somewhere, Link. He must be hiding.'

'I should have guessed. Paske!' he called. 'Where are you? You've got customers.'

The librarian peered around one of the bookshelves, his face as white as a sheet. 'Has it gone?' he whispered, his eyes darting around the room.

'Has what gone?' asked Link, following Paske's nervous eye movements.

'I think your father's here, upsetting him, mistress,' said Sprag.

Eydith turned to Link, 'My father's here.'

'Uh.' That explained it.

'There's something in here,' said Paske. 'It keeps pulling books off the shelves, floating them into a reading room and flicking through pages. It's got lots in there now. If I go and try to put them away, it throws things at me.'

'As a ghost, your father has some poltergeist abilities,' Sprag explained.

'Just stay there a moment, Paske' said Eydith. The pair strode into the reading room. Link slammed the door behind them. *Is he still in here, Sprag?* Eydith thought.

'Yes, mistress.'

Where?

'Behind the table.'

'I'll speak to him, Sprag. Then I'll tell Link what's happening.'

'Yes, mistress. But to save you that, I will let the young wizard hear.'

'You can do that?'

'Now that he knows, mistress, it will be easier to let him in on conversations. Not all of them, of course.'

Link was pleased. He hated being shut out now that he knew they communicated. It seemed a bit rude, too, for them to be talking privately in front of him!

She went to the table and sat opposite her invisible father, putting Sprag down beside the open books. The pages of one began turning unaided.

'What are you doing?' asked Eydith.

'It occurred to me...' said Wimlett, without looking up, 'that Dennis has the Drum. Now he wants the staff. He knows that he can only use the Drum properly if he has the staff.' Wimlett paused for a long moment. 'And if any wizard has the Drum on its own, and tries to perform... well, anything could happen. It has some mischief in it that the staff helps to keep in check.'

'I'm Sprag,' moaned the staff.

'We know all that. Sprag told me,' said Eydith. 'So why have you got all these books out?'

'Because I can't remember the damn words of the spell I wrote, which will bring the Drum and the staff together. I wrote it down in a library book, but I can't remember which one.'

'Trust you,' sighed Sprag.

'It's seventeen years ago, you know!'

'Mistress, we need that librarian,' said Sprag.

Yes, of course. 'Link, ask Paske for the last book my father handed in before he died. We need what's written in it,' said Eydith. 'Please.'

Link found Paske crouching behind his desk.

'Do you still have a record of the last book that Archchancellor Wimlett borrowed?'

'Wimlett? Why him? Of course,' he snapped, affronted that anyone might think he didn't. Grudgingly, he delved through his index system, found it, and sullenly skimmed it across the polished counter at the waiting wizard.

'And be sure to return it.'

Link was about to enter the reading room, when he stopped. 'I haven't got the book,' he admonished himself. He read the card and hurried to the shelves. Eventually he found what he was looking for on a remote high shelf in a dim and cobwebbed alcove. He made his way back to the reading room, inspecting the cover as he walked. Intrigued, he paused to flick through the pages. 'My word! I didn't know we had this kind of thing in here.'

He sat next to Eydith, and put the book on the table. 'Is this the one?' he asked, wondering if there was some mistake.

'Yes, that's it,' said Wimlett. 'Well done, lad.'

'I didn't know you read this kind of thing,' said Sprag, indignantly.

'I don't,' replied Wimlett. 'And neither does anyone else. That's why I chose it to write in.'

Link peered across at the book, one eyebrow raised, and commented, 'I certainly didn't know it was in here… Interesting, though.'

Eydith gave him a withering look. He glanced at the page where Wimlett had opened it. The pages started fluttering back and forth, as Wimlett searched the spells, employing his erratic poltergeist ability.

Finally, the book lay still. 'I've found it,' he announced.

Eydith and Link stared at the page, and then at one another. Eydith then looked where she thought Wimlett was sitting. 'What sort of writing is *this?*' she wondered.

'Do you like it?' said Wimlett, proudly. 'That's my tiniest, neatest handwriting, I'll have you know.'

'It's awful. I can't read a word of it.'

'Oh, come on…' said Wimlett, 'it's not *that* bad.'

Eydith ran her fingers over the writing. Sprag could probably read it to them.

Sprag could. But it was difficult to read verbatim, aloud. Easier to tell her in his own words. It was basically saying things they already knew. Not a spell at all, as far as he could tell.

And Sprag knew he was right when Wimlett went quiet. The staff picked up his annoyance and disappointment. The old wizard seemed to have written at such length in the book's margins about the benefits of uniting the Drum and the Staff that he'd forgotten to add the spell that would accomplish it.

After listening to mentions of the Drum and staff working together for the umpteenth time, Eydith looked at Link. 'We have to get the Drum away from Dennis,' she said.

Link nodded thoughtfully. Something had occurred to him. 'So, it must be Sprag that Dennis is looking for,' he said, not realising how late he was to the party. 'And if we get the Drum, then we'll have the power to deal with Dennis.'

'Precisely,' said Sprag, charitably.

Wimlett cheered up when he located the spell that Sprag had missed. It was cleverly woven into the narrative of the Drum and staff. But he wasn't pleased to find that the spell was inert. It wouldn't respond to him, or any of the others. He guessed ruefully that the spells in the book would respond only to the current Archchancellor. Dennis. The Drum contained these same spells along with hundreds more. And all that stood between those spells and Dennis was the staff. Or rather the lack of it. Wimlett decided not to wait till tonight to catch up with Dennis. He announced his departure, bade them farewell, and drifted off through the nearest wall.

37

Jook and Psoddoph finished their breakfasts at the hotel and loaded the few odds and ends that they'd used overnight back onto the cart, warily avoiding the crossbows. Dennis lifted a corner of the canvas, to make sure the guards had loaded the Drum. When he was satisfied that everything was how it should be, he made himself comfortable and flicked the reins.

He was almost whistling a happy little tune as they rolled out of town. He'd learned that the stable master's wife was the town gossip. When he finally got away from her, he'd satisfied himself that the staff wasn't there. So, the original plan was still in effect.

A sign at the edge of town read 'Prossill that way'. It was written on a finger pointing to the right. Beside it on the post was another finger pointing left, that read: 'Not that way'.

38

Wimlett left the university by walking through walls until he was outside and back in the sunshine. Without thinking, he took a long deep breath, and leant against a wall. As a ghost, neither of these things should have been possible, but he found that sometimes they were. He was working on a theory about it, which he'd run past Naphrat next time he showed up. Today he'd simply enjoy it. Whatever was in the air this morning was pretty good stuff. He took a few more really deep breaths and then set off towards the Tong Plain.

He really needed transport. He could still use his faithful old donkey, because they both occupied the same spectral plane, now. The problem was that Wimlett never knew when Muffin was going to show up, as he now circled the planet like a low-orbit satellite. If there was little or no wind, his acute hearing could pick up the sound of the ghostly cart before it reached him. All he had to do as it passed was time his jump right, and steer Muffin in the direction he wanted to go.

He was hoping Dennis wasn't too far ahead of him. Life would be easier if he could get over his fears and take to the air. Though how he'd fare with the air currents up there, he wasn't sure. He would have to take his courage in both hands before long, as speed was becoming essential. Dennis may be headed off on a fool's errand right now, but he'd be back and it would only be a matter of time before the Drum betrayed the staff. The only reason it hadn't happened already was that Sprag hadn't been in his original form when Eydith first brought him into the building. But that cloak of his pole-like appearance had since been shed.

A few minutes down the road Wimlett heard a cart trundling along behind him. *Ah...* he thought, but it wasn't Muffin. It was just another traveller getting an early start. He pointlessly stepped off the road to allow it to pass, and hopped up on the tailboard.

Half an hour later, he noticed a dust cloud on the horizon approaching at great speed. This time it was Muffin with the wheel-less cart on his latest orbit of the world. He was going to pass quite close...

Wimlett stood up and prepared himself for a leap that he hoped would propel him into a cart moving at subsonic speed. The donkey was close now. Wimlett took a deep breath, gauged the distance and, as the cart whizzed by, he launched himself into the air with a scream. 'Aargh!'

And missed.

He continued travelling at speed, caught in the spectral slipstream created by donkey and cart, and he screamed some more as he bounced along the road ahead of his original transport. He was about fifty yards further on when he finally sprawled to a halt.

The horse pulling the cart that Wimlett had been on panicked at the sudden rush of wind that went by. Wimlett heard the thunder of hooves, the rattling of the cart, and the terrified cries of a man desperately trying to regain control. Wimlett watched, wide-eyed, as it careered towards him, and started too late to shift himself.

The flying hooves thundered through his ribs, the wheels passed through his legs, and, caught in a second rush of air he went tumbling along the road again.

When he finally came to rest, he lay there, deathly still. 'Oh, the pain! The agony!' he wailed. After a moment, he thought about what he was saying. 'What pain? You haven't got any pain, you old fool,' he muttered. 'You're a ghost, remember? You're dead!' But he was still having problems learning to adjust his old sentient reactions.

That was it!

That was what was going on! His theory finally crystallised. Even though he was incorporeal and rationally he knew he could come to no physical harm, he was still reacting instinctively with his old corporeal instincts. It was all in his mind. Not that that made it any easier to deal with. It was strange how people thought that discovering something was all in their mind was the answer. It wasn't, but it was a step towards an answer. Wimlett felt sure of that. He got up and dusted himself down, until he realised the dust was swirling through him, and wasn't on him. The horse and cart had disappeared over the horizon.

Wimlett had had enough for one morning and decided to walk back to the university.

***

'Back so soon?' said Sprag, with what sounded like a suggestion of disappointment.

'I couldn't get a lift,' said Wimlett, curtly.

'I could always transport you,' suggested Sprag, helpfully. 'Where do you want to go?'

'Really?' Wimlett wasn't convinced, but said, 'I want to get just this side of Prossill.'

'Mistress?' said Sprag, 'Do you know where Prossill is?'

'Yes... er, it's about ten days west of here.'

'Hardly a map reference, but it'll have to do. As you may have heard, your father wants to go there.'

'And how exactly do you intend to get me there?' Wimlett scoffed. 'Because there's no way I'm riding you like a broomstick.'

'Nor any way I'm going to let you,' returned Sprag. The staff glowed momentarily, and before Wimlett realised what was happening its aura had enveloped him. He was stretched out as if made of elastic, and catapulted forward at great speed as he contracted back to normal size. There was a crackling noise in the air, followed by the sound of a minor sonic boom. 'You're on your way,' Sprag shouted after him, silently adding, 'probably faster than you'd like.'

Just on the edge of hearing, a scream faded into the distance.

'Has he gone?' asked Eydith.

'Oh, yes, mistress, didn't you hear him?'

Eydith realised she must have, and grinned, 'I don't think he was quite expecting that.' Then she wondered, 'Would it work for me?'

'Yes, mistress,' he said, confidently. But then he back-tracked. 'Probably. But in your case, I would limit it to shorter hops. Because, unless you can see your destination, you might find yourself landing in an awkward or dangerous place. Okay for ghosts; not for humans.'

'Worth considering, though,' she said.

39

Wimlett arrived in an awkward place. His impromptu magical flight ended with him inside a house of sorts somewhere on the Tong Plain. He landed with his head poking through a wall and his body on the other side, giving him the appearance of an exhibit in a trophy room. Not that anyone would see this indignity, he reminded himself. And being a ghost meant that it wasn't a pressing problem. Though, he reflected peevishly, being a ghost hadn't saved him from being slammed through rocks, bounced over cliffs, and shredded by trees on his rapid journey there. And now he found himself peering into a sparsely furnished room that was occupied by an old woman and a girl. They were sitting side by side on a bench-seat that ran the length of one wall.

The old woman looked up. 'Yes?' she snapped. 'What do you want?'

Wimlett was surprised. 'You can *see* me?' he said.

'Course I can, I'm not blind,' the old woman replied.

'But I'm a ghost,' he insisted.

'And I'm a witch,' she said. 'And don't I know you from somewhere?' She scrutinised him while scratching at a large wart on her chin. Unexpectedly, it came off and she hurriedly turned her face away. 'Yes! That's it. You're that wizard, Wim... Wim... something or other...' She stared at him again, and the wart had moved.

'Wimlett,' he obliged.

'Stop interrupting when I'm thinking,' she snapped. 'Wim...Wim... Wimlett! That's it.'

'The very same, madam. At your service.' Upon which he started to emerge into the room.

'Stop right there, mister!' she ordered, with such urgency that Wimlett froze mid-step. 'I've seen ghosts before. You got any clothes on? There's a young girl in here.'

'Of course I have clothes on,' said Wimlett, testily. 'I wouldn't enter a room without them. Besides, I have a daughter about her age.'

'All right, just being careful, that's all.' And looking aside at the young girl, she pulled a quizzical face and said quietly, 'A wizard with a daughter?' The girl also looked intrigued. But neither of them pursued it.

Wimlett sat himself on the bench-seat that ran the length of the opposite wall. 'Where am I?' he asked.

'Don't you know?' asked the girl, implying, *how can you not know where you are*?

'Well,' said Wimlett, 'I asked to be put down somewhere near Prossill.'

'Put down?' said the old woman. They were studying him closely now and making him feel uncomfortable. To avoid eye contact, he stood up and looked out of one of the windows. He scanned the horizon for a moment to try and get his bearings. 'You obviously know who I am, but I can't say I remember either of you. Have we met... er...?'

'Esmerelda,' the witch said, holding her head high. 'Esmerelda Swampshott.'

Wimlett decided immediately to keep it strictly to Esmerelda – or Esme, on better acquaintance – or he'd probably finish up calling her something awful.

'And this,' she went on, 'is Florence, me apprentice.'

Wimlett acknowledged Florence, who blushed slightly, and was evidently enough of a witch already to be able to see him, too.

'Where is this place?' Wimlett asked, again.

'Well,' replied Esmerelda, 'We're about a day and half from Prossill now, but last week we were five or six days away.'

'Has it moved closer?' asked Wimlett, puzzled.

'Don't be daft, man. How can it move? It's nailed down.'

Wimlett let it go for now. He looked around to see if her broomstick was handy. She was in such a quirky mood that she might hit him with it. Instead, he was surprised to see she had what looked like a wizard's staff resting against the seat on the other side of her. He'd have to ask her about that. But not right now. He glanced at Florence. She seemed to anticipate his gaze, and turned away. So he stared out of the window again, across the vast Tong Plain that stretched away to the skyline. Out of the corner of his eye, he saw the witch studying him again.

'I know where I saw you last,' she said, pointing an accusing finger at him. 'Years ago, it was. You were in the Piggin Wissall that night when the trolls wrecked it. You looked a lot, lot younger then, but something about you tells me it was you alright. I sense these things.'

Wimlett was beyond surprised. 'You remember that? You were there? I'm sorry but I don't remember seeing you.'

'After the first hour, you wouldn't have seen *anyone anywhere*,' Esme started. 'You were under the table, rat-arsed, if me memory serves me rightly, and destined to spend the night in the gutter, if that young barmaid hadn't taken pity on you and had you taken up to her room.'

'Up to her room?' Florence put a hand to her mouth.

'Don't fret, young Florence,' said Esme, 'nothing really disgusting happened. At least, not while this *gentleman* was conscious.' Then she looked at Wimlett. 'They say you had a lot to answer for that night. But, by my reckoning, I don't know how you could've been responsible. It wasn't easy to piece it together because someone with powerful magic put a spell on the city that night.' She paused for her and Florence to exchange knowing glances. 'I felt it, but I could only see through it a bit. Enough to know it wasn't your fault. Though I don't know what you were up to with that vanity potion you must have been using. Really! – a man in your position.'

'It's a long story,' said Wimlett.

'No doubt,' she said.

Wimlett chose not to elaborate. Instead, he found himself saying, appreciatively, 'You're quite a witch, Esmerelda! You've got it worked out closely enough.'

Now it was her turn to blush. 'Call me Esme,' she said, looking away, out of the window.

Waiting for the awkwardness to ebb away, Wimlett turned to the window himself. Nothing had changed so he went across the narrow room to the windows on their side. Outside there were a few trees, a couple of barns and some flat-bed carts, with bored looking horses idling between the shafts.

Seeing him peering out, 'Who are you waiting for?' Esme asked.

'I'm not waiting for anyone.' the wizard replied. 'But I'm on my way to find somebody.'

'What's his name?' she asked, bluntly. *Nosily* in Wimlett's opinion. But there was something about her he liked.

'Dennis, Archchancellor of Havrapsor.'

'Dennis?' she repeated the name quickly, as if to get it out of her mouth in a hurry. 'Oh, *him*.'

'You know him? Have you seen him?' Wimlett's interest was aroused. Florence, too, was suddenly alert.

'No, not since...'

'Not since when?'

'Not since I saw him last time, of course,' she said, truthfully, but exasperatingly.

'When was that, then?' he tried.

'About nine months before this one was born,' she said. The room went quiet as Wimlett digested this. Nine months before...

He leaned in closer. 'Florence is your... daughter?' he said.

Her face softened. 'Yes,' she replied, and smiled at the girl,

'And Dennis is...

'No, no, no, no, no,' she said. Perhaps protesting too much, thought Wimlett. 'I saw Dennis a few days after my own... close your ears, Florence... impregnation. He was in what was left of the Piggin Wissall's bar asking after Triona. He mistook me for her. Easy mistake. That's when I saw him,' she reassured Wimlett. 'The spell on the city that night robbed me of the memory of the father. It was the same for Triona. But we both suspected, as you were in her bed some of the night, you probably had something to do with it.' She paused, looking at him, waiting for him to confirm or deny.

But Wimlett was processing it all. He seemed to have landed among people who knew his story. People who sympathised with him, even. Was this Sprag's doing? He doubted it. Naphrat's? Maybe. The Powers That Be? Who knew?

'So, you know Triona?'

Esme snorted. 'My own twin sister. I should think I do!'

He stared at her. Triona's twin? How was that possible? *Esme is an old hag*, he thought. *And the girl is only sixteen or seventeen. She's far too old to have a child so young. Even allowing for her witch's powers.*

He leaned in more closely. He'd guessed the wart was false, and he could now see that she wore a lot of earthy make-up. She was certainly a lot younger than she appeared. Added to which, Florence, who would be Eydith's cousin, if all this were true, did look vaguely like Eydith. She had a similarly shaped face, the same eyes, and the same long, elegant fingers.

'We haven't been that close for years, Triona and me,' Esme interrupted his thoughts. 'We lost touch. Had a bit of a falling out. My fault really, I suppose,' she said, grudgingly, prompting a disapproving look from Florence. 'But lately I heard she was worried about Eydith – her daughter – going off out into the big world on her own on some mission. You know what these youngsters are! So, I thought it might help patch things up between us if I went out to find the daughter and see how she was doing. Maybe steer her back home, if need be.'

'This is amazing!' exclaimed Wimlett falling back in his seat, almost dropping through it. Regaining his composure, he said, 'Forgive me, but this is truly amazing.'

It was their turn to listen incredulously, as Wimlett explained how he was part of Eydith's mission. The only interruption was Esme's 'Ah,' when he confirmed Eydith was his daughter. He finished by mentioning how Naphrat was helping him.

'Death's helper?' said Esme, a little aghast.

'The very same,' said Wimlett. 'He's okay, really. He looks out for her now. Like some kind of angel on her shoulder.' The incongruity of the picture threw him for a moment. 'She will be very important one day... you mark my words.'

'Important for what?' queried the witch.

'Havrapsor!' he said, thrusting out his chest, a little pompously. 'And probably a lot more besides.'

'It's full of layabouts and worse, now Dennis is Archchancellor.'

'Exactly,' agreed Wimlett. 'It needs someone like Eydith to sort it out. As my daughter, she believes she has the right to study to become wizard. And so do I.'

'Good luck getting that passed Dennis, she said. 'I say we make her see sense and get her back home.'

'Good luck with that, too,' said Wimlett, chortling. 'You really don't know Eydith, do you?'

Esmerelda changed tack. 'Just fancy,' she said, a little wistfully, 'little Eydith, your daughter. That makes us sort of family, don't it?'

'It certainly does.'

Suddenly, the whole room lurched. There was a clanking of metal and the shrill sound of a whistle. The scenery at the window began to move slowly to Wimlett's right.

'At last,' said Esmerelda, with a sigh.

'What magic is this?' said Wimlett, enormously impressed.

'It's not magic, you fool. It's some clunking great invention, by one of those... er... people who invent things,' said Esmerelda, struggling.

'An inventor,' Florence obliged. 'It's called *a train.*'

'Thank you.' Esme smiled. 'Quick, isn't she?' she added, rolling her eyes. Wimlett stared transfixed at the moving picture in the window and, as he discovered, the opposite window, also.

40

In the library, Link was eyeing the book in which Wimlett had written his spells. Eydith was about to pick it up but he got there first. He opened it at the first page.

'Wow!' he said, and started flicking through the pages, making various noises like, 'Cor,' and 'Well I never...'

Eydith gave him one of her dark looks from across the table. 'Don't be so disgusting,' she muttered.

'Do you know what this is?'

'I have no idea,' she replied, and stuck her nose in the air.

'It's about cra...'

She held up a hand to stop him.

'Look,' he began, 'It's a fact of life, that's all. Sewage.'

She cringed.

'The book is about plans for a sewage system under the university, and under all the roads of Kra-Pton.' He snapped the book shut, and turned it to read the author's name. 'Oh... it's by E. Kra-Pton, himself,' he read. 'A bit before my time.'

'What's a, you know, *system,* anyway?' Eydith wondered, her curiosity getting the better of her. 'Sounds as disgusting as it looks. Not that I looked too closely.'

Opening the book again, he found a relevant page. 'It's a lot of tubes and tunnels that do away with the buckets and things that you keep under your bed,' said Link, doing his best to interpret the illustrations and diagrams. 'And, best of all, it means *indoor privies*!'

'That's really disgusting,' she maintained. 'And, you shouldn't be looking under my bed, either.'

'I was speaking generally,' said Link. 'And I disagree. I think it's a wonderful idea. Especially if it does away with outdoor privies. They can be hell on a chilly morning.'

'That's all very well,' said Eydith, 'but where would you put one indoors?'

'It would have to go upstairs, obviously,' said Link.

'Supposing you haven't got an upstairs,' Eydith argued, 'you can't put it on the roof.'

She changed the subject. 'I have to learn some magic,' said Eydith. 'Or have you forgotten?'

'No,' said Link, shaking his head. 'But with Sprag, you don't need much help from me. He knows all you'll ever need.'

'This is true, mistress,' said Sprag. 'Take me to the books where we left off. Touch the spines of the books with me. I will connect with the contents and channel them to your memory. It still takes time, but less time. And you still have to learn how to use what you receive, of course. Nobody can teach you that.'

Eydith picked up Sprag, and went to the section of the library that held all the old spell books, Link went to a reading room with the 'sewer' book.

Sprag was seriously understating it when he said the process would still take time. He was able to relay information at an astonishing rate. Though perhaps he hadn't reckoned on Eydith's capacity to absorb magic.

While he waited, Link thumbed through the book on sewage systems. He found it fascinating, and became lost in it. He felt the possibilities should be seriously explored. The city would be much more hygienic. Normally, he wouldn't have used a word like 'hygienic', but he'd found it in the book a lot and liked the sound of it. On some mornings in the city, especially in the summer, and with open sewers in many streets, the place was anything but hygienic.

Eydith finished and wandered back. 'You were right, Link. It didn't take long. Are you all right, Sprag?' The staff had gone unusually quiet.

'I have what you would call a headache, mistress. I will be all right.'

'I'm going to borrow this book!' Link announced.

'You know best,' said Eydith, doubtfully.

'I'll leave a note for Paske.' He scribbled on a piece of paper, and signed it with a squiggly flourish. 'I've also told him I wasn't responsible for that square indent on the front, in case he tries to fine me for it.'

Back in Eydith's room, they sat in silence while Link read and Eydith processed the magic she'd received. Sprag idly wondered where Wimlett had finished up. He tried to locate the old wizard's mind – something which had been hard enough to do when he was alive. Now he was a ghost it was going to be almost impossible. He smiled at his little joke and it eased his headache.

41

Wimlett sat watching the countryside roll by. Esmerelda and Florence sat eating cheese and apples, and making juicy crunching noises each time one of them took a bite of an apple. As he sat enjoying the novelty of the train, he felt something scratch at his mind. Then it moved away. And then come back, as if trying to attract his attention.

'Ah, there you are,' said a voice intruding on his thoughts. Wimlett banged his head with the heel of his hand, like a swimmer getting rid of water from his ears. 'Don't do that,' said Sprag. 'It's taken me ages to find you... where are you?'

You wouldn't believe me if I told you, thought Wimlett.

'Try me,' said Sprag, in his head

Well, thought the late wizard, *you asked for it. I'm sitting on a bench in a small room on wheels, looking through a window at the countryside rolling by. And the room is one of a dozen or so rooms, all joined together and being towed along by a large kettle on wheels.*

Sprag quietly grinned. He was an amused piece of magical wood while digesting these little gems of information. Then Wimlett thought again: *Are you still there?*

'Yes, but you keep fading,' replied Sprag.

It'll be all right in a moment. We're going under some trees. It's probably interfering with reception. Wimlett just about finished when Sprag received a load of static. The staff frantically tried to track Wimlett's thought patterns – and suddenly picked him up again. 'Where are you?' he asked again, this time with some urgency.

Somewhere in the vicinity of Prossill. And I've seen a staff exactly like you.

'Have you seen Dennis, yet?' Sprag wanted to know.

No, I think he's still on the road. And I'd guess, from knowing when he left Kra-Pton, he'll be getting close to the desert by now.

'Did you say something about a staff?'

Yes, replied Wimlett. *For a moment, I thought it was you... you know, when you were more flagpole-like.*

Sprag thought about it. 'Do you think Dennis might actually be on the trail of that one? – thinking it's me?'

That's a thought. You could be right. At that point, the train began to enter another wooded area and the connection wavered.

'Excellent,' said Sprag, hurriedly. 'And if you see him, or find out where he is, you must let Eydith know.' There was a clicking sound, followed by a soft purring noise. Sprag had left Wimlett's mind.

Are you still there? Wimlett thought. *Hello? Hello?* 'Blast, he's gone.'

'Who's gone?' Esmerelda snapped at him. 'You been drinking again?'

'Sorry,' said Wimlett, aware of his surroundings again. 'I was just thinking aloud.' It had been a while since he'd looked at her properly, and now he noticed that the skin on her face was crazed, like a dried up river bed, and her wart had gone. Before he could stop himself, he said, 'You look terrible. What's happened to your face?'

'Oh, Mother,' said Florence, 'your disguise is all cracked.'

'What? Oh, no!' cried Esmerelda, swivelling away into a corner of the carriage. She rummaged through her luggage for her looking glass. When she checked her reflection, more make-up fell off. 'It's all that chewing's done it,' she scowled.

'Why don't you wash it off and just be yourself?' suggested Wimlett.

Florence agreed. 'Yes, Mother, why not? We can take care of Dennis without doing it in disguise.'

'I'm not so sure, young lady. He's a very tricky customer.'

'Take care of Dennis?' interrupted Wimlett. 'I thought you were looking for Eydith.'

'Same thing,' said Esme bluntly. 'If she's gone to that university – and Triona said she would – then she's going to run into trouble with *him*. And, no offense, but I gather from what her mother says, that Eydith's probably as stubborn as *him*. So there's going to be fireworks. And she's going to need help.'

'More help than you two,' said Wimlett. 'Look, we're both after the same thing. We both want to help Eydith, and we both want to sort Dennis out. We should work together. Eydith has a promising young seventh-level wizard working with her. And I have Naphrat with me...' He broke off while Esme screwed up her face, dislodging more make-up. 'If we all work together, we'll stand a better chance.'

'Where are they, then?' asked Esme, unconvinced.

'Kra-Pton, at the moment.'

'Well...' said Esme, reluctantly. 'I don't know.'

'I think we should accept Wimlett's offer, Mother. He's right. We need all the help we can get. You've said it yourself: Dennis can be very nasty. And his magic is very powerful.'

Wimlett, put more pressure on. 'We could get in each other's way if we don't work together. Which will be to Dennis's advantage.' That seemed to do it, and finally they agreed – Esme reluctantly, and Florence smiling with relief.

It was settled that Wimlett would head back to the university, while Esme and Florence continued to Prossill. They would get a room at The Magic Finger, a tavern situated near the Town Hall, which was a landmark no-one could miss. There they would wait for him and the others.

Wimlett stuck his head through the carriage wall to disembark. And pulled back sharply. He hadn't reckoned on how fast thirty-five miles an hour would be for someone planning to jump. He stood for a minute, plucking up the courage. He felt the eyes of the two women on him, and glancing round it occurred to him how attractive Esme was with hardly any make-up left. She looked like Triona, of course, and he found himself wishing he was mortal again. He smiled at her nervously, and put his head back through the wall.

He knew the more he thought about it, the harder it would be, so this time he just screwed his eyes shut and jumped. He felt the wind racing by, buffeting him, but he resolutely kept his eyes shut waiting for it to abate. When he felt nothing, he warily opened an eye, and found himself standing up to his waist in the ground.

Smiling inwardly, he floated himself to ground level and began wondering how best to get home. He'd have to keep an eye out for transport. The direction he needed to go was back up the track, so he'd follow that. He glanced up and down before stepping on, and nothing was coming. All he could see of the train was a distant plume of smoke.

After about fifteen minutes of walking, Wimlett heard something clattering along the track behind him. He turned and saw a small cart travelling towards him. There were two men standing on it, each pushing a see-saw lever arrangement that seemed to power it along. He turned his eyes to the sky, 'Thank you,' he whispered. Which was a good thought at a bad time. This moment of inattention, and a miscalculation of the thing's speed, resulted in a startled 'Aargh!' as the machine ploughed into him. He'd been surprised into solidarity once again. But it had worked in his favour this time. Because now he was sitting on the little cart, happily on his way home. Well, at least as far as the end of the track.

42

Dennis was roughly half-way to Prossill. He and his two guards had begun to cross a desert region. It was early in the day and the sun wasn't too hot yet, but the vultures were circling overhead already. Jook saw them.

'I didn't think there'd be birds in the desert,' he mused. 'I wonder what they find to eat.'

'Us,' said Psoddoph, bluntly, 'if we don't make it.'

'Can we go another way, boss?' asked Jook.

'This is the quickest way,' grunted Dennis. 'We're certainly not wasting time skirting round it to the north. It won't take long.'

Jook sat quietly shielding his eyes from the sun and watching the vultures circling lazily overhead. Psoddoph rummaged through the box under the seat, and eventually pulled out two battered old straw hats. 'Ah... here they are,' he announced. 'Would you stop a minute, boss?'

Dennis sighed impatiently, but tugged on the reins to bring the horses to a halt. 'What is it now?'

Psoddoph jumped down and put a hat on each of the horses. He looked up at Dennis, then said, grimly, 'If they don't make it, neither do we.'

'Yes, good thinking,' Dennis conceded, and almost added a 'thank you'. But only almost.

Dennis got the horses moving again. Jook watched the vultures again. They seemed to hold a morbid fascination for him. They reminded him of seagulls wheeling around in the sky – and made him feel uncomfortably like a fish. 'There's more of 'em now!' he called, his anxiety mounting with each new arrival. The others ignored him, and concentrated on keeping the cart moving across the loose sand. Jook decided to keep his observations to himself.

The sand rolled by as monotonously as the hours. The sun reached its zenith and became uncomfortably hot. Dennis, in his black robes (obligingly, as the villain of the piece) was warmer than the others, whose clothes were lighter and reflected some of the heat. Dennis knew they needed to travel faster, but he was loath to push the horses in this heat in case they took offence and died on him.

He even thought about telling the two guards to get off and trot beside the cart, but he knew how reluctant they'd be, and then there'd be an atmosphere. And although he enjoyed some silence from time to time, he also appreciated having people around to curse. His mulling over of these things was interrupted when he saw the tracks of carts and hoof-prints crossing the sand in front of them.

'Look!' he shouted, slowing the cart and standing up. 'Tracks! Get down there and see which way they're heading, Jook.'

Jook thought Dennis would have been better able to see that better from up there, but he kept it to himself.

The tracks ran north/south, and south was the general direction they should be going, so they followed. They'd stumbled on a trail that was in regular use. They made better progress now, as the sand had been compacted by other travellers, and the cart didn't keep sinking. Even the vultures decided they'd probably make it after all, and wheeled off in search of more hopeless travellers. But as time went on, Dennis began to have reservations. *What if we're following a horde of barbarians?* He thought. *And what if we catch up with them?* Then he tried to think of something else.

They followed the trail around and between, and sometimes over the dunes. At the top of a particularly high dune, they looked down the slope of a long valley. At the bottom was a small makeshift town made up of tents and caravans, clustered around an oasis. It was a market town. Hundreds of people milled around. Shouting or being shouted at by the many stall holders whose stalls lined the untidy streets. There were dogs, horses, goats, camels, and whole flocks of chickens. The whole place was alive.

'We might learn of a quicker way of getting out of this desert down there,' said Psoddoph, thinking aloud.

Dennis hadn't thought of that, but it was possible. 'Yes, and perhaps I could trade in these horses.'

The cart rolled gently down the slope, giving the horses a few easier minutes, and when they reached the outskirts of the settlement, Dennis steered them into the shade behind one of the larger tents, scattering chickens in all directions.

'Jook, you come with me,' said Dennis, then looked back at Psoddoph and added, 'look after the cart. We shouldn't be long.' Psoddoph thought he'd sooner go with Dennis and have a look around. Jook thought he'd sooner stay with the cart and away from Dennis.

'Just mingle, and don't attract attention,' said Dennis, as he and Jook reconnoitred. They wandered among the tents and stalls, picking up various trinkets, turning them over and putting them down again, as if intelligently looking for hallmarks or pottery marks, because that's what everyone else did at these markets.

As well as the bric-a-brac, there were baskets of fruit and exotic herbs, cooking utensils and livestock, especially chickens. Everywhere, chickens! The birds were in the makeshift roads, the stalls, the wicker baskets, the sacks and even the beer tent!

Jook wasn't sure what Dennis was looking for, but he saw it first. 'Look, boss. A magic shop!' he called, pointing at a tent with a sign over the entrance that read:

HASSAN'S EMPORIUM OF MAGIC

'Ah, this is more like it,' said Dennis, quickening his step. Jook hadn't realised how quickly his master could move, and was suddenly left standing, as Dennis almost took to the air in his haste to get to the tent, everyone parting before him. Jook had to weave his way through the crowds and the chickens to catch up. The wizard was poised on the threshold of the tent, waiting for him.

After the wall-to-wall sunshine of a few seconds ago, at first it was very dark inside. But at least it was cool. Dennis had stopped just inside, allowing his eyes to get accustomed to the gloom, when a small hunchbacked man materialised out of the darkness.

'You vish to buy, gentlemen?' he asked, in a voice and an accent that Dennis and Jook thought they recognised, but couldn't quite remember where they'd heard it before.

'We're just browsing,' said Jook, who never did like pushy salesmen. The man nodded, and backed away into the gloom. Jook picked up an ancient-looking oil lamp. 'This looks nice,' he said, 'could do with a bit of a clean, though.'

Dennis snatched it away just as Jook was about to give it a good rub on his sleeve. 'Don't *do* that,' he snapped. 'You never know who or what's going to come out of one those things.' Dennis gingerly put the lamp back on the table, and added, 'Just don't touch anything, there's a good chap. You're making me nervous.'

Jook was minded to sulk now, just to teach him not to treat him like a child. But the wizard had spotted what he was looking for. Not so much spotted, as tripped over, scattering chickens as he went. On the floor where he landed was a pile of carpets. He reined in his enthusiasm and started turning back the corners, making out he was feeling the pile. 'Yes, this is what we need,' he said, not too loudly, grinning to himself, as he got to his feet.

Jook was not impressed. 'What do we need a carpet for? We're in a desert, or haven't you noticed? We going to upgrade the cart?'

'You're missing the point,' he said, as he leaned forward and whispered in Jook's ear. 'These are *magic* carpets. Some of them. And not just single-person rugs like we get back home. We could fly out of this desert *with the cart* on one of these.'

Jook's eyes lit up. This was more like it.

'Shop!' Dennis called out.

The man seemed to materialise in front of them. It was quite unnerving.

'You vish to buy?' asked Hassan, his smile and his eyes widening in anticipation.

'No,' said Dennis, 've vish... I mean *we wish,* to trade.'

'Oh,' said the man, deflating. 'Vot haff you got to trade vith?'

'*A fine horse,*' stated Dennis, intimating that this might be his only offer.

'And vot do you vont for zis 'orse?' asked Hassan.

'Why, your emporium, of course.'

'My emporium?' Hassan repeated, in disbelief. 'My emporium for a *horse*? You must be bloody joking!'

'Okay,' said Dennis, stroking his beard, 'what about this pile of old carpets, then?'

'No vay,' said Hassan, shaking his head. 'You don't even get a doormat for vun 'orse.'

'It's a very good horse,' stressed Dennis. 'It's got four legs, two eyes – it can probably see for miles, in fact. And if it wasn't for a missing tooth, this horse would be perfect.'

'Vot else you got?'

'All right, I'll give you the reins as well.'

'Vot sort of carpet you vont?' asked Hassan, in the vague hope of turning things to his advantage.

'Quite a big one,' said Dennis.

Jook looked on in wonder. He'd lost the thread soon after the bartering started. Hassan started lifting the corners of the carpets to show Dennis the various sizes available. The wizard eyed them critically, mentally measuring them for the task he had in mind. Eventually, Hassan pulled out one that Dennis thought would be suitable. It was big enough to cover the floor in his bedroom, he estimated, for when he got it home, and sufficiently big enough for the purpose of carrying the cart and the three of them to Prossill and back home.

'This one will do,' said Dennis, admiring his choice.

'I vont more zan vun 'orse for ze carpet zat big,' Hassan whined. It looked like the bartering was about to start all over again.

'How much more?' snapped Dennis, narrowing his eyes, menacingly.

'Vot about...' Hassan paused, mentally running through his list of wants. '... Two 'orses? If you 'ad two...?'

Dennis smiled. For a moment, he thought Hassan was going to ask for money. He'd played the man well: holding back about his other horse. After haggling for a few more seconds – just for the look of it, as far as Jook could see – they agreed on both the horses in exchange for the carpet, and he sent Jook back to get them.

***

'What is he *thinking*?' said Psoddoph. 'Getting rid of both the horses! Supposing this *magic carpet* doesn't work?'

'Well, at least we know where they are if we need to *borrow* them again,' said Jook.

'Yeah, I hadn't thought of that,' said Psoddoph, cheering up. 'Give me a hand to unhitch 'em.'

Dennis was waiting with Hassan by the tent curtain when Jook returned. 'Vot fine 'orses you brink me,' said Hassan, smiling. 'Are you sure you vish to part viz zem?'

'Oh, yes,' said Dennis, emphatically, thinking, *I was never more sure of anything in my life.* He stood back as Jook led the animals into the tent, closely followed by Hassan, who seemed anxious to take the reins. He seemed to be moving with some effort now. He was dragging his left leg. There was something familiar about the man.

Dennis suddenly realised who he was dealing with. And there was a problem! This little barbarian had the horses, but Dennis hadn't yet got a carpet. He glanced around, but it was missing. 'How on Crett!' He reached into his mind for a suitable spell to get him and his guards out of this situation. He was tiring of finishing second in this encounter.

Jook interrupted him. 'Have you got the carpet?'

'No,' hissed Dennis. 'That's what's bothering me.' Dennis shared his suspicions. 'Take a closer look. I think we're dealing with Herman the Barbarian.'

'I thought I knew that accent,' Jook whispered out of the corner of his mouth. 'Right,' he added, 'I'll speak to him.'

Dennis nodded, keeping a more severe magical solution in abeyance for the moment.

Hassan was petting his new acquisitions, oblivious of the two men in his emporium.

'Herman,' said Jook, to see how the man would react.

'Vere?' said the man, almost twisting his head off as he turned.

'No,' said Jook. 'You, are Herman. The Barbarian.'

'No, no' retorted the little man, dismissively. 'I am *Hassan*. I am Herman's bruzzer. You know me, ze second hand carpet dealer.'

'You look like Herman to me,' said Jook, unconvinced, whilst adopting a threatening stance.

'I voz a barbarian vunce,' said Hassan, a little wistfully, recalling his former life as a nomadic plunderer. 'But I voz not barbaric enough. It voz ze vife, you know. After a ferd child voz born she started puttingk an herb in my drinks. I voz getting like Herman, you know? Almost permanently asleep. Did you know zat?' He dropped the reins and limped slowly to a canvas chair with 'MANAGER' crudely stencilled on the back, and sat down.

He pulled out a clay pipe, and patted his robe, looking for something to light it with. 'Haff you got a light, soldier?' he asked. Jook pulled a box of matches from his tunic. Hassan looked searchingly into the bowl of his pipe. 'Perhaps you haff some tobacco, also?' he asked, offering the pipe to Jook for inspection. Jook grudgingly measured a small amount out.

'Right,' said Jook, when Hassan had sucked his pipe to life, 'we'll take the carpet, and be on our way, shall we?'

'Hold it! Zere is vun more zing!'

'What?' asked Jook, warily.

'Vot about a drink? You know, just to seal ze bargain.'

Jook looked at Dennis, and uncannily heard his boss's voice in his head, *Tell him, no. He might still have some of that stuff his wife was giving him.*

'Thanks for the offer, Hassan. But, we're in a bit of a hurry,' said Jook, thrusting out a hand to signify goodbye. 'Let's just shake on it.' Unexpectedly, Hassan grabbed it and hauled himself upright. Having steadied himself, he raised a hand and clicked his fingers, summoning two men who dropped the rolled-up carpet on the shop floor.

Dennis stopped scanning the vengeful spells in his repertoire and relaxed.

'I'll get you ze receipt,' said Hassan, sighing, and limped over to a knee-high table. He came back and presented Dennis with a note, along with a small, red leather-bound book, which Dennis stuffed into one of the many pockets secreted within the folds of his robe.

Jook heaved the rolled-up carpet onto his shoulder, not realising he was facing away from the exit. Then he twigged. Fortunately, as he turned round without thinking, the rolled carpet was prevented from clearing a shelf of amulets and shrunken skulls by its sudden impact with the side of Dennis's head. Jook didn't see the wizard's lips moving, but he did see words with blue edges flaring in his mind.

Aloud, he just snapped, 'Please be more careful.'

Hassan appeared in front of them. 'Give my regards to Herman ven you see him.'

'I'll do that,' said Jook, as he began to steer his way through the throng of people. And chickens. 'Why are these desert villages always full of chickens?' Jook wondered. Dennis didn't bother to answer.

When they found Psoddoph, he had three chickens.

'For later,' he explained.

'Right, boss,' said Jook, looking over the side of the cart. 'Where'd you want this?'

'Not *in* the cart, you idiot. Just a minute,' replied Dennis, as he sized up the situation. 'Bring it round here.' Jook dumped it on the ground behind the cart. Dennis kicked it gently and it unrolled. Psoddoph stared at it without uttering a word.

'I don't suppose you've ever seen anything like this before,' said Dennis, proudly.

'No, boss. You're dead right there,' Psoddoph agreed, and went on incautiously, 'It's bloody awful.'

Dennis blinked.

Jook stepped forward, 'Excuse me, boss.'

'Yes, what is it *now*?' said Dennis, still smarting from Psoddoph's remark.

'Well, I'm no expert, you understand...'

'Yes, yes, all right, get on with it, man.'

'But I think it might be upside down,' said Jook, and quickly took a step back to avoid anything that Dennis might inflict on him.

Dennis eyed it for a moment, then lifted a corner. 'Hmm... you could be right,' he conceded, and began to drag the carpet away from the cart to give them room to turn it over.

When the job was done, the carpet lay before them looking as it would one day when it finally adorned Dennis's bedroom. The design was panel Persian, though it had no panels, and was certainly not Persian. It had seen better days, and was probably about to see worse.

'That's better,' said Psoddoph, nodding approval. 'That's more like it.'

'Now we roll the cart onto it,' said Dennis.

The two guards nodded, put their shoulders to the cart and pushed, thinking, *what do you mean 'we',* as they did so.

Then they waited for Dennis to tell them what was going to happen next.

43

Somewhere in the south-west of Kermells Tong, Wimlett was enjoying the turn of speed he was experiencing on the rail cart. Obviously the two men working the handles didn't know he was there, although the one at the back, facing forward, thought he saw a man-shaped heat haze, but he put it down to the vibrations of the cart affecting his vision, and thought no more of it.

They were coming to the end of the track and started to slow down. And like most mechanical contrivances – which tend to develop little idiosyncrasies – this one was no exception. It enjoyed the clickety-clacking, and the smell of burning oil on its axles, and it was never in a hurry to slow down.

The two men were familiar with this, and slowed it down sufficiently to jump off safely about two hundred yards before it hit the buffers. Wimlett didn't notice them leave. He sat there, looking with interest at a collection of shed-like buildings to the left up ahead.

The cart suddenly stopped. The rear wheels bucked and threw him headlong through the air on a surprisingly long trajectory. In flight, he said what he always said when something like this happened… 'Aargh!' It concluded with a splash, as he landed in a pool in the front garden of a little house.

Wimlett allowed himself a little smile. He sat in the water reflecting on the weirdness of making a splash. It was fair enough that he could forget he was immaterial – but how could water do that as well? 'Ah', it dawned him. 'Of course.' Whenever he was distracted into forgetting he was a ghost, he didn't only temporarily experience the illusion of solidity, he became briefly truly solid. Which was interesting, and also a little worrying. But he seemed to survive it.

The little house was interesting, too. It appeared to be made of marzipan and lollipops. Over the door was a sign which read:

Esmerelda's Cottage

And underneath, was a smaller sign, which read:

I don't mind you eating the flowers,

But leave the ROOF alone!

'Don't see too many of your sort round 'ere,' said a little voice.

Wimlett turned in surprise. 'Who said that?'

'Me,' replied the little voice.

Wimlett looked around the pond and saw a small, bearded man sitting on a toadstool on the edge. He had a jolly red face beneath a large, blue floppy hat, and wore smart red jacket and yellow trousers. 'You've ruined a good day's fishin' you know?' he said, though he didn't sound particularly upset about it.

It occurred to Wimlett that he was talking to a garden gnome. He glanced around him, and into the murky water of the shallow pond, but couldn't see any fish. This came as a great relief, because, apart from the pain from forgetting he was a ghost, and from the panic he occasionally experienced from flight, fish in ponds were among the highest items on his hate-list.

'You can see me?' Wimlett asked.

'Well, me concrete eyes don't see abstract things, of course, but I can see you alright.'

'Actually, I am a bit abstract. But never mind. Have you caught anything, yet?' he asked, conversationally.

'Nope. Never 'ave,' replied the gnome.

'What bait are you using?'

'Bait? What's bait?' asked the gnome, his concrete neck creaking under the strain of looking up at Wimlett as he stepped out of the pond.

'Well... worms, maggots, that sort of thing,' explained Wimlett, as he stepped back into the pond and sat on the grassy edge, as there wasn't enough room for two on the gnome's toadstool.

'Where would I get those from?' the gnome wondered, although not really wanting to know.

'You'd dig them up. Out of the ground.'

'I can't do that!' exclaimed the gnome. 'I'm a fishin' gnome. I fish. Diggin' gnomes dig.'

Wimlett was curious. 'How long have you been fishing... these waters?'

The gnome thought for a moment. He held his forearm up into the sunlight and studied a small dial strapped to his wrist. 'I've been sat here for nearly twenty years, now.'

'Don't you ever get bored?' asked Wimlett.

'What? Me? Bored with fishin'? No... never.'

'But you've never caught anything.'

'That's the *whole* point,' stressed the gnome. 'As soon as I catch something, it will lose its mystery. Then I'll have to find something else to do. And what else can you do with a fishin' rod?'

Wimlett considered this, but decided not to test the gnome's sense of humour. Seeing no fish nearby in the pond, he changed his position, took off his pointy-toed shoes, and wiggled his toes in the water. It had been a good many years since he'd done that, and his thoughts went momentarily back to his childhood visits to the sunny shores of the Southern Ocean 'Yeah, you're right, there's not a lot else you can do with a fishing rod.'

'I could swap it, I s'pose,' said the gnome, thoughtfully. 'But I don't fancy a spade, or a rake.'

'What about a wheelbarrow, or a swing?' Wimlett suggested.

'A swing sounds good. How does that work?'

'You just sit on it and wait for the wind to move you.'

'That wouldn't be too long, then. I suffer terribly from wind,' said the little figure. And right on cue, he produced a sound like tearing cloth from somewhere around the top of the toadstool.

Wimlett quickly stood up. 'Well, it's been nice to chat,' he said, hurriedly, trying not to breathe any more than necessary, even though he didn't have to. 'I should be going now.'

'Oh, so soon? Perhaps I'll see you again sometime.'

Before Wimlett could say another word, the air about him shimmered and was filled with the crackles and colours of magic – magic with the fingerprints of Sprag all over it, if he wasn't mistaken. He found himself rushing through the air – many times faster than he'd travelled on the rail cart. With his eyes clamped tightly shut, he kept reminding himself he was a ghost, in case he hit something.

44

'Ah, there you are,' said Sprag, as Wimlett whooshed into Eydith's room at the university. The old wizard felt as if he'd been snatched up by a whirlwind and deposited abruptly many miles later.

Even though Eydith couldn't see him, it was obvious from the disturbance that he was back. She could see what he'd brought with him, too.

Link was in the room too, and he was first to ask the question, 'Why have you brought a garden pond with you?'

Wimlett looked down, and sure enough, there it was. Complete with weeds and lilies. And Sprag's sometimes hit-or-miss magic had placed Wimlett in the middle of it. But thankfully, it had left the flatulent gnome behind.

'Oh, dear,' said Sprag, before Wimlett could say anything. 'I think a little refining is needed on that outreach spell. I'm still not absolutely sure where your boundaries are.'

'I think you may have crossed them,' said Wimlett, dryly, stepping clear of the pond.

Sprag went quiet, concentrating. The air in the room crackled and the pond launched itself in a rush of wind back to where it belonged.

Eydith looked at the wet patches on the carpet where Wimlett had trodden. She pointed her fingers at them and delivered an orange charge of magic, causing a cloud of steam and smoke to fill the room.

Link rushed to the window and tried to open it quickly, but it was a long time since this had happened to it, and the window wasn't going to give in without a struggle. But neither was Link, and it was touch and go for a while.

When the smoke had cleared, they all stared disapprovingly at the carpet. 'You'd have done better to let it dry on its own,' said Link, shaking his head at the charred holes.

'Okay, it was a little hotter than I intended, that's all,' said Eydith, defensively, and raised her hand again.

'No! I'll mend it. We don't want you burning the university down just yet!"

Eydith accepted the offer. She was advanced with her magical knowledge, but was still getting to grips with the practical side. Link snapped his fingers and the carpet began to weave itself together again, pattern and all. When it had finished, it was Link's turn to feel foolish.

'Never mind,' said Eydith. 'If we just walk on the new bits, they'll eventually look as worn as the rest of it.' She glanced towards where she guessed Wimlett was. 'What have you been up to, Father?' she asked.

'Just the important bits, please,' said Sprag.

'Well, down south they've invented a new means of travel. It's much faster, and more comfortable than a cart. It runs on wheels, just like a cart, but the wheels run along on two long strips of iron laid side by side.' He paused to note he had their interest. 'And there are lots of carts all joined together – well, not carts exactly, they're more like little rooms, and they call them carriages. And they're all pulled along by a large kettle-thing belching smoke and steam. Very impressive it is. And it runs up through the forest lands into Prossill.'

Sprag looked into his store of future knowledge. 'It's called a railway,' he explained.

'That's a good name for it,' said Wimlett. 'Though I'm sure they called it a train.'

'It's both,' intoned Sprag.

'Do go on, Father,' Eydith goaded him.

'All right! Where was I? Oh, yes, the railway – as you say it's called.... That reminds me, Eydith, I met your aunt and your cousin on it.' He paused let that sink in.

Her eyebrows arched and her mouth gaped on hearing something so unexpected. 'Aunt Esmeralda and Florence? You met them? On this train thing?'

'And that's where I left them,' he said, following on with another piece of interesting information, 'They are looking for Dennis.'

'Are they mad?' said Link, more as a statement than a question.

'No, far from it. And it's likely that Dennis is looking for *them*, too.'

'What would he want with them?

Sprag intervened. 'Dennis is not looking for them in particular. As we know, he's looking for the staff that activates the Drum. He's following rumours – or rainbows – that someone in or around Prossill has it. It's very likely, mistress, that aunt and cousin of yours would create a ripple or two of uncommon magic around them. He's detected it, or word has reached him about it, and he's guessing that the staff – me – is the cause.'

'My aunt Esme is a witch,' said Eydith, thinking that might help explain it.

'That's not enough, in itself, to explain his interest,' said Sprag. 'But her magic may be unusual and of interest because it bears a family likeness, however tenuous, to your father's.'

'You're clutching at straws, Sprag,' said Wimlett, dismissing the notion out of hand. 'Getting back to it, Esmeralda is after Dennis because they want to help you, Eydith.'

'Help *me*?'

Wimlett explained, recapping some family history that Eydith was already familiar with and kept nodding as he spoke.

She was a little affronted that her aunt felt she needed her help. She was seventeen now, not a little girl anymore! But she was glad to hear that her mother and aunt were getting back on better terms after so long.

'What're they like?' she said finally. 'It's been so long since I've seen them.'

'They're okay,' said Wimlett, prepared to leave it at that.

But Eydith wanted to pursue it further. 'Just okay?' She stared expectantly at the empty space her father occupied.

'Well, yes. Oh, how would I know? They look all right. They behave themselves. They're house trained.' He stopped abruptly and added, 'Probably.'

Eydith and Link began to laugh. 'You're hopeless, Father.'

Wimlett blushed, but it didn't show.

Linkwood broke the mood with, 'I don't know about them helping Eydith, I think we'd better help them. They can't face Dennis on their own.'

'I've already put it to them, that we join forces,' announced Wimlett. 'They want Dennis dealt with; we want Dennis dealt with. So it makes sense. And the more of us the better. They are headed for Prossill on the train. Dennis is headed that way, too. So that's where we should be going. And we need to be quick about it, or they might confront Dennis before we get there, with disastrous consequences. As Link rightly says, we need to make plans. But the first thing to do is find the fastest way for us all to get to Prossill. We can work out what to do when we get there.'

They sat around the table, thinking. Except Sprag, of course. He lay across it, his runes wriggling. He was weighing up whether his powers of transportation were the answer, whether they would be powerful enough for all of them to travel together. He felt he could do it. He also felt he could locate Dennis. The Drum itself was concealing its whereabouts. No doubt it had worked out that it might otherwise betray the staff if Dennis ever got near it. Sprag would have to be wary of that.

'I know!' said Eydith, brightly. 'Maybe Sprag can transport us to Prossill ahead of Dennis. We can wait there and make our plans once Sprag has located him.'

Are you a mind reader now as well? thought Sprag. 'Yes, mistress. I have been giving it some thought. I have been attempting to pinpoint Dennis for some time, but he is elusive. Though I am beginning to recognise his mental pattern, which is characterised more by the absence of something than it is by the presence...'

'A conscience,' suggested Wimlett.

'I have been alert, also, for signs of the Drum, with which I have an affinity. The Drum is with Dennis, we know, so that could be our way to find him once we reach Prossill.'

'Makes perfect sense,' said Wimlett. Eydith and Link nodded eagerly.

'I believe I can transport us all together using the spell I used for Wimlett.'

'Seriously?' queried Wimlett, remembering how unpleasant that was. 'There's no way flesh and blood is going to survive that.'

'I've considered the safety of everyone,' said Sprag. 'And the process will be less stressful for those with body mass to slow it down.'

'You didn't consider *my* safety without body mass.'

'Exactly,' said Sprag, 'there was no need.'

Wimlett grunted and fell silent.

Sprag went on, 'It will also take us longer, because we cannot make the trip in one flight. We will need to take short hops – only as far as we can see the terrain ahead – so that we avoid tall trees, high rocks and buildings.'

Wimlett was about to add a thought on that, but was cut short.

'There,' said Eydith, clapping her hands. 'That's settled then. We'll leave tomorrow.' And then she turned to look directly where she knew Wimlett was. 'Now tell me more about my aunt and cousin.'

45

'Have you flown one of these things before, boss?' asked Jook.

'A smaller one,' said Dennis, 'but not since I was a student. But you never forget. And once you've flown one, you can fly them all, I suppose.'

Psoddoph went quiet. He didn't like to say anything, but that last remark was not a confidence builder.

'Right, boss,' said Jook. 'I'm ready.'

'Good man,' said Dennis. 'What about you, Psoddoph?'

'Ready as I'll ever be,' he said, gripping a wheel of the cart with both hands.

With a cursory glance around to check that everything was safely aboard – the cart, the three of them and all their stuff – Dennis looked down at the carpet, and then pointed to the sky. 'Up!' he shouted at the carpet. Nothing happened. He repeated it, louder. 'UP!' Still nothing.

'What was that book Hassan gave you with the carpet, boss?' asked Psoddoph. 'The red one.' He had a shrewd idea it was the manual. And an even shrewder idea that it would come in handy about now.

'What? Oh, yes, the book.' Dennis fished around in the folds of his robe. 'Got it,' he said, waving it in the air.

'Right, boss. What does it say about going up?' asked Jook, enthusiastically, leaning over him.

'With a horse, you'd only have to slap its arse, and away you'd go,' mumbled Psoddoph.

'Will you stop moaning, and be a bit more supportive,' Dennis demanded. 'I'm trying to get us out of here.'

'Yeah,' agreed Jook, 'more er... what 'e said.'

'Right, now let's concentrate on what it says,' said Dennis, scanning page one. 'Oh, no *wonder* it wouldn't work. It says you have to speak to it *politely*.'

'But, boss,' Jook interrupted. 'You don't speak polite. It's a foreign language to you.' Then he said, 'OUCH!' as Dennis made one of his ears turn red with the practical magic of a flick.

'Okay, come on, then,' said Psoddoph, trying to sound enthusiastic. 'Let's give it a try.'

'*I'll* give the order,' said Dennis. 'No-one else. Now – is everyone ready?'

'Yes,' said the guards in unison, fingers crossed.

'Carpet...' said Dennis, in the mildest tone he could muster, 'up, *please.*'

Three stomachs suddenly grew exceedingly heavy, as gravity kicked in, two-or-three-fold, it seemed. The carpet responded very favourably to the wizard's polite request. He'd said, 'Up', and that's where it was going. Like a rock from a catapult.

'Hold on!' shouted Dennis, rather unnecessarily. They were hanging on for dear life.

'Do something!' yelled Jook, trying to make himself heard above the rushing air.

Dennis's reaction was late – and ill thought out.

'Carpet, DOWN... Please!' he screamed as politely as he could.

He should have said, 'Stop!' then, 'Down', and then, 'Slowly'. The carpet smoothly slammed itself into reverse. The three men covered their mouths with one free hand while clutching the cart with the other in a desperate attempt to hold onto their breakfasts, but the rapid descent of the carpet was making that nigh on impossible. Dennis struggled to get his thoughts together. Even a spell was beyond him, and it might take too long to recite, anyway. He had to regain control of the descent, or, sometime in the next few seconds, the last thing they'd all see would be the insides of their boots.

'Carpet! Stop...please!' he screamed.

'Aargh!' cried the guards, collapsing to their knees. Dennis had braced himself for the sudden stop, and managed to stay more or less upright. What saved them was the flexibility of the carpet, and the fabric's ability to absorb their momentum.

The Carpet hovered about fifty feet up, with its passengers seated on the edges and peering over. 'Before we try any more of the advanced stuff,' suggested Psoddoph, 'it might be a good idea if you read the book all the way through?'

'Yeah,' agreed Jook, less keen than before, 'this is getting bloody dangerous.'

'All right! Don't keep on!' Dennis snapped, climbing up onto the cart. He sat down and opened the book. After reading a few paragraphs, he looked down on the guards and announced, 'That's it. I know all I need to, now!'

Psoddoph's heart sank. 'Famous last bloody words,' he mumbled.

Dennis put the book away and clambered down onto the carpet's edge. 'Right, carpet,' he said, slowly and deliberately, 'Slowly, down, *please*.' The carpet began a more leisurely descent, and when it was a couple of feet from the ground, Dennis called, 'Stop...! Please.' The carpet jarred to a halt, right where he intended. 'There you go,' he said, smugly, 'nothing to it.'

Dennis decided that now he'd mastered 'up' and 'down', he would try a bit of 'forward' and 'reverse'. The way was clear behind them. 'Right, carpet, ready?' Dennis asked, not really expecting a reply, 'Turn please,' and just as the carpet began to rotate, he added, 'Slowly.' When he judged the carpet to be lined up with a sizeable gap ahead between two tents, he requested it to 'Stop, please.' He rubbed his hands together gleefully as the carpet responded. 'Carpet,' he said, 'forward... slowly, please.' His delight didn't last long.

Something was wrong. Sideways was not what he had in mind. 'Stop, please,' he called in exasperation. 'Now what's bloody well wrong with it?' he groaned.

'Can I see the book, please?' asked Psoddoph, politely. This new civility was infectious. Dennis glowered and handed it over. Psoddoph, like many casual readers, started flicking through from the back. This type of person usually hates surprises. In a lifetime of casual reading, he'd discovered that the best bits were rarely at the beginning. Again, that proved to be correct. For there at the bottom of the third page from the end was a very important addition to the text. It was on a slip of paper glued to the page, and headed *erratum*. He read it out slowly.

The makers of this carpet apologise for having made

an orientation error when cutting. The front and rear are in fact the sides,

and the sides are now to be found at each end. Pleased bear this in mind

when giving directions. Once again, we apologise for any

inconvenience this may cause.

Dennis, on one of his rare trips into the slummy areas of Kra-Pton, had learned a very expressive word that was new to him, and he felt that now was as good a time as any to use it. 'Shit!' he muttered. 'There's always something.' And had he known about the carpet's faulty manufacture, he would have insisted on a discount. Though he didn't stop to think how he could have got ten percent off two horses.

The carpet hovered beneath them, waiting. Dennis thought the only way to sort it out would be to move it away from the tents and experiment.

And when he'd got the general idea, he would chalk the directions on it for reference.

Under his polite instructions, delivered through gritted-teeth, the carpet rose to a safe height above the surrounding tents. There were a few upturned faces below, hoping for a repeat performance of the last death-defying descent. Dennis re-read the part about 'forward' and 'reverse'. After several misjudgements, he finally got the hang of it, and got the carpet heading south.

The guards became less tense. Dennis kept the *User Guide* handy, and scoured the horizon for tall things to avoid. There were hardly any in the desert. He was able to fly low, skimming the surface at about five or six feet. Later on, they'd have to get above the trees.

46

They made good time across the desert. Dennis experimented with the speed of the carpet, and found a rate that was comfortable for all. He was pleased again for a while. He even conceded that they should land at the next waterhole and have something to eat. Though chiefly because it gave him an opportunity to test his skills at landing in a waterside clearing among trees.

'That's the only trouble with eating outside,' Jook complained, as he swatted another fly.

'What's that?' asked Psoddoph.

'Half the bloody insects in the neighbourhood want a share.'

'If you will cook fish,' Dennis griped, 'what do you expect? The smell's everywhere.'

Jook considered this, swatted another fly off, and then threw the partly cooked fish back into the lake.

'What did you do that for?' asked Psoddoph.

'It crossed my mind,' said Jook, 'that I don't know what those flies 'ave been standing on before they walked all over it. But I can 'ave a good guess.'

'Well, what's to eat now, then?' asked Dennis, irritably.

'Nothing,' said Jook, 'less of course you feel like magicing something up.'

The Drum was listening.

One of the things Dennis didn't approve of was wasting magic on trivialities like cooking. They considered flying on to find the next settlement or town, but just then a chicken in the cart clucked its own death warrant. 'That'll do!' He brightened. 'Chicken for dinner. Jook... see to it.'

'I don't mind plucking it,' said Jook. 'I don't even mind cooking it. But I ain't killing it,' he stated, flatly.

Dennis swivelled his head to Psoddoph, who answered before Dennis asked the question. 'Don't look at me, boss. I can't do it either.'

'Some tough guys you two are,' he muttered. He flexed his fingers as he stalked to the cage. He gave the contents the once over. The three birds stared back in that odd way that chickens have of putting their heads first on one side, then on the other, as if trying to decide which way up you are. The wizard peered through the bars and saw three eggs almost hidden in the straw. 'You don't know how lucky you are, chickens. Now move away, I want those eggs.'

They stood back obediently, and as soon as his hand was in the cage, they attacked it.

'That does it!' he screeched. The chickens continued to watch, heads on one side, then the other, waiting for him to try it again. He eased the door open and shot his hand in with the speed of a striking snake, grabbing a bird by its neck. He snatched it from the cage, slamming the door on the other two.

There was a squawking and a flapping until Dennis finally let it slip from his grasp. The bird landed in front of him, shook its head and attacked his legs. Dennis screamed a spell and directed his hands at the feathered fury. A crackle of something hot and magical filled the air

'Feel better, now, boss?' asked Jook.

Dennis fixed him with a dangerous glare, and Jook covered his face.

Psoddoph collected the bird from the ground, sat down, tore off a leg, and offered it to Dennis, who took it in silence.

'Hmm... not bad,' he commented, a little placated. 'A bit overdone, perhaps. But not bad.'

When they'd eaten, Dennis sat on the ground with his back against a cartwheel and stretched. The sun had moved beyond the taller trees and they had some shade. Psoddoph took his cue from this and got in the back of the cart to put his feet up. Which didn't leave much room for Jook, who took a stroll down to the edge of the lake. He sat down and stared at the glistening water. After a few minutes, he picked up some flat stones and began skimming them across the surface.

Psoddoph shut his eyes and was hoping for a nap but an irritating blue light kept pulsing faintly in the corner of his eye. He thought it would probably go away, but when it didn't he opened his eyes and saw it was coming from the canvas covering the Drum a few feet away. He stirred himself to lift a corner of the canvas. The Drum was slowly pulsating, not threateningly, he didn't think, but he thought he'd better call Dennis.

'What's happening, boss?' he said, when Dennis arrived at his side.

'I don't know,' said Dennis, intrigued. 'It's never done this before.'

He tried to read the Drum as he would a person, but drew a blank. *Not too different from reading Jook, in fact,* he thought, smiling to himself. Except that this felt deliberate.

What was happening had indeed not happened before. The Drum was beginning to sense the staff searching for it. The magical rapport between the two was asserting itself, albeit weakly at present. The pulsating blue light was a homing beacon, alerting the staff to its whereabouts. The beacon was designed to help re-unite the staff and Drum, and at that moment the Drum was doing all it could to make that happen.

'Keep an eye on it, Psoddoph,' Dennis ordered.

Dennis went back to the fire, and to his slumber against the wheel.

The Drum continued to pulse with its eerie, blue light for another minute, and then it glowed brighter than ever, then stopped.

Psoddoph called out and told Dennis, who returned to take a look. When he arrived, the Drum flared red. Experimentally he moved closer and then away from it, and saw that it flared every time he went close.

'What is it with that Drum?' Dennis whined.

'It seems to have taken a dislike to you, boss,' said the guard, leaning back out of Dennis's reach.

But Dennis looked up to where the sun was glinting through the lower branches of the trees, telling him it was mid-afternoon, and told him to go and get Jook, because they were leaving.

'Come on!' snapped Dennis, irritably, as they ambled back from the lake. 'We haven't got all day.'

Psoddoph shook his head. Unless he'd missed something, he considered that 'all day' was precisely what they did have, and longer if necessary.

Dennis stepped onto the carpet. He felt in the folds of his robe for the User Guide. First, he pulled out a rather attractive bunch of paper flowers, followed by a pair of white doves, and flinched when an irate little rabbit scratched him. 'What the...!' He cursed, and noticed the Drum flaring red again under its canvass. It had obviously inherited some of the humour of its previous owner along with his spells.

Dennis almost lashed out to deliver a chastening flare of his own, but stopped himself. It would do him no good to harm the Drum, even if he could, which was doubtful, and the local effect of such an artefact being hit with an offensive spell didn't bear thinking about.

Psoddoph shook his head in sympathy, which almost earned him a chastening flare. Then he stepped onto the carpet and picked up the book from the ground, offering it to Dennis. 'This what you're looking for, boss?'

Dennis grunted and snatched it from him, and flicked through the pages. Then he announced, 'Right. Got it! I remember it all now.'

Jook's heart sank as he, too, stepped aboard. He braced himself as Dennis cleared his throat, and spoke softly to the carpet. 'Carpet... Up, slowly, *please*.'

Obediently, the carpet rose slowly. Dennis chuckled and rubbed his hands together. 'Carpet, stop, please.' The carpet hovered over the shoreline, waiting for further instructions. Before moving off, Dennis walked around the narrow perimeter, looking for the chalk marks he'd made to show him the orientation, but they were missing. He was about to yell at the guards for being so careless, but saw a brief red glow under the canvas in the back.

He cursed again, and sat down. He put his head in his hands and tried desperately not to weep. He was beginning to hate the Drum, and hate this carpet, too, almost as much as he'd hated the horses he'd traded for it. At length, he pulled himself together. 'Think!' he muttered, angrily to himself. 'Why do these things happen to me?'

Jook heard him, and resisted the temptation to tell him, but Psoddoph's mouth was already in gear and headed for trouble. 'Things probably don't like you, boss,' he said, wishing he'd phrased it more tactfully. But, at least he was the other side of the cart and Dennis couldn't reach him.

The wizard spun angrily. 'I don't know why!' he snapped. 'I'm a nice person.' And Dennis *really* believed this, as, oddly, most terrible people do.

Jook almost choked.

'Don't let things upset you so,' said Psoddoph, calmly. 'Just pretend it didn't happen, and move on. We can chalk the marks back on. Take a couple of deep breaths.'

'Yes, that's probably best,' Dennis whined. Then he sighed deeply. 'That's better,' he said, 'now, let's get going, shall we, carpet?'

The carpet continued to linger in the air.

'Very slowly...' said Dennis, mentally preparing himself to be thrust into whichever direction the carpet was going to go... 'Forward, please.'

It gently moved backwards.

'Stop, please!' Dennis ordered.

'You see?' said Psoddoph, helpfully, but not helping. 'You had an even chance, and you got it wrong. That's all.'

Jook buried his face in his hands.

Dennis shuffled round to the other side of the cart.

'The important thing is...' said Psoddoph, kindly, 'that you didn't get angry with it.'

Jook cringed again.

Dennis sat down dejectedly and looked over his shoulder. Then, in the calmest of voices, he told Psoddoph to, 'Piss off.' After which, he turned his attention back to steering the carpet. Prossill was still a fair way off.

47

The flight to Prossill continued uneventfully through most of the rest of the afternoon. Dennis's polite course adjustments were well received. Both he and the carpet were behaving themselves. The desert was slipping by below, and showing signs of handing over the business of landscape to some greenery.

Dennis was daydreaming a lot about the staff, and how powerful he was going to be when he had it. He'd rule the land with an iron fist. No-one would dare oppose him. He would tax the rich and bleed the poor, and have everything he ever wanted. He might even have enough power to expand his influence right across the world. How could Wimlett and all those other dim-witted Archchancellors have been so incredibly short-sighted with all the power they had!

Behind him, the Drum glowed with swirling currents of anger, which faded when Dennis was jolted from his reverie. Fortunately for Dennis, on its own, the Drum's innate powers were restrained. Neither could it weald any of the spells it held. But it could withhold them, even to an Archchancellor – and certainly one without the staff!

'Look! Down there, boss!' shouted Psoddoph, pointing leftwards. 'That strange little house. Did you ever see one like that?'

'I've seen one,' Jook piped up. 'That'd be a witch's house.'

Dennis peered over the edge of the carpet. Something clicked in his brain. He was curious. Maybe he could learn something here. He politely requested a smooth descent. He was really getting the hang of this.

Soon, the three men were standing at a picket gate set in a low white picket fence. The fence enclosed a neat house made of gingerbread, lollipops and marzipan. Dennis pushed the gate with his toe and walked in. The two guards followed close behind. At the front door, he looked up and read a nameplate with a notice under it:

Esmerelda's Cottage.

I don't mind you eating the flowers,

But leave the ROOF alone!

Dennis glanced back at Jook, who was nearest, and whispered, 'I've heard of this woman. She's a witch. My sources tell me she may be responsible for some of the uncommon magic detected out this way. She may well have the staff, or know where it is.' He pressed the bell push, and his thumb sunk into the gingerbread.

Jook couldn't help himself. 'Glad my sauces never talk to me like that. It'd put me right off me dinner.'

Psoddoph groaned. He never knew for sure if his friend was joking when he said things like this. But he knew it was a bad idea.

Redeeming himself, Jook said, 'That's great news, boss.'

'Yes, isn't it?' Dennis chuckled.

Jook studied the sign under the cottage nameplate, but gave up and had to ask Psoddoph.

'It says the witch doesn't mind us eating the flowers, but to leave the roof alone.'

'Well, she doesn't seem to be home to stop us.' Jook looked around the garden, his eyes widening as he saw the rows of candyfloss and chocolate roses. Then he caught sight of the liquorice-all-sorts, and fruit-drop tree standing temptingly in a corner. But the roof looked even better. He loved marzipan. He looked around to make sure no-one was watching and reached up to break a piece off the corner.

A little voice said, 'Oi! Can't you read?'

Jook could only say, 'Ouch!' as the gnome by his feet stabbed him in the leg with the end of a fishing rod. Normally gnomes pretend they can't speak or move, but this one knew there was no point the moment he saw a wizard with the guards.

Psoddoph looked down and grinned at the gnome. 'Hello, little feller, what's your name?'

'Questions! Questions! Always bloody questions!' the gnome ranted. 'Why can't you just say something without asking a question? I never ask questions, now, *do I?*'

Dennis came over to investigate. 'Oh. What have we here?' He grinned and squatted down for a closer look.

'Oh, no. Not another one.' The gnome sighed hugely for one so small.

'He seems upset,' said Dennis, looking at Psoddoph. 'What have you done to him?'

'Nothin', boss. Honest,' said Psoddoph. 'Apart from ask him his name, that is. Then, he gave me a load of lip.'

'Oh, did he now?' said Dennis, furrowing his brow. He snatched up the gnome and dangled him at arm's length, level with his eyes. 'Now, little man, when one of my guards asks you a question, you answer. Understand?'

The gnome squirmed and wriggled, almost catching Dennis in the eye with his fishing rod. After some ineffective lunges, and some failed attempts to twist himself around to bite Dennis's hand, he gave up. 'Okay, okay,' he blurted in his high-pitched voice. 'What do you want?'

'That's better,' said Dennis. 'Your name will do for a start. I always begin with the easy ones.'

'Arfer!' the gnome replied, grudgingly.

'There, you see, that wasn't difficult, was it – *Arfer*,' Dennis cooed.

'Look, mister...'

'Dennis,' he interrupted.

'*Dennis*, stop messin' about – and put me down.'

'I think that's a good idea, boss,' said Jook. 'After all, we don't know where 'e's been.'

Arfer made a mental note to 'get 'im' for that.

'Are you going to behave?' asked Dennis.

'Oh, yes,' Arfer lied, peering at him from beneath his painted stone eyebrows.

Dennis put the gnome back on the ground, and no sooner had Arfer regained his balance, than he rushed at the wizard's legs and bit him. Then he scrambled for the comparative safety of the other side of the pond. Dennis hopped around clutching his shin. 'Grab him!' he yelled. 'Now! The little...!'

Jook went round one side of the pond and Psoddoph the other, to trap Arfer between them. But Psoddoph hadn't got far when he was hit in the shins by a gnome with a garden rake. This new arrival was now about to slam the rake down on Psoddoph's toes, but the guard stepped back just in time. Angrily, he drew his sword and waved it at the gnome, who scampered round the pond to join Arfer.

Jook was dealing with another problem on his side of the pond – a third gnome with a wheelbarrow. The gnome had steered it with deadly accuracy and at a fair lick of speed, into Jook's calves, causing him to stumble and step into the pond. His boot came off in the mud. One of his *best pair*! And now he was angry, too.

He chose to ignore the gnomes for a moment. He sat on the edge of the pond, lifted his water-filled boot out of the water and shook it. This was hardly a good time for a time out. There was a crash, followed by a stabbing pain in his back. The gnome rammed him a second time and pitched him forward into the pond.

Jook sat covered in the mucky stuff that grows in ponds, and slapped the surface of the water hard. 'That's it! I've 'ad it up to 'ere wiv you little buggers!' He saluted just above his eyebrows, to indicate just how far he'd had it up to. He clambered out of the water and lunged fiercely at the nearest gnome – the one about to swing his rake and sink the tines into Psoddoph again.

He caught the rake and wrenched it from the little man's hand. He then flung it at the gnome with the wheelbarrow, who tilted his barrow forward to shield himself. The tines pierced the wood and remained firmly embedded. Still in a rage, Jook picked up the barrow and rake and slung them at the ground as hard as he could. But gnomes' equipment doesn't break so easily. He looked around for something to smash it with.

All three gnomes were now grouped on the other side of the pond, laughing at the guards' misfortune. But their faces froze when they saw Dennis enter the fray. He looked like a man with murderous intent as he raised his hand. There was a crackle of magic in the air, and an orange light speared from his fingertips and engulfed them. Instantly, they were bound together in tightly coiled ropes and slumped to the ground. Like all gnomes, everywhere, when snared, they cursed and struggled. But to no avail. They should have been happy to be alive. But apparently not. Captives rarely count their blessings.

Psoddoph hurried around the pond to get his hands on them. Jook was more intent on picking bits of pondweed and lilies from his clothes. But a quick word from the wizard, and a snap of his fingers, sent all the remaining slimy stuff back into the pond.

The Drum glowed.

'I'm all wet, boss,' moaned Jook, hoping a little magic might come his way, too.

'Tough!' snapped Dennis, as he stormed around the pond towards the gnomes.

'But, boss...' Jook wailed.

Psoddoph squatted in front of the gnomes. 'You've done it now,' he gloated. 'He's furious. I wouldn't mind betting he'll turn you into something nasty. Permanently.'

'Nah...' said Arfer, 'he wouldn't do that. Would he?'

'Oh, yes he bloody well would!' Dennis barked. 'Now, what's it to be? Toads? Frogs? Hedgehogs or snakes? No, I know what I'll do.' He leered at them. 'Statues! I'll make you all permanently what you pretend to be!'

'No!' yelled Arfer. 'Not statues! Anyfing but soddin' statues.'

'Okay,' said Dennis, as if relenting. 'Gnomes are supposed to know things, aren't they? Or so the saying goes. And I need to know things. First, tell me who lives here?'

'Esmerelda Swampshott and Florence,' Arfer replied, quickly.

'Careful, boss,' Jook warned. 'He could be lying.'

'No, I don't think so. Nobody would make up a name like that.'

'What, Florence?' said Jook, quizzically.

'No. Idiot. Swampshit!' snapped Dennis.

'I just knew you'd get it wrong.' Jook grinned.

'That's enough, now,' cautioned Psoddoph, tugging at Jook's sleeve. 'Not while the boss is angry, or *you* might end the day as a frog.'

Dennis ignored them and turned back to the gnomes. 'Where have they gone?'

'Who?' said Arfer, forgetting what was going on.

'Esmerelda and Florence!' Dennis snapped. 'Why don't you pay attention when I'm talking at you?'

'Prossill!' answered all three gnomes in unison.

'Why?'

'They're looking for a Drum, or so Esmerelda said,' said Arfer, peering past Dennis at the cart. 'But you've got it, haven't you?' he added, accusingly.

'Never mind about that,' Dennis sidestepped, then added, 'Does she happen to carry a staff, this witch?'

'Well, not a staff, as such. She 'as a broomstick, nat'rally. Though, finking about it, it don't have a broom on the end, so you could call it a staff, I s'pose.'

Dennis caught his breath. His heart skipped a beat. 'When did they leave? How long ago?'

'I don't know,' whined Arfer. 'I just sit 'ere fishin' all day, you know how it is... Might've been a week... I lose track of time once I dip me rod in the water,' he said, staring glassy-eyed by way of a demonstration.

'All right,' said Dennis, as evenly as he could manage. 'How did they leave?'

'Bolt upright, she was. Both feet on the ground,' said Arfer, truthfully. 'Not like sometimes, when she staggers a bit and falls over,' he added, sadly.

'Drinks a lot, does she?' said Dennis, getting sucked into a conversation that he might easily lose control of.

'No, not really,' Arfer sighed. 'Just enough to make her fall over sometimes.'

'Shame,' said Dennis, squatting down. 'It must be awful when she gets like that.'

'Yeah...' Arfer agreed, with a faraway look. 'Brews all her own stuff, you know,' he added, brightening.

'Does she now?' said Dennis.

'Yeah. Keeps it locked away round the back. Would you care for a drop? It's good stuff,' enthused the gnome. 'And I know where she keeps the key.'

Dennis felt a sudden dryness in his throat. It had been a while since he'd sampled something. 'Wouldn't mind.'

Arfer smiled a crooked smile. 'You'll have to untie me.'

The wizard waved a hand, and the ropes fell away and slithered back to wherever Dennis had conjured them from. 'All right,' he said, feeling a kind of hypnotic compliance creeping over him.

'Don't listen to 'im, boss,' Psoddoph urged. 'It's a trick.'

'Nooo,' said Dennis, reassuringly. 'I think we could all do with a beverage. It's been a while. Not many taverns in the desert.'

Arfer struggled to his feet and waited while the other two scurried away.

Unseen, the Drum glowed, with a dim orange light.

'Follow me,' said Arfer, rubbing some life back into his arms as he strode round to the back of the house.

Around the corner there was a small building that wasn't constructed from anything edible, though the brickwork bore little resemblance to real bricks. It had a strange-looking door, painted green, with a row of holes along the top and bottom, and a highly polished brass handle. Some runes of a sort that Dennis hadn't seen before were burnt into a piece of wood that seemed nailed to the door as an afterthought.

Arfer lifted a nearby flowerpot, grabbed the key and squeezed himself under the door. He'd never have reached the keyhole anyway. And now that Arfer had the key with him, Dennis couldn't follow. Dennis huffed and listened. He could hear the sounds of bottles being opened and the gentle clinking sounds they made as they touched the sides of the tankards they were being emptied into. He heard voices, too. It seemed like the other two gnomes had made their way there, too. He stood closer and tried to look through one of the holes across the top of the door. It was pitch dark in there.

'Careful, boss!'

'Ouch!' Dennis yelled, clutching his ear. A long, sharp stick was waving from the hole next to where he'd been looking.

'Cor, you were lucky there, boss,' said Jook, grinning involuntarily, 'If I 'adn't called you just then, that little bugger could've 'ad yer eye out.'

Dennis stepped back a couple of paces, aimed his fingers at the door, and released a fireball.

Unseen, in the cart, the Drum glowed.

The door also glowed momentarily, and the fireball glanced away towards Jook, who dived to the ground as it sailed past, hit a tree, and went spinning back towards Dennis. He made a rapid sign in the air and deflected it away. The ball took on a life of its own, and did a complete circuit of the house to come at Dennis from the rear.

'Look out, boss!' Psoddoph cried.

Dennis said, 'Whoa...!' as he ducked, and sidestepped in one ungainly movement. The fireball lost momentum and fizzled out on the grass. He tried again. The second fireball went spinning over the roof. Seconds later, there was a loud splash and a hiss of steam from the pond.

'What's that door made of?' Jook wondered. It seemed to shimmer.

Dennis reached out cautiously to touch it. Before he got close, a shaft of searing, white light arced between his fingers and the door handle. He snatched his hand away and muttered a colourful curse. From behind the door, came a shriek of gnomic laughter, and Arfer called out, 'You'll never get us in 'ere, wizard!'

'I've got a feeling he's right, boss,' said Psoddoph.

'I can wait,' snapped Dennis. 'I want that little bugger.'

'What for, boss?' said Psoddoph, quietly. 'He's told you what you need to know.'

'He just *burned* my finger,' said Dennis, blowing on the slightly blackened digit.

'Why don't we go and have a look in the house?' suggested Psoddoph. 'If he thinks we've gone, he might come out.'

Dennis considered this, while cooling his finger. 'The witch must have left some protection on that side of the building. A witch's spell wouldn't normally resist me, but I think the Drum's reinforcing it.'

'It doesn't like you,' Psoddoph reminded him, trying to commiserate.

Dennis shook his hurt finger for a moment, to the alarm of the guards. 'I know what we'll do…'

'Yes, boss?'

'We're going. Now!' Dennis shouted at the door.

'Hic!' came the muffled reply.

The three men stomped noisily round to the front door. Jook tried the handle. 'It's locked, boss,' he said, stating the obvious.

'Of course it's locked. What did you expect?' said Dennis, looking skywards for sympathy. 'Sometimes…!'

'What, boss?'

'Oh, never mind. This door may be shielded, too.'

Jook tried the handle again. Then he had a brainwave. And knocked. Nothing happened. After a few seconds, he turned to Dennis. 'There's nobody in.'

Dennis cuffed him across the ear. 'We *know* there's nobody in!' he shouted, in exasperation. 'I've already tried the gingerbread bloody bell! Remember?'

'Let's go,' said Psoddoph, trying to diffuse the situation before Dennis did something Jook would regret, and he started to walk away.

'Just a minute,' Dennis whispered. 'I'll just have another look round the corner to see if that little runt has come out yet.' Psoddoph shrugged and followed.

Around the corner, the door was still shut, but Dennis crept up to it anyway and stood quietly listening. The gnomes were singing a sad lament about the more disgusting habits of the lank-eyed porcupine. To give them their due, it was probably some of the best close-harmony singing to be heard anywhere in the land. Even with the impromptu 'Hics' that were developing into a refrain of their own.

'It's no good, boss,' said Psoddoph. 'I reckon they're in there till midnight now.'

'Damn! Just one whack, that's all. One *good* whack, that's all I want.' He punched the palm of his hand and winced when he caught his blistered finger.

'P'raps next time, boss. Come on, let's be on our way to Prossill.' Psoddoph took the disconsolate Dennis by the hand (he winced again), and walked him back to the cart.

48

It was barely dawn when Link tapped on Eydith's door. She woke promptly, having slept only lightly, and not much, from thinking about the journey ahead of them today. 'Sprag,' she whispered, 'are you awake?'

'Yes, mistress,' came the creaky reply. 'Though what I do is not actually sleep. But for simplicity you can call it that.'

'Pedantic as ever,' she said, smiling weakly.

'I try, mistress.'

'Can you wake up father? I don't want him being blown around the room when I open the door.'

'I'm awake,' said Wimlett, testily. 'I've been awake for ages.'

While Eydith had been sleeping, Sprag had been busy refining his magical connections with her and her father. She could hear Wimlett's voice quite clearly now, and if she concentrated hard enough, she could just make him out, sitting transparently at the table. He looked very like a ghost, in fact. She smiled as she watched him stroking his beard, deep in thought.

Then came a rat-a-tat...tat, and she got up to let Link in.

'It's the big day,' he said eagerly, slipping past her. 'Are you all ready?'

'Yes, I was planning to go in my pyjamas.'

'Ah, sorry, yes.'

'But I won't be long sorting myself out.'

'In the meantime,' said Sprag, 'you can lie back on the bed while I enhance your connection with myself and Wimlett, so that we can all see and hear one another better. I have worked out how to do it. And, who knows? – it might even help,' he finished, unable to supress a little sarcasm.

The process took about twenty minutes. He got up a little dazed and confused to find that Eydith had sorted herself out, and that the ghost of Wimlett was seated at the table. He nodded a 'hello' to him.

'Right,' said Eydith. 'I think we're all about ready now.'

'You haven't eaten anything yet, my girl,' said Wimlett. 'We have a big day ahead of us.'

She wanted to protest, but no sooner had she thought about breakfast, than a bowl appeared on the table. It was filled with a thickish grey paste that she hoped was porridge. *How did I do that?* she wondered, looking at it suspiciously. *I'm going to have to be careful what I wish for.*

'I've been teaching you in your sleep,' answered Sprag, still connected. 'And don't worry – it won't be so quick to fire off, now that you know it can happen. I just hope it works properly, that's all.'

'So far, so good,' Eydith reassured him, sampling the porridge. She ate till she was full, and Link finished it. He approved of what she'd produced. Though that wasn't much of an endorsement: most things edible met with his approval.

'Okay,' she said, finally, grabbing her small shoulder-bag. 'Let's check the passage, and be off.'

Wimlett put himself to good use by literally poking his head through the door. 'All clear.'

***

Hardly anyone was around in the early-morning streets, as the group made their way to the outskirts of the city. The inhabitants of Kra-Pton were not the earliest of risers. The only people the party encountered were a few night-watchmen, and the occasional drunk settling down in the gutter for the day.

Once clear of the city perimeter, Wimlett led Eydith and Link to the road that he'd travelled previously. They could relax a little, free of the possibility of running into anyone Link knew from the university, who might wonder what they were up to.

As they strolled, Eydith wondered about the practicalities of the flight, while Link explored the inner cavity of his left ear.

'As I see it,' she said, 'when we fly, it will be best, and save time, if we all travel together. Is that possible, Sprag?'

'That is exactly what I have in mind,' said the staff. 'You will hold onto me, Link, will hold your other hand, and your father will hold Link's other hand. That way we will all be transported together.'

'And now would be a good time to try it,' said Wimlett, 'if everyone's okay with that?'

They were. They were walking across open country for the first few miles, and had the advantage of being able to see where they were going when they took off. It would be good practice for when they had to navigate obstacles like trees and hills.

Link was very much in favour. It meant physical contact with Eydith! He grabbed her hand in readiness, and it felt pleasingly warm and soft. What he didn't know was that she could hear his thoughts when they touched. She was flattered. And what *she* didn't know was that he had *those* sorts of thoughts about her. But for the moment, she decided not to embarrass him by letting on.

Then Link reached out for Wimlett's hand, and a flaw in Sprag's plan became evident. Wimlett's hand passed right through his. 'Eydith! Can you or Sprag do something here? I can't hold a hand that's made of nothing,' he said, shaking his hand in the air where the ghostly mage's hand was.

'I can make him more solid,' said Sprag. 'But only one part of him, and just for a while.'

Wimlett's right hand slowly materialised, and Link tentatively reached out to take it.

'It won't bite you, you know,' said Wimlett.

Though Link thought it just might, he steeled himself for the crackle of static magic, or worse. What he got, though, felt like a handful of ice-cold rubber. His immediate reaction was, 'Yuck!' But like a true hero, he hung on.

'Well, I've held better hands, too,' said Wimlett, shaking his head.

Sprag couldn't risk making any more of Wimlett's body solid. He would be carrying enough weight as it was. But he was pleased to know that parts of the old mage could be made solid. It might prove useful. Though Naphrat's magic was not easy to interfere with, nor was it something that Sprag would interfere with lightly.

They were ready for their first flight. There was very little preamble. The staff shimmered. They were whisked from the ground and travelling faster than they'd ever done before. Except Wimlett, of course. Eydith thrilled to the speed. Link, on the other hand was worried, and felt the urgent need to say something. 'Eydith! Get Sprag to fly higher!' he called.

'What's the problem?' she called back.

'Shouldn't I be flying as well?'

'Yes, of course!'

'Then why am I running along beside you with my legs going like a windmill in a gale?'

Sprag lurched higher. Then, 'Hold on a minute!' Link shouted. 'I've dropped Wimlett!'

Sprag slowed to a stop, and Link released his grip on Eydith's hand, forgetting that Sprag was still about six feet in the air. He let out an 'Aargh!' that surpassed even one of Wimlett's cries of panic for volume, intensity and duration.

He landed further on than Wimlett, but being solid, didn't roll quite so far. The old mage passed right through him, giving him that unnerving icy feeling of someone walking over his grave. Though, how anyone would know what that felt like, Link wasn't sure, and certainly wouldn't be investigating it right then, or ever.

Link got up slowly, checking that no bones were broken, then turned to look for Wimlett. He could see his solid hand, its fingers flexing, lying nearby on the dusty road, and then saw the outline of the rest of him, and gave a sigh of relief. He couldn't be any deader, of course, but Link didn't want the old wizard to come to any harm on his account. Eydith would be very cross indeed. He looked around and saw her suspended from Sprag, just above him. The staff had helpfully dropped a few feet. He clasped her hand in his again. Then reaching down, he took Wimlett's hand to help him up. Expecting some weight behind it, he tugged, and was soon reminded, as he fell back in the dust, that ghosts are considerably lacking in pounds and ounces.

'Will you two stop messing about,' Eydith called, as she descended to the ground with Sprag. 'We haven't got all day.'

Link muttered something. Wimlett made a sort of 'Hmph' sound.

'Okay,' she said, trying to stay calm, 'let's try that again, shall we?'

Like paper-chain dolls, the three of them took to the air once again, and made for the horizon, where a line of trees marked their landing place, and the jumping off point for their more hazardous second leap.

I wonder where Dennis is, Eydith thought.

Sprag was listening, but he left her to her thoughts. His role was mostly to guide and protect. As much as possible, he'd leave her to make her own decisions, and her own mistakes. And, to date, she'd done well. He projected a part of his awareness into the eyes of a large bird that was flying overhead, and scanned the yellow grass of the Tong Plain where they were now. He was looking for signs of human life. One life in particular. Dennis. There was no trace of the man. He tried for the Drum, and couldn't locate that either. It was no surprise that they were out of range. But it helped to keep his senses honed.

The sun was higher now. The travellers were glad of the cool breeze that accompanied each flight. They flew on past the Low Hills and across the Blue Grass Plain where the cow herds grazed. They made regular stops to get their bearings, and to rest their aching arms. It was not an ideal a way to travel, dragging each other along in this fashion. Eydith and Link had been giving it a lot of thought. At the next stop, they sat in silence, rubbing their aching wrists, arms and shoulders.

'There's got to be a better way than this,' Link complained. 'My arm's dropping off.'

'Any ideas, Sprag?' asked Eydith.

'I know it's hard on you,' said the staff, 'But if we carry on as we are, and then head south to find that railway Wimlett found, we can continue on that.'

'That would help.' She looked at Link and Wimlett. 'What about you two?'

Eydith could almost see her father fully now – he was nodding, albeit grudgingly. Link could come up with no better idea. So, after half an hour's rest, they set off. Thankfully, it wasn't long before they veered south to the railway. After a dozen or so longish arm-aching flights, they landed by a colourful little cottage.

◄─◄❮❯►─►

49

Dennis maintained the carpet at a steady speed, skimming over the tree tops, high enough to avoid getting snagged. He felt better now they were on their way again. The sky was blue, there were fluffy white clouds scudding in the breeze, and a few inquisitive birds keeping the travellers company. He was quite enjoying himself, though loathe to admit it.

Jook lay in the back of the cart, staring at the sky. Psoddoph sat under the cart in the shade, polishing his sword, the sound of which was starting to irritate Dennis.

'Stop playing with that thing and put it away,' he said, shortly.

Psoddoph complied and Jook smiled as he heard the familiar swish of a steel blade sliding into a leather scabbard, and the satisfying click, as the finger guard stopped it. 'It's not as if you ever do anything with it,' Dennis added, meanly.

'Yes, I do, boss,' snorted Psoddoph, rather hurt.

'Oh, yes. I forgot,' Dennis mocked. 'You trip over it quite a lot. And open jars sometimes.'

Psoddoph ignored him. Jook sighed. Dennis looked around at the landscape passing below. *All this will be mine one day*, he thought.

The Drum observed and did nothing.

As the morning wore away to midday, the sun became so bright that Jook, who had stretched out on his back to pass the time looking at shapes in the clouds, had to shut his eyes tight, and cover them with a kerchief. Even then he could see the redness behind his eyelids. He could see the occasional shapes and shadows of the birds passing around them, too. One of them seemed quite large, he thought. He dismissed it as being a bit closer than the others, probably looking to scavenge food from the cart. But then it passed again, more slowly this time, causing the sun to darken significantly. A *biggish* bird? *Not those bloody vultures again, surely!*

He kept his eyes shut, and waved an arm to shoo it away. The wingbeats sounded extraordinarily loud. But he wasn't too bothered. There were some sizeable birds in these parts. But maybe he should just take a peek. He didn't want the thing pecking and stabbing around him for the food store.

After a minute, Jook cracked open one eye and let it focus. He opened his other eye. It focused more quickly. Then he swallowed. Loudly.

He'd heard of these things, but he'd never actually seen one. In fact, he thought the last one was killed by some barbarian hero, about thirty years ago. Yet here was one, large as life, perched at the end of the cart. He lay there, frozen to the spot, watching the beast fold its leathery bat-like wings and take a piece of coal from a pouch somewhere among the scales that covered most of its body. It popped the coal into a mouth packed full of the most lethal looking teeth he'd ever had the misfortune to gaze upon.

The creature ran its claws down the back of its horse-like head, and vainly patted a few loose strands of golden mane back into place. Jook considered his options, which were startlingly few. But, on the plus side, the creature had been there for a few minutes, and it hadn't attacked him. He began to feel marginally less terrified. The beast ignored him, and carried on preening itself. 'Are you there?' he breathed, as loudly as he dared, and tapped on the floor of the cart.

'What's up?' answered Psoddoph.

'Can you come up 'ere a minute?' whispered Jook, urgently.

'What is it *now*?' Psoddoph complained.

'Look, just come up 'ere will you. And be careful.'

'What? Oh, all right, I'm coming.' Psoddoph pulled himself out from under the cart, stretched, blinked and yawned. It was that kind of day. 'Okay, what do you want?'

'Don't make any sudden moves.' said Jook, pointing at the back of the cart.

Psoddoph's eyes followed the line of Jook's arm, and settled on the beast. He stared at it, open mouthed, for a very long moment. 'Shit,' he murmured. He knew that Dennis was close to his feet, and reached out tentatively with a toe to prod him. 'Boss?' he whispered, 'Come and see this?'

Dennis swiped the foot away, indignantly, and stood up to see what was going on 'It's a bloody dragon!' he yelled, half in awe, half in panic. 'Jook! Get rid of it!'

Jook had frozen in the throes of trying to assess the range of the thing's fire power compared with how close he was. But Psoddoph, now back under the cart with Dennis, was not fazed by the beast. He seemed let down by it. 'I remember you once saying they were the biggest beasts in the world,' he accused. 'It ain't that big.'

'It's a baby,' said Dennis, trying to calm himself. 'And do you know what that means?'

He shrugged.

'Its mother won't be far away. And if she turns up, we'll have big trouble.'

Psoddoph said a bad word. Then embellished it.

Jook remained transfixed, as the baby dragon took another piece of coal from a breast pocket, it seemed, and, after giving it a quick polish on its rump, tossed it into the air and caught it in its teeth. It swallowed and gave a little belch, sending out a small spout of flame. Jook sat up very slowly. He was considering waving his arms about and yelling to scare it away, when the sky darkened and he heard the sound of leathery wings beating. The carpet tilted. He looked over his shoulder, knowing exactly what he would see. Mother.

'Magnificent!' Dennis couldn't help but be impressed at the sight of the biggest dragon he'd ever seen or heard of.

'Yeah,' said Psoddoph. 'And let's not forget *terrifying*!'

Dennis was lying under the cart a short way from Psoddoph. The tilt from the beast's weight made the cart slip, but only as far as the wizard's legs, which acted like a brick wedged under a wheel to stop it rolling. He grimaced, silently hiding the pain, and whispered to Psoddoph to take the shiny sword he lavished so much care and attention on, and actually use it to strike down the dragons!

'Have you thought this through, boss?' asked the guard, in a vain attempt to put off the inevitable.

'Look! I pay you to guard me,' Dennis protested. 'But most of the time I seem to be protecting you two!'

'But I've never fought a dragon, boss. And this one, well...' He sighed, deeply, drew his sword, and moved out from under the cart. The baby dragon had flown, and was circling nearby. The mother was growling and preening herself like a cat, with one eye on Jook who was cowering in a corner of the cart in easy reach of a breath of flame.

Psoddoph's fear was overcome in part by seeing the plight of his friend. He knew he had to act quickly and decisively. And although it was the most worrying thing about the situation, the fact that the beast's attention was fixed on Jook, was also the most favourable thing about it. The dragon didn't notice when he slipped quietly around behind her. He wasn't a brave man, by any stretch of the imagination, but he was no coward either.

He stood, sword in hand, behind the enormous beast. All he had to do was plunge the sword into her, and – job done!

'No, I can't do it,' he told himself. 'Not in the back. It's not fair.' He raised his sword above his head with both hands, and brought the flat of it whistling down with all his strength across the dragon's tail. There was a loud slap and an even louder roar. A great jet of flame flared upwards from her nostrils, she spread her leathery wings, beat them noisily, and climbed into the air, her offspring following in her wake. They were moving away.

The carpet bobbed dangerously and then righted itself.

'Satisfied?' said Psoddoph, looking down at Dennis, who was still under the cart.

The wizard smiled. 'That's more like it.'

Jook leapt off the cart and scrambled to relative safety underneath with the others. 'Did you see those things?' he gasped.

'I'm not blind,' said Dennis.

Psoddoph knelt with his sword still in his hand, watching the dragons shrink to specks in the distance. He was pleased with himself. His first fight with a dragon, and he'd dealt with two of them with a single stroke. In the distance, the specks circled a couple of times and soared higher. Satisfied with his day's work, he turned to Dennis, 'It's all right now, boss,' he said, milking the moment, and posing heroically as he sheathed his sword. 'They've gone.'

'Would one of you mind moving the cart now?' Dennis pleaded, still pinned.

Jook obligingly put his shoulder to it.

'No, no, no!' the wizard yelled. 'The other way!' Why did he just know that would happen?

Dennis withdrew his leg and began to massage the pain away.

Psoddoph was keeping an eye on the dragons. Was it his imagination, or were those specks getting bigger? 'Boss?' he said, keeping his voice as level as possible, 'I think they're coming back.'

'What?' he snapped, scrambling to his feet. He looked where Psoddoph was pointing. 'Oh, no. I told you to *kill* them, didn't I? Eh, didn't I?' he railed. 'And there's three of them now!'

A third dragon, improbably bigger than the mother, was leading the trio and homing in on the carpet.

Under the canvas it was dark. The Drum was glad.

Dennis was doing some of the most agile thinking he'd done in years. He was too young to die, besides, he had plans, and being flame grilled by three overweight lizards wasn't one of them. 'Calm down,' he told himself. 'Deep breaths.' He had the presence of mind to realise that if he started barking orders to the carpet, he would risk tipping them all into oblivion. He considered launching a fireball at the beast, but couldn't be sure what the Drum would do with it. Also, he'd read somewhere that a dragon could swallow a fireball and return it with interest. He had an idea, and without letting it go cold, he yelled at the carpet. 'Carpet! Take evasive action!' then added politely, '... *Please.*'

The carpet turned, as if sizing up the situation, and went into a steep dive. There was a united cry of, 'Yaargh!' as the passengers grabbed something to hang on to. Their breath left their lungs as they plunged; their knuckles blanched, and their faces turned a strange shade of green.

The leading dragon peeled away from the formation and dived at the carpet. A blast of orange flame roared from its nostrils and spat through the air where the carpet had been only seconds before. The second dragon attacked from below, flying up passed them. The speed of the air rushing by tilted the carpet dangerously, but it banked steeply, holding on to its passengers by sheer gravity.

The carpet stopped plummeting and soared back into the sky, narrowly avoiding a small blast from the baby dragon. The two larger beasts, mother and father, caught up with each other, and were treading air directly ahead. Dennis looped an arm through one of the cartwheels to secure himself better. He closed his eyes, and promptly opened them again, because he could imagine far worse things happening than he could see.

The carpet stopped, and hung in the air, as if waiting for the dragons to make a move. Daring them almost. They were lazily beating the air, watching. The carpet pulled back a few feet, like a long-jumper preparing to run, and then it shot forward. The guards watched, paralysed, as they mentally counted the seconds to impact, wondering who would be first to break down and scream. Even when terror-stricken, they still held onto their soldiers' pride.

The carpet raced to within feet of the lead dragon before it veered away, narrowly avoiding the blast of crimson fire coming at it. The two big beasts folded their wings and dived after their quarry, plummeting like giant birds of prey. Great gouts of flame leapt ahead of them as they followed. The sky was bright and hot behind the carpet. The smallest dragon joined the fray and sped passed, clipping the carpet and almost sending it spinning. Without warning, the carpet stopped, almost propelling the cart and three men into empty air, but tipping back to save them. It turned to face its attackers, and started moving straight at them.

'What the hell's it doing now!' screamed Jook.

'I'm buggered if I know!' Dennis yelled back.

Psoddoph had every faith in the carpet, but kept his hands over his eyes.

The carpet advanced, seemingly heedless of its own flammability. Or of its passengers'. The creatures craned their necks forwards and roared. The men braced themselves. But instead of searing fire, there was only a cough and a splutter, as a token flame snaked lazily from the both dragons. Their fires were out. They'd forgotten their need to stop for coal. But they continued to pursue and harry the carpet, which now took evasive action almost casually, as it swung around to get back on Dennis's original course.

There were trees ahead. Lots of them. A forest, in fact, and they were heading for it.

The carpet dropped down and began to slalom its way skilfully through the trees. It slowed and landed gracefully, to the applause of the two guards, in the first clearing it found that had an overarching canopy.

'What the hell are you two doing?' barked Dennis incredulously. 'Clapping a carpet, for goodness' sake!'

'It did a great job, boss,' said Psoddoph.

'It's a bloody carpet!'

The dragons veered away knowing they couldn't follow. They wheeled about on the breeze over the tree tops for a while, looking for a way in. Eventually, they gave up and settled on some high branches. 'It's no use, Deidre,' sighed the biggest dragon. 'We'll never find them down there.'

'Oh, dear, Norman,' sighed Deidre. 'It's so annoying when they do that. And I so wanted to scorch that little bugger who whacked my tail with his sword.'

'Oh, let's let them go, dearest,' said Norman. 'You know I don't really care for that sort. And all the adrenaline makes them too spicy, anyway.' Then he had a thought, 'Let's go and visit that castle over the Green Mountains. You remember? There was a nice selection over there.'

'Ooh, Norman, I do remember,' she cooed, and peering into the forest, after the meal that had escaped, she added, 'those grey ones down there are all right, at a pinch, but a bit stringy. I would've liked a taste of that one in black though.'

'Darling… they won't be half as nice as those at the castle. You know – the bright shiny ones with the soft centres?'

'Oh, all right, you've convinced me… JUNIOR!' she roared, as she looked around the horizon. 'Oh, where's that little bugger got to, now?'

50

'That's Esmerelda's place!' shouted Wimlett, 'I knew you could find it, staff.'

Sprag didn't answer. It would only start another argument. Besides, he was searching the vicinity for the Drum. He'd sensed what he thought was its homing call, but it was weak, and he wasn't sure. Eydith and Link walked up to the little gate and went into the garden. There were flashes of movement around the pond, as the garden gnomes rushed back to their places. Link reached the front door and tried the handle. It didn't move.

Eydith went to a window, eager to see what her aunt's home looked like inside. She saw a neatly furnished room, with floral design covers on the chairs, and lots of brass and copper ornaments hanging from dark wooden beams. And in the big open fireplace was a big black cauldron. The interior wasn't made of confectionary, she noted, especially the fireplace and chimney! The shelves above it were stocked with potions in bottles, and to one side of the hearth leaned a besom with a stout broom handle.

She made her way back to the front door and reached out to knock.

'There's nobody in,' said a little voice.

'Stop messing about, Link,' said Eydith.

'It wasn't me.'

'I know who it was,' said Wimlett, pointing at a smartly dressed garden gnome with a fishing rod held out over the pond.

'Hello, wizard!' Arfer called out. 'Funny fing you know. Don't see no ghosts for years, then you see the same one twice in a week.' The gnome shook his head, 'Funny that, ennit?'

'I suppose it is,' said Wimlett. 'Caught anything yet?'

'No, not yet,' said Arfer, happily.

'Been fishing long?' asked Eydith, politely.

'Always this nosy, is she?' said Arfer, ignoring Eydith and speaking to Wimlett.

'Hush your tongue, gnome. She might make you catch something.'

'Oh, no! Please don't do that,' Arfer pleaded. 'I wouldn't know what to do with it, anyway.'

'Gnomes know things,' said Sprag, directly into Eydith's mind. 'It's an adage, but there's truth in it, believe me. I sense this creature knows where Dennis is, mistress.'

'Right,' she said. 'How do I address a gnome?'

'Well, firstly, as you would a human,' said Sprag. 'If that doesn't work, treat him like dirt. If you still don't get any sense out of him, I'd advise kicking him into the pond. They're obstinate little things.' The staff had a discernible chuckle in his voice.

'I'll try the first option,' said Eydith, bending down beside Arfer. 'Hello, gnome. What's your name?'

'Questions! Always bloody questions!' he snapped.

Eydith stood up and made a show of drawing her foot back. If he didn't respond to kindness, she'd skip treating him like dirt, and move directly to the kick into the pond. But before her foot connected, Arfer spoke up.

'All right! All right! It's Arfer!' he said, hurriedly.

'Right, mister Arfer gnome. I think you might have some information I want.'

'Have I?' said Arfer, still trying to be difficult. Though, as a gnome, he didn't have to try: it came naturally.

'Where's Dennis?' She stared him straight in the eye.

'What's he look like?'

'Tall, dressed in black, has a smarmy smile and a short temper, and has two guards with him.' She was resisting the urge to add emphasis with prods in his chest from her rather vicious looking finger nail.

'Oh... *that* Dennis,' said the gnome. 'Well, last I 'eard, he'd got a magic carpet and was flying to Prossill.'

'Where is he now?'

The gnome looked down. 'He was camped on the edge of the desert, by a small lake,' he said, tapping the side of his nose. 'But now, he's hiding in the Old Forest.'

'Why? What happened?' asked Eydith, raising an eyebrow.

Arfer looked down again, and Eydith realised he was studying a miniature crystal ball. 'Ah... yes. I see. He's been attacked by dragons,' Arfer reported, then stopped. The ball had gone cloudy. He held it up to one eye and peered in. He shook it, then banged it a couple of times on the concrete toadstool he was sitting on. There was a fizzing sound and smoke came out of it. At which point he tossed it on the grass, muttering something about 'getting what you pay for'.

'There,' said Eydith. 'That didn't hurt did it? Well, not as much as it might have,' she added quietly, as she stood up.

The gnome breathed a sigh of relief at what seemed the end of his ordeal, but Eydith turned back to him. 'One more question...' she said, bending – 'Has he still got the Drum with him?'

'Oh, yes. He doesn't go anywhere without that.'

'Thank you. You can get on with your fishing now – or rather you're not-fishing.' Then she stood up and joined Link, who had been watching from the doorway.

They were making progress. 'You handled him well,' said Link, smiling at the sight of the disgruntled little fisherman. 'I think we ought to find somebody who works with the new railway, and find out how to get to Prossill.'

'The railway's over that way,' said Wimlett, recalling his impromptu flight from the buffers to the pond, and a little annoyed that they didn't ask him. 'And what am I – invisible?' he said, grumpily, adding, 'Oh, *yeah*.'

'Not so much now, Father. Not to us, anyway.' After a short walk they found two men, one leaning on a sack-trolley, and the other sitting on some crates. Both of them straightened up when they saw Eydith and Link coming.

'Hello, miss,' said the man on the crates. 'What can we do for you?'

'When's the next transport to Prossill?' she asked, politely.

He looked up at the sun, and scratched his head. He looked past the buffers and along the track. 'About an hour... I reckon,' he said. There was no sign of a timetable; he was making an educated guess. Seeing her quizzical look, he explained, 'It's early days, miss, and things are still happening a bit, like, 'as and when', if you know what I mean? The train comes and goes, like, when the guvnor says so.'

'Okay,' said Link. 'We'll come back in about an hour.'

For something to do, they took a stroll around the various sheds and huts that made up the terminal. After a while, Eydith slipped her hand into Link's. They hardly noticed it happen. It just seemed like the natural thing to do.

The place was busy. Carts were rolling into the yard, and goods were being unloaded, and put in position to be hefted onto the train's flatbed trucks. Link could see farm tools, metal plates, building materials, timber, and sacks of grain. Link was thinking: *This must be a worthwhile investment. This railway has possibilities. Perhaps extend the track down to the river. Sailing ships don't even need fuel. Then, what with my design for the sewers of Kra-Pton... If only I had the money, I could make a lot more here.* The irony of that wasn't lost on him. But he was of having an entrepreneurial turn of mind.

The hour went quickly. And as they walked back past Esmerelda's cottage, they noticed puffs of steam and smoke coming along the track.

Eydith paused and looked over the little fence to say goodbye to Arfer. He didn't notice her as he reeled in his line for possibly the millionth time, and smiled with relief when his hook came up empty again. She grinned and followed Link down to the track.

'There's somebody who might know something,' said Link, pointing out a tall, smartly-dressed man wearing a very official looking hat with lots of gold string woven onto it, who hardly needed pointing out. Up close, he was even taller. He smiled down at Eydith, and seemed like a friendly and easy-going man, and not at all superior, like his height and general bearing.

'Hello, my dear,' he said, in a deep, booming, but amiable voice. 'What can I do for you?'

Eydith cleared her throat. 'Er... we were wondering how much it would cost to go to Prossill.'

'Well, now,' replied the man, who might have been a station master had there had been a station. He pushed his hat back and rubbed his chin. 'This will be your first trip, then?'

'Yes, sir,' said Eydith, resisting the urge to stand on tiptoe.

'In that case – seeing that you've asked, and aren't intending to sneak on board – the pair of you can travel as my guests.'

'What?' said Eydith. 'You mean... for free?'

'Of course,' said the man, smiling broadly. 'A special for first-timers. After all, it's my railway. And I like the look of you two.' He beckoned them to follow. They went along the train until they came to the part he was looking for. 'This is my carriage,' he told them. 'Well, they're all mine really, but this one and the one behind are private.' He climbed the polished brass steps and opened the door for them.

'Hmm... this is nice,' said Link, admiring the well-upholstered armchairs and the low, varnished oak table. 'Very nice.'

'Yes, it is, isn't it?' the man agreed. 'Please make yourselves comfortable. Once everything's loaded, we'll be on our way.'

'How long will it take to get to Prossill?' asked Eydith.

'Oh... only about a day and a half.'

'That quick?' Link remarked.

'Yes. But I must leave you for a few minutes, now,' said the man. 'I need to make sure everything's going smoothly.' He excused himself, ducking under the door frame.

'This *is* nice,' whispered Eydith. 'We're being treated by the owner himself.'

'Yes,' said Wimlett, joining in. 'Last time I was on this thing, I was hanging on a wall.'

Eydith and Link sat staring out the windows at the activity outside. 'You know,' said Link, 'I think we'll be in Prossill before Dennis.'

'That would be good. It'll give me some time to catch up with Esmerelda and Florence. And we can plan what we're going to do to get hold of the Drum and deal with Dennis,' said Eydith.

'Sounds almost too easy when you say it,' cut in Wimlett, ruefully.

Eydith heard him vaguely, because she'd found herself looking into Link's eyes at that moment. She hadn't paid that much attention to them before, but now, after their stroll around the depot, she felt drawn to them. They were very dark, almost blue black, like her own. And when they weren't on her, his eyes were on everything else that was going on, very alert. He saw how she was looking at him, and his cheeks reddened slightly.

'Do you think the owner would mind if I moved this chair?' he wondered. 'I don't really want to travel facing backwards. I'd much rather see where I'm going.'

'I don't think he'd mind,' she replied. 'But you don't have to make up excuses to come and sit next to me, you know.'

He gave her a nervous smile, and shifted the chair. 'Did you bring any food?' he asked, as he sat down.

'Ah, now we're getting to it, aren't we?' she accused him. 'You want to be nearer my food.' She picked up the little sack she carried with her. 'Only some apples and plums I collected from the kitchen.'

As they settled down to eat, there was a shrill blast from a steam whistle, and the train began to move forwards in a series of jolts, as the driver fought with the controls. 'We're off,' said Link, excitedly, and looked for somewhere to deposit his apple core. There was nowhere, so he ate it, stalk and all.

'Would you like another?' she asked, as she leant towards the sack again.

'No, that was fine,' he replied, stifling a belch.

They both leant back into the comfortable chairs and watched the countryside roll by, gathering speed. With the motion of the carriage and the repetitive clickety-clack of the wheels, it wasn't long before Link dozed. Eydith looked around for something to amuse herself with. There was nothing. The carriage was beautifully furnished, but totally devoid of entertainment, not even something to read. Her mind went to Sprag. 'Are you awake?'

'Mistress, I never sleep,' said the staff, a little exasperated at having to keep reminding her. 'I have only planes of consciousness. I'm trying to find the Drum. I can feel it on the very edge of my senses.'

'Sleep *is* only another plane of consciousness, isn't it?' she came back, thinking, *well, if he wants to be pedantic...*'

Sprag ran that past himself, and stayed quiet.

'Do you think that gnome was telling the truth?' she wondered.

'I think he was saying what he knew, mistress. However, as far as I can tell, the Drum is not moving, so the carpet must be aground somewhere north of here.'

She glanced across at Wimlett. 'Where are we meeting Esmerelda and Florence?'

'At the Magic Finger tavern, near the Town Hall,' said Wimlett. 'I'll go ahead and find out exactly where, and get back to you.'

'So, we have to hang around the train sheds at Prossill till to you decide to come back, do we?'

'No, my dear,' said Wimlett, returning the sarcasm. 'You can find a tavern near the sheds, or go for a walk around the town, and we can meet somewhere of your choice.'

'That sounds better.' She perked up.

'Don't worry, mistress,' said Sprag. 'I'll find him.'

The connecting door to the next carriage swung open and the tall man ducked and came in. 'Sorry about the bumpy start,' he apologised. 'Driver couldn't get the brake to disengage properly, but it's all right now.'

At the sound of that booming voice, Link woke up and stretched. 'Are we there yet?'

The man laughed. 'We've only been travelling for about twenty minutes.'

'Ah,' said Link, looking around. 'Do we go all the way without stopping?'

'Oh, no. We have to pick up wood and take on water. First stop is in about three hours.'

'I can't wait that long,' said Link, worriedly.

'What's the problem?'

Link stood up and beckoned the man to lower his head, so that he could whisper in his ear. 'I need a privy,' he said, as quietly as possible.

A smile touched the man's face. 'Come with me.'

Link followed him out of the carriage, across the adjoining verandas, and into the next carriage. The man turned and said, 'I didn't want to embarrass you in front of your young lady, but we don't have one. It's a wonderful idea, though. We all make sure we go before we set out.'

'What am I going to do, then?' asked Link, hopping from foot to foot.

'Well, you can stand on the open veranda between the carriages, if you like,' he replied, licking his finger and holding it out of the window to see which way the wind was blowing. 'Should be alright at the moment.'

'That'll have to do,' said Link, disappearing through the door.

When he returned to the big man's carriage, the man was not in the sitting area but in an adjoining part. The door was open, and Link could see him sitting behind a table. He was writing or drawing. He looked up and motioned for Link to join him.

'Better now?' he said, grinning.

'Much. Thank you.'

'By the way, my name is Hector,' said the man, resting his pencil on the desk and standing up.

'Linkwood. But I prefer Link.' And the two men shook hands, hector hesitating only momentarily over how clean Link's hand was.

Link looked down at the large rudimentary drawing on the table. 'What are you doing?'

'Well, it's your idea, actually,' said Hector. 'You just inspired me. I'm designing a travelling privy.' He invited Link to take a look. 'Though I think it's going to need a wash basin,' he added, looking at the hand he'd just shaken.

Link was in his element, and eagerly studied the drawing. After a few minutes, he said, 'May I make a suggestion?'

'Of course, dear boy,' said Hector. 'What do you have in mind?'

'I could be wrong here, you understand... But don't you think it would be better *inside* the carriage? Perhaps at one end, partitioned off.'

'Hmm. What about...' Hector hesitated... 'You know... nasty whiffs – the old smellaroos?'

'Put a vent in the roof,' proposed Link. 'One that faces the rear of the train.'

'I see,' enthused Hector, 'to let the bad air out, and another at the bottom here to let good air in.'

'Kind of,' said Link, patiently. 'People don't want to be standing or sitting in a gale. So put intakes underneath to the sides, and facing the front from where the warmer air from the engine is coming.'

'Wonderful!' said Hector, scrapping his first design. 'Are you an inventor, too?'

'No,' grinned Link. 'I'm a wizard. You're the inventor.'

'Not really,' said Hector, modestly. 'I see a need, and set out to fill it. I like to help. I'm just er... er... a very rich man who draws things and gets other people to build them. That's all.'

Link's thoughts went to the sewers in Kra-Pton. It wasn't a particularly pleasant place for them to go. What should be in the sewers was often running in the gutters for everyone to see. *Perhaps later*, he thought, *if I get to know him better, I could ask this man to help with that. It would certainly take a lot of money, and he just said he was very rich.*

Hector looked at the ceiling for inspiration. 'That's it!' he said, jubilantly. 'I'll put one in every carriage. That'll stop people having to walk up and down the train.'

'Good idea,' agreed Link. 'I'll leave you to it, then.' And with that, he left and went to find Eydith.

As he walked in, she looked up. 'You've been a while,' she said, patting the chair next to her, inviting Link to sit. He told her about Hector, and his plans for adding privies to the train, but he didn't mention the sewers yet. He wanted to work on that idea some more before telling her.

The sun was getting low, and the redness of dusk was straddling the horizon. The carriage was darkening. He looked around for some lighting. There didn't seem to be any. Just as he was thinking it might be up to one of them to provide something magically, a man in uniform entered the carriage. He wore a badge saying ENGINEER, and when he'd politely wished them both, 'Good evening,' he took two oil lamps from a box on the wall, checked them, lit them, and hung them on hooks at each end of the carriage. They filled the area with a soft, yellow light. It wasn't a colour Link would've chosen, but he knew he could change it when the engineer had gone.

Shortly after he left, a young woman arrived with a tray of sandwiches, a large jug of ale, and two glasses. 'Compliments of Mr. Hector, sir,' she said, bobbing down on one knee as she placed the tray on the low table. Link gawped unthinkingly at her.

He eventually thanked her and managed to drag his eyes away from the front of the woman's revealing dress, and caught sight of the look he was getting from Eydith.

When she'd gone, he prepared himself for the verbal barrage that he was sure would follow. But Eydith let it pass.

Eydith picked up a sandwich. 'I didn't know I was this hungry.'

'Me neither,' agreed Link, tucking in, pleased that the subject had moved on so quickly. He was first to sample the ale, and was quick to remark that it was too good to knock back in two or three big swigs – his usual style.

Wimlett heard, and wafted over. He couldn't drink it, not without the help of Naphrat, but the smell was the next best thing. He inhaled and floated gently to the ceiling. It was *that* good. Now, though, having one solid hand, he tended to float on one side. It acted like ballast. But it meant he didn't have to spend the night touring the ceiling. The bread was crusty, the cheese was thick; there were pickled onions and the ale was good. 'It's all right for you, Sprag,' Wimlett grumbled. 'You've got no nose to tell you what you're missing.'

The staff was not going to be drawn. 'Yes, it does have its advantages at a time like this.'

'I'm sleeping elsewhere tonight,' Wimlett stated.

'Where?' Sprag asked, just curious.

'One of the luggage trucks.'

'Don't get blown away,' Sprag warned.

'I've got this hand, you know,' he said, as he walked to the door.

As usual, he walked through, but this time he stopped abruptly, as though he'd jammed his brakes on. He was outside, but his solid hand was trapped inside. It didn't go through walls and doors any more.

Link watched the hand bang against the door a couple of times, and grinned. 'He'll be back in a moment.'

She grinned back. 'I wonder if he was as daft as this when he was alive.'

'No, not quite, mistress,' said Sprag, feeling defensive of his old master. 'To give him due credit, in his prime, he was an excellent Archchancellor.'

Then, as predicted, the hand, followed by the rest of the ghostly wizard, re-entered the carriage. 'All right!' he snapped. 'I'll stay here, but you two had better behave yourselves!'

'I don't know what you mean, Father,' said Eydith. Link picked up his glass and took another sip.

Soon, it was completely dark outside. Link lowered the lights, and Eydith began to doze. It wasn't long before she was fully asleep. He put his cloak over her and settled himself down. It wasn't long before he, too, was sleeping soundly.

Wimlett was worried. He didn't want to sleep until he could satisfy himself that if anyone opened a door, he wouldn't get blown away. His hand would stop him being blown out through a wall, door or window – which wouldn't be a bit of a wrench, and not a pleasant awakening! But there was still the problem of a thoughtlessly *opened* door or window. He'd be whisked away into the airstream of the train. Eventually, he swallowed his pride, and asked Sprag for help.

'Hold me in the middle with your solid hand,' Sprag directed. 'Sideways, I'm too long to go through doors and windows. And I can summon enough control over my movement to ensure I remain horizontal should you be caught in a breeze. I can ensure your grip stays firm while you sleep, too.'

Wimlett gratefully complied. He was happy now. It might still be a wrench if he got blown, but it seemed safe enough. He closed his eyes and was soon asleep on the floor.

The train rumbled on through the night. Apart from the headlight, the only light left burning was the one in Hector's workshop. He was busy. He was determined to have his privy design on the drawing board before morning, when he would proudly present it to Link. He admired the young wizard's creative ability, and hoped that now he'd met him, he could persuade him to visit again, and more often. *New people bring new ideas to the table*, he mused. He felt he'd worked alone for too long, and was getting a bit stale. Really good inventions were occurring less frequently.

51

The next morning Eydith and Link were woken up by the sound of Hector knocking.

In the dawn light, they saw they were travelling across the plains and farmland that stretched down to the Southern Ocean.

'Good morning, everybody!' Hector's voice resonated around the carriage and was a better wake-up call than any rooster.

Wimlett awoke in pain, or rather the memory of it from his physical life. Hector had trodden in him. Then the big man took another step forward, and Wimlett screamed a silent scream as Hector stepped on his solid hand. It was the first time in a very long time that he had experienced real pain, and he was not best pleased.

Fortunately, Hector knew immediately that he'd trodden on something. He moved his foot and looked down. Wimlett whisked his hand away fast and out of sight under a chair. Hector caught a brief glimpse, though, and said, 'Pesky spiders. We get them sometimes, but they're quite harmless.' He was about to stoop down to remove it, but Link, who'd watched the whole episode, reached down ahead of him and said, 'Don't worry, I'll sort it out.' He made a big show of catching and tossing a non-existent spider from the window.

Hector was followed into the carriage by a girl with a tray bearing tea and toast for breakfast. Link kept his eyes on the food and off the girl this time, while Eydith smiled to herself.

They settled down to watch the scenery and pass the time chatting for an hour. Wimlett took the opportunity to get to know better the young wizard who was showing such an interest in his daughter. Link was pleased, and a little awestruck when he thought about it, to be chatting like this to the old Archchancellor. He'd never known him personally, only from the bad reputation that Dennis had given him. And now he knew that the majority of the old university staff were right in not believing a word of it.

They felt the train slowing and broke off their conversations when they stopped by a farm house to take on water.

'We will stop here for an hour or so,' Hector announced, popping his head round the door. 'So, if you want to stretch your legs, or get something more to eat, there's a farmhouse about fifty yards away, and the lady there will be happy to oblige.'

'Perhaps we can freshen up?' said Eydith, hopefully.

'Of course, my dear!' boomed Hector. 'Link, come with me first, please. I have something to show you.'

Eydith left the carriage and walked to the farmhouse along with some passengers from other carriages, while Link followed Hector to his workshop.

'Here it is!' said Hector, proudly.

'So it is,' agreed Link.

'What do you think of it?'

'Well… it's certainly a privy,' said Link.

'Yes, and I've put a water tank in that space just there in the wall above, so it washes down when you pull this lever,' Hector enthused.

'What's that little room there?' Link wondered, pointing at an adjacent space on the drawing.

'Ah… that's where the attendant sits. You know… to take the money.'

'Money? What money? You can't charge people for doing what comes naturally.'

'Oh, no. *I'm* not. But the attendants will, or they won't get paid. I shall lease out these privies to the highest bidders, and they can charge people a fixed fee for keeping them clean, and well stocked. And the brass-work well polished, that sort of thing.'

Link smiled. 'You certainly know about business.'

'Well,' said Hector, 'what do you think of it?'

'It's… it's, well… it's…' Link stuttered, struggling for the right words.

'I knew you'd like it,' said Hector, beaming. 'Let's go and get some food.'

The two men walked down to the farmhouse. As they passed the engine, Hector paused for a second to watch the gangs loading the wood and filling the water tank, and men who'd been slacking suddenly became animated and purposeful.

In the carriage, Sprag was under the table, next to Wimlett, who had retreated there to nurse his painful fingers. It wasn't long before the engineer from the previous evening came in and took the lanterns down, checked them, and put them back in the box. Wimlett realised a little late that his hand was where it might be seen, so he snatched it away.

The engineer looked down, thinking he'd heard a noise. Sprag kept perfectly still. He didn't have many other options. It was probably the thing he did best. Curious, the man stooped down and picked him up. Was it his imagination, or did the strange markings on this length of old wood move? Sprag didn't want to alarm the man with anything sudden or aggressive, but neither did he want to be taken. He needed to do something low-key that wouldn't arouse the man's curiosity even more. He asked Wimlett to create a diversion, but the wizard pointed out that it would probably be construed as coming from the staff. He said, 'Can't you get into *his* mind and make him go away?' Sprag said he was attuned to wizards not railway engineers.

'You're just going to have to send him a jolt of magic.'

'It's certainly tempting,' said Sprag, 'with his unwizardly hands on me.'

They waited to see what the engineer would do. 'You might come in handy,' the man said, holding up the staff, 'for reaching the high-up lamps around the buildings.'

This had gone on long enough, and Sprag was about to take action when he felt a familiar mind approaching.

The door swung open and Eydith stepped in, appalled at what she saw. 'I'll take that, if you don't mind!' she demanded fiercely, clearly brooking no argument.

The engineer snapped to attention abruptly, and let the staff fall towards her. 'As you wish, ma'am.' He touched his cap meekly and left.

Wimlett got up. 'He doesn't know how lucky he was that you came back,' he said, and cackled, 'I think he was in for a shock.'

Not far behind Eydith, on their return from the farmhouse, Hector hauled himself up into the cab of the engine, to check on things (though really because he liked sitting there), and he left Link to make his own way back to his carriage.

'Hector said we should be there sometime this afternoon,' said Link, as he lowered himself into the chair next to Eydith. In a short while, the whistle screamed and the train started moving again. More smoothly this time. Link guessed that Hector must be driving.

'Mind that big spider,' said Eydith, when Link had settled.

Link leapt from the seat and in record time, he was standing in the carriage doorway looking back nervously from the safety of a half-closed door.

'I thought so,' she said, and started laughing helplessly.

'You...'

52

The train was only a few miles outside Prossill now. Eydith was looking forward to seeing Esme and Florence again. It had been a long while. Link was thinking about the sewers of Kra-Pton. They were in his thoughts a lot lately, and his acquaintance with Hector had made him more determined to do something about them.

He'd discovered that once Hector was fired up by an idea, it wasn't long before it became a reality. The fact that the railway had come into existence in only a few short years was proof of that. But the problem facing Link was how to make money from a sewage system. That was the incentive required to get Hector involved. Not that Hector was overly materialistic, but he was pragmatic. He knew he couldn't maintain his hobby if he'd used up his funds, plentiful though they were.

'What are you looking so serious about,' Eydith asked, interrupting his thoughts.

'Oh, nothing,' he lied, sparing her a conversation about sewage. 'Just tired.'

'It was a long journey,' she commented.

'Yes, and now I'm looking forward to getting off and feeling the ground under my feet again.' He stretched his legs out in front of him.

'It's been comfortable though,' said Eydith.

'Oh, yes. I'm not complaining. I just feel the need for more space, that's all.'

'Hector's been very kind. We'll have to find a way of repaying him.'

'I think I may have already done that,' said Link, looking pleased with himself. 'I gave him an idea for an on-board privy, which he's designed, and thinks will make lots of money for him.'

The train was slowing down.

Hector ducked and came in. 'There in about two minutes,' he boomed. 'Have you enjoyed your trip?'

'Oh, yes,' said Eydith, for both of them. 'A very novel experience. And saved us a lot of time. Thank you very much.'

'No thanks needed. Your friend here,' he pointed at Link, 'has probably earned me a hundred times over what your fares might have been.'

'Er, does that mean I can have another ninety-nine trips for free?' asked Link.

Hector pulled a face. 'What about fifty?'

'Done!' Link grinned, offering his hand to shake on the deal.

Hector flashed a smile, and released one of his booming laughs as he took Link's hand.

'When are you going back?' asked Eydith. 'We can join you, if we're ready by then.'

'I've got a few things to do, and a few adjustments to make to the train. Probably just a few days. I might see you, then.'

'I certainly hope so,' she said, smiling.

The train ground to a juddering halt. Hector's pained look, as he steadied himself, told them he needed to spend more time in the cab training his driver. *A swift clout round both ears would probably do it,* he thought. Eydith picked up Sprag, and Link picked up her bag. She then stood back, allowing him to open the door gallantly, as he liked to. He stepped out and thumped to the ground, out of sight.

'Other side!' he called back, while scrambling to his feet. 'The platform's on the other side.' He wasn't nervous around her anymore – but clearly sometimes still a little distracted – and he grinned to himself for not noticing the platform wasn't there.

Eydith turned away, so he wouldn't see her giggling. He dodged under the carriage and squeezed up onto the wooden staging that served as a platform. He was in time to open the door for her. She stepped down and sniffed the air. 'It's better than Kra-Pton,' she noticed straight away, taking a deeper breath.

'What is?' asked Link.

'The smell.'

Link hadn't noticed. He sniffed. 'There isn't one.'

'Exactly,' she said.

He looked around for a way off the platform, and spotted a gate.

'This way.' He strode off, leaving her standing.

'Wait a minute!' she called, trotting after him. When she was by his side, she slipped her hand into his, and they strolled to the gate together. They hadn't gone more than a few paces when she pulled him up sharply... 'Where's father?'

Sprag answered, 'He's probably waiting till everyone's gone, mistress.'

'Why? Nobody can see him, but us,' Eydith replied.

'His hand is still solid, mistress. He doesn't want to frighten anyone. I offered to make it invisible again, but he refused. He's decided he wants to keep it for now.'

'I suppose we'd better wait for him, then.'

Inside the carriage, Wimlett watched impatiently while the other passengers milled about on the platform. He sat in one of the big armchairs with his visible hand under a cushion. He saw Eydith and Link go, and was eager to join them, but the young woman tidying the carriage was a problem. He sat watching her go all around the place with a bunch of feathers tied on a stick, and a yellow cloth, dusting here, polishing there.

She got to the chair next to him, picked up the cushion and gave it a shake, turned, plumped it, then placed it neatly back into the chair. Wimlett sneezed, silently. The young woman turned her attention to the chair Wimlett was sitting in. He swallowed hard, and prepared his eardrums for a scream. She grabbed the cushion and pulled it through him, revealing his 'severed' hand. The cushion fell from her fingers. She cupped her hands in front of her mouth, too shocked even to scream. Then, she turned and ran.

She didn't think to close the door behind her, and Wimlett was feeling in a playful mood so he ran after her. Seeing the hand floating after her, she found her voice, and began running in blind panic up the platform.

'I do believe this is him now,' said Sprag, as the screaming woman rushed by.

'Father! What have you been up to now?' cried Eydith, trying hard not to stamp her foot.

Wimlett shook his head and laughed. 'You should've seen her face when she picked that cushion up.'

'Can't you behave?' she scolded. 'Just for ten minutes?'

Link looked away and smiled, wishing he'd been there.

The dusty road into Prossill wasn't busy today. Just a few people leading donkey carts, and a few make-shift stalls scattered at intervals. Eydith lingered to browse, but Wimlett was anxious to make contact with Esmerelda. 'I'll be off then,' he said.

'Where did you say we'd find you?' Eydith asked him.

'The Magic Finger, next to the Town Hall. You can't miss it, apparently.'

'Keep out of trouble,' she begged. 'If you can.'

53

Wimlett hopped up on the back of a passing cart going into the city. He hid his hand in some straw. He'd tried walking and drifting along in a ghostly fashion, but it was a little breezy today, which hampered his progress. Which was odd, because breezes should pass through him. Perhaps Naphrat could explain it sometime, or do something about it. Perhaps he could also explain how his invisible eyes could collect the light by which he could see. It should pass through. Same with the vibrations of sound in his ears. If he was invisible and immaterial, he should be both blind and deaf.

Since he'd last been to Prossill, the place had sprawled out a lot, engulfing some of the surrounding villages. The suburb he was entering had been one such village, and from what he recalled, the place needed engulfing. It was a slum then, and it was a slum now.

The driver of the cart was nervous. His eyes were darting in all directions like he was expecting trouble. He didn't have long to wait. He was soon confronted by a pair of ruffians, who stepped out in the road as if from nowhere. The nearest one grabbed the donkey's bridle, the other slipped around the back, and leapt onto the tailboard to attack the driver from behind.

Wimlett was having none of this. A disembodied hand flew out of the straw and grabbed the man by his throat. The fellow panicked when he couldn't find the arm that should be attached to the hand, to prise it loose. He couldn't see or hear anyone, but he knew from the grip squeezing his windpipe that fresh air was soon going to be in short supply. He also had just enough brain cells to work out that he was a ruffian in serious trouble, and he eventually went limp.

The other man came forward, and was met by a disembodied balled fist that struck him squarely on the nose. He recoiled in terror, and with a good dose of eye-watering pain, and tumbled back into the road, senselessness.

The unconscious villain in the cart was now being robbed by Wimlett. The old mage was delighted to find twelve gold coins and two silver ones. He felt he ought to give the driver something for giving him a lift into the city, and put a silver coin on the seat beside him, tapping it as he did so, to attract the man's attention. The driver looked down, horrified. Not only at the sight of the detached hand, but also at the thought of owning something that someone might kill him for.

When he was sure nobody was looking, he snatched up the coin and rammed it into his pocket. He urged the donkey on. *What had just happened?* he wondered, trying to make some sense of it, but failing. He looked over his shoulder, at the unconscious villain lying in the straw. *Oh no!* He realised he was carrying one of the city's most notorious villains. Even the barbarian heroes avoided this one. His mind was in turmoil. What with the first silver he'd ever owned in his pocket, and a very dangerous man – the man most likely to take it off him! – In the back of his cart, he didn't know what to do next.

He knew his choices were limited. Should he take the man to the Watch and collect his reward first, or, more pressingly, should he knock on the nearest friendly-looking door and ask to use the privy?

He was warming to the idea of owning the silver coin. And the reward would mean another one. Possibly a gold one. He was really going to be a target! But it was still alluring. He steered the cart to the Watch House. *They're bound to have a privy there.*

A few yards further on, he stopped to bind and gag his human cargo. Satisfied that the man was secure, he covered him with straw to hide him from prying eyes, and continued on his way.

Wimlett sat beside the trussed-up villain with his gold coins clasped firmly in his hand, which was likewise hidden in the straw. He watched the buildings go slowly by, hoping the driver would eventually pass The Magic Finger, which was on the main thoroughfare through Prossill. But the cart hadn't gone far before a very large man stepped out of a dark alley, and grabbed the donkey's bridle.

'What have we got here?' The big man said, smirking menacingly.

Really? thought Wimlett, *Again, already?!*

'Oh, no, not again,' the driver mumbled, echoing Wimlett. Even as a local, he couldn't believe twice in ten minutes. He reflexively moved his hand to his pocket to feel the coin.

'Oh, you have something of value?' said the big man, who was a little smarter than he looked. 'Well, it will cost you whatever it is to get by me.'

An unseen hand was stealthily being drawn from the straw. It spread the twelve gold coins carefully on the boards. Wimlett then unsheathed a lethal-looking dagger from the belt of the villain lying next to him.

The driver was so fed up, he decided to throw caution to the wind. After all, some unseen power seemed to have taken him under its wing today. Hadn't it just taken care of two would-be robbers – one of them, the worst of the lot! It could handle this one man, couldn't it? Big as he was. 'I've got nothing to give you,' he said, defiantly.

The big man laughed at him, and beckoned into the shadows of the side alley. Six more evil-looking ruffians emerged, brandishing axes, knives, swords and nasty, spikey balls on chains.

'We don't want no trouble,' said the leader, still grinning. 'Just hand over your coins, and we'll be off... won't we, lads?'

The lads grinned, showing a motley collection of teeth and gaps.

Wimlett dropped silently off the back of the cart and slipped into the shadows. One of the robbers felt something touch his back. He turned, but saw nothing. It happened again. By sheer luck, Wimlett had picked on the man with the shortest fuse. The man snarled, turned to the man nearest to him, thinking he was responsible, and rammed a mailed fist into the side of the man's head.

The man reeled back. He cursed and rubbed a rapidly swelling ear. A large red lump was rising on his face. Having collected the few wits he had, he angrily drew his dagger, and lunged at his attacker, slashing the man's sleeve and cutting his arm.

'That's enough, lads!' the leader bellowed. 'Let's not fight amongst ourselves, now.'

'Keep out of this, Gilbert,' snarled cut-arm, not taking his eyes off the man with the knife. 'I've 'ad enough of 'im keep touchin' me, an' that.' He drew his double-handed axe from his belt, and the two men squared up.

Just then, one of the other robbers fell to the ground inexplicably. Wimlett had knocked him senseless with the weighty pommel of the dagger. The other four looked at each other.

'Who did that!' demanded Gilbert, angrily. Three men shrugged their innocence. The fourth staggered forward and slumped to the ground, a dagger between his shoulder blades. Everyone looked decidedly spooked.

Wimlett stealthily removed an axe from the belt of the first man that fell, and retreated to the gloom of the alley. Two of the remaining tough guys turned and ran.

Gilbert stood his ground, assessing the situation. 'What the hell's going on?!'

Cut-arm and red-face forgot their differences for the time being and fell in beside Gilbert. 'Who *are* you?' the big man asked the cart driver, who was affecting nonchalance, digging at something under his fingernails with a small knife. He looked down, thinking, *More to the point, who shall I tell these buggers I am.* After a few seconds, *I know*, he thought.

'I'm Seamor the Stabber, a barbarian hero from the Tong Plain.'

Cut-arm looked at his comrades and whispered, 'Never 'eard of 'im.'

'I'm new in these parts,' Seamor added hurriedly. 'Before that I was in Kra-Pton, and before that I was in the Land of Corin, and before that...'

'All right, all right, we get the picture,' Gilbert interrupted. 'You've been around a bit.'

'I could tell you of many places, far beyond the four horizons. Wild places, beyond even yonder... further than wherever... but perhaps not today. Now, if you'll just stand aside, I'll leave you in peace.'

'Yeah,' said Gilbert, quietly. 'I think maybe we'd better let 'im pass, lads.' He winked at the others, and added, 'Before he bores us all to death.'

Seamor stood up, 'Oh, there is one more thing!' he called, as the men were slinking away.

Gilbert turned, 'Yeah? What's that?'

'Would you be so kind as to put these bodies on my cart? Otherwise the place will be full of flies in an hour or so.' Seamor was enjoying this.

The villain's slouched back, shoulders sagging, and unwillingly heaved their dead comrades onto the cart. 'Is that *all?*' asked Gilbert, through clenched teeth.

'Yeah, anything else, your hero-ness?' said Red-face, sullenly sarcastic.

'Yes, thank you for reminding me. Got any gold, silver, copper? You know... coins, that sort of thing.'

Red-face went redder, and, for a second or two weighed his options before digging deep into his pockets and slamming two copper coins down on the seat next to Seamor. The others followed and lightened their pockets of a few more copper coins. After this they slunk back into the shadows. It was some consolation that at least they'd remained dishonest enough to hold back all their silvers, and on the strength of that vowed to get very drunk, later.

Seamor was pleased with himself. He tapped the donkey and continued on his way to the Watch House. Wimlett hadn't had so much fun in ages, and hopped back on the cart as the donkey laboured by.

Soon, they were on wider streets. There were shops, and people walking about and looking in windows. Street peddlers were selling sausages in buns. There were jugglers trying to keep all their balls in the air. Street musicians entertained with involuntary variations on familiar themes. It was all part of the noise and bustle of a living, breathing city.

The road became smoother, pressed and polished by millions of feet. Wimlett sat with his feet hanging over the edge of the tailboard, taking it all in, wishing he could walk among the crowds as one of them, fondly remembering how he used do that in Kra-Pton. He sighed, almost audibly, over the way things had turned out. Death had its compensations, but he didn't care for the permanency of the thing. But then, he thought, nothing lasts forever. So maybe not even permanency. That cheered him a little. What cheered him even more was the sight of a sign hanging from a bracket above a door.

The Magic Finger

He rummaged through the straw in the cart, found his coins, and dropped silently to the road. A moment later, he was outside the tavern, looking at the tables with their brightly coloured parasols cluttering the pavement and forcing people to walk in the gutter. What he needed now was someone to open the door so he could get in.

He waited. It looked like it was going to rain. 'Serves them right,' he muttered, 'tempting fate leaving their stupid umbrellas out here.' He continued to wait, but nobody passing wanted to go in. 'I could be here all evening,' he whined to himself. Then it struck him, and he looked down at his solid hand. *What a stupid old fool I am sometimes. I can let myself in now.* Pleased that Sprag wasn't around to relish the moment, he pulled the handle. It was heavier than he expected, and being a ghost gave him no weight to put behind his hand. *If I had my magic, I'd have this thing off its hinges so fast...*

He gave it one last mighty heave, just when someone opened it. Their combined effort swung the door back so fast that the man leaving fell back into a handy chair, while Wimlett was flung across the bar.

As he sailed through the room, he hurtled between a large barbarian and his drinking companions, and with his arms flailing he managed to slap the man in his cauliflower ear. The man yelled in surprise, dropped his tankard, and drew his dagger to attack whoever was nearest.

A troll, whose name was Flint, was playing a sort-of piano in the corner. He stopped when he saw the men fighting, and wondered what was going on.

Due to an accident at birth, Flint was no ordinary troll. His mother had been frightened by an explosion in the quarry where she was working. The explosion coincided with a stray flash of magical lightning caused by two wizards duelling in the next valley. The combined effect somehow blasted

Flint from his mother's womb, and, it would seem, to the very front of the queue where the brains were being handed out.

Whereas the normal run-of-the-mill troll was slow-witted and quarrelsome, lacked brain to mouth co-ordination, and had a problem doing two things at once, like thinking and walking – this sort-of pianist was of a different breed. Nevertheless, Flint still felt the ancestral urge to join in if a fight was looming.

He didn't get up immediately, because somebody had foolishly jogged his sort-of piano and caused the lid to drop onto his fingers. He wasn't in much pain – and being a troll, even if he was in agony, he'd find somewhere private to scream, rather than let anyone see. He raised the lid, and sat and watched the barbarians, to see if the argument got any more heated,

He was about to begin playing again, when a careless drinker nudged the instrument again, causing the finely balanced lid to drop once more. This time he pulled his fingers away in time. He sprang to his feet, and bopped the careless man on the head with a granite-like fist. The man stood motionless, grinning inanely at some private *son et lumière* going on behind his eyes, then dropped to the floor, and lay there. Somewhat still.

A deathly hush fell over the drinkers, including the two barbarians, who'd been close to blows. Flint stared across at them, and they took their cue from the man on the floor and postponed their quarrel. They were no match for an angry troll.

Wimlett had landed in a pool of spilt ale, and was emerging from under the counter. He stood up and placed a silver down in front of the bartender. The man looked down at it, not noticing the unattached hand that had put it there, then he looked this way and that for whoever had put the coin there. Then he screamed, and fled. *Strange man,* thought Wimlett. Then he saw something in the long mirror behind the counter, and stepped back.

He stared hard at where his reflection would be if he had one. There was something there – something not quite himself, though. In fact, when it came into focus, *nothing* like himself. No wonder the barman bolted. And if you thought that a bar couldn't go any quieter than it did a moment ago, you'd be wrong. Drinkers were examining the contents of their glasses more closely than usual. Some rubbed their eyes and shook their heads in an effort to clear the apparitions from their minds.

A skeletal hand settled briefly, on Wimlett's shoulder, before passing through it. He turned…

'Hello, Wimlett, old friend,' said a sepulchrous voice. 'I thought I'd find you here.'

54

Wimlett knew immediately the dark shape that had glided into place beside him. If the voice, which sounded like the low rumble of boulders being ground on the sea bed, hadn't given him a clue, then the overly long scythe across his shoulder and the ornate Life-Timer hanging from his belt certainly would have.

'Hello, Naph. What brings you here? Business or pleasure?' asked Wimlett.

'A bit of both, really.' He tapped the Timer. 'And a man's gotta drink, you know? Keep body and soul together and all that.'

Wimlett thought he saw the makings of a grin on the Dark Angel's face. 'Well... whose is that?'

Naphrat held the Timer up and studied it. 'It has the name Gilbert on it,' he said, not appearing too interested. 'And I've got lots more in here.' He opened his cloak, revealing several rows of Life-Timers arranged on hooks that didn't seem to be attached to anything.

'Reckon there might be a spot of bother then, do you?'

'Looks very likely,' replied Naphrat, hollowly. 'Knowing you were in Prossill, and this is your kind of place, I thought I might get here early and catch up. Where's that barman? A man could die of thirst in this place!' He looked down at Wimlett. 'I read that somewhere.'

Warily the barman sidled back to his station behind the bar. Wimlett couldn't help noticing the man was in a kind of trance, seeing only what his brain preferred him to see. The disembodied hand, and the tall stranger with a deathly pale face, holding a scythe, were a trick of his imagination. These people were just ordinary folk out for a drink, that was all. *Must hold that thought! Must hold that thought!*

Something occurred to Wimlett. 'How come people can see you, Naphrat? I thought only my kind could do that.'

'Most of the time that's right. But with a little effort on my part – actually a *lot* of effort, which is why I don't do it often – I can sustain it for a while. I can even modify my appearance a little to make myself more acceptable – certainly long enough to order a few drinks. Speaking of which, what are you having?'

'Well,' said Wimlett, puzzled for a moment by the notion that what stood next to him could be considered in any way acceptable. He eyed the array of bottles behind the bar, and said, 'I wouldn't mind some of that red stuff, but I'll need some help to drink it.'

'Not a problem. I can finish it for you.' Then the penny dropped. 'Ah, I get it.' Upon which, he waved a trumpet-sleeved arm over Wimlett, who felt a cold glow trickle through him. 'No point of a drinking buddy who can't drink.' Then to the barman he said, 'Two large glasses of that red stuff there.'

Naphrat put two green, oxidised copper coins on the bar, probably earned while he was acting Ferryman. 'No,' said Wimlett. 'I'll get these.' He replaced Naphrat's antique copper coins with a gold one. The barman picked it up and tried to bend it in his teeth, then tossed it into the till and began counting out Wimlett's change – all two hundred and seventy-two coins of it, making four piles on the counter.

'Your change, sir.' The barman grinned nervously at where in the air he'd placed the hand's face.

'Keep it,' said Wimlett, waving the hand dismissively. He wished he had a few pockets. There was probably enough money piled in front of him to buy a major stake-holding in the tavern! He picked up his glass and looked into Naphrat's infinitely hollow sockets. 'You mentioned there might be trouble?'

'Depends,' said Naphrat, noncommittally.

'On what?'

'Well... I came here tonight on a hunch.'

'I didn't think I saw your horse outside,' quipped Wimlett, instantly regretting it.

Naphrat ignored him. One shouldn't joke with Death or His assistant, but as the man was already dead, perhaps he'd earned the right. 'I heard a lot of the Life-Timers acting up. So I checked the Ledgers, and here I am.' He glanced around the room, with a professional lack of eye and nodded. 'I think the sooner I take this lot, the better.' He picked up his drink and took a sip. And, as always, when Naphrat drank, Wimlett found himself looking at the skeletal ribcage in front of him, expecting the liquid to be sloshing straight out. But it never did.

Naphrat drained the glass and banged it down on the counter. The barman picked it up. 'Same again, gents?' he asked.

'Why not?' Naphrat nodded creakily, rocking back on his heels.

Wimlett was about to put another gold coin on the counter from his clenched fist, when the barman held up a hand. 'These are on the house,' he whispered. He could afford to be generous after the tip from the first round.

'This is *my* kind of tavern.' Naphrat smiled, and Wimlett studied his face for a moment. He really had only one expression. Deadpan was never more appropriate. But he had the strange ability to convey a smile, or any other expression, without moving a bone of his face. The same was true of Death.

Flint began to play the sort-of piano again, and the drinkers' interest in the ghoulish company waned. They got down to the serious business of trying to drink the ale faster than the barman could pull it. The barbarians were getting rowdy again, and starting to sing the opening verse of a well-known farmyard ballad about a chicken and a pig, but they couldn't remember the last few lines and it finished up with one of them trying to order eggs and bacon. This broke down into hoots of laughter, a great deal of thigh slapping and cries of... 'More ale, wench!'

Wimlett turned to see what was going on. He hadn't noticed any *wench* when he came in. But, then, he did enter at quite a speed. Then he saw her. And blinked. What was *she* doing working in the bar?

Florence was gathering tankards and she looked miserable, completely out of her element. She ran back to the counter to get them refilled, and then scurried back to the drinkers who took advantage of the fact that her hands were full. As she squeezed between the tables, she suffered the humiliation of being slapped and pinched in places no man had ever been before.

'Could you pass me a bottle of that blue stuff?' Wimlett asked the barman, pointing at the biggest bottle on the shelf.

'Course, sir,' the barman obliged. 'Would you like me to pour?'

'No, that's all right,' Wimlett replied, suddenly realising he could be heard, curtesy of Naphrat. 'Just give me the bottle.'

The barman was impressed. No-one had ever drunk even a quarter of bottle of Blue Viper on their own before. Wimlett took it and marched over to the table where Florence was still being tormented by the group of drunken barbarians. He stood for moment, taking in the faces. One was familiar. It was Gilbert the Giant, recovering from his recent humiliation at the hands of Seamor, the reluctant hero.

Wimlett had almost killed Gilbert earlier. *But, better late than never.*

Florence could see Wimlett's hand weaving across the room towards her, gripping the Blue Viper. But instead of being alarmed or threatened she was oddly mesmerised. The hand seemed to be motioning her to move away from the table, so she stood aside. When she was clear, the hand lifted the bottle high and brought it crashing down on Gilbert's head. Naphrat was instantly on hand swinging his great Soul Reaping scythe at the drunken giant.

A brawl broke out among the other drunken barbarians at the table who hurried to strip the late Gilbert of his belongings. They pounced on the corpse together and started going through his pockets, wrenching rings off his fingers, and pulling silver chains from around his neck. This sort of thing had become customary among barbarians. There was nearly always trouble when it came to dividing the spoils left by a death. Fights inevitably broke out. Daggers were drawn, axes thrown, and faces punched. So now they saved everyone a lot of trouble by immediately stripping their dead relatives or comrades of everything they owned, leaving nothing to argue over. Barbarians from other tables dived over to get a look in, too.

Then SLAM! Down came the lid of the sort-of piano, across Flint's fingers.

Once was probably an accident. Twice was pushing their luck. Three times was just plain bloody stupidity! In one move, he stood up and pushed the instrument away. It should have been the chair he moved back, but he was in no mood for niceties. He shook his throbbing fingers, then pushed back his sleeves. He spat on his palms and rubbed them together, creating sparks.

He barged into the pack of scrapping barbarians and started by cracking a couple of heads together, then followed that with a few wall-bangers, and a window flyer. Naphrat was nimbly flashing about with his scythe, helping the fatally damaged on their way to wherever they believed they were going. Wimlett had his fingers trodden on and opted for the safety of the beams under the ceiling. He propelled himself up with his good hand and watched the battle as it progressed beneath him. Flint was swinging his granite fists with unerring accuracy, making sounds like WHAM! POW! SMACK! and KERUNCH! each time he connected with the bone-hard head, or ale-softened belly of a barbarian. There was definitely a sort-of grin on his face.

Above the din of the brawl, the sound of bells could be heard outside, distantly at first, but getting closer and closer, until it couldn't get any louder and suddenly stopped. The tavern doors burst open and in charged a dozen officers of the Watch. Seeing the bodies of the unconscious and dead littering the floor, they formed a line. Then the Sergeant started to bark orders.

'Crossbows out men! Load 'em up, and... *wait* for it!' The officers raised their weapons and selected their targets. But the order to fire was a long time coming. Slowly, the young officer nearest the Sergeant turned his head.

The Sergeant had disappeared.

The officer looked down. *Ah... there he is*. Being next in the chain of command, the young man reluctantly assumed the role of Sergeant. 'Fire! For god's sake. Fire!' he yelled, panicking.

The men broke ranks and rushed to the door. 'Where?' said one, sniffing the air. 'Where?'

'No! Fire the bloody crossbows, you idiots!' he yelled.

The men of the Watch regrouped, and the air was filled with crossbow bolts aimed at nothing in particular, bouncing off stone walls and glancing off copper topped tables, ceiling beams and smashing through windows. One bolt hit a barbarian, but the force of its impact had been slowed so much by the time it reached him, that it fell harmlessly to the floor. One passed through Wimlett. Another ricocheted off almost every available surface in the bar, and returned like a homing pigeon to strike the leg of the Watchman who'd fired it. He gave a shriek of pained surprise, and then grinned as he sat down, relieved to have a valid excuse for sitting out the riot.

At the bar, the barman sat on the till, protecting it from all-comers with a large axe. He swung it to great effect against would-be looters. Shortly, the landlord arrived and stepped in to relieve him. He was such a thug that even drunken barbarians gave him a wide berth.

After the bolt passed through him, Wimlett decided to move. The safest place seemed to be behind Flint. The stone man was felling all before him, and Naphrat was at his elbow, reaping and finding it difficult to swing his scythe accurately, as he was contending with a severe bout of hiccups.

Wimlett had second thoughts about his proximity to the troll. Perhaps under the bar was safer. But he decided against that as well. There were already more feet sticking out from under the bar than the bed of the old woman who lived in a shoe. The door to the rooms upstairs looked the best option. Gingerly he pulled himself back along the beam to a place over the door, pausing occasionally to adjust his invisible robes. Clutching the remainder of his gold coins made it difficult, but he wasn't going to let them go. He dropped onto a table, and from there to the sawdust covered floor. One foot found the floor, the other found a half-full spittoon. His 'Yuck' was almost audible. Being a ghost, none of the foul contents of the spittoon clung to his foot, but that didn't prevent him from feeling like they had.

The door was open just wide enough to get his hand through. The rest of his invisible body passed easily through the woodwork. The passage was dimly lit. Getting his bearings, he saw another door opposite, which he guessed led into the yard where the stables were. And to his left was a door to a privy for patrons of the bar. And to his right... was Florence.

'I didn't think you were ever coming out of there,' she said, from the half-light of the passage.

'Are you all right?'

'Yes. Come on. Mother's upstairs.' She walked a few paces, turned off the passage, and ran up a stone staircase that led to the room where she and Esme were lodging.

55

Esmerelda was sitting in a chair by a stone fireplace, staring into the flames. A face in the flames stared back at her and stuck out its tongue. She made a rapid sign at it with her hand, causing the face to flinch and disappear. She hardly acknowledged Wimlett's arrival.

Oh, dear, he thought, *she's in one of her moods.* He turned to Florence. 'Why are you working in the bar? That's no place for you.'

'There was a card by the door saying they needed bar staff. Mother thought it would be a good way to keep an eye on Dennis when he gets here. It's job-share, we take it in turns.'

'What do you mean, 'when he gets here?' He might go anywhere in Prossill.'

'Mum's a witch,' she said, simply, assuming it was explanation enough.

Esmerelda rocked her chair. 'And we need to know when he gets here.'

'Why didn't you get a room at the front to watch from a window?'

'Staff don't get front rooms,' she snapped, 'I've asked.'

Wimlett shrugged. There was no point in arguing.

'You should have been down there just now, mother,' said Florence, animatedly. 'There was a fight!'

'I thought I heard something. Why didn't you come and get me? You know I like to watch a good bar fight!'

'It's probably over by now... the Watch came.'

'Oh, that's what all that bloody bell ringing was about, was it?'

Esmerelda went to the window and looked down. Seeing one or two officers being treated in the yard at the rear, she moaned, 'Sod it! That's just typical; I missed the wagon.' She stormed to the door, admitting to herself – and *only* herself – that Wimlett was right after all about the vantage point of the window.

'Where are you going?' asked Florence.

'To see the landlord. I *want* a better room!' She yanked open the door and marched out, slamming it behind her.

'I think I'd better go with her,' said Wimlett. He started towards the door, then stopped. 'Here, take these,' he said, offering Florence the gold coins. 'They might come in handy.' And his physical hand was aching from gripping them.

Her face brightened. 'Why, thank you!'

Downstairs, the bar was still noisy, but not as much as when he left. He pushed the door and slid inside. He glanced around and saw Esme arguing with the landlord. Naphrat was still standing shoulder to shoulder with the troll, a grin on his expressionless face – a trick which only a Reaper could pull off. The bar was less crowded now, due to the bodies littering the floor.

Six members of the Watch were still standing, surprisingly. Most of the surviving drunken brawlers were seated, tied in groups of three or four, the others were in the process of being tied. Naphrat was right, something was going to happen, and it did.

Flint was quiet now. There was no opposition, so he went back to his sort-of piano, sat down and dragged it closer. Naphrat wiped his scythe on the clothing of the nearest corpse, slung it over his shoulder, and produced a list from his robe. He walked around the corpses, ticking off names and checking Life-Timers.

Wimlett watched curiously, he'd never seen the Angel of Death at work before. Naphrat stalked the room, his shoulders occasionally going into spasm. He'd still got hiccups. Then he clattered to a stop, re-counted the bodies and ran his finger down the list. 'Someone's missing!' he declared, sonorously, and a little theatrically.

Wimlett looked across with concern. 'Missing?'

'Yes, you heard me. Missing.' He twirled around, scouring the room once again, his cloak flying out around him, and halted in a dramatic pose. 'Where's Dennis!'

Wimlett cleared his throat. 'Ahem. Er... he's not here, yet.'

Naphrat drew himself up to his full height, and his jaw dropped as he turned to his friend.

'But we are expecting him,' Wimlett assured him, hurriedly.

'I've just about had it with him! He's always late, or something happens, and he slips through my fingers!'

Wimlett glanced involuntarily at Naphrat's knotted, and ancient fingers, and couldn't help thinking that they were the sort you'd want to slip through pretty quickly. He heard the despair in his voice. And was that a tear running down his bleached bony face? No. Condensation, more like. But there was a look of resignation in those impassive features that he'd never seen before.

'This time I'll wait,' growled the Dark Angel. 'And I'll have him.' He leant on a battered table, which started to creak under his weight, trim of figure though he was. Then it collapsed completely. He kept his balance and snatched up a half-finished tankard of ale from another wonky table. He tested a chair and sat down to drink.

Wimlett sat opposite. 'Have you heard from Death lately?'

'No, but I might write to Him when I get back. See if He's had enough, yet, because I bloody well have. I didn't mind doing this for a couple of years, but I think He's taking advantage of my good nature now.' He slammed a bony fist down on the table, almost splitting it in two, 'Let's have another drink.' He stood up and moved to the bar where Esme was arguing with the landlord about moving her to another room.

She stopped talking when she heard Naphrat's clicking feet approach and stop next to her. When she saw him, she covered her mouth with her hands.

Naphrat gave her the benefit of his expressionless smile, and, deeply and hollowly, said, 'Hello. What's your name?'

'Esmerelda, sir. Esmerelda Swampshott,' she replied, nervously, her head tilting deferentially.

He looked at his list, not expecting to see her name, but it was amusing to do it sometimes. 'Landlord! Two more glasses of that red stuff, and whatever the lady wants.'

Esme passed out and slid down to the floor. The Grim Reaper was the last person she ever expected to buy her a drink.

'Oh, dear,' said Naphrat. 'It's been a long time since I had that effect on a lady.'

Wimlett knelt and felt her wrist with his solid hand. He knew better than to try to loosen any of her clothing. 'Just fainted, that's all,' he announced.

'Oh, and a glass of iced water to revive the lady, landlord,' Naphrat added.

This could get interesting, thought Wimlett.

Naphrat splashed it in Esme's face and she burst into life again. 'What the hell's going on? Who did that!' she stormed, dragging herself unsteadily to her feet.

'That's more like it,' Wimlett observed, amusedly.

Esme glanced around, furious, challenging the culprit to own up. She stopped when she came to the vacantly grinning face of the Dark Angel, and she remembered what had just happened. 'B... begging your pardon, sir,' she stammered, and bobbed her knees. Her joints cracked with the effort, and Naphrat nodded approvingly. Then he asked resonantly, 'What would you like?'

To Esme, it was as if all her birthdays and Solstice celebrations had arrived together. One of the most powerful beings in the Unknown Universe had asked her what she wanted. It was difficult not to be greedy in such a situation, but she didn't want to start too big. Something not too difficult, but which was bugging her right now.

'I want a room at the front of this place, but *he*...' she pointed out the landlord, 'says I can't.'

Naphrat was kicking himself for not being specific. He was asking what she wanted to drink, that was all. 'What's wrong with the room you have now?' *Why do I do it?* He asked himself. Conversations like this always dragged on and dragged him in.

'It's at the back and I can't see the street from there.'

'It's like any other street,' said Naphrat, trying to dissuade her. 'Not that picturesque.'

'Well, Dennis will be coming down this one, and I want to know when he does!'

'How strange.' Naphrat beamed, impossibly. 'So do I. But he's rather late, though not in the good sense of being dead.'

'He has something I want,' she snapped, feeling more confident knowing they had something in common.

'Yes,' said Naphrat, nodding. 'I know the problem.'

'Well, if it's all the same to you, I'd like to deal with him first,' said Esme, rather forgetting herself and almost of a mind to roll her sleeves up.

'I think you'd better get in first. What I have in mind is somewhat permanent.'

'It's a deal,' she said.

'I'm glad about that.'

Naphrat swivelled his skull towards to the landlord. 'About this room the lady wants...'

'Er... yes,' said the landlord, swallowing hard. 'Er... there appears to be one available all of a sudden.' Thuggish though he undoubtedly was, he wasn't going to argue with this. He took one of the numbered keys from the hooks behind the bar and dropped it on the counter noisily.

'I thought there might be,' muttered Naphrat.

'Now, I'll have what he's having,' Esme snapped, glaring at the landlord.

Finding himself dealing with a crabby witch and the Angel of Death himself (not that he was properly aware of what either of them were), the landlord was seriously regretting giving his barman the rest of the night off.

Naphrat downed his drink in one, and banged the glass down on the counter. 'Right,' he said. 'I'll be off. I'll leave Dennis to the good lady Esmerelda and the rest of you, for now.'

She smiled at the Reaper. A compliment's a compliment whoever it comes from.

'So soon?' said Wimlett.

'Yes, I've got most of those I came for.' He stalked to the door. 'Catch you later.'

Wimlett followed and stood in the doorway to watch him climb into Bruno's saddle and ride off into the late evening sky.

When Naphrat was a mere speck among the stars, Wimlett went back inside, where the men of the Watch were applying bandages to survivors, and laying out the less fortunate. Esme finished her drink, gave the landlord one of her looks, and went upstairs to give Florence the news about the new room. Wimlett floated after her. They began packing almost immediately, and as they'd travelled light, there were not many trips to make down the passage.

Wimlett joined them in the new room, and with nothing to do while they were sorting out and settling in, he went to the window and looked out. 'Oh, dear, I'd forgotten about them!'

'Who?' asked Florence, going to see who Wimlett was talking about.

'Eydith and Linkwood. They're coming down the street.'

56

Earlier that evening, after a short stop at a farmhouse for food and comfort, Dennis and his two guards returned to the carpet. Jook climbed into the cart while Psoddoph sat down and leant against a wheel.

Dennis seemed preoccupied. He remained standing, looking down at Psoddoph. 'Do you think he's come out yet?'

'Who?' said Psoddoph.

'That gnome,' said Dennis, punching the palm of his hand.

'Maybe, boss.'

'When we're done, I'm coming back this way,' muttered Dennis. 'I want him to suffer.'

Jook was listening in. *Why does he want to make so many enemies?* He wondered, at a loss to understand his boss.

The Drum glowed a little, and dimmed.

The wizard seated himself at the front of the cart. But instead of instructing the carpet to rise, he sat staring at the sky. The guards waited expectantly for him to get them moving again.

When nothing happened, 'We're ready, boss,' said Psoddoph.

'What for?'

'Well… to go. When you're ready,' said the guard, growing a little concerned over his master's behaviour.

'Oh… yes. This thing doesn't get going on its own, does it?' He blinked a few times as if engaging his wits, and rummaged through the folds in his robe for the book.

'Oh, no,' sighed Jook, 'I thought he'd got the hang of it by now.'

'What's that!' said Dennis, sharply, turning around.

'Nothing, boss,' Jook replied, lamely.

Dennis leafed through the book for a minute then stuck a finger in the air to determine the wind's strength and direction. The carpet lifted at his command. He was still seething over the gnomes, and the carpet sensed it and flew jerkily. Jook and Psoddoph held on.

Dennis's anger cooled in a while, and the carpet began to fly smoothly. Psoddoph relaxed to take in the scenery, dangling his legs over the edge.

Jook decided on a quiet smoke, and rummaged in his pockets for a cigarette. It had been a long time since he'd last smoked, and his head spun a little, though mainly because this wad of tobacco had been used many times before, and had matured over the months. He rarely threw a butt away. He found that five butts made a reasonable new smoke. And five butts from these recycled smokes produced yet another new smoke. Which was why this one, which was probably an eighth or ninth generation product, made him giddy. He eyed it suspiciously and thought how lucky he was, to be lying down at this altitude.

After a while, Dennis located the railway tracks below them and began watching them, mesmerised by the elongated 'Λ' that disappeared over the horizon. He almost dozed, and only snapped out of it, when he nearly collided with a tall tree. He veered safely away, barely in time.

Psoddoph grabbed the wheel behind him, but Jook failed to grab anything in time. He pitched forward and hit his head on the Drum. The deep boom shook the air about them, violently rustling the upper branches of the tree they'd dodged. It shook Dennis, too. He decided to put the carpet on auto-pilot, asking it to fly them to Prossill, avoiding anything tall and hard. That done, he peered over the back of the cart, to where Jook was lying rubbing his head.

'What are you doing to the Drum?' he demanded.

'It's not me, boss,' said Jook. 'I slipped and banged me 'ead.'

'Well, it's never made a sound like that before,' said Dennis, stroking his neat blonde beard.

'I suspect that's because it's never bin 'it with an 'ead before,' said Jook, feeling the tender spot above his left ear.

The Drum glowed, brightly.

'Hit it again!' Dennis ordered.

'Really?' queried Jook. But he did as he was told, careful to use the other side of his head. The Drum resonated even more deeply and loudly this time – out of all proportion to the impact of Jook's timid head butt. The three men covered their ears. Jook's jaw dropped and he lost his smoke.

57

Eydith and Link ambled along the street in Prossill, stopping occasionally to look in shop windows. Most of the shops had closed for the evening, or were in the throes of closing. In one of the windows, she noticed Sprag's reflection glowing softly, pulsing at about her heart rate. *What's the matter?* She thought.

The staff was also emitting a low hum in her mind, at the same frequency as the glow. Link noticed the staff blinking. 'What's he doing that for?'

'I don't know,' she said, shrugging. 'But I think I should put him down for a moment.' She gently laid the glowing staff on the cold flagstones, and crouched down beside him. The glow went out, and his voice suddenly crackled into her mind, 'Hell, that's cold! Pick me up.'

'I thought something was wrong,' she said.

'No, I'm all right. I can sense the Drum and I was scanning to see how far away it is.'

'That's good news,' said Eydith, brightening. 'And we can't be far from the place where we're supposed to meet my father and the others.'

The staff glowed steadily brighter. 'They're somewhere close, mistress. I can sense your father.'

Eydith picked him up and looked around at the buildings on the street, looking for a particularly imposing one that might be the Town Hall. It was there up ahead alright, but she saw something else first, as did Link.

'Look!' He pointed at a cart that looked like a large cage on wheels. There were two large horses in the shafts, each with its head in a nosebag the size of a dustbin. 'It's a Watch patrol wagon out on business. There's been a disturbance at that bar.'

'Why do I get the feeling we've found your father?' said Sprag.

They crossed over towards the wagon and immediately saw the sign swinging over the establishment where it was parked. 'Yep, this is the place. The Magic Finger,' said Link. He led the way between the tables with the colourful parasols. He tried to push the door open, but it swung only half way back because of something on the floor behind.

The obstruction was a bruised and bloodied barbarian who hadn't yet been attended to by the Watch. They stepped over him and some of the others that still littered the floor. It wasn't as though this was an everyday occurrence in Eydith's life, but in the short time she'd known her father and Link, she'd grown to accept that wherever there were wizards, there would probably be casualties and the Angel of Death in attendance before too long.

She saw the landlord near the bar, and didn't like the look of him. She called over, 'We're looking for two people called Esmerelda and Florence. Can you tell us if they're staying here?'

The landlord's shoulders sagged. He was expecting an order for drinks. 'Yeah, they're here. Upstairs. Room three, over the front.' He indicated the side door with his thumb.

'Can we go up?' Eydith asked, already making for the door.

'Why not, everyone seems to be doing as they please here tonight.'

The pair went through the door. Beyond, it was dark. Eydith made to summon a little magic light but something in Link's mind triggered a warning. She was still a little new and dangerous at this. He quickly spread his fingers, and a bright orange flame lit up the passageway as it arced towards a torch in a bracket on the wall.

'I was going to do that,' she hissed.

'Yes, I know,' said Link. 'But you do tend to overdo things a bit sometimes.'

'That carpet was an accident! *All right?*'

'Okay, okay!' He grinned, raising his hands defensively. 'You're getting the hang of it. It's just that being an Archchancellor's daughter you're a bit more powerful than us normal magicians, so it's harder to control. But you're doing okay, believe me.'

She was a little placated, but not entirely. 'Good!'

He took the torch from the bracket and led the way up the stone steps. At the top, door number three had a strip of light showing underneath. It seemed like the only occupied room, but perhaps the neighbours were not back yet, or had turned in early.

'I don't like this place,' Eydith whispered. 'It's creepy.'

'Shush, you're making me nervous,' whispered Link, as they reached door. Just as he was about to tap, it swung back, squeaking on hinges that had never been oiled. The light from the room widened to flood the landing.

The smiling face of Florence peered round the door. 'Eydith!'

'No, I'm Link,' he said, sticking a thumb in his chest. 'This is Eydith,' he announced, and knew better than to stick a thumb in her chest.

Florence smiled. 'Come in, we're expecting you.'

The cousins hugged before Esme called, irritably, 'Who is it?' Florence told her that Eydith and Link had arrived. 'Bring 'em in, girl, and shut the door, the light's escaping.'

Link stood back, letting Eydith pass, and followed her in. Esme was sitting in an armchair by the fireplace.

'Come in, come in, child. Sit there.' Esme indicated the chair opposite her.

'Hello, Aunt Esme.' Eydith kissed her cheek and sat down. Her father's ghostly form joined them. 'Hello, Father. What happened downstairs?'

'Nothing to do with me,' he replied, picking up on the accusation. 'Two barbarians had an argument, and well... one thing led to many other things. You know how it is?' Everyone on Crett knew how it was. It was said that *The Barbarian Book of Pleasantries* was one of the slimmest volumes in the Unknown Universe. Whereas their *Book of Crass* ran to nine volumes.

Link smiled and went to stand behind Eydith's chair.

'Where's yer manners girl?' said Esme, 'Introduce your young man.'

She flushed a little on hearing link described like that, but things were certainly moving in that direction.

Florence went to fetch drinks while Eydith and her aunt caught up, chatting cautiously around delicate family matters. But at least the worst was water under the bridge now, and Esme was doing her best to heal the old rift between her and her sister. Eydith was both confused and amused at how Esme could be so considerate in such a grumpy way.

When the conversation slowed, Sprag glowed softly, and whispered into Eydith's mind. 'I feel a kindred spirit in this place, mistress. Something from long ago is tugging at my mind.'

She glanced around and for the first time noticed a stout length of weathered wood, like a flagpole, propped up beside the fireplace. Sprag had led her gaze to it. 'What's that?' she asked, aloud, sloping her head towards it.

'Oh, that's mother's broomstick,' Florence replied. 'It's supposed to be quite a rare one. Made of some special wood, she says.'

'It is, *too*,' stressed Esme. 'A long-extinct kind of fruit tree, handed down through generations, yer know.' As a broomstick it was lacking the all-important broom at one end, but Eydith chose not to comment. 'Used to be twice as long as that, though,' Esme added, pointing at the pole. 'Somewhere along the way, one of our ancestors, a wizard called Fickling, they say, had two sons, and when he lay a-dying he couldn't decide which one to give it to, so he had it cut in half.'

'Shame,' said Eydith, mentally measuring the pole and imagining its original length. 'He must have been very tall.'

'Well over seven feet, they say, an' a very gifted wizard he was, too,' Esme answered softly, with a trace reverence.

'He must have been to have cut a staff,' Eydith agreed. 'He wouldn't have had any trouble dealing with Dennis.' She took Sprag, who was still glowing, and placed him next to the pole. *Just as I thought, exactly the same length.*

'Mistress,' said Sprag, 'I think it's my other half.'

'I didn't know you had another half.'

'It was many centuries ago, I'd almost forgotten, mistress.'

'Can it speak?'

'No,' said Sprag. 'Although it does have *some* magic.'

'What can it do?'

'It can fly.'

'Is that all?'

'Almost all.'

'Don't you miss it?'

'No. My... um... 'personality' could not be divided, so I am completely whole without it. I am the half which was given to the older brother, who was so much more of a wizard than the younger could ever be. The father knew my abilities would be wasted on the younger. In his wisdom, he gave the appearance of dividing the staff equally, while placing all of my gifts and powers in the older brother's half. The power of flight, which makes it an excellent transport for a witch, was added to my other half by a spell, as were a few other minor abilities in order to make the division appear fair.'

'Wow, he certainly was a wise one.'

'Indeed, mistress. The older son was a founding father of Havrapsor, which is how I came to be there to be handed down to each new Archchancellor.'

'Wow,' said Eydith again, looking at the two almost identical staffs. The difference was that, on closer inspection, Sprag had runes where the other one merely had grain. 'And here you are, reunited with... does it have a name?'

'No, mistress.'

'What are you up to, girl?' said Esme, not taking in what Eydith was doing. And Eydith quickly decided it was best not to tell Esme that she owned the considerably better half of a powerful staff, while she (Esme), owned the considerably lesser half! At least, not just yet.

'Just admiring your broomstick.'

'It does the job,' said Esme, dismissively. Then, 'Have you seen Dennis?' she asked, pulling a face at the distastefulness of saying his name.

'I was about to ask you the same thing,' said Eydith.

'Naphrat was in here earlier, and he was looking for him too,' said Wimlett.

'Naphrat can't take Dennis,' snapped Esme. 'Only Death Himself can take a wizard or a witch. A wizard like Dennis won't surrender his soul to Naphrat's scythe.'

'That's something I hadn't thought of,' confessed Wimlett, now giving it some thought. The situation had probably changed, he thought, now that Naphrat was running things. Though it bothered him a little when he considered that, as far as he knew, no wizards or witches had died in a remarkably long time. Not even himself. *That's probably why the job was botched. Not only that bloody Timer. Esme could be right. I need to get this sorted out the next time Naphrat shows up. And where's Death when you need Him? What if a wizard's Timer runs out while He's gallivanting about on vacation? What on Crett was he thinking, going on a break?*

People say Death's a big mystery, and certainly Wimlett couldn't make sense of Him, sometimes.

Appropriate to his train of thought, Wimlett watched out of the window as the bodies of some barbarians were being dumped into the back of a wagon. The walking-wounded were being shepherded up the street to the jail. He stuck his head through the glass, to get a better idea of what was going on, and overheard snippets of conversations from below that went... 'Look! It's 'erbert the 'orrible – 'e's gotta be werf two gold pieces... even dead.' And, 'Blimey, look at these two! Gotta be werf at least one gold a piece.' He saw a senior Watch member shuffling through papers that must have been Wanted Posters. Then, 'All right, lads. Big bonuses tonight!' It seemed there could be joy even in the midst of death.

It was almost dark, and Wimlett took one last look up and down the street. He could see no sign of Dennis, so he drew back inside. 'I don't think Dennis will be arriving tonight,' he said. 'We might as well all try and get some sleep.'

'Yes,' said Esme, sternly. 'And it would be as well for us all to be up and about *early* in the morning.' Her words seemed laden with prophetic import, and the others shared meaningful glances. But she just thought it might be a good idea. She poked the fire, sending a shower of sparks up the chimney.

58

The silver disc of Crett's moon was hauling its way into the sky with about as much conviction as the sun had that morning. The cosmologists put its reluctance down to gravitational anomalies which they couldn't understand. But it was just sheer laziness.

The sun and moon were still worshipped fanatically in some places by the two main religious sects on Crett. One by day, the other by night. And, if it hadn't been for a rogue devotee drawing some revealing graffiti on a wall, neither sect would have known of the other's existence. Neither of them was sure which of them had drawn it. And when all was said and done, it turned out that each, in a roundabout way, worshipped the other's astronomic obsession anyway. The sun and moon themselves were absolutely baffled by all this, hated all the attention, and were only too pleased for cloudy days and nights when they could keep well out of it.

There were no clouds tonight, and as the moon struggled lazily to its place in the star-strewn sky, a frost crept over the plain below. The carpet slowed, and the breath of the three men was visible, trailing behind it. Dennis pulled his robe tighter around him, and looked hard for somewhere to land.

'That looks all right!' called Psoddoph, pointing to a spot by the side of a stream, 'What do you think, boss?'

Dennis grunted agreement and a little offhandedly asked the carpet to land. The result was the stream coming up to meet them faster than anticipated. Dennis had to politely scream some adjusted instructions to slow them down. They settled gently and thankfully a few feet from the water's edge.

They'd been high when he first saw the stream, and now they were down, they discovered it was quite a wide a river. It had a greenish hue, and smelled a bit, too, from pollution. The three men stepped onto the grass and stretched their stiffened limbs. 'Get some wood, Jook. We'll have a fire and warm up a bit,' ordered Dennis.

Jook went off, muttering something about a bit of *what?*

Dennis glared at his back. *It's a good job I need him,* he thought. *But one day...*

Jook didn't hang about. It was cold and he didn't like the descending dark very much. Neither did Dennis, for that matter. The Drum kept giving him nightmares. It managed to induce a recurring one about him walking in the Dark Dimensions with the Things. And the Prince of the Underworld was beckoning, and Dennis didn't want to go. But he couldn't say no, and was relieved to be jumped from sleep by the Things lurching out of the darkness to get him. So, Dennis preferred the place to be a bit brighter.

Jook returned with his arms loaded with wood, and laid it where Dennis pointed. Then the wizard aimed his fingers at the sticks and muttered an incantation, and a flame shot out. *Same old magic,* he smiled to himself, and crouched down on the edge of the carpet.

'There's something nice about a fire, Jook,' said Dennis, in an attempt at a pleasant tone, pushing his shadowy thoughts away.

'Yep,' agreed Jook. 'Keeps the wolves away.'

'Yes, I suppose it does... *What wolves?*'

'I dunno, boss,' said Jook, with a shrug. 'None in particular. Any wolf, I suppose. It just a saying, that's all.'

Dennis settled down. 'That wood's burning fast. Go and get some more, will you?'

'I'll go,' offered Psoddoph, fancying a bit of exercise, and relieving himself. He walked a few yards to an old, rotting tree that had fallen down.

'Thanks!' Jook called after him.

An owl flew silently overhead, then swooped on something small and furry that scurried under a bush.

'Do you ever wish you were something else, boss?' said Jook, straining to hear the squeals coming from under the bush.

'I will be something else,' said Denis. 'I will be ruler of the land. Perhaps more.'

'No, I didn't mean that,' said Jook. 'Something interesting... like a bird, or a cat. Something like that.'

'No!'

That should have been an end to it, but Jook's thoughts were still running. 'I wouldn't mind being a wizard,' he said, idly pushing the last sticks into the flames.

'You? A wizard?' mocked Dennis. 'You'll never be as wizard as long as your... oh, never mind. But you could be a frog if you like.' He flexed his fingers, menacingly.

'No, I don't think so, boss,' Jook declined. 'Wrong end of the food chain.' But his thoughts rolled on, undeterred.

The owl flew up into a tree to devour what it had just murdered.

'No, I couldn't possibly be an animal. I couldn't eat mice, or creepy-crawlies.' Jook chewed experimentally, trying to capture the experience. Dennis shook his head, hardly believing this conversation, but before Jook could carry it on, Psoddoph came back with the wood.

'Put it by me here,' said Dennis. He sat staring into the flames, ignoring the guards. Jook went to sit with Psoddoph. Later, the two men drifted into sleep, lolling on one another, but Dennis sat up all night keeping the fire going and watching the flames. Sleep wouldn't come. The Drum had been acting strangely. The staff may be nearby. All sorts of things were whirling in his mind.

Eventually the moon waned, and the sun showed itself tentatively on the far horizon. The sounds of night died, and the sounds of the dawn stirred. Dennis, in spite of his lack of sleep, was wide awake. He pushed the last stick into the fire and stood up, stretched, breathed deeply, and began coughing from the smell of the river.

It woke the guards, who stretched and yawned their way back to consciousness, rubbed their eyes and looked around to see where they were. They, too coughed with their first breaths, and looked at one another reproachfully.

'It's the river,' said Dennis. 'You'll get used to it.'

The fire died, and the three men got back on the carpet. Dennis decided to follow the river upstream, as the pollution it carried could only be coming from a large town. And hereabouts that could only be Prossill. He summoned the carpet respectfully into the air, high enough to see if the horizon held any clues, and saw that the railway tracks followed the river anyway, so he wasn't going to get there any quicker. He thought about getting the carpet to fly faster. Its top speed, according to the manual, was about fifteen percent more than they were doing. But no. He shrugged, telling himself there was no point. It would make little difference, and more speed meant more chance of an accident, which would slow him down even more.

A glance behind told him that Jook was watching the sky. Puffs of tobacco smoke were drifting into the air. The carpet started to shudder. Ah... Psoddoph was vigorously polishing his sword again. Perhaps, if he made it any sharper, he might trim his beard with it. And Psoddoph's reaction to that would be interesting.

Each man was in his private world. It was the most peaceful time that Dennis could recall for weeks. And he hated every second of it. He wanted action, and he wanted the staff. And the way the Drum was acting up, strongly suggested it was sensing the staff. He rubbed his hands together. *Soon,* he thought, *I shall have them both. And then it won't be making mischief – it will do as I say!*

He fully expected the Drum to respond in some way to that thought, but it stayed quiet.

All that concerned Jook right then, was that they must be nearing a city at last. He wondered what the food would be like. Although he wasn't too fussy, just so long as it was hot and hanging over the side of the plate.

Psoddoph looked at his reflection in his gleaming blade. *I could do with a haircut,* he thought. *A proper one. Not like the ones I get at the barracks. Cook's always using the basin that fits me for spotted dick, too, and who wants a haircut with a basin that's had a spotted dick in it? When I get enough money,* he vowed, *I'm going to buy my own basin.*

Dennis saw the city first. It was still a long way off, but he could make out some taller buildings. And an even taller spire that was probably erected in honour of some god or other, or possibly all of them, it was that tall. Jook sat up, and Psoddoph moved to the edge at the front of the carpet, just below Dennis.

Inside an hour, they were approaching the suburbs, and levelled off at a lower altitude to have a closer look. They were passing over a part of the city that more than adequately qualified as 'outer city deprivation'. 'Look at the state of this place,' Dennis muttered.

'Not a good idea to land around 'ere, boss,' said Psoddoph. 'If we leave the cart, there won't be anything left when we get back.'

'I think you're right, we'll look for somewhere a bit more upmarket.' He asked the carpet to take them high above the rooftops again.

They flew around looking at other parts of the city – where the houses didn't have corrugated iron sheets for windows, and where there weren't bits of broken carts and old mattresses strewn across unkempt lawns. Slowly the scene changed, and the buildings below them had well-manicured lawns front and back. This was more like it. 'We'll land and find out where we are,' said Dennis.

'That looks like a friendly place,' said Psoddoph, indicating a trim little cottage, with window boxes brimming with flowers adorning the front of it.

'Yeah,' Jook said, eying the place. 'Looks friendly enough, boss.'

Dennis was about to tell them he was quite capable of picking a spot himself, but instead settled the carpet on the front lawn of the cottage. Out of courtesy to the owner, he supposed he ought to announce himself and explain their temporary presence. He led the guards up to the quaint yellow door, and rattled the brass letterbox. Almost immediately the door swung in, and they were confronted by a little, white haired old lady dressed head-to-toe in black. She peered round the door and her eyes went swiftly from the three men to the cart parked on her lawn.

'Good morning. My name is Dennis,' he started, smarmily. The guards, standing one each side, nodded enthusiastically and pointed at him.

'He's Dennis,' they said in unison, as if some sort of authentication was needed.

'Stop doing that!' snapped Dennis. The old lady smiled as if she suddenly recognised them.

'Oh, you're early, but do come in. I'll be ready in a minute,' she said, leading them into her living room. They exchanged quizzical looks and followed her inside, where, instead of the room being laid out nice and neat and cottagey, all the furniture was lined up by the door, the carpet was rolled up, and the centre of the room was stacked with boxes. 'Right,' she began. 'Where do you want to start?'

'Sorry?' said Dennis.

'Don't be,' she said. 'I know the ropes. I've done this lots of times. Usually, you start with the big stuff, then the small stuff, then the fragile stuff. Then me! I'll ride up with the driver.'

'There seems to be a bit of a misunderstanding here, boss,' said Jook, with remarkable insight, nudging Dennis's arm.

Dennis, restraining his sarcasm, whispered that he thought it might be the case, and to the lady, he said, 'Excuse me, madam, but were you expecting somebody?'

'Well, I was. But you're here now.' She smiled, sweetly.

'No, I'm not,' said Dennis.

'Yes, you are, *silly*,' she insisted. 'I can see you.' She went to prod him, but he saw it coming and leaned back.

'No, I didn't mean I'm not here, I mean, I'm not who you think I am.'

'You mean... You're not, 'MOVE IT WITH DENNIS'?'

'No madam. I'm the Archchancellor of Havrapsor University.'

'Are you sure?'

'Positive.'

'You look like 'MOVE IT WITH DENNIS' to me, young man.' She leaned in and scrutinised his face. With that, her brow furrowed, and a tear of disappointment ran down her cheek.

'Don't cry, lady,' said Jook, putting a comforting arm around her shoulder. "E does 'ave that sort of effect on people sometimes. Tell you what – I'll speak to 'im.'

'No!' said Dennis, before Jook could open his mouth. 'Definitely not!'

'But, boss...'

'I said, NO!' said Dennis, flatly.

'But, boss. We don't even know where she wants to go.'

'No, and I don't know where I want to go yet, either,' Dennis snapped.

'Perhaps I can help,' the old lady volunteered, her lip still quivering a little. 'I've often told people where to go.'

'I don't think you want to hear this, boss,' whispered Psoddoph, reaching up to put his fingers over Dennis's ears, and then thinking better of it.

Dennis raised a hand to emphasize what he was about to say, and the old lady grabbed it and looked at his palm. 'You're going on a long journey,' she intoned, looking soulfully into his eyes.

'I've just finished a long journey!' he said sharply, and then thought, *that's all I need, an old woman who reads palms.*

'I can see that. But it's not over yet.' Before he could snatch his hand away, she gripped it tighter and studied it more closely. 'Looks to me like you're going round again,' she grinned, then turning his hand over. 'Maybe even a third time by the look of all this.'

Dennis looked at the ceiling and began tapping his foot. 'Have you quite finished?'

'No, not quite. I see you're looking for something... *a stick?* Maybe. No. A staff.'

She had his attention now. 'Tell me more. Let's sit down and do this properly,' he said, smiling engagingly, or so he thought. 'While my men here load your furniture.'

Jook smiled, too, knowing he'd kind of got his way. Psoddoph looked around at some of the heavy-looking chairs and sideboard, wondering if the carpet would take the weight.

The old woman turned business-like. 'Will you just be wanting the palm reading?' she asked, 'or the cards as well?'

'Just the palms,' said Dennis, knowing his patience would only extend so far.

'First, you must cross my palm with silver.'

He grudgingly dug inside his robe and produced a tiny silver coin, which she eyed critically, but took it anyway.

She lifted his hands to within an inch of her face, and started. 'There's a whole world in the palms of your hands, you know.'

'Yes, I'm sure there is,' he said, quickly, trying to skip the mumbo jumbo.

'Aha!' she said.

'Yes?'

'I see the staff you seek.'

'Good, good.'

'It's on the other side,' she said, cryptically.

'The other side of what?' prompted Dennis.

'Can't see properly. Could be a building. Could be a passageway. Could be a room. Could be... all of them. Could be...'

'Anywhere,' Dennis finished for her, exasperatedly. 'Can't you be more specific than that?'

'I can only say what the palms say,' she said, sniffing.

'How convenient,' he mumbled.

She was merely following the first rule of palm reading, which is: you can't be wrong if you're not specific.

'Well, thank you, I suppose,' he said, moodily, glad he hadn't paid more. He thought he heard her mutter, 'You get what you pay for.'

'Mark my words,' she said, solemnly, repeating, 'You will find the staff on the other side... of a building... a passageway... a room.'

'Or anywhere,' he finished for her, faintly mockingly.

The two guards got on with moving the furniture, knocking paint off door frames and grazing knuckles, until the only things left in the room were the two boxes Dennis and the old woman were sitting on. They went outside and sat in the garden to wait. Jook finished a roll-up he'd saved, while Psoddoph made sure the furniture was safely stowed on the cart. It looked severely overloaded. And it was as well that Dennis could afford a sturdier transport than most.

Very soon, Dennis and the old lady emerged from the little cottage.

She looked at the cart. 'Oh, dear. Some-one's stolen your horses.'

'I don't need *horses*.' Dennis said, a little too dismissively. 'I've got a magic carpet.'

'Don't you take that tone with me, young man!' she snapped. 'I'm not just a gullible old woman.'

He toyed with a number of responses to that, but settled with, 'I really do have a magic carpet. Look, the cart is on it.'

She walked closer. 'Oh, beg your pardon. I didn't think those things were around anymore. Not in Prossill, anyway.'

'There are still a few,' said Dennis. 'Now, where would you like to sit?'

'Oh... Up with the driver, as always. That will be fun.' She grinned widely, exposing a variety of teeth, climbed a little hesitantly onto the cart and sat down triumphantly.

Dennis leant against a wheel and looked up at her. 'Where are we going?'

'To my sister's house, please.'

'Right. Good. And where would that be?'

'It's right near the Town Hall,' she replied. 'A nice place. Except for that awful tavern opposite.'

'Do you happen to know the way?' he asked.

'Yes, of course,' she replied, adding a trifle haughtily, 'I *have* been to my own sister's, you know.'

'Good. Because you'll have to direct us.' He clambered up beside her. 'Are you ready?'

'Oh, yes.' The old lady beamed, jigging about on the seat, gleefully. 'It's that way.'

'Right, hold on tight,' said Dennis. 'Carpet, up gently... please,' he called. The carpet strained under the weight for a moment, then lifted steadily. He requested it to go forward at a modest pace, and the carpet duly obliged.

'I haven't seen the city from up here,' the old lady squealed. 'Isn't it exciting?'

'Yeah,' said Jook from behind, stifling a yawn.

'You don't know when you're well off, young man,' she told him.

'I do, lady. Believe me, I do,' replied Jook, softly.

'Where's the Town Hall?' asked Dennis.

The old lady swivelled around and pointed at a distant tall building with a domed roof. 'Over there! You can't miss it.'

Psoddoph didn't like the sound of that.

After a painfully slow crossing of the town, Dennis circled the dome, waiting for her to get her bearings. They came down just a little faster than usual because of the weight, and he had to do some quick thinking. About ten feet from the ground, he asked it to rise. The carpet's momentum took it almost all the way down, and before it could start going up, Dennis asked it to go down again. The carpet stopped.

'I'm impressed, boss,' said Psoddoph, nodding his head. 'Very impressed.'

'Is that it?' The old lady was disappointed that the ride was over.

'Afraid so,' said Dennis.

'Can't we go round again?'

'Nope. This is it. Down you get,' said Dennis, holding out his hand to help her. It looked gallant, but he didn't want to waste time explaining and sorting everything out with her sister if she fell down and injured herself. He winced as she launched herself past him.

But she landed safely and nimbly on the pavement. She straightened her dress, pulled back her shoulders, marched up to the front door, and swung the knocker, hard.

⸺⸱⸻⟨⟩⸻⸱⸺

59

'Come over here, quick!' hissed Wimlett. 'Look... down there.' He pointed down into the street. The others crowded around him, trying not to be in him, and craned their necks to see what had grabbed the late wizard's attention.

'It's Dennis!' said Eydith, her eyes widening.

'What's he doing?' asked Link.

'He appears to be helping that old lady off his cart,' said Eydith, frowning, and trying to make better sense of what she was watching.

'What?' said Esme. 'That's not like him at all. Helping her *under* it would be more his way.'

'His two guards are with him as well,' said Link, also trying to figure out the scene in the street below. 'What *are* they doing?'

'Taking a load of old furniture into that house,' Eydith observed, needlessly. 'Like they're helping her move in.' They could all see that much for themselves. But she needed to say it to believe it.

***

Down below, Jook and Psoddoph trotted back and forth up the front path unloading the cart. Dennis went inside the house with the old lady and her sister, to avoid the heavy lifting. Jook said as much as he struggled with a large box and pushed the gate open with his foot. And now Dennis had unhelpfully closed the front door behind him. The old lady's sister saw him and went to open it for him. Grillo, the woman's small dog, also saw Jook, as it scampered around the side of the house to investigate the new arrivals. It seized the opportunity to begin attacking Jook's ankles.

'Kick his balls!' the sister yelled when she opened the door. Jook thought it a little harsh, but he was used to taking orders, and assumed she knew best. He adjusted the angle of the box so he could see Grillo, and swung his foot with such force that he lifted the yelping terrier into the air.

'No! No! No!' she yelled. 'Not his testicles! His balls, there on the grass!'

Jook was at a loss for words. Grillo limped painfully into the house and hid under a chair, from where he barked and growled at the guards as they went in and out. But now his bark was a couple of octaves higher than before, and it would be days before he would frighten anyone again.

In just under an hour, the cart was clear of furniture, and from their vantage point at the upstairs window, Wimlett and the others could now see what remained.

'I can't see the Drum,' Wimlett said to Eydith.

She shook her head slowly. Noticing Sprag against the wall by the window, she picked him up and held him against the glass for a better view. It seemed daft, but also the right thing to do. She felt him enter her mind, and realised that, in truth, he was always there, but mostly at a respectful distance.

'It's under the canvas, mistress,' he said. 'I can sense its presence strongly.' The staff glowed warmly, and down in the street, she saw a corresponding soft orange light filtering through the canvas.

Wimlett noticed, too. 'One of us needs to keep watch from here, so we don't lose track of them, while you decide what you're going to do next, Daughter.' He sounded serious.

'Any suggestions, Father?'

'I'm thinking,' said the old mage, stroking his transparent beard with his visible hand. 'We need to keep a close eye on them. Watch for an opportunity. Size up the opposition we can expect from the guards. That sort of thing. Link can't go down there. Dennis would recognise him.'

'Huh!' Link scoffed. 'I'm not even sure he knows I exist. Dennis doesn't exactly fraternise with seventh-levels,'

'But we can't take a chance. It's best he doesn't know we're here. It gives us the advantage. And we can't risk a confrontation yet, either. Esme can't go, he might remember her, or her twin sister. He might even remember Eydith from her visit to the university. That leaves just me and Florence.'

Eydith walked away from the window, and sat by the fire. 'Do you think Florence could do it, Father?'

'Do what?' he replied, absently.

'Have you lost the thread of this already?' she scolded.

'No, of course not. But you haven't told me what you want her to do, yet.'

'Give me a chance. Steal the Drum, of course. Or cause a distraction so that one of us can do it.'

'She could cause a distraction. She shouldn't try to steal the Drum by herself. For a start, it's bulky. And it'll be guarded, we can be sure of that.' He tugged his beard again. 'And we certainly shouldn't attempt it in daylight.' The fingers of his solid hand tapped a rhythm on the window-board while he mulled it over. 'Let's none of us forget how tricky and dangerous Dennis is.'

'Too right!' Esme joined in, enthusiastically.

Eydith agreed they should wait till dark. 'Dennis will be away from his guards. I can't see him staying in the same room. He'll probably have them watching the Drum in turns throughout the night.'

'I'm sure he will. So, we will need to trick them into leaving it unguarded.' When no-one spoke, he added, 'At the first opportunity. This very night, if possible.'

They had the outline of a plan. And there were no dissenters. The details would be worked out on the hoof, when they knew more about the comings and goings of Dennis and his guards.

'He's coming out,' Esme whispered from the window. Not that Dennis could hear, but she was getting a little nervous now that all the talk was becoming reality. She stepped back in case he looked up.

Dennis stood chatting with the old sisters. The conversation drew to a close when he pointed at The Magic Finger. He touched his forehead politely and walked purposefully across the road. One of the old ladies gave the guards a coin each. They smiled graciously, and Jook apologised once again for his earlier misunderstanding. He hoped that Grillo would soon get his bark back out of the auditory range where only other dogs could hear it.

Psoddoph followed his master across the road. The two men threaded their way through the tables fronting the tavern, and went inside. Psoddoph was just close enough behind to catch the door in his face as Dennis let it go. He usually let Jook go in front on these occasions, but he'd been left minding the stuff.

The Magic Finger was near empty at this time of day. Dennis looked around for a table, wondering what on Crett had happened to the place. There weren't many left standing after last night's riot, but he spotted one that might support a few pints and told Psoddoph to move it closer to the window. Then he strode to the bar.

'Two jugs of your finest ale, landlord. And today's menu,' he said, as he cast another eye over the splintered state of the room. 'Get trolls in here, do you?'

Welt, the thuggish-looking landlord grunted something affirmative, and stood to attention, his weasally eyes glinting at the sight of strangers in his tavern. 'Right you are, sir. Two jugs. I'll send 'em over.'

Dennis walked back to where Psoddoph stood looking through the window. 'What about chairs?' asked Dennis, casually.

'Oh, you didn't say, boss.' Psoddoph glanced quickly around the room and saw some stacked in a corner. He pulled out a couple that looked safe enough, tested them, and proceeded back to the window. He'd only gone a few steps when a cold, hard hand rested on his shoulder.

'You got my chair,' rasped a gravelly voice.

Psoddoph was not getting the friendliest of vibes, and looked over his shoulder at a broad, craggy face.

'Dat's my chair you've got,' Flint repeated.

Psoddoph swallowed hard, and looked down at the chairs. They looked identical. In fact, they looked identical to every other usable chair in the place, as far as he could tell. Though admittedly some were differently damaged. How could this troll – not usually the brightest of creatures, though this one did seem to have of spark of something in its eyes – how could he possibly know which one was his? Psoddoph raised one of the chairs. 'This one?' he mouthed.

Flint slowly shook his head.

Psoddoph shook his head in sympathy, and put the chair down. 'This one?'

Flint nodded slowly.

'Where do you want me to put it?' he asked, wishing he'd phrased it better.

'Over dere,' said Flint, pointing at the sort-of piano.

Psoddoph didn't want any trouble, especially with someone made of enough stone to build a luxury privy, so he took the chair to the sort-of piano, and placed it at what he considered a comfortable distance for the troll to play. Or sort of.

The landlord opened a door at the side of the room and yelled, 'Florence!' When she appeared, he told her to take the drinks to the gentlemen by the window.

Bells were ringing in Dennis's brain. *Florence. Not a common name in these parts.* He began racking his brains trying to think where he'd heard the name recently. *Got it! That's the name of the girl with the witch, Swampshit – the witch with the broomstick without a broom on the end! Could that be...?* Florence arrived at the table, and stood the two jugs down in front of them. 'Thank you, my dear,' he said, in a tone as smooth as ruffled silk. 'This is for you.' He gave her a small copper coin.

Psoddoph hadn't seen him do that before. Ever. He almost choked on his first sip of ale. Perhaps being continually polite to the carpet, and then the sisters, had affected him. But he doubted it. Dennis was only nice when it suited him. Florence bobbed a curtsy of sorts and thanked him.

'What a charming girl,' he mused, as he watched her glide gracefully back to the bar, where she tripped.

'Oh, come on, boss. She's hardly more than a child. Besides, I didn't think you wizards went in for that sort of stuff.' Psoddoph eyed him across the rim of his jug as he took another swig.

'There are guidelines for wizards on such matters, but not rules. It depends how one interprets them.' Which was pretty liberally when one was Archchancellor. Even more so when one was Dennis. Switching the subject to something more germane, he said, 'Cast your mind back a few weeks,' he said. 'That Cottage. Those gnomes.'

Psoddoph nodded, hoping this wasn't going start another angry outburst.

'Well, don't you remember? The girl with the witch who has the broomstick that's probably a staff, was called Florence.'

Psoddoph nodded, looking a bit vague.

'Well, the serving wench here is called Florence. Didn't you hear?' Dennis whispered. 'And how common a name is Florence around here, or anywhere, come to that? I'm almost certain that must be her. They were heading for Prossill. It would be too much of a coincidence.'

Psoddoph was thinking that her being in the tavern where they were sitting right then was the thing that would be too much of a coincidence.

Florence returned with the Menu of Day. It had probably been the Menu of the Day before as well, and the Day before that, all the way back to when the place first opened. She handed them a copy each and waited at the table. Which is after all, what waiting at tables is all about.

Psoddoph looked up at her. 'There's not much of a choice, is there?'

'Only two, sir,' she replied.

'What's the other one, then?'

'You can have it hot, sir,' she smiled, sweetly. 'If you want it cold, you can have it now. Hot is about half an hour.'

'Okay,' said Dennis, cheerfully, 'Make it three... Hot. We'll drink our ale, and return in an hour. Where's the landlord?'

'I'll fetch him for you, sir.'

In a moment, Welt was standing at Dennis's table with a tea towel draped over one arm. 'What can I do for you, sirs?' he asked.

'We need a stable, or a barn, for a couple of nights,' said the wizard. 'Can you oblige?'

Welt smiled benevolently. 'There's no need for that, sir. My *rooms* are quite reasonable.'

'No,' said Dennis. 'You misunderstand. It's not for me. I don't want to sleep rough. I have a cart that I want locked away while I'm here.'

'I think I might find an empty stable for that alright, sir. What about your horses?'

'You don't have to worry about that,' said Dennis, obliquely.

'We have a magic carpet,' said Psoddoph, obtusely. He received a sharp kick under the table.

'And where would this cart on a *magic carpet* be right now, sir?' asked the landlord, trying desperately to maintain an expression that wouldn't betray his wondering what the current market value of such a thing would be, if it went 'missing'.

'Just across the street,' said Dennis, quietly controlling his anger.

Welt peered through the window and there, sure enough, was a cart on a carpet. And only one guard.

'Are there are just three in your party, sir?' Welt inquired, trying to stay as business-like as possible.

'Yes,' said Dennis, gravely, trying to warn him off. 'Me and my guards, who are very good at what they do.'

'Yes, sir. I'm sure they are. How many rooms?'

'One for me and one for them. They will guard my cart in shifts,' said Dennis, pointedly.

'Right you are, sir,' he said, grinning. 'I'll arrange all that. You can fly your cart in, in about half an hour. Just give me time to empty a stable.' He'd quickly worked out it would be easier to relieve Dennis of the carpet if it wasn't locked in the barn.

Florence made sure she was busying herself close enough to catch the conversation, and when Welt turned away to occupy himself behind the bar, she quietly slipped upstairs to tell the others.

Dennis and Psoddoph went out in the street. Jook had taken all the crossbows off the cart a while ago, but he nursed one on his lap as he sat guarding the Drum. He smiled broadly when he saw Dennis and Psoddoph coming. He raised a hand to acknowledge them, and to signal to a small group of young ruffians that had congregated, that he was no longer alone. They retreated to a nearby alley.

'Any trouble?' asked Dennis.

'No, boss. Nothin' I can't handle.' He patted the crossbow, and the other two hopped out of the way sharply.

'Good,' said Dennis. 'I've got a place to keep the cart, but it won't be ready for another half hour.' The ruffians heard this, and they moved back out of the alley. There were more of them.

Eyeing the gathering gang, Psoddoph suggested, 'It might be a good idea to get it off the ground now, boss.'

Dennis looked at the gathering of apprentice cut-throats. 'You could be right.' And in moments the carpet was airborne.

***

Florence burst into the upstairs room. The others were gathered around the window, watching the carpet with the wizard and his guards hovering only a few yards away. 'Dennis is staying *here!*' she announced.

'Hush a minute, child,' Esme scolded her.

The ruffians were fast losing interest, perhaps deterred by Psoddoph brandishing his brightly polished blade and blinding everyone in the sunlit street. And the cart was out of reach. Dennis noticed people watching from their windows, but he wasn't concerned with them. It was to be expected. It wasn't every day they saw a cart flying on a carpet.

Florence kept out of sight, to one side of the window, as did Eydith and Link. Only Esme and Wimlett could see what was going on. Esme's time with Dennis was a long time ago, and she thought she'd changed too much for him to recognise her. Immediately, anyway. As for Wimlett, Dennis shouldn't be able to see him at all. Though you never could tell with someone as magically tricky as Dennis.

Florence told them what she'd heard.

'Do you know which rooms they're in?' asked Eydith. 'We could get Father in one of them before they arrive.'

'I'll find out,' said Florence, and hurried back to the bar.

'I'll need to be careful,' said Wimlett. 'For all I know, he might be able to see me. Or sense me. He's pretty sharp you know! He's been honing his powers for a long time. I'll go into the guards' room, which will hopefully be next door to his.'

Down in the bar, Florence studied the guest register on the pretext that if the new arrivals needed room service, she'd know where to find them.

In the corner, Flint was playing a sort-of sad lament on the sort-of piano.

'Oi! Flint!' the landlord shouted at him. 'This isn't a funeral parlour. Liven it up a bit, will you!'

Flint picked up the tempo. Florence saw her opportunity to slip back upstairs with the information they needed. 'The guards have the room directly opposite us, and Dennis is next to them, towards the stairs.'

'Is there another way out of here?' asked Wimlett.

'Along the passage in the other direction. But it's very narrow,' Florence warned.

'What have you got in mind, Father?' asked Eydith.

'We don't want to keep going passed Dennis's room. He might hear us. Or we might run into him.'

'Yeah,' said Eydith. 'We're a bit too close for comfort. I didn't expect this.'

'They're still down in the street,' Esme chimed in. 'You've got time to get in there before they come up.'

'They won't be here for another twenty minutes, Mother,' said Florence. 'The men are still clearing out a stable for Dennis's cart.'

'Better to be early, than caught,' said Esme. 'We don't want him bursting in and catching Wimlett in the middle of poking around or something, do we?'

'No, Mother,' Florence mouthed.

'Good! Wimlett, off you go,' said Esme, waving him away.

He obeyed.

Link opened the door and felt a chill as the ghostly mage drifted past. The door to the guards' room opposite was half open and Wimlett slid in. This was the room Esme and Florence had been in before, so he immediately got his bearings. He found a suitable spot to settle, against the wall separating this room from Dennis's. Helpfully, there was a large chair he could sit behind and hide his hand. He made himself comfortable, and then carefully leaned through the wall. Luckily, instead of emerging inside the wardrobe a couple of feet to his left, his head came out into the room.

He had a good view across Dennis's room, especially if he stood up, which he now did. He stepped into the room as far as his material hand would allow, and satisfied himself that he'd picked the perfect place for reconnaissance.

Out of curiosity, and because he had some time to kill before Dennis and his men arrived, he decided to check out the wardrobe. He stepped inside. It was dark and dusty. It smelt musty, too, until he remembered he no longer had a sense of smell. This set him to thinking. He wondered if he could use this forgetfulness to his advantage. Was there any way he could induce forgetfulness, temporarily, to give him back his senses, and even some solidity? It was an appealing idea. *But how do I make myself forget I'm a ghost on demand?*

A moment later he successfully – and totally – forgot he was a ghost when he saw the dark outline of someone standing at the other end of the wardrobe. He was briefly ninety-five percent human when he shrieked. Only the short section of his upper arm that went through the wall remained ghost. Had he not frozen in terror, he might have torn his arm off trying to get away. He breathed a deep and grateful sigh of relief when he realised that he shared the wardrobe with an old dressing gown on a hanger. He slowly dematerialised. 'This is ridiculous!' he scolded himself. '*I'm* supposed to be the one around here who makes people jump!'

He counted to ten, and made himself calm down to concentrate on the job in hand. He wafted out of the wardrobe and took another quick look around. *I'll come back when Dennis has sorted himself out.* He withdrew to the guards' room where his solid hand protruded eerily from the wall.

60

Dennis was tiring of all the waiting around. He steered the carpet up over the tavern to see where the stables were. He located the stable yard, and estimated that it was about big enough for them to land there.

'Looks a bit tight, boss,' Jook commented, guessing what his boss was thinking.

Dennis just murmured, 'Hmm,' and rubbed his chin, thoughtfully. 'It probably only looks small from up here.'

'Jook might be right, boss,' said Psoddoph. 'There's not much room if we... you know, need to make a quick get-away.'

'And why would we need to do that?' asked Dennis.

'Well, we are here to steal something, that's all,' said Psoddoph, with a slight shrug of his shoulders.

'Stop worrying – we'll be all right.' And with that, Dennis started the carpet on its descent. More by luck than judgement, when they touched down the main stable doors were directly in front of them, allowing for the misorientation of the carpet, which Dennis hadn't.

Jook pushed the doors, but they didn't budge. They opened outwards. 'That's just bloody typical!' he moaned.

'What's the matter, *now*?' asked Dennis.

'The doors are the wrong way round, boss,' Jook whined. 'I can't get 'em open because the cart's in the way.'

Dennis released a long sigh, and took them back to roof level. 'Right,' he said. 'This is what we'll do. You,' – he pointed at Jook – 'When I move closer, step gently down onto the roof, make your way to that gantry platform into the hayloft, and go down and open the doors. Push them right back, mind you. Then I'll bring the carpet down.'

'Good idea, boss.'

'Yes, I know.'

When the carpet was a couple of feet above the roof, Jook took a deep breath and launched himself. With both feet. There was an ominous creaking the moment he landed, and he quickly tried to reverse the manoeuvre, twisting round to grab hold of the carpet. Which was never going to happen, as he'd already started to drop through the roof. There was a loud crack as the old timbers gave way under him

He landed almost softly with a dull thud and a loud groan on some bales of straw. He lay still for a moment, recovering some of the wind that had been knocked out of him. He seemed okay. He tentatively moved his limbs, and took in his surroundings.

Above him, in a ragged circle of light, two faces peered down from the edge of the carpet. When they saw he was sitting up, Psoddoph beamed with relief. But the look on Dennis's face was thunderous.

'You fool!' he yelled. 'Have you any idea what it will cost to have this lot repaired?'

Jook rolled out of the light and made an obscene gesture in the air.

'No!' shouted Dennis. 'More like five, I shouldn't wonder!'

'Don't worry about me boss. *I'm* not hurt,' Jook called back, sarcastically. He stepped back into the shaft of light and looked up. 'It was an accident, boss. I didn't do it on purpose!'

'I distinctly saw you jump,' snarled Dennis. 'When I'd said *step down gently.*'

'Yeah, but...'

'With both feet!'

'But...'

'Enough! Go and open the doors. We'll discuss it later...' He paused. 'At bonus time.'

Jook slouched over to the doors and pushed them fully open flat against the outside wall. Instead of the sunlight flooding in, the yard was in semi darkness. The carpet was eclipsing the sunlight as it slowly descended towards him. He stepped back and waited for the wrath of the wizard to descend on him along with it. But it didn't.

The Drum glowed momentarily. Dennis was wearing a stupid grin, signifying he'd thought of something. He stepped off the carpet and strode into the stables, where he headed for the shaft of light and looked up at the damage. There was no-one around, so he raised a hand and muttered something not in words. The splinters of timber scattered around the floor flew back into place, as if time had reversed for them, and the hole no longer existed. Dennis was much relieved. He was a little wary using magic around the Drum because he sensed the mischief in it. He was also pleased for the opportunity to rehearse that spell. Much as he didn't like to waste magic, he didn't want to get rusty.

The smile faded quickly, though. He banished it the moment he felt it had hung about long enough. Dennis was unlikely to have laughter lines if he ever reached old age.

He looked around the stable for the most suitable of the half dozen stalls to house the carpet and the cart. None were exactly 'tailor made' for the job, and most were being used as storage. One or two had horses in them. Then he saw the one furthest from the doors had been partially cleared, but still needed some rubbish shifting out of it. The landlord's men weren't that thorough.

'Thanks, boss,' said Jook, eying the magically repaired roof. 'What shall we do now?' he asked, trying to make amends. 'Shall we drag it in, or will you fly it?'

Dennis sized it up and decided to fly it in. 'That way, anyone trying to steal the carpet will have to get the cart off it first,' he explained. 'But before I bring it in, you two need to finish clearing the floor in there, sharpish.'

'He nearly said please,' said Psoddoph, aside.

'Nah.'

'Is everything satisfactory, sir?' said a syrupy voice that wasn't there a second ago.

Dennis and the two guards turned as one. It was Welt, the landlord.

'It would appear so. For now,' Dennis replied, guardedly. 'Do you have a key for this stable?'

'Oh, yes, sir. Two, in fact. One for you,' – which he handed over – 'and one for me,' he said, patting his pocket.

Dennis took the key and put it in the folds of his robe. 'Hmm,' he breathed and raised an eyebrow at Psoddoph, whose look told him he didn't trust Welt either.

'Can I get into the bar directly from here, landlord?' asked Dennis. 'Or do I have to go around to the front?'

'You can go in through that door over there.' He pointed to an arched doorway which had the word 'Privy' written on a board nailed to the lintel.

'It goes through into the bar, sir,' the landlord said, attempting a grin. 'Now, would you like me to show you up?'

'Just point me in the general direction. These two show me up enough as it is, and they don't need any help from you,' he said.

'I like your sense of humour, sir.'

Psoddoph stepped in front of the man. 'He doesn't have one,' he stated, firmly in Dennis's defence.

Welt was no pushover, but he took a step back, not wanting to antagonise paying customers. 'Right, then,' he said, 'your rooms are ready now, and dinner will be about ten minutes.' Bowing from the waist, he slipped away.

'I don't trust him one bit,' said Dennis, turning to his guards. 'Which one of you is going to take first watch?'

They looked at each other and shrugged.

'Look, if you've got to take a vote... then I'll take the deciding one: Jook can do it.'

'Okay, boss. No problem,' he said, cheerfully, and went to sit on a hay bale.

'Hold it!' barked Dennis.

'What's up?' asked Jook.

'Here's the key. And bolt the doors when we've gone?'

The guards had the end stable ready by the time Dennis had steeled himself for the manoeuvre – his first attempt at indoor flying. It went faultlessly. He stepped smugly into the outer stables area – both guards willing him to trip over – and stood admiring the precise positioning of the carpet.

Now, apart from a broken-down old cart in another stall, the only other occupants of the entire stables were a couple of docile horses on the far side, and the bales of straw here and there that Jook had met earlier, plus the usual bats and ravens.

The other two headed off to find the bar and then their rooms. After bolting the doors and turning the key, Jook climbed onto the cart and sat down. The rest of the world was finally shut out. He looked for something to occupy his time. *I could play I spy with my little eye,* he thought. *But everything would be prefaced with 'd', for dark.*

He looked for a lamp. *There's always a lamp in these places. Or they'd never catch fire, would they?* The problem with looking for a lamp in the dark, is that you needed a lamp. While he thought about it, he noticed that the stable seemed lighter. There was a glow coming from behind him. 'Oh, it's you,' he sighed.

The Drum glowed.

61

Dennis and Psoddoph found their way back into the bar and sat at the table by the window.

'Hello again, sir,' Florence greeted them with a smile. 'Your meals will be ready in a couple of minutes. Can I get you a drink while you're waiting?'

'You see,' said Dennis, looking at his guard, 'a bit of civility goes a long way... Yes, my dear, what have you got? You know... what's best today?'

She didn't have a clue. She looked up at the ceiling, trying to remember some of the names she'd seen on the bottles behind the bar. *Oh, yes*, she thought, 'The mead is very good this time of year, sir,' she replied, hoping it was the right thing to say.

Dennis knew nothing of mead either. 'Right,' he said, 'That'll be it, then. Two big jugs of your finest mead, my dear.' And off she went.

'Are you sure, boss?' said Psoddoph, a little anxiously. 'Only, mead can be pretty potent stuff, if you're not used to it?'

'Nonsense,' insisted the wizard. 'It's just a drink.'

Psoddoph wasn't that used to it himself. He was a moderate drinker, unlike most of his ilk When Florence placed the jug in front of him, he took a small sip and put it down. Dennis, on the other hand liked to drink. There were always nice wines on the tables back in the dining room at the university, especially on the Archchancellor's private table. His experience with mead, however, was zero.

Psoddoph found the mead a little sweet for his taste, and the jugs were large, so he didn't match Dennis swig for swig. He'd heard about the sort of headaches it could leave you with. Florence glided across the room with two plates of food, and banged them down on the table.

'This looks rather...' Dennis paused, '...interesting.'

'It's hot, boss,' said Psoddoph, arming himself with a knife and fork. 'So it'll do me.'

Dennis stuck his fork in the brown wad he thought must be meat. To his surprise it was quite tender, and the knife went through it. Neither man noticed the dull footfalls approaching, but there was no not-noticing the voice.

'You want some music?' asked Flint, the troll who played the sort-of piano.

Psoddoph looked at Dennis. 'I think it might be wise, boss,' he said, assessing the challenging look on the troll's stony face.

'Why not?' Dennis smiled appropriately.

'Anyfing special you'd like to 'ear?' asked the lugubrious troll.

'Nothing comes to mind,' said Dennis. 'You play me your favourite tune.'

'I ain't got one. I don't like any of 'em, specially.'

'Oh, dear me,' said Dennis, trying to humour him. 'Don't you have just one that you dislike a little less than the others?'

'What uvvers?' asked Flint. 'I only know one; I just play it at different speeds with different notes.'

'In that case,' said Dennis, quietly, 'I'd like to hear you play it very moderately.' When the troll didn't budge, he added, 'And with different notes.'

'Right,' said Flint, and shuffled back to the sort-of the piano, plonked himself down and started to play. Sort of. It wasn't that bad, actually. A bit repetitive, but not bad. Sort of good, in fact.

The tavern was a lot busier than when Dennis and Psoddoph had first arrived. Customers were sitting at the tables that were safe to use, chatting and drinking, or just waiting for their meals to be brought, soaking up the ambience created by the troll.

Dennis was a methodical eater. The sort who starts with the meat, then eats the peas, then all the chips. He'd got to the chips. Most were okay, but with his attention half on the troll, he absently stuck his fork into an overcooked one. It was as brittle as ice, and exploded under the pressure of his fork. The plate was shattered.

Both men smiled apologetically at the neighbouring tables. Dennis looked around and snapped his fingers at the landlord. Welt saw him, but chose to ignore him for a moment, thinking, *who does he think he is? My best customer?* He motioned to Florence. 'See what he wants on the window table, lass.'

She saw Dennis trying to attract attention and picked her way to him between the tables. 'What's the problem, sir?' she asked, politely, ignoring the mess in front of him.

Dennis looked up rather sheepishly, 'I appear to have damaged the plate.'

'Looks like you've smashed it to bits, sir. But, don't worry, I'll put it on your bill.' She held up the corners of her apron, scooped the fragments into it, and walked off. Dennis couldn't believe what he'd just heard.

'She's going to charge me for that!' he whined, looking across to Psoddoph for support.

Psoddoph raised his jug to hide his grin. And Dennis, with nothing left to eat, picked up his own jug. The guard had finished eating, not that he was full. He just didn't fancy picking shards of china out of what was left on his plate. 'I think I'd better get back to the stable and let Jook come in now, boss.'

'I suppose so. But first we'll go and look at the rooms.'

'Right,' said Psoddoph, getting up.

'Are you going to finish that?' asked Dennis, looking at the remains of the mead in Psoddoph's jug. He'd left about a third of it.

'No. I've had enough,' said the guard, pushing his chair away from the table.

'It's pretty good stuff.' Dennis lifted the jug and downed the contents in one continuous gulp.

Bloody 'ell, Psoddoph thought. *Those jugs are really big. He's had about three normal jugs, I reckon. And he's not used to it.*

Dennis banged it down on the table. 'Aaah, that was nice.' When he began to stand, Dennis felt every pair of eyes in the room looking at him, waiting with interest to see if he would make it to his feet, and actually walk. When he was upright, some were offering odds on how many steps he would take before he went down. His head seemed clear enough, but he could sense a numbness creeping up his legs. He desperately wanted to get outside into the fresh air.

He took a deep breath and steadied himself against the table, then made a lurching step towards the door leading to the stable yard. Going upstairs to the rooms didn't seem like an option at that moment. But so far, so good. The numbness hadn't reached his knees yet, so he took another step. *Why don't they look away?* He wondered, foggily, *haven't they seen anything like me before?* He set off walking as if stepping over things that weren't there.

With Psoddoph by his side, he reached the door and rested against the wall. There was a round of applause, and cries of, 'Well done!' and 'We didn't think you were gonna make it, feller!' But the cry that hurt most was, 'I told you... that's a silver you owe me!'

Psoddoph guided Dennis outside, where the wizard took a very deep breath, went as stiff as a board, spun round and fell back. From the cobbled ground, he looked up at the sky for a moment, then mouthed, 'Oh, shit,' and passed out.

Psoddoph looked down at the sorry sight, enjoying the moment. 'You can't stay there, boss,' he said, chuckling to himself. Dennis groaned something about leaving him alone. Psoddoph ignored him and pulled him into a sitting position, before hoisting him onto his shoulder. He carried him fireman-fashion back inside and up the stairs to find his room.

Florence rushed upstairs to tell the others when she saw Dennis stagger out.

Once they were updated, Eydith went to the door and was just in time to catch Psoddoph struggling to open the door of Dennis's room. On impulse, she slid into the poorly lit hallway. 'Would you like some help?' she asked, as she stepped out of the gloom.

'Blimey miss, I didn't see you there,' he wheezed. As he turned, he banged Dennis's head on the wall.

Eydith managed to wince and smiled at the same time. 'I see you have a burden.'

'Ever since I've known him, miss. And, yes, thank you, miss. If you'd push the door for me…' he panted. 'Not much natural light in these places. Wouldn't hurt to put a few windows here and there. I think there must have been a tax on 'em at one time.'

Eydith opened the door, coughing and treading loudly to alert Wimlett to conceal himself, if he needed to. She craned in and looked around the room, but couldn't see an unattached hand anywhere.

Psoddoph dropped Dennis onto the bed and stood up, stretching his aching back. Dennis groaned and moved a little. He opened an eye to see his trusty guard standing over him. 'Good man,' he murmured, and closed it again.

But Dennis wasn't done yet. Suddenly, both eyes sprang opened and he stared at the ceiling. His hands made a grab for the sides of the bed. He held on tightly, because the room was spinning and the bed was trying to throw him off.

'Psoddoph!' he screamed. 'Find some rope! Quickly!' Dennis shouted. 'Tie me to the bed. It's trying to throw me off!'

There was no point arguing with him. Psoddoph looked around. There was nothing. But in the wardrobe, he found an old dressing gown with the cord still in it. He untangled it and began tying Dennis down. This was another moment to be savoured. They were coming thick and fast.

'More rope!' yelled Dennis.

Psoddoph looked appealingly at Eydith, who was hanging back out of the line of sight.

'I'll get some,' she said, and hurried back along the passage.

Florence was standing at the door. 'What's happening?' she hissed.

'I need some rope. Quickly!' said Eydith. 'Don't ask!'

'There's some in the cupboard at the top of the stairs,' said Florence. She dashed to get it.

'More rope!' yelled the drunken wizard. 'I don't think I can hold on much longer. More rope!'

'All right, boss. I've got some here,' said the guard, as he added more loops to secure Dennis to the bed.

Psoddoph tied him down so tightly that all he could move were his toes and his head. At last, Dennis felt safe. He closed his eyes, and immediately went to sleep. 'That should hold him for a while,' Psoddoph reckoned.

Eydith grinned furtively.

'I'd better find my room, now,' said Psoddoph, as they tiptoed to the door. It was almost dark, so he paused to light a torch on the wall before he left.

Eydith was in the passage first, and directed him to the next room. 'Not bad,' he muttered as he walked to the window. He looked down into the deserted stable yard and in the flickering torchlight recognised the doors they'd taken the carpet through earlier. Then, he remembered Jook. *I must let him go and get something to eat,* he thought. *He must be starving.* He had one more look around the room. 'Better than the barracks, that's for sure,' he said, approvingly. Then he made his way down to the stables, savouring the thought of telling Jook what had happened to Dennis.

---◈◀▷◈---

62

Florence and Eydith watched the guard go, and went into their room. Link and Esme were sharing a bottle of something bordering on the colour purple. Link was swaying a little from side-to-side and almost asleep. Esme was awake and staring glassy-eyed at Eydith.

'I don't believe this. We've hardly been gone a few minutes. And I've just seen one drunkard. Is he drunk?' Eydith asked her aunt.

Esme looked long and hard at the young wizard, and then nudged him with her toe. 'Are you drunk yet?' she slurred.

Link opened his eyes. 'Nope, but it won't be long at this rate, I shouldn't think.'

'See, I told you I could drink you under the table, didn't I?' she cackled, very witchlike, and Link obligingly slid down out of sight.

Florence was dumbstruck for a moment. 'Oh, Mother, what am I going to do with you? We really need to keep our wits about us now. Surely you know that?' she scolded her, more in dismay than anger. Esme wouldn't look her in the eye. Did this mean she might have to *apologise*? The last time she did anything like that was... no, she couldn't remember. She didn't think she'd ever apologised to anyone ever before. Not even hypocritically. Whether that put her ahead of Dennis or behind him in the ethical stakes was a tricky one. Though she was inarguably a better person. But, then, who wasn't? She would have to think fast. She wasn't about to break the habit of a lifetime by saying 'sorry'.

Change the subject!

'I think he's tired. It must have been that long journey,' she tried, lamely.

Florence remained unimpressed. 'Mother, he's been here for hours, now.'

Esme's mind started to race. There had to be a way out of this. Suddenly, it came to her. 'He started it!' she blurted, pointing at the dozing Link. This was not strictly true, but it off-loaded some of the blame. And as the saying goes: 'a blame shared is a blame halved'. Florence shook her head in disbelief. She knew when her mother wasn't being honest.

Eydith wasn't convinced either, though she doubted that Link was totally blameless. She pushed him with her foot. 'Come on, Link. Wake up, we've got work to do.'

He peeped out from one eye when he heard her voice, and sat up, striking his head on the underside of the low table. He went back down again, hitting his head on the floor, and rolled onto his side, moaning and clutching both sides of his head. Eydith moved the table aside and knelt beside him.

'That serves you right!' she said, a little harshly, her annoyance competing with her growing fondness for him. 'Now get up.'

Link managed to haul himself upright. 'That's better, I think I must have dozed off. I was so extraordinarily tired, for some reason.' He spent some time working through the word 'extraordinarily'.

'Oh, so Link isn't drunk, Mother. It's just you! Please sort yourself out. We need to get on. Dennis is also drunk – *very* drunk – and in his room tied to his bed. One of his guards has gone down to the stables to give the other one a break from guarding the Drum. This could be our chance. But Eydith and I can't do everything on our own. This could be our chance to grab the Drum.'

Esme almost apologised, but stopped herself. 'I'll mix myself a cure,' she said, snapping her fingers. A smoking potion materialised obediently.

'That looks like the stuff that got you in that state in the first place, Mother.'

'Yes, it's called a hairy dog – no, a 'hair of the dog.' So saying, she downed it and slumped back in the armchair. Whereupon her eyes opened as though someone had switched her on. She was back. She even had the presence of mind to waft some of the thick smoke from her 'hair of the dog', which hung in the air, in Link's direction. It swirled in front of his face while he stared at it stupidly. And as he didn't have the gumption to inhale it, the vapour found his mouth for him.

Esme's new-found attention went to Florence. 'Where did you say Dennis was?' she asked, remarkably soberly.

'That's what we came back to tell you, Mother.' Florence closed her eyes and tried to summon her usual patience. 'He's drunk and tied to the bed in his room. The guard that brought him up has gone to tell the one in the stable to go and get himself something to eat.'

'That's excellent,' said Link, now able to put one thought in front of another again. He had an idea. 'Eydith, get your father. He's got some haunting to do.'

Eydith went across the passage, found the guards' room unlocked, and prowled around for a couple of minutes whispering 'Father' as loudly as she dared. She concluded he must have seen or heard what had happened to Dennis, and had decided it was safe to go into his room. She didn't like the idea, but she made her way next door, found that unlocked, too, and crept in. She stood stock-still and held her breath when Dennis stirred and mumbled something indistinct. Once he'd settled back down, she breathed again and glanced around. 'Father?' she whispered. 'Where are you?'

'I'm in here,' came a muffled reply.

'Where?'

'In this bloody wardrobe. That stupid guard shut me in.'

She opened the door, and the hand floated past her. 'How did that happen?'

'It was a masterpiece of synchronisation,' he began. 'I held onto the back of the guard's tunic when he went out of his room. And I stuck with him when he went to check on Dennis...'

Dennis shifted slightly at the sound of his name, and Eydith signalled her father to talk more quietly.

'I was still hanging onto his tunic to keep my hand out of sight, when the guard decided to have a nose around. He opened the wardrobe and found an old dressing gown which he took a fancy to. He'd probably never owned one. He put it on and started admiring himself in the long mirror inside the door. That's when I transferred my hand to the dressing gown, thinking I could use it to hide in when he left.'

'And it didn't occur to you that he'd put it back in the wardrobe?' Eydith added for him, to complete the explanation.

'Well... no, that was the flaw in the plan.'

'In your 'masterpiece of synchronisation'?'

'Well, up until then, it was.'

Eydith laughed as quietly as she could. 'Come on, we're going down to the stables.'

'What for?'

'Link has an idea, and it involves you doing some haunting,' she said, figuring he'd warm to the idea.

'What, the wailing and the chain rattling, and everything?' he cooed, predictably. 'I haven't had a good clank for ages. Or a wail, come to think of it.'

Eydith rolled her eyes. For an ex-university professor, he could be pretty dumb at times. But endearingly so, she had to admit to herself, secretly smiling.

Florence returned to the bar to keep an eye on Jook, while Esme watched Dennis's room to warn the others if he emerged.

Eydith, Link and Wimlett met by the stable door, and together they searched for a gap big enough for Wimlett's hand to pass through.

'This place must be watertight,' she complained. 'There are no gaps anywhere.'

'Why don't you just knock?' suggested Link. 'I'm sure he'd let you in. And the idea is to distract him.'

'And scare him,' added Wimlett.

Sprag vibrated disapprovingly in both her hand and her mind at the suggestion that she should go in. But it was probably the best idea.

Eydith took a deep breath and hammered on the door.

'Who is it?' called Psoddoph, a bit fed up that his quiet time had been interrupted.

'It's me. I got you the rope, remember?'

She heard the guard's weary footfalls as he shuffled to the doors. 'What do you want?'

'I just thought you might like some company,' she replied, pushing Link out of view should the door open. 'It must be very dark in there. And...' she paused meaningfully, '... lonely.' When she mentally stepped back and thought about what she was doing, she thought. *This is not me at all. So why am I doing it so well? And quite enjoying it?*

Link had it in mind to ask her a similar couple of questions sometime.

63

The girl was right. It was very dark. Psoddoph couldn't see much at all. There was a narrow beam of light from somewhere above, that was all. He fumbled with the bolts and tried to open one of the doors, then remembered to use the key that Jook had passed to him. He swung the door back just enough to allow her to squeeze through, accompanied by Wimlett's unseen, solid hand. Link hung back out of sight.

Psoddoph wasn't at all sure what was on Eydith's mind. He'd never had a proper girlfriend in all his young life, so he was interested but unsure of himself in this situation. And, whilst she was very pretty, he thought he might have feelings for the girl in bar, Florence.

Though what Eydith intended wasn't at all what he imagined.

They felt their way around the cart to a pile of hay in the corner, and sat down. Wimlett, visible only to Eydith, though not very in this light, kept a close eye on them. 'This is cosy,' said Eydith, shuffling closer. 'What shall we talk about?'

Psoddoph was glad of the cover of darkness, as she wouldn't see his reddening face. He was beginning to think that this was going to go a lot further, and it occurred to him that when the guards' captain had said they would be trained for every situation, that wasn't entirely true.

'Well...' he said, and stopped in mid-sentence as an unseen hand tapped him on the shoulder. He turned and came into rapid contact with a chunk of wood. The next thing he saw was a constellation of stars going nova inside his skull, and some little birds twittering as they circled around outside it. He lost consciousness thinking, *the pictures in the kids' story books were right all along.*

Eydith winced at the thud. 'Oh, dear. I hope you haven't killed him.' She bent forward and checked he was still breathing. 'Is that your idea of scaring him? What did you hit him with?'

'I didn't hit him, I just tapped him on the shoulder.'

'I hit him, mistress,' said Sprag, reminding them of his presence. 'He should sleep for a couple of hours if I judged it right.'

'But how did you manage...' Eydith decided she didn't even want to know. 'Shall I tie him up?'

'No, he won't be going anywhere. Now let the young wizard in.'

Sprag glowed brightly, giving her plenty of light to see her way. From the cart, the Drum glowed too. Bats and ravens left their roosts and sped around her through the opening doors. Link fended them off as he stepped in, then immediately shielded his eyes. 'What's happening? Why's it so bright in here?'

'It's Sprag and the Drum. I think they're too close!' she called.

'Then separate them fast!'

'NO!' shouted Wimlett. 'Let them communicate. The time for battle may be soon!'

Battle? Thought Eydith and Link. Both had not thought of the coming encounter with Dennis in quite those terms.

All three jumped, as the canvas covering the Drum was flung aside.

The light of pure magic flared in the stable, crashing through the spectrum and adding colours that only magic can produce, accompanied by inexplicable sounds audible only to those who could see the cascades of magical light. Outside, the stable yard was in total silence.

A minute passed and the Drum glowed more softly. Only the occasional burst of silver sparks illuminated the darkness. The staff glowed like a white-hot poker.

'You must pick it up, Eydith!' Wimlett's voice seemed to boom in her head. She looked fearfully at the staff.

'Pick it up!' her father's voice boomed again.

'You must be joking! It's seriously hot! Look at it!'

Link nodded vigorously in agreement.

'No!' her father insisted. 'It's only light!'

She reached down, but drew back.

'Pick it up. Now!' he yelled, with a harshness she'd not thought possible from him. 'And take it to the Drum.'

She swallowed hard and made a grab for it. She held it aloft, away from herself. The Drum came alive again and filled the stable with a fresh cascade of light. The staff, not to be outdone, shone like never before. Hugely thankful that there was no searing pain, or smell of burning flesh, she held the staff above her in both hands and solemnly approached the Drum.

She could hear voices in her head, reciting archaic rimes, all speaking at once. Knowledge was passing through her mind from all directions, across ages and cultures and worlds. She was no longer aware of the stable around her, nor of Link or her father. She was bathed in the Light of Knowing and the Wealth of Understanding. Simultaneously, she was drawn into the black velvet night of the Parallel Existence, where the Other Things dwell. But she was filled with the power to keep them at bay. The entities slunk away from her.

Link watched through half closed eyes, and the gaps between his fingers. Eydith was standing with her arms raised, facing the Drum, enveloped in light. He felt Wimlett's presence beside him, and realised he was standing stupidly with his mouth wide open. 'What magic did you put in that Drum?' he asked the ghostly mage.

'I can't take credit for all this. There are spells from all the Archchancellors in our history, circulating in there.' After a moment he added, 'It looks very impressive, though, doesn't it?'

The lights were dimming fast and the magical display was ebbing. Link pushed the doors slightly to allow some daylight in. Eydith dropped to her knees with the staff still held aloft, as if in prayer, or offering the staff to some unseen deity. Finally, Drum and staff dimmed completely and in perfect unison. Link made to approach her, but checked first with Wimlett, who nodded. She seemed dazed. He knelt beside her, unsure what to do next. He touched her arm, and she turned slowly to face him. Her eyes locked on him and he wanted to draw back, but couldn't. Her eyes were ethereal, like golden orbs. They were focused intently on a spot somewhere at the back of his mind, far back, at a place he'd never been to himself, or even suspected existed.

'Hello, Link,' she said, in a voice that came from far away, yet was so intimately close.

'Stop messing about. You're making me nervous.'

The golden orbs dissolved into the midnight blue, flecked with stars that appealed so much to him. 'Are you alright? I've never seen so much magic before in my life!'

'I'm fine. Honestly.' She took a moment to adjust to her surroundings. 'Now, let's grab that Drum and get out of here before that poor man wakes up.'

Link cast an eye over the guard. 'That's quite a bruise he has there. Must remember not to upset Sprag.' He climbed on the cart and took hold of the Drum. He'd only seen it from a distance and hadn't realised how big it was. But it wasn't too heavy. He shifted it to the side of the cart, jumped down and lifted it off.

Wimlett had a thought. 'Put something under the canvas, so they'll think it's still there. It might give us time to get away before they start hunting for it – and for us.'

'A good idea, Father. There must be something around here we can use.'

'Stop wasting time, child. Use your magic!'

She raised the staff and thought Drum-shaped thoughts. Sprag glowed and delivered a charge of blue light. It hit the canvas, which responded by flexing itself into the very shape it was when covering the Drum.

'Good,' said Wimlett, approvingly. 'Now let's get it back to the room.'

The Drum was awkward to carry. Link checked for straps so he could wear it like a drum major, but there were none. He did the best he could, first negotiating the stables, and then the narrow doorways and up the stairs.

Esme was waiting anxiously when Link almost fell into the room and slammed the Drum on the floor. 'Watch out!' she chided him 'You'll break it...' Her voice trailed off when she saw the patched state of the Drum and added, '...again.'

Link dropped into a chair, pleased with himself, and took a proper look at the magical instrument. Eydith joined him, 'It doesn't look like much, does it?' she whispered, in case the Drum heard. 'Look at all those patches.'

Wimlett was appalled. 'What on Crett have they done with it?'

'Never mind that,' said Link. 'We now have the staff *and* the Drum! Doesn't that make you pretty much the most powerful person on the planet, Eydith?!'

Wimlett jumped in quickly to inject some reality. 'Not until her ability catches up with her knowledge, it doesn't. She not even a fully-fledged wizard yet. That takes time. Maybe not so much in her case,' he had to concede. 'But it'll still take time. The staff and Drum will limit what Eydith can do before she's ready. Against Dennis, though, they wouldn't stand much of a chance. They wouldn't resist him for long once he applied himself to the task of tapping their power.'

'Think of all that power in the wrong hands,' Eydith murmured.

'It doesn't bear thinking about,' said Link. 'And that's why we're here, doing what we're doing.'

'Precisely,' said Wimlett, pointedly, and from much experience. 'It's about not letting the wrong people wield power, far more than it's about wielding it for yourself. If you want it for your own ends, then you're one of the people who shouldn't have it.'

Esme had been pacing around the Drum while this conversation was going on, eyeing it suspiciously. 'Is that really it?' she sneered. 'I was expecting something much grander than that.'

'It's more than you can see,' said Wimlett, giving the shorter explanation. 'Now, you all need to get yourselves packed up and out of here before they notice it's gone.'

One of the perks of being a ghost was having no luggage.

⚬⚬⟨⟩⟨⟩⚬⚬

64

Psoddoph came round. He felt his bruise and winced. He rolled over and got to his knees, where he knelt for a moment, trying to remember what had happened.

A young woman came to mind. She had sat down beside him. That was nice. He savoured that for a moment. That was all he could remember. Something, *someone*, must have whacked him on the head. He looked around. She was gone. Obviously. He stood up and looked at the cart. *Phew!* The Drum was still there. He panicked when he patted his tunic and the key wasn't there, but thankfully he found it in the door. He locked it, and slumped down on a bale of straw to rest and let his head clear.

65

Mere yards away, Jook was sitting in the bar of The Magic Finger. He was nursing a large tankard of ale, idly watching passers-by through the window, when the clatter of a plate being slammed onto the table in front of him claimed his attention.

He looked up into Florence's smiling face. 'I think that's what you said, sir. Hanging over the side, is that right?' She licked some gravy off her thumb.

Jook picked up the knife and fork. 'Magic.' He set about carving the steak. Florence wiped her hands on her apron and returned to her station by the bar.

The door to the stairs opened slightly. 'Psst!' her mother's head was just visible through the crack. 'Come on,' she hissed. 'We're going.'

Florence sneaked out and followed Esme up to the room where Eydith, Link and Wimlett were waiting.

'We've got the Drum,' said Eydith, excitedly. 'Get your things, we're leaving.'

'But I haven't had my wages, yet,' she complained.

'And I haven't paid for the room,' said Esme. 'So one balances out the other.'

'That's not fair, Mother,' Florence pouted, as she started collecting her belongings.

'Of course it's fair. No wages, no rent.'

'What I mean is: that means *I'm* paying for the room.'

'So it does. Never mind, girl. These things happen.'

'Don't worry,' said Eydith, quietly, 'I'll make sure you have it. How much would you have been paid?'

'About two silvers.'

Eydith looked away and closed her eyes so that no-one would see them become gold. When she opened them, in a matter of seconds, they were normal, and the deed was done. 'Look in your left pocket.'

Florence felt five metallic discs. When she took them out, her eyes widened. She was holding five golds.

'I can't take these,' she said, offering them back to Eydith. She already had the golds that Wimlett had given her earlier.

'Keep them,' Eydith insisted, and closed her hand over Florence's. 'But keep quiet about them, and don't let anyone but us *see* them.'

'Are you coming?' asked Link, impatiently. 'It'll be getting dark soon.'

'It's dark already,' Esme corrected him.

'I meant in here,' he said, reaching up to douse a torch.

66

In his room across the passageway, Dennis was regaining consciousness. The torch Psoddoph lit had burned low. His head was pounding, and when he tried to move, nothing happened. *I'm paralysed*, he thought. He managed to get his head off the pillow and he could see his pointy-toed boots at the bottom of the bed. He could wriggle his pointy-toed feet, so that was good. He also noticed that for some reason he was tied to the bed. He let his head to flop back on the pillow. 'Oh, bugger,' he said, to himself. 'I hope nothing pleasant happened while I was asleep, and I missed it.'

'Psoddoph!' he yelled, 'Where are you?!'

But Psoddoph was out of earshot, sitting minding the cart, and minding his own poor head.

Dennis shuffled about, but the ropes were not going to slacken or break. 'Can I use magic?' The words fell on no ears but his own. His answer, very civil in the circumstances was, 'Of course you can, Dennis. You're a wizard, aren't you? Yes, of course I am,' he replied, knowingly. His next question was, 'Why do I always talk to myself when I'm on my own?'

'Now... what sort of magic will get this rope off me? What about a *rope untying* spell?' He suggested to himself. *Am I actually being sarcastic to myself?* He wondered. 'No, for an untying spell I need to be able to see the ends to direct them. So, what about burning the rope?'

'Yes. Excellent idea,' he congratulated himself. 'Concentrate. Oh, my head,' he moaned. He picked a spot on the rope, and said a few appropriate words, willing the rope to burn. A small area began smouldering. He stared harder, and added another small incantation. Smoke started to get in his eyes, and he saw a flame flicker into life. He was beginning to regret this course of action. 'What have you done?!' The ropes were burning through, and the bonds were loosening, but his robe was also on fire. Not thinking it through, he craned his head forward and blew hard on the flames. Flames love a good air supply, and they began to grow with the encouragement he was giving them. 'Oh, shit!'

'You need water!' he told himself. 'Lots of it, and bloody quickly by the look of it.' It was difficult to concentrate on anything but his burning clothes. Thankfully, he got his thoughts together and focused them on the cloud of smoke forming above him.

'Please turn into a rain cloud,' he pleaded, and managed to twitch a hand at it, in an abrupt magical gesture. *'Please.'*

The smoke contracted into a solid black storm cloud, and Dennis heaved a sigh of relief – followed swiftly by 'Ouch!' when a small fork of lightning singed his left eyebrow. He didn't think he'd included that in his spell. He hadn't, but the Drum, sensing his magic from the room across the passageway, had. Then, from a childhood habit, he was about to count the seconds until the thunder clap, to tell him know how far away the storm was, but there were none to count. The storm was directly overhead. About four feet overhead. And more rain than he would have thought possible fell from this one small cloud. The Drum couldn't take credit for this, it was all down to his panic overloading the spell. But thankfully, the fire was rapidly extinguished and his hands were free at last.

Across the passageway the Drum glowed, while Sprag remained inert.

Dennis wriggled free and stood up. His head spun for a moment, and he held onto a table to balance himself. By degrees, his head cleared and the vertigo passed. *Oh, shit,* he thought, *look at the state of the bed. What am I going to do about that?* It was severely charred and soaking wet.

His clothes were wet through, too, and sticking to him. Even worse, they were *cold* and wet and sticking to him. His shoes were no better. His dry clothes were in the cart. He opened the door slightly, and peered down the gloomy passageway. There was nobody about, so he squelched as quietly as he could to the top of the stairs, and padded his way down to the small arched door that led out into the cobbled stable yard.

It was almost dark when he tapped on the stable door. The sudden noise roused Psoddoph. 'Who's there?' he asked, defiantly.

'It's me, Dennis,' he hissed through the narrow gap where the doors almost met when they were closed.

'Just a minute, boss,' said the guard, easing himself up off the straw bale, and moving his head about to test how it was.

Dennis hopped from foot to foot outside. 'Oh, do come on, man, for goodness' sake.'

After what seemed forever, which is often the case when you're waiting in cold soggy clothes, Psoddoph slid back the bolts, turned the key, and creaked one of the doors open. As soon as there was room enough, Dennis pushed passed him, almost knocking the guard off his feet. 'You're up, then?' said Psoddoph, a little too chirpily.

'Where are my dry clothes?' Dennis barked, as he stalked to the back of the stable.

'Must be still in the cart, I s'pose, boss. Nobody's touched anything. Is it raining out there?'

'No!' said Dennis, squelching around the cart in the gloomy stable. 'I don't want to talk about it. You can give me the key back now.'

◦━◦◦◦◦◆▶◦◦◦◦━◦

67

A few moments after Dennis left his room, the occupants of the room opposite were ready to leave theirs. Wimlett poked his head through the door and checked that the passageway was clear. He withdrew it and nodded to Link, who opened the door and let the others file past before picking up the Drum. Wimlett hung back to make sure Dennis was still secured in his room. Esme, although she could see Wimlett's imprint on reality, accidently put her hand through him. She shuddered, not realising how cold the space he occupied was, and withdrew it quickly, resisting the urge to say something that might hurt his feelings. She settled for. 'Yuck!' Which did.

'He's not there,' whispered the old mage.

'But he was tied down,' said Florence.

'Well, he's got away.'

Eydith pushed the door open and looked inside. 'There's been a fire in here, the bed's all burnt.'

Link frowned. 'We'd better watch out. If he's gone down to the cart, he may know the Drum's missing by now.'

'I'll go and tell the landlord about the fire,' said Florence. 'Knowing him, he'll want to talk to Dennis about it right away. That might delay him for a while.'

'How on Crett am I going to get this Drum downstairs and through the bar without anyone noticing?' asked Link.

'With some difficulty, I imagine,' replied Esme, helpfully. 'But there are only three people we have to worry about noticing it. No-one else will care.'

'Now Dennis is about, I can't go out the front in full view,' he said. 'I'm taking it back to the room until we sort out how we're going to do this.'

Wimlett agreed with him, and already had an idea. 'Eydith, get what's left of the rope from Dennis's room. I think we can lower the Drum from the window. And with any luck, we can make a dash to Hector's railway before anyone sees us.'

'Is it heavy?' asked Eydith, referring to the Drum.

'No, not really… just awkward,' replied Link. 'I'll lift it onto the ledge. Then I'll go down and wait for you and Florence to lower it down to me.'

'I'll come with you,' said Wimlett, 'and watch the street. Esme, you'd better come as well.'

Esme picked up her bag and followed Link and Wimlett down through the bar, all of them keeping an eye out for Dennis and his guards.

Eydith and Florence held the Drum poised on the brink. It glowed softly, pulsing like a heartbeat. Perhaps it was the fear of what might happen to it if it fell.

Link appeared in the dim lamplight on the street below. The street was helpfully dark and empty. The two girls gripped the rope and eased the Drum over the ledge and down. It weighed very little between them, and they lowered it to the ground without incident. They didn't hang around. They reached the bar just in time to hear the end of a bawdy song from Jook, accompanied by Flint playing the sort-of piano.

Florence looked for the landlord. He was at a table with four mean-looking characters. They seemed deferential towards him, signifying who was boss. She approached them warily, and waited at a respectful distance for someone to notice her. One of the mean characters saw her first and tugged Welt's sleeve. He beckoned her to the table. 'You look troubled, lass. What's the matter?'

Although the landlord was a thug, he always managed to conduct himself in what resembled a gentlemanly manner when ladies were around. Florence told him what she'd seen in Dennis's room, embellishing it as much as she thought she could get away with, and strongly hinting that Dennis might be about to leave without reporting it.

'Right,' he said, grimly. 'Leave it to me.'

She smiled meekly and backed away. She walked casually to the front door where Eydith was waiting, and they both watched the landlord and his four henchmen walk to the stairs and disappear from view.

'Come on!' said Eydith, urgently. 'Let's go.'

On the far side of the bar, Jook and Flint had worked out another routine, and were entertaining the crowd again, allowing Eydith and Florence to slip away unnoticed.

Welt burst into the room that Dennis was using and stopped abruptly when he saw the damage. His colleagues slammed into his back, knocking him across the room and almost through the opposite window. The others landed in a heap by the bed.

'You all right, Welt?' asked one of them, looking for his leader.

'Sheesh!' came the reply. 'It's all wet down here!'

There was silence for a moment. Then one of them, having felt that the pot under the bed was upright, sniffed the water on his hand, said, 'Oh... that's all right, then.'

The four men struggled to their feet. 'Can't see much damage in 'ere, guv,' said another of them.

'Can't see much of anyfing really,' volunteered another. 'Anyone got a torch? The one in here's finished.'

'However did you work that out?' snarled Welt. 'Get the one from the wall in the passage.'

'Oh, right,' said the smallest of the men, when the others all looked at him expectantly. A man called Lofty. A moment later, Lofty was back empty handed.

'Where's the bloody torch, then?' asked Welt.

'It's right where you said, guv.'

'Well, why isn't it here?'

'Er... I can't reach it, guv.'

Welt bordered on a torrent of abuse, but instead sighed and said, 'How about finding something that will allow you to reach it?' his condescension bordering on civility.

Lofty beckoned the tallest member of the group, a long limbed, muscular man called Stubbly, who followed him into the passage. When they reached the torch, Stubbly lifted him up to get it.

Welt held the torch aloft, illuminating the room. 'Oh, no. Look at this!'

'Yeah...' chorused the others.

'Right, lads,' said Welt. 'Let's go and find this Dennis.' He marched back down to the bar.

Jook and Flint were still entertaining the crowd. Welt took in the room. Dennis wasn't there. Jook caught sight of him and noticed the angry look. He stopped singing, and whispered to the troll to keep on sort of playing while he went to find out what was going on.

'Anything wrong, guv?' asked Jook.

'Yeah, I'm looking for that odd type who came in here on a carpet.'

'Haven't seen 'im for ages,' said Jook.

'You were with 'im, weren't you, soldier?'

'Why? What's 'e done?' asked Jook, noncommittally.

'He's set fire to one of my bedrooms.'

'No, never seen 'im before in my life, guv,' said Jook, maintaining eye contact, as he'd heard that was the most convincing way to lie.

Welt didn't know whether to believe him or not. 'He must still be here somewhere. Stubbly! Lofty! Check the stables! You two,' he said, glaring at the others, 'come with me. We'll check outside.'

68

Dennis had changed into his dry clothes, and was feeling better. He'd gotten used to his wet pointy-toed boots now they'd warmed up a bit. He started issuing orders to Psoddoph, who for the sake of decency (and that some things are difficult to un-see) had looked away while his master was changing. 'You go and turf Jook out of the bar. I'll go back to the rooms and make sure we haven't left anything.'

'Are we checking out, boss?' asked the guard.

'That's the general idea.' Dennis made for the door.

But Psoddoph was unsure about leaving the cart.

'We'll only be gone a minute. Don't worry, I've locked it. Just push the main doors shut behind you.' So saying, he marched back up to the room.

As Psoddoph closed the doors, he noticed the PRIVY sign over the door that Dennis went through. It reminded him he needed to pay a visit. He went through and turned aside into the toilet. While standing there, in the comparative silence of his own tinkling, he heard Welt's two henchmen pass through on their way to the stable yard. He didn't know who they were, but he caught enough of their conversation to work it out. With all due haste, he tidied up his loose ends, and made his way to the bar.

The room was filled with smoke smells, and, apart from Jook's singing, and the sort-of accompaniment of the troll, it was fairly quiet. Psoddoph went and sat right in front of his comrade, and mouthed, 'Come on, we're going. Now.'

Jook sped up the song, bringing it to a rather premature ending, a few bars ahead of Flint. He whispered in the troll's ear, 'Carry on partner. I have to go.' Thinking his soloist had gone to relieve himself, the troll rejoined the tune he was sort of playing and the two guards exited through the privy door.

Dennis checked the rooms and satisfied himself that they had left nothing behind. He was about to hurry off, when he noticed the door opposite was slightly ajar. A mixture of curiosity and suspicion took hold of him. Curiosity, because he'd not noticed that door open before, and he'd thought that they were the only guests on that floor. Suspicion, simply because it came naturally to him. He nudged the door with his pointy-toed boot.

The place was empty so he stepped in. And could not believe what he saw in the dim light from the passageway. The very prize he'd been searching for.

The staff!

It was propped against the wall by the fireplace. Totally unattended. He took a step towards it, then halted. *Was this a trap? It was too easy.* How could it be right there as if waiting for him? That wasn't the way things usually worked for him. But then it all came back to him. *Good grief! That dotty old woman, the palm-reader, was right! The staff was 'on the other side', just as she'd said.* And from his room, it was on the other side 'of a building', on the other side 'of a passageway', and on the other side 'of a room'. *Remarkable!* For a silly moment he felt he should have paid her more.

No-one was about. Not believing his luck, he rushed in and grabbed it, then ran as fast as he could down the narrow steps at the other end of the passage. His route was dimly lit by almost-spent candles, some of which flickered out as he swept by. In his haste to get away, he got a little lost. The passage became narrower, until he came to a tiny door that was so low, he practically had to crawl through. He could hear the sound of the sort-of piano, and the drone of voices. He stood up to find himself surrounded by broken tables and chairs, and realised he was in the corner of the bar where all the wrecked furniture had been stacked after the brawl a couple of days ago.

Just as he was about to step into the open, the landlord and two of his ruffians came in. They went storming upstairs, followed by two other odd-looking characters who'd entered through the privy door.

He knows, Dennis thought. And when they'd gone, he moved to that same side door and headed through to the stable. Once there, he swung both doors back as far as they would go. 'Psoddoph! Jook!' he yelled, urgently.

'But I've only just got 'ere, boss,' Jook moaned from the back stable, misunderstanding.

'No, idiot!' he hissed. 'Are you both there?'

'Yes, boss. We're here,' they droned in unison.

Dennis joined them. 'Good! Get this door open wide and get on the carpet before the landlord and his men get here!'

'Oh,' said Psoddoph. 'They know what you've done, then.'

'Quiet, and get on the cart. I won't tell you again.'

'We're on it, boss,' said Jook.

Dennis climbed onto the seat, and muttered, 'Carpet... up, please.' The carpet rose, and he asked it to go backwards. The carpet went forward. At least he'd remembered which way round it was. He negotiated the area outside the stalls, only to find that the main doors into the yard were closing in front of him. Welt and his gang had found them. Their escape route was well and truly cut off. He requested the carpet to stop, as politely as he could through gritted teeth.

The carpet hovered.

Dennis thought.

Jook and Psoddoph each picked up a crossbow. Judging by the thunderous looks on the five faces looking up at them, they all thought it fair to assume that explanations were out of the question.

The wizard looked up at the roof. There was no way through that. It was easy from the other side. Jook could bear testimony to that. Dennis picked up the recently acquired staff. He had a notion that he might think more clearly with a powerful staff in his hand. But before he could settle in for a really good think, the threats and abuse started from Welt and his gang.

'You can't escape. You might as well come down,' said Welt, loudly and without menace. Which seemed somehow more menacing.

'Yeah... down,' agreed a thick voice from somewhere in the gloom.

'Open the doors so we can see you properly!' Dennis called back.

This prompted a scraping sound, as Jook struck a match and held it up. 'That any better, boss?'

'You fool,' Dennis hissed. 'Put it out. I want to see *them* – not let them see us!'

'Okay, boss,' said Jook. He dropped the match over the edge. It didn't go out. It set fire to the stalks of dry straw that littered the stable floor. Fanned by the draught coming under the doors, the flames spread rapidly in all directions. While it burned brightly and quickly, it wasn't doing any harm. There wasn't enough loose straw in any one place to sustain a flame longer than a few seconds. But sparks were drifting dangerously into the air.

The men on the floor were flailing their arms, knocking sparks from their clothes and causing tiny points of red light to go dancing and swirling up to the rafters, where the carpet was hovering out of the gang's reach.

It was getting smoky up there. Dennis and the guards were finding it difficult to breathe.

'Can't you do something, boss?' asked Psoddoph. 'Magically, say?'

Dennis stood up huffily and threw his hands up, remembering his last performance as a firefighter hadn't gone so well. 'I'm thinking, all right?' There was a clattering sound from above them.

'Great, boss,' said Jook. 'That's done the trick.'

Dennis had raised his hands so abruptly, that the staff he was clutching had inadvertently punched a hole in the roof. Smoke was funnelling out. But it was also dragging the sparks up around them.

'I think we'd better move, boss,' Psoddoph suggested, strongly, 'before we all go up in smoke.'

Dennis didn't dwell on a lengthy reply. He moved the carpet to a safe distance from the hole.

'Oi!' shouted Welt. 'Ain't you satisfied with setting fire to one of my bedrooms? Are you trying to burn the bloody stables down as well, now?'

'Oh, shit,' muttered Dennis. 'Well, at least we know for certain he knows about that.'

'Course 'e knows, boss,' said Jook, 'some bugger's grassed you up, I reckon.'

Dennis was beginning to panic... No, he was beginning to lose patience. Which could mean that others *might* need to panic. Which was how he was trying to sell it to himself. He looked down at the gang. 'Open the doors!' he demanded. 'Or, you'll be sorry!'

There was a moment's silence, which was followed by the swishing sound of swords being drawn.

'Swords won't be of any use to you!' crowed Dennis. 'My men are armed with the latest multi-bolt crossbows, or whatever they call them.'

'Psst,' said Jook, close to Dennis's ear. 'That's not quite right.'

'Well, I don't know *exactly* what you call them. This is hardly the time...'

'No, what I mean is: we've got the crossbows...'

'Yes?'

'But we can't find the bolt things.'

Dennis slumped. He was at a loss, for the moment.

'What's the matter, lads?' mocked Welt. 'Why don't you shoot us with your crossbows? Not having trouble finding the arrowy things, are we?' he added, scornfully.

'Because it's too soddin' dark!' Jook yelled back.

'Oh, no it isn't!'

'Oh, yes, it is!' Jook insisted.

'It's not that at all. It's because *you don't have the arrowy things.* We've got them!

'Oh, no,' moaned Psoddoph. 'They've got a key. They must've taken them when I went to get Jook.'

'You'll have to use your highly polished sword, then, won't you?' snapped Dennis.

'I spent hours cleaning that. I'm not getting blood all over it. Take us down, please,' Psoddoph said, politely, addressing the carpet. Then, as they began to lower, he unexpectedly snatched the staff from Dennis's hand.

Dennis was aghast. He hadn't issued any commands, but the carpet was descending anyway. He'd not seen any point in enabling the carpet's voice-recognition option mentioned in the manual. Till now, that was.

'Come on, Jook,' said Psoddoph. 'Time to earn our keep.'

Suddenly the air filled with the strange and unexpected sound of swords bending and snapping, and clattering to the ground as they were parried and hit by a magical staff in the hands of someone who only knew how use it as a weapon. He'd been handy with the quarterstaff in his teens. Jook waded in with both gauntleted fists flying, while Dennis crouched under the cart trying to think of a spell that would give them some light. He couldn't risk using magic offensively in this dark and confined space, because he might hurt one of the guards, or worse, himself – especially if he hit the staff and it reacted.

He closed his ears to the grunts, and the thumping of fists and staff, and concentrated on making light. He summoned a little magic to produce just a little light, and a small candle appeared on the wall. 'Oh, good,' he whispered. 'Now just a bit bigger, please, if you don't mind.' He added a minor incantation and the candle became a torch, burning brighter.

He could see his guards in action. And from memory, this was the first time. He was impressed; they were quite good, considering they were outnumbered more than two to one. He decided to even the odds. *Here's a little spell I've always wanted to try.* Light flashed from his fingertips, hitting the air beside the guards, and mirror images of Jook and Psoddoph appeared, standing shoulder to shoulder. Welt was now faced with two of each, and a wizard.

From the point of view of the villains, whose line of work usually involved no more than robbery with some low-key threats and abuse, this was no longer a healthy scenario. Welt decided to retreat. His henchmen, although usually slower of thought, were already backing towards the doors. He found himself dealing with the four guards on his own. He threw his dagger at one of the replicas and ran.

The five villains hit the doors at the same time, knocking them wide open as they tumbled out into the yard. The replicas of Jook and Psoddoph gave chase, giving the real guards time to clamber back onto the carpet, and Dennis time to manoeuvre it out and into the sky. Welt and his cronies scurried back to the bar to nurse their wounds and their hurt pride, and to down a long drink or two. The replica guards faded when Dennis no longer concentrated on them – which became increasingly impossible once they were out of his sight – and the two real ones sat on the edge of the carpet, breathing heavily.

Dennis guided the carpet out over the rooftops, looking for somewhere to set it down. He wasn't at all happy about flying at night.

69

'Are you sure this is the right way?' asked Esme, of anyone who might be listening. 'Do you know where you're going?'

'It's difficult to tell in the dark,' replied Eydith. 'I think we'd better find an inn to stay until morning.'

Wimlett agreed. 'This place is barely safe in daylight. I can't imagine what it's like at night.'

Florence saw a shape move into the shadows ahead of them, and whispered, 'I think we're about to find out.'

'Father,' whispered Eydith. 'Some of your ghostly stuff could be handy here.'

'Should be interesting,' said Wimlett, moving ahead of them.

A tall shape stepped out of the shadows in front of them. They heard the swishing sound of a sword being unsheathed. The streetlight glinted off its razor-sharp edges as the handler moved it in loose circles in front of them.

'I'll take all your valuables, please,' said the figure, quietly and assertively.

'No, I don't think you will,' whispered Wimlett, in the would-be robber's ear. And by way of confirmation, a disembodied hand was holding the man's own knife at his throat.

'Er... let's not be too hasty, friend,' said the figure. 'Perhaps we could discuss this...'

'Yes, *friend*,' answered Eydith. 'And at the end of this discussion, perhaps we'll take all *your* valuables.'

'Yeah,' Esme piped up, in her best gangster voice (which was also her worst). 'How does that grab yuh?'

'Er... no. I don't think that's what I had in mind,' said the young man, with no fondness for role reversal. 'Perhaps I could relieve you of just a *few* of your valuables, then? Come on, that's how this is supposed to work.'

'You can't relieve us of anything,' retorted Eydith. 'You don't appear to grasp the situation. We have the upper hand. My father has your own knife pressed against your throat.'

'Yes... it had come to my attention, miss. But *I am* the robber here, not you.'

'Well, you're not very good at it are you?'

'Well, no... Not yet, I suppose. I'm still practising, you see.' He swallowed hard, and felt the point of the knife prick his throat.

'Have you been practising long?' asked Eydith.

'What time is it?'

'Just after midnight, I think.'

'That makes it about half an hour, then.'

Wimlett lowered the knife, and the young man relaxed slightly.

'Look,' said Florence. 'We're not giving you anything, so you might as well go home.'

'I can't do that,' he said, nervously. 'If I go home with nothing, my mum won't half be cross, and I won't get any supper.'

Eydith smiled and pointed her hand at the road beside him. A beam of light shot from her fingers creating a small explosion and a shower of sparks near his feet. The figure spun on his toes and took off down the nearest alley. 'MUM!'

'I've seen her do worse trying to light the fire in her room,' remarked Link, drolly, as he picked up the Drum.

'Why did you let him go?' asked Esme. 'He's bound to tell others we're here... all alone... in the streets, at midnight.'

'He was so young,' Eydith replied. 'And, anyway, he'll be in enough trouble without any help from me. And I should think the only people he'd be sending after us would be his worst enemies.'

'Did you pick up your staff, Mother?' asked Florence, not seeing it.

Esme looked concerned. 'No, I thought you had it. You were the last one out.'

'I haven't got it!' said Florence.

'Are you sure?'

'Mother, it's *five* feet long!'

'Don't make excuses, girl!' snapped Esme.

'Stop bickering, you two' said Eydith.

'You don't understand, Eydith,' said Florence, gravely. 'That staff is not as harmless as you might think. It's more than just a witch's broomstick. In fact, although mother coaxes it into flying sometimes, it's not a broomstick at all. It has hardly any powers, but it is possessed.'

'Only a small demon,' Esme cut in 'A lippy little whatnot, too. But that's not the point.'

'We can't go back for it,' said Eydith. 'Dennis could be looking for us by now. He's not slow at putting two and two together.'

Mother and daughter went quiet. Florence was glad of her cousin's intervention. But Esme was sulking.

Consoling her, Eydith said, 'I'm sure Sprag can locate it for you. And we can get it back as soon as the opportunity arises.'

Esme grunted something best not heard.

Wimlett walked ahead of the party, to give them an early warning of anything untoward that might lie ahead. They trekked uneventfully for half an hour, or more. On the outskirts of the city they saw the lights from Hector's platform glowing dimly in the distance.

Link was flagging from carrying the Drum. 'How are you doing?' asked Eydith.

'It gets heavier the further I carry it,' sighed Link.

'Where are we going?' asked Florence, a little further along the road.

'To Hector's railway, of course,' Eydith replied.

'No, after that.'

'Back to Kra-Pton.'

'Is that wise?' asked Florence, doubtfully.

'We have to face Dennis sometime,' said Eydith. 'And that's where he'll be headed.'

'Yeah,' agreed link, 'He can't stay away from Havrapsor too much longer. He'll have stuff to do piling up on his desk, I'm sure. Not that he does that much. From what I hear, he's a master of delegation.'

'Do you know, Florence, he had me escorted out of the university?'

'Women aren't allowed in. Though, thinking about it, I'm sure women can visit. So, why ever did he make you leave?'

'I told him I wanted to be a wizard. And I said my father was a wizard, so according to the rules of admissions, I should be let in, woman or not. I've read them carefully, and they say, "The *child* of a wizard should be admitted" – No mention of boy or girl.' She paused for a moment, when something else occurred to her. 'Is your father a wizard, as well, Florence? If he is, then maybe we can both get in?'

Florence chose not to answer.

So Eydith carried on. 'Dennis took the Archchancellorship by corruption and threats. We know that. He blackened my father's name, too.'

'Not that everyone believed him,' Link interrupted quickly, and was rewarded with half a smile from Eydith.

Her eyes glowed with anger, as she thought of the gross injustice of it. 'Someone's got to stand up to him. He's got to go!'

'Do you really think we can do it?' Florence asked, not sounding too sure.

'I have the staff. And I have the Drum,' Eydith replied.

'Dennis may well have my mother's staff by now. And if so, he may discover he has a little demonic help,' Florence reminded her.

'I'm trying not to think about that,' said Eydith.

'Well, p'raps you should,' interrupted Esme, still a bit crotchety about the missing staff. She was walking a few steps behind, listening to the conversation. 'Though good luck to him getting help from that little b...'

'Mother!'

'And there's still a chance he may not realise it,' said Eydith.

Wimlett could hear them, too, and waited for them so he could join in. 'Dennis will be furious when he knows he's lost the Drum. He'll be questioning everyone in sight. And he'll work it out, you can be sure. Then he'll be after us.'

'But surely he won't have enough power to harm us without the Drum?' Eydith tried, hopefully.

'I know the Drum,' said Wimlett. 'And on its own it might have been more of a hindrance to him. And I think I know Dennis well enough to know that he'll work out what that staff is and what it can do. With access to a demon, he might be reckless enough to call on the Powers from the other Dimensions to get what he wants,' said Wimlett, gravely.

'Father, I'm sure I have enough power to stop him now,' Eydith insisted.

'You're still learning. You may have more power,' said Wimlett, 'but Dennis has more experience. And a ruthless streak. So beware.'

'Let's not forget you also have help,' said Link.

'Yes, I have all of you,' said Eydith, indicating them, with a sweep of her hand.

'And there's also a whole university full of wizards who will probably help,' said Link. 'If we get there and enlist them before Dennis gets back. Most of them will be pleased to see the back of him.'

'Dennis has a flying carpet,' Florence reminded them. 'He'll get there first.'

'I doubt that he'll want to fly at night,' said Eydith. 'So he probably won't get going till the morning.'

'I hope so,' said Florence, and shivered, not at the cool night air, but at the thought of Dennis roaming the skies looking for them. 'It's so open here. If it was daylight, we'd be seen easily from up there. At least we'll be safe on the train.'

70

Dennis and the guards flew slowly and cautiously for some time. Below them, all that was visible in the light of the half-moon was rooftops, and more rooftops.

'Why don't you head out into the country, boss?' asked Psoddoph. 'We'll be up 'ere till dawn at this rate.'

'Yeah,' moaned Jook. 'I don't like it up 'ere in the dark, either.'

Dennis didn't argue for once. He let the carpet drift across the city limits. He thought they weren't far from the river, where he could set it down for the night. They flew on but the river was nowhere in sight. He remembered it was full of all manner of things which put a dull film over it, making it unreflective even in daylight. That would explain why he couldn't see it below.

It didn't occur to him that he was flying in entirely the wrong direction.

The guards watched the dark landscape creep past below, anxiously straining their eyes for somewhere to land. They kept pointing out possible places, but Dennis paid them no heed. In his mind, he knew that the river was down there somewhere, and just because he couldn't see it, didn't mean it wasn't there. His flew closer to the ground, and more slowly. He didn't want to land in the stretch of mud along the riverbanks. After a while, he had an idea.

'Jook!' he called. 'I need to know if we're over firm ground. See if you can lean out and pick up a rock, will you?'

'Okay, boss,' Jook obliged. He laid belly down on the edge of the carpet, trailing his hand over the side.

'Got one yet?' asked Dennis.

'Not yet, boss. How big do you want it?'

'As big as you can manage.'

'Right.' He leaned out further. Just ahead, in the gloom, he saw a pointed stone, about twice the size of his fist. He made ready to grab it. Next moment, it was right there. He grabbed it firmly and the carpet slid out from under him. He found himself lying flat in the dust, clutching a pointy stone that was still in the ground. He tried to lift it, but it wouldn't budge. He scooped the dirt from around it, only to discover that the more he dug, the more rock there was. Unknown to him, he was trying to uncover a mountain that had become progressively covered in sand, shale and earth from the beginning of time. It wouldn't budge, so he picked up another stone, scrambled to his feet and chased after the carpet. 'Come back, boss. I've got one!'

Dennis turned the carpet around, and coasted noiselessly back. 'It doesn't matter now,' he muttered. 'I was going to drop it to see if it sank or made a splash,' he added, 'But it seems we've dropped *you* and you didn't sink or splash, so I have my answer.'

Jook stamped on the ground. 'Pretty firm 'ere, boss.'

'I know.' Dennis sighed heavily. 'I know. I really should have shoved you over the side in the first place.'

Dennis landed the carpet. The weight of the wagon made no impression on the ground. He sat down on the edge of the carpet with Psoddoph beside him.

'What now, boss?' asked Jook.

'We wait,' Dennis replied.

'All right… what for?'

'Daylight, of course. What else would we wait for – Winter Solstice?'

'Oh,' said Jook. 'Daylight. That long.'

'Look' – Dennis rounded on them, not letting on that he agreed – 'You're the ones who wanted to stop. So, shut up now, and take a nap, or something.'

Jook didn't feel like taking a nap. He sat down in the dirt and looked around in the semi-darkness for something to do. The only things around were stones, pebbles and rocks. He put a stone in front him and tried to balance another on it. It slid off. He tried another, with the same result. There was a small bush a few feet away, and he thought it might be more amusing to throw stones at that. He threw one, hitting it first time, and was pleased with himself, so he threw another. It was too easy. He wanted something smaller to aim at. Or a larger rock to throw.

In the shadows was a rock, half the size of a football. As soon as he grabbed it he realised his mistake. It was soft and it gave off a horrible smell. 'Yuck!' It was beginning to hurt. He tried to shake it off his fingers. He wasn't sure if it was biting or stinging – though the debate was short and academic. Eventually he shook it free and whatever it was scampered to safety under the bushes.

Not knowing what had attacked him, Jook had a dilemma. Did he put his fingers in his mouth? Or wipe them down his clothes?

Dennis sniffed the air. 'I think I smell a Lesser Spotted Bog-Trotter,' he announced. 'Anybody see it?'

'So that's what it was,' said Jook. 'It went under that bush.'

'You mean you saw it?' said Dennis.

'It bit me on the 'and, boss,' Jook whined. 'It 'ad me fingers. Not poisonous, is it?'

'That depends. Well, don't just sit there, go and find it,' Dennis ordered. 'They're delicious.'

'I'd rather not, boss. I'm not *that* hungry,' said Jook, adding, 'and what do you mean, it depends?!'

'They're poisonous in their mating season, that's all. You should be alright.'

'Well, thanks for nothing,' said Jook, sullenly, inspecting his fingers.

'Oh, is *that* what that smell is?' said Psoddoph.

'Of course,' replied Dennis. 'You didn't think it was *me*, did you?'

'No, boss. But I don't think I could eat anything that smells as bad as that.'

'Whatever gave the idea I was going to share?'

'In that case I'll go look for it, shall I?'

'Don't bother,' sighed Dennis. 'The moment has passed.'

They all settled down again. Jook had the stinging sensation in his hand and a bad smell on his fingers. So, there being nothing else, he wiped it on a stone by his foot. Which wriggled and clamped onto him before dropping to the dirt and running back under the bush. He yelped and cursed, and ran at the bush and trampled it flat. But the creature was long gone. He heard its distant squeals mocking him.

The three men sat in silence dozing fitfully for the next few hours waiting for the sun to rise.

At first light, Dennis stirred and picked up the staff he'd stolen from Esme's room and stared at it. As he did so, his eyes widened and his jaw dropped. He caught his breath as it dawned on him that he now had exactly what he wanted. Where on Crett had his brains been all this while! *The Staff and the Drum!* He stood up quickly. 'Come on!' he announced enthusiastically to his bleary-eyed companions, 'We're going home!'

Psoddoph yawned, and stretched lazily. 'What's the sudden rush, boss?'

'Don't you see?' said Dennis, holding the staff in one hand and pointing at the outline on the cart with the other. 'Staff and Drum!'

The two guards were suddenly wide awake. 'It's bonus time!' they cried merrily together.

'What?' said Dennis. 'Oh… yes. We'll talk about that later.'

'How much later, boss?' asked Jook, not wishing to be too blunt.

'When we get back to the university.'

'Right,' said Psoddoph. 'Let's go!'

Dennis took the carpet up into the early morning sky. 'Can either of you see anything that looks like a river?'

'No, boss,' Jook replied, shielding his eyes and wincing when some tooth-shaped marks on the side of his finger touched his forehead. And was that his imagination, or did he hear some distant squeals of delight at that moment.

'I think it's on the other side of the city,' said Psoddoph. 'Back that way.'

Taking his bearings, and conceding the guard was probably right, without actually saying so, the wizard turned the carpet. There was an urgency about the way he snapped out his requests now, and he had an air of confidence that had been lacking these last few weeks. They held him in high respect, generally speaking, for his position and power, and as the one who held the purse-strings and would *eventually* pay their wages. But for once it was rare and good to have him filled with bonhomie towards them.

It wouldn't last. Sooner or later, the meaner Dennis would resurface.

They flew back over Prossill, and Jook spotted the dome of the Town Hall. 'Do you think that old lady's dog's any better, yet?' Psoddoph wondered aloud.

'Hope so,' said Jook. 'Might teach the little bugger a lesson, though, next time someone knocks on the door,' he added, smirking.

'Would you like to go down and ask?' suggested Dennis, affably.

'Okay, boss,' replied Jook. 'That would be a nice gesture.'

'Well, forget it!' snapped Dennis, back in character. 'This flight's non-stop to Kra-Pton. We don't stop for anything.'

'Cheers,' said Jook, ruefully, and then, 'But can you slow down a bit, boss?'

'What for?' Dennis replied, sharply.

'I can't keep me match alight at this speed.'

'That'll save you some smokes then, won't it? We hold this speed.'

Psoddoph unsheathed his sword to clean it. It helped him think. He noticed a few nicks and a couple of blood stains from the fight in the stable. He polished vigorously, but the nicks would be a job for the blacksmith. He thought about asking if they got paid expenses, but it didn't seem like the right moment.

'There's the river!' shouted Jook, pointing at the brown, muddy ribbon that wound its way across the Plain. Dennis made a slight adjustment to the carpet's flight path and leaned back, smugly.

71

'Look! There's Hector!' Eydith shouted, and began running towards the staging that served as a platform.

Hector heard her and turned. His eyes shone, and his lips parted in a broad smile, revealing his magnificent white teeth. 'Eydith!' his voice boomed out, 'And Link! You just made it. We leave in five minutes.'

'It's good to see you again,' said Eydith, returning his smile.

'You've got company, I see,' he boomed.

'This is my cousin, Florence. And this is her mother, Esme.'

Hector touched his peaked cap, in salutation. 'Hello, Florence and Aunt Esme.'

Esme cringed. She hated that, but, in this case, she took it in good humour. She instantly liked the look of this man. She smiled sweetly, acknowledging him.

Hector turned his attention to Link. 'Joined a band?' he asked, jovially.

'Oh, this?' said Link, lowering the Drum to the ground. 'No, just taking it back where it belongs.'

'Is it all right if we take it on board?' asked Eydith.

'Of course. But it'll cost you one of those rides I owe you.' Hector only half-smiled as he said it, confirming what his tone had already conveyed: that he was not being unfair, just properly business-like. He seemed keen to teach Link these things.

'I wouldn't have it any other way. But I insist on paying for Esme and Florence,' she said, flatly.

Hector rubbed the back of his head. 'I thought you might say that, but I don't know how much would be appropriate for my friends – or, rather, friends of my friends.' He thought about it. 'What about one silver... each?'

Eydith felt generous and gave him two each.

Hector considered this. 'How can I refuse? But now I insist that you use my carriage.'

'Agreed,' said Esme, quickly, before anyone could argue.

The business done, the four of them and the invisible Wimlett, who always travelled free, followed Hector up to the carriage and climbed aboard. Eydith considered paying her father's fare, but thought she would spare Hector the conundrum.

'This is nice,' Esme remarked, admiring the décor. Florence agreed and sat in a large armchair by a window.

'Make yourselves comfortable,' said Hector. 'I'll be back in a couple of minutes.' He stepped off the carriage and walked along to the engine, which was belching smoke and building up a head of steam in readiness for departure. Shortly after, the whistle shrilled, and the train began to gather speed.

Hector was soon back, and he was looking for Link.

'I've been looking forward to seeing you again,' he said, very pleased, and showing those excellent teeth again. 'Would you mind if I borrowed him for a moment?' he asked Eydith.

'No, of course not,' she replied, deciding not to comment on her implied possession of him.

Link got up. 'What can I do for you?'

'I've something to show you in the workshop.'

Before he left, Link whispered to Eydith, 'Keep an eye on the Drum.' He'd become rather protective of it after carrying it so far. Though she hardly needed reminding.

The two men entered Hector's unique mobile workshop, which doubled as his research and development office. He motioned Link to sit. Spread across the centre table was a map showing the land East of Prossill, stretching across the Tong Plain, past Kra-Pton and further east into the Land of Corin.

'What do you think?' asked Hector.

'I think it's a map,' said Link, not sure what Hector expected him to say.

'So far, so good. I see you haven't lost your powers of observation,' said the big man. 'But it's more than that. See this red line from Prossill to here?'

Link craned forward to see where Hector was pointing.

'The blue line is my existing railway,' – he traced it with his finger – 'the red is where I propose to extend it.'

'Phew!' whistled Link. 'That'll take an age.'

'A year or two, at least. I'll need assistance if I'm going to do it any quicker,' said Hector, his tone becoming more serious.

'Can't help you there,' said Link, good humouredly. 'I'm not much good with hammers and nails and bits of wood.'

'If only it were that simple.' Hector leaned back from the table, straightened to his full height, and sighed deeply. It was the first time Link had noticed that his carriage was a little higher than the rest. 'What I need from someone like you, is ideas, not muscle.'

Link studied the map and became a little more business-like. 'It's certainly a bigger job than the line you've already done.'

Hector ran his pencil along the blue line to a point where it crossed a broader blue line. 'I can get the track as far as here without a problem, but this is a wide river.'

'And you'll need a lot of materials for a bridge strong enough to take a train.'

'My calculations show that even my best designs would buckle under the weight. And if I use iron, the temperature changes in the area between day and night are significant, and the stresses could warp the bridge and the track. If I use wood, the beams will have to be enormous, and the lowest ones will rot in a few years because the river floods regularly.'

'What's the ground like by the river?'

Hector had examined it and it wasn't too solid. He pointed his pencil at a place further up the river. 'There's a quarry there,' he said. 'Where I can get stone to lay a foundation on either side to build from.'

'There's your answer.' Link smiled, triumphantly. 'Don't just build the foundations from stone, build the whole thing from stone!'

Hector wasn't sure. 'That's alright for footbridges. But trains, I don't think so.'

Link was more than sure. 'You've got so fixed on the idea of using metal and timber, because that's how you've built your railway, that you're missing the obvious. And don't think small stone blocks for footbridges – think big stone blocks for a railway bridge! The quarry must be able to cut big ones. Stones are as strong as anything.'

Hector sat back in his chair. 'And it doesn't warp or rot,'   he said, the light coming on at last. He'd dismissed stone as too old-fashioned for his modern railway, but... 'But that means I've got to drag huge, heavy stones along this road.'

'Build a boat!'

'A boat?' echoed Hector.

'You can bring the stones down from the quarry on a barge.'

'Well... I hadn't thought of that, I must say,' enthused Hector. 'I knew you'd come up with something, my boy. These things need younger brains sometimes.'

Hector was undoubtedly an excellent engineer, but Link wondered sometimes where he was when the common sense was handed out. But maybe, as the man said, is was more a matter of bringing fresh brains to a situation.

'Link, I'll give some thought to designing it now! Thanks. Would you like a drink?'

'No,' replied Link, holding up a hand. 'Not just now.' He turned to leave, but remembered something else. 'By the way, how's your mobile privy coming along?'

'Works a treat,' said Hector, beaming. 'There are two on the train now, and I've redesigned the new carriages with one at each end.'

'You'll need them if you take the track all the way to Corin,' commented Link. 'Or you'll be making lots of stops along the way.' Mention of privies made him suddenly uncomfortable. He glanced around. 'Where's the nearest one?'

'Right behind me.' Hector beamed and indicated a newly-created door. His personal privy.

'But of course,' said Link, approvingly.

72

'Where's that young man of yours got to, Eydith?' asked Esme.

'Sorting out some ambitious scheme with Hector, I expect,' she replied. 'He'll be back soon.' She smiled to herself at what Esme had just called him.

Link came back on cue and sat beside her. 'Everything alright?' he asked.

'Yes, fine,' they chorused.

'Good.' He glanced around, reassuring himself that the Drum and Sprag were there. The Drum had a disembodied hand resting on it. And the staff was leaning against the carriage wall beside Eydith.

She happened to glance out of the window at that moment, and, to her surprise and dismay, she saw a dark, oblong shape drifting overhead, overtaking the train. 'Oh, no! Look! Up there!' She pointed, animatedly. 'That has to be Dennis!'

They crowded at the window on her side.

'Damn,' breathed Link. 'He'll be there long before us.'

'With the wrong staff and no Drum,' observed Wimlett, allowing himself a little chuckle.

'Do you think he knows, yet?' said Florence.

'I doubt it. If he knew that, he'd probably have worked it out that the culprits had escaped on this train out of Prossill, and he'd be in hot pursuit. The fact that he's flown right over us means he thinks he's won.'

They watched in silence as the carpet disappeared from view up ahead.

73

'Did you see that thing down there?' asked Jook.

'Some new-fangled travelling contraption, I've heard talk of,' said Dennis.

'Makes a lot of smoke,' remarked Psoddoph. 'Worse than dragons.'

'Almost worse than Jook,' said Dennis, not missing an opportunity to get a dig in about his smoking habit.

'Hah,' snorted Jook. 'Don't think it'll catch on,'

'Nah,' agreed Psoddoph, sheathing his sword.

Dennis steered the carpet dead ahead, quietly musing how he was going to rule Kermells Tong. His favourite subject. The guards watched the horizon, and yawned occasionally. A rush of air made the carpet rock slightly.

Jook couldn't believe his eyes. 'Did you see that? – a donkey with its arse on fire?'

'Pulling a cart with no wheels?' asked Psoddoph.

'Yeah.'

Psoddoph considered that for a moment. Only crazy people saw things like that. 'No. I didn't see nothing.'

'Me neither,' said Jook, quickly.

'I caught sight of a dragon, though,' said Psoddoph, looking deadly serious.

'Where? Where? Where?' said Jook, frantically scanning the sky in all directions.

'Relax. Only kidding.'

'Well don't!' interrupted Dennis. 'Not about things like that!'

'No, boss,' came the mumbled reply.

That had the effect Dennis desired... silence. Just the sound of the breeze in the treetops, which he would one day own. *Can you own a breeze?* he wondered.

They all maintained silence for some hours, until Jook broke it, asking casually, 'Are we flying back across the desert, boss?'

Dennis made a big show of looking over the edge. 'No,' he replied, eventually, and with sarcasm so heavy it was a wonder the carpet stayed aloft. 'Unless it has turned green.'

'Okay, *will* we be flying over the desert?'

'No. We'll be following the track to the end, staying south of the desert. I might stop for an hour then, before we cross the Tong Plain. Hopefully we'll be the other side of Snake River, the day after tomorrow.'

'Thanks, boss,' they chorused. 'That soon. Wow.'

None of the men had fully appreciated till now how much faster the carpet was compared with the horses and cart they'd used on the outward journey. They were all agreeably surprised when they saw the end of the railway track ahead. Dennis took the carpet lower. From this height, he could better make out the sheds and other buildings that radiated from the end of the track. He had some unfinished business to take care of nearby.

He requested the carpet to rise, for a wider view. And when they flew passed the end of the depot, Jook saw it first.

'Look, boss. There's that little house made of sweets and stuff.'

Dennis seemed to have reserved his meanest scowl for this very moment. A couple of frolicking rabbits, who'd been curiously watching the carpet approach, saw him and went racing to the bottom of the deepest burrow to hand.

Dennis stepped off while the carpet was still a couple of feet from the ground, and marched into the garden.

'Oh, no,' sighed Psoddoph. 'He's after that bloody gnome again!'

They trotted after him.

The gnomes had seen the carpet land and had run to the cover of Esme's ale cellar.

Seeing no gnomes in the garden, Dennis rushed around to the green wooden door and banged on it with the staff. 'It's me, gnome! You'd better come out or I'll level the place to the ground!' There was no reply. He rapped on the door again. 'Do you hear me, gnome? It's me, Dennis! The last thing you'll ever see!'

He waited again for a reply. All he got was a stifled belch, followed by a giggle. Then another giggle, and another, until someone said, 'Shh!'

Psoddoph touched Dennis's arm. 'I think they're all in there, boss.'

Dennis slammed the staff down and cursed.

'No good losing your temper, boss,' said Psoddoph, soothingly.

'*And why not,*' said Dennis, a tear welling up in his eyes. 'I have just smashed this staff down on my foot.' He raised it and began working it round in painful circles. 'Get me the Drum,' he ordered, 'I'm going to give the Drum and staff their first outing together under my control.'

Jook sauntered round to the front of the cottage, breaking a piece of marzipan off the roof as he went by. He paused to watch it repair itself. *Magic. If it can do that,* he wondered, *why does the sign tell you not to eat it?* He decided not to hang about to find out. Just in case. At the cart, he lifted the canvas to find a shimmering drum-shaped nothingness. He stared at it, dumbfounded, for a full minute, and let the enormity of the situation dawn. He even feared it might be magical revenge for eating a piece of roof. But that was not an explanation he was about to offer Dennis! He now had to pluck up the courage to go back and face his master.

'Where is it, boss?' he asked, trying an approach that didn't implicate him.

'The Drum?' said Dennis, curtly. 'In the cart, of course, man. Under the canvas, where you put it.'

There was no way this was going to go well.

'I looked there. There's just a sort of nothing,' Jook explained.

'Don't be stupid, man!'

'Boss,' Jook insisted, 'the Drum's *not* in the cart.'

Dennis strode back to the cart, but his foot was painful so he broke into a galloping limp. The canvas was thrown back and a shimmering drum-shaped nothingness was mocking him. He poked it with the end of the staff and it vanished in a shower of sparks. Dennis's jaw moved up and down, soundlessly.

'I *told you*, didn't I!' said Jook, judiciously taking a step or two away from him.

'First, I'm going back to get that bloody gnome!' said Dennis, seething. 'Then...' The thought went unfinished as he hobbled round to the back of the cottage.

At the green door he muttered a spell. As he did so, he hit the door with the staff, expecting a better result than last time. The door stayed put, but the staff rang like a great sonorous bell, vibrating up its length, through his hand, up his arm, and into the rest of his body, shaking him like a leaf in a storm. For him, the world was going in and out of focus, but for Jook and Psoddoph, it was Dennis who was oscillating in and out of view. Through it all, however, one thing was appallingly clear to him – he felt no presence whatsoever in the staff of all the accumulated spells that it should contain.

When the reverberation had died, the silence was broken by a peel of laughter from the cellar. Dennis limped wordlessly back to the carpet, and sat in the cart. When the two guards were aboard, he sullenly asked the carpet to take them back to Havrapsor University, as fast as possible. He'd lost the Drum. He'd stolen the wrong staff. He'd hurt his foot, and now he was getting a headache.

He was not a happy wizard. If the guards had anything to say, they were definitely keeping it to themselves. The slightest sound or action around him might trip the wire that set him off. They held on tightly and sat quietly for the rest of the journey.

⚬━◉◄❮❯►◉━⚬

74

Hector was slaving over a hot drawing board. Unaccountably, visions of Esme were filling his mind. *Who is this woman?* he wondered. *She reminds me of someone. Where have I seen her before?* It was no good; he couldn't concentrate on designing the bridge. He put his pencil in the desk-tidy where the motion of the carriage wouldn't roll it to the floor, and leant back in his chair, locking his fingers behind his head.

Esme was thinking about him, too, and she was using her witch's powers to put thoughts of herself into his mind. From her seemingly idle chatter with Eydith, she had found out he was a very rich man. She thought he was quite handsome, too. And... well, she couldn't remain single all her life. Even though she was a witch. And Florence could do with a good father figure.

He was a very pleasant man, well mannered, if perhaps a bit noisy. But she put that down to having to make himself heard above the noise of the train all the time. She concentrated harder, willing him to come to her. She could sense his shyness, and mentally planted the suggestion that he use Link as a go-between.

That did the trick. Hector pushed the chair away and stood up. He stuck his head round the carriage door. 'I'm having a spot of bother with this bridge, Link. Can you spare a few minutes?'

Esme's heart soared at the sight of him, which didn't go unnoticed by Eydith and Florence, who exchanged quick glances. Link followed Hector back to the workshop, and, once inside, Hector told him the real reason for wanting to see him.

'Who is that lady?' he asked. 'For some reason, I cannot get her out of my head.'

Link smiled, knowingly. 'I take it you mean Esme?'

'Yes, that's the one. The older lady. I really would like to know more about her, if you don't mind me asking?'

'Fire away. What do you want to know?'

Hector looked uncharacteristically awkward and fidgety. 'Well, what's her background? Where does she come from? Do you know whereabouts she lives?'

'Taking that last one first, she lives at the end of your tracks. The end where we're headed, that is. I'm surprised you didn't know,' said Link. 'Her house is right by your terminal. Why don't you call on her? You could find out more about her, then, than I could ever tell you. Or would you like me to approach her for you? Get the lay of the land, so's to speak. Lay the ground, as it were?'

'You would be doing me a great favour,' said Hector.

'I take it, then, that you have more than a slight interest in this lady, Hector?' said Link, smiling in a friendly, conspiratorial, man-to-man way.

'I think... yes, would about sum it up. I've never been particularly drawn to anyone till now. I've been an old bachelor so long.' Hector spoke more softly now. Nothing like his usual volume. 'She is an attractive woman; wouldn't you agree?'

'Yes, I would,' Link agreed. 'But she has a temper with a bit of a short fuse,' he warned.

'I will teach her to control it,' said Hector, confidently.

'D'you know anything about her at all?' asked Link.

'Yes, nothing,' said Hector, confusingly, then finishing, 'except that she excites me.'

'She's a witch,' said Link, flatly, taking the plunge,

'Most women are, from what I gather,' said Hector, with a faraway expression. 'But this is the first one whose spell I have fallen under so completely.'

Link sighed. 'I appear to be under the spell of a wizard, myself.'

'Aha!' laughed Hector. 'Young Eydith.'

'The very same.' Link sighed again. 'But at least she lives in a proper house.'

'What do you mean?' Hector asked.

Link wondered how to tell him that the object of his desire lives in a cottage made of confectionary? 'Well...' he started, and stalled, but there was only one way to tell it: 'Esme lives in a cottage made of lollipops and marzipan.'

'She does?' said Hector, raising a bushy eyebrow.

'She does. And what's more,' he added, picking up Hector's pencil, and drawing a little x on his map, 'the cottage is right here. Right in the direction you want to lay more track.'

'Then there's nothing else for it,' said Hector. 'I will have to ask her to marry me, and take her away from all this.'

'Don't be too hasty. You don't know how she feels about you, yet.'

'Come,' said Hector, 'we will ask her, now,'

'So soon?! And what do you mean, 'we'?' asked Link, in astonishment. 'And what happened to the cautious approach? – to me making proper introductions first, and taking things at a steady pace?'

'I don't believe there's anything to be gained from that. It's now or never. And I'll need you beside me for moral support.' With that, Hector took Link by the arm and both men marched into the carriage where Esme sat looking out of the window.

At the sound of them barging in, the three women looked up.

'It's all right, ladies. Don't get up,' Hector announced.

Esme smiled at his attempt at humour. Then Hector quickly stepped forward and knelt in front of her. 'Esme...' he began, warmly.

'Yes?' she replied, forgetting to feign surprise.

Hector stood up, and turned to Link. 'Good, that's settled, then.'

'What's settled?' asked Esme. Though she had a good idea.

'I think you've just agreed to marry him,' said Link, grinning broadly, and helpfully attempting to move things forward.

'I have?' Esme frowned, a little disturbed by the speed of her own magic. Then after a long pause, she repeated herself, suddenly delighted. 'I have!'

Florence's surprise was quickly followed by her congratulations.

'You don't mind?' said Esme.

'Of course not. It's about time you settled down.' She beamed her approval at Hector.

Eydith joined Florence in wishing them well. Wimlett kept quiet, and kept his hand out of sight. There was an unspoken mutual consent that this was hardly the time for him to be introduced to Hector. He smiled his congratulations.

But Hector's face became solemn. 'You'll have to leave your little cottage, I'm afraid,' he said, preparing himself for conflict.

'Agreed,' said Esme, without fuss. 'But there are things I need to get from there, first.'

She slumped back into her seat, astonished at how quickly things had happened. As well she might! She knew enough about her own magic to know she could never have accomplished it on her own. She wasn't *that* good. Which pleased her. She wouldn't want to think she'd enchanted him into marrying her against his will. No, this was one of those times when magic had merely followed in the wake of destiny. It was so quick they hadn't even courted, or got to know one another properly. There would be time for that. He hadn't even bought her an engagement ring. She looked down at her bare third finger. Perhaps they'd move straight on to the wedding ring.

Wedding ring! *There was a wedding to plan, a dress to make, a venue to find, people to invite...* Hector's voice interrupted her flurry of thoughts.

'Agreed... my dear,' said Hector. 'Anything you like. Now, Link! Follow me, please.' And he dragged the startled wizard back to his workshop.

'Thank you for that,' said Hector, smiling broadly, when they were away from the women.

Link couldn't wipe the grin off his face.

Hector stood by the window, his hands clasped behind his back, watching the countryside roll by. 'We must have been travelling faster than I thought. We'll be stopping soon to take on wood.' He sat down at his desk, and, after staring at the map for a while, he picked up a pair of dividers and walked them across it.

'Do you know,' he said, 'when I've finished this track to Corin, I might consider building a canal from Prossill down to the coast, just there.'

'Have you thought about laying another track alongside the one you've already laid?' Link suggested, having suddenly seen the benefit.

Hector laughed at the apparent absurdity of it. 'What purpose would that serve?' I already have one track; why would I want another?' But his curiosity was aroused. 'Explain.'

'With a second track you could run another train in the other direction at the same time. You wouldn't have to keep people waiting so long. I notice you have a lot more passengers today than a few days ago when we came. It's getting popular. People might lose interest if they have to wait around too much.' Then it occurred to him, 'But you only have one train, so...' He shrugged.

Hector brushed that aside. He was seeing possibilities. 'I have another engine being built. A better, faster model, too. I was planning to run it on the new track. But now you've got me thinking, young man. I could run the two trains on the entire track. One each way. It's a huge extra expense, though...' He stalled, and Link thought that was the end of it. 'But so much more efficient. And that means more profitable.' His eyes brightened. 'Link, you're a wizard!'

Link could only agree.

75

The train chugged to a halt beside a wood yard. Hector stepped off, followed by Esme, taking his proffered hand to alight ladylike. It now appeared that whenever she was in his presence, she followed him around like a puppy, and hung on his every word. She was even happy to have Hector show her around his wood yard! Florence hadn't seen her mother so happy in ages, and her affection for Hector had stripped years off her.

For the rest of the journey, Hector sat in his carriage with the party, chatting and napping, and making plans for the coming weeks and months – Esme and Hector, a wedding; Hector and Link, a new double-track railway, and a stone bridge.

Eydith and Link were also thinking about the coming confrontation with Dennis.

Florence sat quietly. It was hard to know what she was thinking.

Night fell, and the rhythmic sounds and motions sent everyone to sleep. Except Wimlett.

The presence of Hector in the carriage had made things difficult for Wimlett. At the first opportunity, he slipped unseen into Hector's adjoining carriage. He found a comfortable couch and lay there dwelling on many things as the night rumbled on and slowly turned to morning. Soon they would be saying farewell to Hector and Esme. Her priorities had changed and she wouldn't be making the journey back to Kra-Pton. One less to help them with Dennis, he reflected. Or maybe *two* less, if Florence was staying home now, also. So, they'd finished up no better off than they were before he'd met them! But maybe it was for the best. They wouldn't have to worry about Esme and Florence's safety when they came up against Dennis.

Early next morning, the train stopped a few feet from the buffers with a sigh of steam. Hector motioned the party to stay in their seats. 'Let the platform clear and we can get off in comfort.'

Eager as they were to get off and stretch their legs, on matters of platform procedure, who would know better than Hector? And when they saw the trolleys, handcarts and sack-trucks weaving around the other alighting passengers, and heard all the cussing and swearing going on between them and the porters, they knew Hector was right.

He yelled something from their window and quietened things down. 'Another few cuffs around the ear in the training room is required,' he said, apologetically.

'Maybe you should draw up some rules of conduct for your workers,' suggested Link. 'And some safety guidelines.'

Hector was sceptical. 'Well maybe. I wouldn't want that sort of thing getting out of hand. You have to go a long way to beat a good cuff round the ear.'

When all the crates and barrels had been cleared, he led his party from the carriage.

'Esme, my love,' he cooed. 'I'll carry that bag. Where would you like to go first?'

'Is there a privy around here? I'm busting.'

'Over there.' He pointed.

She scurried away, followed by Eydith and Florence.

'Why didn't they go on the train?' he wondered, a little hurt that his newly-installed on-board privies hadn't been taken advantage of.

'Takes a bit of getting used to while the train's moving,' said Link. 'All that swaying about. I hope they don't take all day. I feel like a landmark with this Drum.'

Hector smiled. 'Perhaps we could wander over to Esme's cottage while we're waiting? I'll get one of my porters to tell them where we are when they come out.'

'I don't think that's a good idea. Esme has some odd little characters guarding her cottage, and I think it would be best if we waited for her.'

'Right,' said Hector, raising a hand in acknowledgement. 'We will wait. From what you say it sounds the safest thing to do.' Then he laughed. 'Maybe I should get you to write some safety guidelines for me, after all.'

The three women emerged, relaxed and refreshed.

At the little white gate, Esme looked around the garden. 'My gnomes are gone!' she exclaimed.

'Perhaps they're gardening somewhere, Mother, or stretching their legs,' suggested Florence.

'I'll stretch their necks if they're not back here in two minutes.'

'You go inside and put the kettle on. I'll see if I can find them.'

'All right, but don't be long.'

'I'll come with you,' Eydith offered, taking a firmer grip on Sprag.

Wimlett tagged along, too, as it promised to be amusing.

76

Hector and Link followed Esme into the cottage, while the others went off in search of the missing gnomes. There were certainly none on duty on the front lawn. People call them garden gnomes, but, as every witch knows, that's a corruption of guardian gnomes. Wimlett and the two girls went round the cottage to check the rear garden, and as they passed the green door, they heard the tell-tale giggle of a drunken gnome. Florence stopped. 'Arfer? Is that you?'

'Heh, heh, heh. Nope.'

Wimlett stood back a few yards, to become a spectator. He felt he'd earned a little light entertainment.

Florence tried again. 'Arfer, I think you'd better come out. Esme's home.'

There was scuffling and scurrying from within, the sounds of bottles clinking, and voices lowered in hurried, serious conversation, with phrases like, 'life not worth living,' and 'in deep slurry,' being muttered regularly, interspersed with the unanimous conclusion, 'probably up to our armpits.'

'I'll count to three,' Florence threatened, 'then we'll take the door off and drag you out.'

'Dennis has... hic... already tried that. What... burp! – pardon me – makes you think... hic ... that... you can do any better?' Arfer called back, defiantly.

'I've got Eydith with me,'

'Has she... hic... – scooze me – got the Drum?' asked Arfer.

'Yes, I have,' said Eydith, before Florence could speak.

There was further muffled discussion behind the door: 'Mumble, mumble, got the Drum,' said one. 'Mumble, mumble, Esme's back,' said another. 'Mumble, mumble, mumble!' added another.

'In deep slurry,' concluded Arfer. There was a pregnant silence.

'We're coming out!' The bolts squeaked. The girls took a step back as the pungent aroma of home-made brews and the flatulent odours that accompanied them escaped into the fresh air. Three tipsy gnomes wobbled out into the sunlight.

'Just what has been going on?' asked Florence, stern-faced and hands on hips. Eydith turned away to hide her amusement as the three gnomes stood in line in front of Florence, their heads bowed. Arfer plucked up the courage to look her in the eye.

'It was Dennis,' he began, slowly, and with gathering lucidity – the instant sobriety that a threatening situation can sometimes bring about, but which might easily lapse.

'Yes, so you said. What about him?'

'He was looking for Esme and the staff.'

'Did you tell him where she was?' said Florence.

'Don't remember.' Arfer shrugged. 'But when I told 'im she wasn't 'ere, 'e wanted to drink all her ale, and that.'

'Hmm...' breathed Florence. 'But you got to the shed first, did you?'

'He was going to magic us into statues! We 'ad to 'ide somewhere.'

'I think you'd all better come inside and tell Esme what's been going on.'

'Is she in a good mood?' asked Arfer, more red-faced than the paint on his cheeks.

'She was worried when you weren't by the pond. Now get inside! All of you!' she ordered, pointing along the side of the cottage.

The three gnomes slunk into the cottage, and upon seeing Hector, they froze into their stationary, public personas, as they reflexively did until they knew who they were dealing with.

'It's all right,' said Esme, 'this is a very dear friend of mine. There's no need to get formal.'

They relaxed, and Hector looked on, intrigued.

Esme examined the three unsteady gnomes. 'Where's your fishin' rod?' she asked Arfer.

'By the pond, mistress,' he replied promptly, but he wouldn't look her in the eye.

'And you? Where's your wheelbarrow?' And you... where's your rake?' she jabbed at them as she spoke, and they flinched. 'So, what's this I hear about Dennis? What went on when he was here?'

Arfer wobbled forward. 'He was 'ere, mistress, with two other men. One of them ate a bit of the roof.'

'Yeah, and 'e tied us up. Tried to make us tell 'im where you were,' said Wheelbarrow-gnome.

'Yeah, but Arfer tricked 'im into letting us go and we 'ad to 'ide in the ale shed.'

'And did you tell Dennis where I was?' said Esme, doing her best to control her temper in front of Hector.

'I don't fink so,' Arfer replied.

'What do you mean, you don't think so?'

'Well, that stuff you brew in there tends to fog the mem'ry a bit.' He stopped talking and screwed his face up. There was a sound like tearing cloth, which came from somewhere a little south of his trouser belt. 'I think I'd better go outside again,' said Arfer, covering his backside as he made for the door.

'Phaw! Haven't you learned to control that yet?' snorted Esme, throwing one of the windows wide open. 'Outside! All of you!' she snapped. Hector took this as his cue to step outside, too. He was finding the low ceiling uncomfortable. And Esme's cottage seemed even smaller now that the others had arrived. He'd become a little bemused, too, by all the intrigue going on. But now didn't seem like a good time to ask about it. He could easily find out later. Though something told him he might be better off keeping right out of it.

'Does Dennis know we've got the Drum?' asked Eydith, joining in the interrogation.

Arfer paused by the door to let Hector pass. 'Yep. That's why were still 'ere.'

'What are you talking about?' Esme glared at him.

'He was going to break down the door with your staff and kill us all to death.'

'Oh, no,' wailed Esme. 'He's got *my* staff. He must have found it in our room. Come here.' She called the gnome back, and when he was close enough, she laid her hand on his head and closed her eyes. Arfer went rigid, more concrete than he'd ever been, as she read his mind. After a minute she opened her eyes, removed her hand, and looked at Eydith.

'Dennis knows he hasn't got the staff he was looking for,' she said, having remotely spied on Dennis's last visit to the cottage, using the gnome's presence, then and now, to make a bridge across which to send her mind. She confirmed that he'd discovered he hadn't got the Drum, too. After which she fainted briefly from the effort, and had to be revived. As did Arfer.

'Well, he knows he's not so powerful now,' said Eydith.

'But we won't be able to surprise him anymore,' said Link. 'We've lost that advantage.'

Eydith was thinking. 'Maybe not completely. But now we have the Drum, we have the upper hand. I don't think he'll come looking for us. He'll stay at the university. We should confront him there before he has time to work out his next move.'

'Yes, but he'll be in familiar surroundings,' said Florence.

'So will Link and father,' Eydith pointed out.

'Well,' said Wimlett, 'the sooner we get started, the sooner it'll be done.' He was looking particularly at Eydith and Link when he said this. Esme and Florence's own plans to catch up with Dennis (for whatever reason) were in abeyance.

'Do you need anything?' asked Esme. 'You know... my gnomes, a few extra spells, that sort of thing?'

Eydith's eye caught the gnomes, who were vigorously shaking their heads, willing her to say 'no'. She rolled her eyes. 'No, I don't think so. But thanks anyway.'

The gnomes grinned widely.

Link touched Eydith's arm, and swivelled his eyes in Florence's direction.

'Oh, yes,' she added, 'there is something we need. We'd still like Florence to come along, if that's all right?'

'Can I, Mother?' she asked, clearly keen.

'Are you sure, child? It could get very dangerous.'

'Yes, Mother. I'm sure. I really am.' She nodded repeatedly as she said it.

'Then go. All of you. Come back safe and tell me all about it.'

77

'Nearly home,' said Jook, as they approached the Snake River.

Soon the city of Kra-Pton was visible on the horizon. The silhouettes of the towers of Havrapsor University were like beacons on a distant shore. The guards exchanged grins, while Dennis kept his eyes staring ahead, as if mesmerised. His feelings were mixed. He was glad to be back, but angry at having failed.

As Dennis watched the university pass below, he snapped out of it. He muttered a few well-chosen words, and steered the carpet down. He brought it to a stop with a gentle bump, landing it in the main quadrangle behind the great gates.

Not being a popular Archchancellor, Dennis didn't expect a cheering crowd. But no-one? And not a flag in sight!

'Didn't they know you were due back today from your... er... fishing trip, boss?' asked Jook, a little incautiously.

'No, I forgot to send a card,' Dennis replied, sarcastically.

'Well,' said Psoddoph, looking in every direction. 'Where is everyone? Is it always like this, or is it the end of term?'

Dennis's face flushed with anger. 'Just put the cart away, will you? Then take the carpet up to my rooms. I'll find out what's going on.' They busied themselves, and he turned back after a few seconds and called, 'Pass me the staff.'

It was one of those surreal moments when Jook thought Dennis was going to say 'please'. But Dennis stalked off to the all-day cafeteria, where there was always somebody.

This time the place was deserted.

He went to his rooms, and collapsed into his favourite armchair, causing a cloud of dust to rise up around him. 'Don't they clean this place while I'm away?' he spluttered. He mouthed a few guttural sounds and waved a hand, producing a light popping noise as a spell tidied the room. His other hand still held the staff.

'What's going on?' he asked himself. 'Why am I reduced to wasting magic tidying a room when I employ menials to do it?' He strutted angrily across to a window that overlooked the quad. There was nobody about, not even a raven. 'Where in the name of *Hell* are they?' he railed, addressing the empty quad and banging the staff violently on the floor at all the absent people.

There was a loud crash behind him, followed by the dull thudding sounds of falling rubble. This was followed by the acrid smell of sulphur filling the room, and a voice cursing.

'Why do they make me do it?' the creature moaned, wearily, as it entered Dennis's rooms, almost demolishing them. 'They know all this dust gets on my chest.'

'Who's there?' snapped Dennis, spinning round.

'Ah... there you are,' said the thing emerging from the dust cloud.

Dennis stepped back. 'Who the hell are you?'

The demon was thinking the same thing. He was usually summoned by a witch. Then... 'Got it in one! Hell is who I am. Your demon! My, you've changed, Esmerelda.'

As the dust began to settle, Dennis could see the being taking shape. 'So you are...?' he said, taking in the creature, mildly amused at its attempts to dust itself down and look presentable. It would never look presentable. He eyed it up and down. There was nothing remarkable about it – a bit hunched and on the short side; but the usual scaly complexion, pointed chin, fiery eyes, clawed hands and feet – if you've seen one demon you've seen them all, really. '... What do you want?'

'I don't want nuffin' mate. You called me, remember.' The demon was adamant.

'I did no such thing.'

'Yes, you did. You invoked me and banged the staff – in the name of Hell, you said. Remember? It was only a minute ago, for badness' sake! Well, as I said, that's me. Hell.' The demon paused, took a long breath to show its exasperation, then went on, 'I bet you were one of them kids that used to knock on people's doors and run away, weren't you?'

Dennis ignored that, but smiled at the memory. 'Well? Where did you come from?'

'Parallel Dimension, mate,' Hell replied, matter-of-factly.

'Oh, no you didn't.'

'Oh, yes I did,' Hell insisted.

'Then why did you come *up* through the floor, and not out of the wall?' Dennis, peered down the hole in his floor, and the two floors below that.

'I was busy,' said the creature.

'Busy?' echoed Dennis.

'Stoking me fires.'

'Oh, yes,' mused Dennis, 'I should have realised. The fires of Hell, no doubt.'

'You've 'eard of 'em?'

'No,' said Dennis. 'I just made that up.'

'Well, all right. I don't care anyway. But now I'm 'ere, what do you want?'

He was about to say 'Nothing, Just go away and leave me in peace, you ghastly piece of...!' but he reconsidered. What might he want from a demon?

'Come on,' said Hell, looking at his bare scaly wrist, anxiously, 'I 'aven't got all day, you know.'

'Well, as I'm your new master, (the demon rolled its fiery eyes at this), I'd like you to find all my wizards and bring them back. I want them locked in the cellars. Then I'd like my Drum back. Oh, yes, and the real Archchancellor's staff.'

'Anyfing else?'

'I'll give it some thought while you're getting on with all that,' said Dennis.

'Don't want much, do yuh?' griped Hell. 'You forgot to mention a kingdom of your own, an' a million slaves and beautiful ladies! I usually do all that before breakfast.'

'Don't get smart with me! I want to show the wizards and the other peasants in this city what'll happen if they step out of line.'

'You'll need some 'elp wiv all you wanna do,' said Hell, amiably, ignoring the gist of the conversation so far. It paused, waiting for Dennis to take up the conversation, but he didn't. '*Won't you?*' it prompted.

'And that's where you come in, is it?' Dennis humoured it.

'Got it in one, again!' said Hell, 'I can see I'm not dealing with an idiot 'ere.'

'Well, that's one of us. Are you sure you can handle rounding up my wizards? You're not a very *big* demon, are you?'

'Course I can 'andle it! And while we're being pers'nal, you're quite skinny, as fat wizards go, ain't yuh? And if your magic was up to scratch, you wouldn't 'ave called me in the first place. Would yuh?'

'I didn't call you!'

'Look,' said Hell, 'if you 'adn't banged that flagpole of a staff and called 'Hell', I wouldn't be 'ere now. Would I?'

It was dawning on Dennis. 'You mean you come with the staff?'

'Well... yeah. You a student in this place? – not a full-blown wizard?'

'Why do you, of all things, come with the staff?'

'Well,' said Hell, looking at his clawed feet, 'there was me and this genie, see. Last in the queue we were, and all that was left was a grotty old lamp, which I really liked the look of, and that nice looking, shiny staff...'

'Yes... go on.'

'Well, we tossed a coin, and I got lumbered with the nice staff.' He pulled a face at it. 'Though I suppose *the Demon of the Lamp* don't sound right, does it?'

A thin smile tried to spread across the wizard's face, but could only hang around the edges of his mouth. 'So, it didn't go well for you,' said Dennis.

'Well, it did in a way,' Hell corrected him.

'How so?'

'At least I can sleep stretched out in a staff. I'd have to curl up in a lamp. Though it would 'ave been really grotty in there,' the creature added, wistfully.

Dennis got back to the point. 'Now, are you going to help me or not?'

'Yeah,' said Hell, thinking it sounded like his kind of mischief. 'Ain't as if I 'ave much choice, is it? But you want a lot of fings fast, by the sounds of it.'

'*Now* would be the time frame I have in mind,' said Dennis.

'Well, if it's that dear to yuh,' said Hell, moving his head the other way, 'what are you gonna give me for the extra speed, like?'

'Anything you like, within reason,' said Dennis, his fingers crossed behind his back. 'When I have all I want, I'll give you anything that's in my power to give you. After I've deducted the repairs to my floors.'

'Huh,' it grunted. 'I need to round up some of me pals first. We'll start at dawn.' There was a theatrical puff of smoke, and the little demon disappeared. He heard it coughing for a few moments.

Dennis shook his head at the hole in his floor. He muttered something and moved his hands mystically. The dust and rubble obediently returned to fill the holes in the floors. To make sure it was safe, he tapped it with his toe. All was well. *That rewind spell has come in handy of late, but mustn't overdo it*, he thought. *Conserve the magic.*

He was certain it was no accident that the Drum had been stolen, *and* the wrong staff had been planted for him to take. Someone was plotting against him. He started to mentally list all those who bore him grudges, disliked him or hated him, but it was so long he gave up.

And none of them was a real threat, as far as he knew. Even with the Drum and the real staff, they would be unable to wield their power without the Archchancellorship. He rubbed his hands together, gleefully. 'Soon,' he said, as he looked out of his window at the city roofs beyond the university buildings, and at the indistinct Yonder Hills, 'all this will be mine.'

78

Esme and Hector watched from the cottage door as Link and the two girls disappeared over the horizon. Wimlett was with them, but of course, he'd disappeared some time ago.

'We could do with some transport,' Link remarked, after they'd walked for about fifteen minutes.

'Yes,' agreed Eydith. 'That must be getting quite heavy now.'

'How did you travel before?' asked Florence.

'We kind of flew, using Sprag,' Eydith explained. 'But there were only two of us then, and Link wasn't carrying the Drum.'

'Three of us,' corrected Wimlett, a little fed up at being left out because he was less visible.

'We need a horse and cart,' said Link.

'Why don't you use your magic, daughter?' suggested Wimlett.

'To conjure up a horse and cart?'

'Something fast enough to get us there before Dennis has time to settle,' said Wimlett.

'Yes, but what?'

'A dragon, perhaps?' suggested Wimlett. But seeing Eydith shake her head emphatically, said, 'Perhaps not, then. What about a carpet, like Dennis?'

She liked that better. 'Good idea, but would it stay solid for long enough?'

'It would if you turned something *into* a carpet, rather than create it from nothing.'

Eydith and Florence rummaged among the few things they'd brought with them. The only thing remotely resembling a carpet was a bath towel.

'Where did that come from?' asked Eydith when Florence held it up. Then she noticed the monogram in the corner:

Property of the Magic Finger.

'I suspect my mother,' said Florence. 'She's of a mind that they are put in hotel rooms as souvenirs.'

'Well, we'll let her off this time,' said Eydith, gratefully.

'It's a bit small,' said Link. 'Do you think we'll all get on?'

'I'll have to stretch it a bit, that's all,' said Eydith, playing him along. Though that was in fact what she hoping she could do. Her eyes glowed, and changed to golden orbs. She held Sprag at the towel and mentally recited what she could see scrolling across her mind.

The Drum glowed softly in sympathy.

The others watched the edges of the towel crawl outwards, as it grew to almost four times its original size. The spell completed, Eydith's eyes dimmed. But something wasn't right. The towel was big enough, but only a quarter of its original thickness. It resembled a fluffy net curtain. Eydith was reminded, once again, that she still had a lot to learn.

'Why did that happen, Father?'

'It's about taking up the same amount of space in reality,' Wimlett replied, casting his mind back over the books he'd read and classes he'd taken in his time at the university. 'Your spell had nothing in it to increase the available matter when you expanded the towel. And when we forget that element of the spell, we call it a bit of a bas...'

'I get the idea, Father,' she interrupted. She recalled a fleeting glimpse of an un-recited part of the spell that she missed in her haste and inexperience.

'But it should still support us magically,' said Wimlett. 'I think.'

Link stepped forward. 'Let's try it'.

'Be my guest,' said Eydith, standing aside.

He warily placed the Drum in the centre of the towel and sat behind it. Eydith trod daintily on and sat in front of the Drum. Florence sat carefully behind Link. Wimlett had worries about his weight, but Eydith wiped the smile off his face when she reminded him of his fear of flying.

'Ready?' asked Eydith. 'I guess I'm the driver. Though I'm not sure what I'm supposed to be doing.'

Wimlett came to her aid. 'Just silently command it with your mind. Tell it to rise... to move forward... and say whatever speed you want. You'll soon get the hang of it. But keep your thoughts in check. If they wander, so will the carpet – I mean the towel.'

'Ready?' she asked again.

The Drum glowed. It seemed it was the only passenger that was.

The make-shift carpet trembled and rose into the air. Eydith turned it towards Kra-Pton. With a little more coaching from Wimlett, she did get the hang of it. She gained confidence and picked up speed. At the Drum's invitation, communicated through Sprag, Wimlett stuck his head inside it, where he could forget he was flying. What was going on in there was certainly distracting! Unlike the others, he was able to forget, for a while, the confrontation that lay in front of them.

—◄❰❱►—

79

In Death's study, Naphrat was studying the ledgers. Dennis's soul kept coming to the top of the list for reaping, but each time, it slipped back down again. He went to the vast Vault of Lives where all the Life-Timers were lined up and stacked up, floor to ceiling, in every direction. Apart from the echoing click of his feet as he walked across the stone flags, the only sound was the gentle hissing of the Sands of Time, flowing through the waists of hundreds and thousands of Timers. Having searched in vain for fifteen minutes, he berated himself for forgetting that what he wanted wouldn't be in there. It was among the Timers of magical beings on the shelves behind Death's desk. He was not used to taking Timers from there. He clumped noisily out.

He ran a bony finger along one of the rows. 'Ah, there you are.' He pulled the Timer down and held it in front of one of the large yellow-flamed candles that lit the room. The sand seemed to flow normally, but if he watched for long enough, he could see that it wasn't consistent. It slowed down now and then, allowing the other Timers to overtake it.

He put it on the desk and sat down in front of the great Ledger to watch. Dennis was back at the top of the page, but after a short while the Timer slowed, and other names in the Ledger overtook him. It was most irregular. Naphrat leaned back in the chair.

'What would Death do?' he wondered. 'More to the point, what am I going to do?' For want of a better idea, he decided to check on Dennis while doing his rounds.

Bruno, Death's larger than life, pale grey horse, snorted as Naphrat threw a saddle across the animal's back. In moments, they were flying towards Kra-Pton. Naphrat always knew pretty much where everyone was. It was his job to know. Particularly when wizards and witches were nearing the end of their mortal time, because he had to be there in person to assist them in shuffling off of their mortal coil.

Not that any had died while Death had been away. Only Wimlett. And he hadn't actually died. Only Death Himself could take the soul of a witch or a wizard. Neither Death nor Naphrat had realised that it was something Death could not delegate. So now Dennis was dodging Naphrat.

Tonight, though, nobody, either magical or normal, was about to meet their maker. It was just a case of Death's helper being on his rounds. Which would probably finish in a tavern somewhere. But first, Dennis.

Bruno cantered easily across the sky, and was soon treading the cobbled quadrangle of the university. The Dark Angel led the horse to the stables, patted him affectionately, hooked a nosebag over the animal's ears and went out onto the streets.

To his surprise, there was great commotion. Demons had surfaced and they were everywhere, causing all manner of terror and vandalism. They were whipping cornered groups of people, and smashing windows and parked carts. Naphrat grabbed one of the terrified people as he tried to rush by.

Concealing his face in his hood, not wanting to terrify the man further, he asked 'What's going on?'

'You'd better run, mister!' gasped the terrified man. 'Dennis has sent demons into town.'

'Why?'

'Nobody was at the university when he got home, is what I heard,' said the man, not quite sure who he was talking to. The voice was so weird, he chose not to look into the hood. 'And he's really pissed off about it.' The man glanced fearfully over his shoulder.

'That's hardly a reason...'

'He don't need no reason. He's Dennis!'

'Calm down a moment, man. Where are the other wizards now?'

'Most of 'em were in the Piggin Wissall when he got 'ere. Now some are hiding. But the demons have captured most of 'em, and taken 'em back to the university.'

'Are they doing nothing about this? Or the officers of the Watch?' asked Naphrat, waving a bony hand in the direction of the carnage, and quickly slipping it out of sight again.

'No, like I said, Dennis has locked a lot in the cellars. And the Watch don't have any jurisdiction around the university. They're lying low anyway.' Naphrat slackened his grip and the frightened man ran off down the street.

Naphrat tapped the side of his skull. 'Funny,' he said, to himself, 'I didn't know universities had cellars.'

He clattered off down the street to the Piggin Wissall, side stepping fleeing citizens, and reaping the odd demon's soul, which unaccountably promptly returned to its owner. Naphrat ran a bony finger along the blade of his scythe. 'Maybe it needs sharpening,' he thought aloud. 'Or I'm losing my touch?' He turned a corner just in time to catch full on, the blast from the pie and mash takeaway. A group of demons had ferried some sulphurous material up from below and lobbed it into the shop. What they had against pie and mash we'll never know. It exploded into the night sky. 'Shit!' he muttered, examining the fluffy white mash, covering his black robe. 'This is not my colour at all. And not a pie anywhere.'

He'd seen enough. He turned and clattered back to collect Bruno. Then went home to get showered and changed.

Back at the dark house, he saw a large scroll jammed in the letter box. He eased it out, and took it to the study, where he laid it on the ebony desk. He removed his white-stained robe and tossed it into the laundry basket in the corner. He often put things in there, and, within moments, they'd disappeared, got cleaned, and reappeared, neatly ironed, and back in one of his drawers. It was a mystery to him. Perhaps he was married without realising it.

Having cleaned up, he rummaged around in the walk-in wardrobe off the study and found another robe. It was one of Death's, and a bit big, but he kept it on anyway, and clattered back to the desk, where he examined the scroll.

It had Death's seal on it (where did He find black wax on holiday?). If he had eyebrows, he would have raised one. He broke the seal and unrolled it.

HELLO NAPH,

I THINK IT'S TIME TO COME HOME. THIS TAVERN BUSINESS IS NOT ALL IT'S CRACKED UP TO BE. THE ONLY CUSTOMERS I GET IN THIS DESERT ASK FOR WATER, AND THEY'VE RARELY GOT ANY MONEY. IT'S TAKEN ME A LONG TIME, BUT I'VE FINALLY MANAGED TO DRINK ALL THE STOCK. AND NOW THE ROOF'S FALLEN IN, SO I'M COMING HOME.

Yours darkly,

D.

80

Naphrat slumped back in the chair. Would his Master be pleased with the way he'd run things? Or full of complaints, criticisms and irony. Naphrat didn't understand irony too well.

He searched for a date on the scroll, or any clue as to when it was posted. It would have been a while ago, because Death always waited for a postman to die whenever He needed to send a letter. As he thought on these things, a bony hand rested on his shoulder.

Naphrat jumped and spun round in the chair. Nobody had ever made *him* jump before! He found himself staring into the empty eye-sockets of Death.

'You nearly frightened the life out of me,' wheezed Naphrat.

I'M BACK! The Grim Reaper grinned expressionlessly at him. It's a well-known fact that people on holidays most often get home before their cards.

'I can see that,' said Naphrat, a bony hand resting on his empty ribcage where his heart would have been thumping if he had one.

WELL? AREN'T YOU PLEASED TO SEE ME? asked Death.

'Yes, Master, of course I am,' Naphrat replied, rising from the chair. He genuinely meant it, too.

NO, DON'T GET UP, said Death, spreading His hand on Naphrat's shoulder again.

'I thought you'd want to get in the seat again. Take over.'

NOT FOR A MINUTE, said Death, sitting on the corner of the desk. TELL ME WHAT'S BEEN GOING ON.

Naphrat leaned back and cleared his dry throat. 'I've had some trouble...' he began.

WHAT? THE OLD BONES PLAYING UP, IS IT? SCIATICA?

'No. It's some of the Life-Timers playing up.'

HOW DO YOU MEAN? said Death, picking up the one beside Him on the desk.

'Well, that one for a start,' he said pointing at the one Death was fingering. 'Sometimes it slows down. And one Timer played up so much a wizard died before his time. That was very embarrassing, I can tell you. One opened up and I almost lost the sand. I turned it over in the nick of time.'

YOU HAVEN'T HAD MUCH FUN THEN, HAVE YOU? Death consoled him.

'No. And on top of all that, Dennis, the Archchancellor, has called up demons from the Parallel Dimension, they're putting wizards in the cellars, and now they're terrorising Kra-Pton.' He described his visit. 'And I couldn't reap demon souls. Why was that?'

HMM, Death intoned. I GOT BACK EARLIER TO DAY, THAT'S WHY, AND NEEDED A REST. I'M NOT AS YOUNG AS I USED TO BE. I DIDN'T GET TIME TO TELL YOU.

'So, did my own power just stop working when you arrived?' said Naphrat.

YES, replied Death, with hollow flatness, BECAUSE I'VE TAKEN IT AWAY. NOT ALL OF IT, OF COURSE, JUST SOME OF THE STUFF MORE RELEVENT TO ME.

'Oh, I see,' said Naphrat.

Death peered into the hollow eye-sockets in Naphrat's chalk-white skull. DO YOU? He said.

'Sorry?'

SEE, repeated Death.

'Of course,' said Naphrat, feeling a little edgy and intimidated.

JUST KIDDING, said Death, ARE THERE ANY WIZARDS STILL FREE?

'Maybe half a dozen.'

ANY OF THEM ANY GOOD?

'There's one Seventh Level, by the name of Linkwood. A girl called Eydith. Quite powerful, she is. Great potential. Learning fast. And her cousin, Florence. But she doesn't know she's a wizard yet.'

WHY NOT?

'Dennis is her father. But she's been trained as a witch. And she hasn't told the others.'

AH. AND IF THIS EYDITH IS SO PROMISING, WHO IS *HER* FATHER?

'Wimlett.'

Death looked along the shelves at the Life-Timers behind the desk, and homed in immediately on an empty space. WHERE'S HIS TIMER?

'Er... it's empty, Master.'

THEN, HE'S DEAD? pronounced Death.

'Er... sort of.'

SORT OF? WHAT DO YOU MEAN, SORT OF? 'SORT OF' IS HOW YOU MIGHT PLAY THE PIANO, NOT HOW YOU MIGHT DIE.

'He was the one who died before his time. Faulty Timer. I gave him twenty years as a ghost, as compensation.'

WE'RE NOT IN THE INSURANCE BUSINESS, NAPH.

'Well I had to do something, Master. It was bloody embarrassing,' he said in his own defence.

ALL RIGHT, I'LL SORT IT OUT LATER. Death drummed His fingers on the desk, leaving some pitted ebony, and thought for a moment. THAT MEANS THEREFORE WE HAVE THREE, MAYBE FOUR WIZARDS AT BEST, THAT MIGHT BE PREPARED TO DO SOMETHING ABOUT DENNIS.

'They are prepared to,' Naphrat assured him. 'And what about us – can we help?' He held back judiciously from saying he had already committed to help Wimlett.

WE ARE TAKERS OF SOULS, NOT ASSASSINS, Death pointed out. WE ONLY REAP WHEN THE SANDS RUN OUT. MIND YOU, SOMETIMES THEY NEED HURRYING ALONG A BIT, I AGREE.

'Will these wizards get any help from us, then?' asked Naphrat.

NATURALLY, replied Death. DENNIS MUST BE STOPPED BEFORE HE STARTS KILLING PEOPLE. AND FROM WHAT I'VE HEARD SO FAR – WHAT WITH DEMONS ACTING ON HIS BEHALF – IT WON'T BE LONG BEFORE THAT STARTS. AND WE DON'T WANT UNTIMELY HASSLE, DO WE? – OR THE OVERTIME.

'No,' agreed Naphrat. 'Absolutely not!'

RIGHT, THEN. LET'S GET ON WITH IT, SHALL WE?

81

The magic towel flew on in silence, each passenger alone with their thoughts about the confrontation ahead of them. Eydith felt their safety was in her hands. Link could look after himself, but had his limitations. Florence, although determined, was vulnerable. The only one she didn't have to worry about was Wimlett, who was already dead.

The outline of the city rose on the horizon, but Eydith could find nothing positive or encouraging to say, just, 'We'll be there shortly.'

Eydith brought them down just outside the city gates.

'One of us should go in and see what's happening,' she suggested. 'Who knows what mayhem an irate Dennis might be creating?'

A disembodied hand rose into the air. 'Best be me,' Wimlett said. 'No-one will see me.'

No one could argue with that.

'Thanks, Father.'

'I'll try and be back in an hour,' he promised.

82

Wimlett passed through the city gates and made a right turn for the university. Panic-stricken people were rushing in all directions. Actually, they were all running more or less in the same direction. The one known as *away*. They were running from the hideous demons trying to round them up, although the reason for this was not apparent. And being a ghost didn't help Wimlett, because he couldn't ask anybody.

He decided to carry on directly to the university. In the general mayhem no-one took any notice of his hand. It didn't take him long. He slipped into a familiar shaded alleyway and made his way to the back of the building. Here was the door he used as a student, after lights-out. He gave it a shove and couldn't believe his luck when it yielded. Dennis obviously didn't know of it.   The lack of cobwebs proved that students still found the route useful. He made his way along a narrow passage which, if his memory served him rightly, should take him into a cupboard in a dark corner of the library. Or a cupboard in the kitchens.

As a student, he'd known enough rudimentary magic to light his way. Now, as a ghost, he had to rely on whatever faint light found its way in. The passage divided up ahead. He didn't remember that. He stood for a moment, recalling his old route. Then he took the other one, the newer one. He wanted to know where it led. There were unfamiliar blasts of cold air coming from up ahead, and he felt something was wrong.

He followed the draught, wishing he had a glove for his solid hand. The air was chilling. The passage had the appearance of having been hewn from solid rock. The light was almost zero. He carried on, clinging to handy irregularities in the wall, not sure of where he was going. Then he reached the end. A slab of solid rock.

'Bloody typical!' he cursed. 'How do I get through that?' He sat on an outcrop of rock, and stroked his beard, wondering if he should turn back, or whether there might be a way through. There were no gaps around it, that he could feel, or a helpful iron ring to pull. Some odd lengths of timber strewn about, probably left over from building work, were no use either. 'Oh, Hell!' he blurted out, in frustration.

In response, it would seem, he heard from below a distant rumbling, followed by the approaching scratchy footsteps of something obviously used to clambering up steep stone walls from deep in the bowels of Crett. He sat still in the near blackness, awaiting whatever was coming.

As it got closer, Wimlett could hear mumblings. 'What's 'e want now?' something was complaining. 'We'll never get this job done if 'e keeps interfering.'

Wimlett felt a sudden urge to sneeze. And he didn't manage to stifle it.

The footsteps stopped. 'Somebody call?' said a rasping voice.

Wimlett didn't answer.

'Is there anybody there?' the demon asked again.

Wimlett sunk himself into the wall. All but his hand.

'Knock once for *no*, and twice for *yes*,' the demon said, sounding wary, as it drew up almost level with the ghostly mage.

Wimlett could just about make out the shape of the demon, and to his own surprise, before he could stop himself, knocked once on a piece of timber propped up by him.

And the demon, whose eyes were better adapted, saw it. 'Yuck! A hand! Yuck!' And it scurried back down the passage repeatedly shouting, 'Yuck, Yuck! And it lied! It's two knocks for *yes*! Yuck! It's 'orrible!'

Wimlett couldn't bring himself to move for a moment; he was so affronted by the creature's reaction. After all, how many things can a demon find *that* disturbing. Then, he experimentally put his head through the slab at the end of the passage, and withdrew it again immediately. 'Dennis!' he hissed.

Dennis looked up, distracted from his reading by a faint voice calling his name. 'Who's there?' he asked, calmly. 'Hell, is that you?' There was no reply. He slammed shut the great *Book of Advanced Spells for the Professional*, and stood up. Esme's staff was leaning against the wall. He strode across the room, snatched it up and began rubbing it vigorously, thinking to himself, *I must remember never do this in mixed company.*

83

There was a distant crash from the Parallel Dimension, followed by rumblings and grumblings, and the scratchy footfalls of demonic feet, getting closer and louder. Suddenly the demon burst into the room.

'What do you want *now*?' asked Hell, impatiently.

'I just wondered where you were,' Dennis replied, cordially.

'You *what*?' screeched the demon.

'Just wondered where you were,' Dennis repeated.

'I was huntin' a wizard, till somebody called me,' snapped Hell.

'When was that?'

'About ten minutes ago.'

'Do you happen to know who was it?'

'Dunno,' said the demon, sounding a little puzzled. 'When I got there, whoever it was, 'ad bin eaten. It was 'orrible. There was only an 'and left. Still movin', it was. *Writhin'.*'

'Yuck!' remarked Dennis.

'That's what I thought.'

'Anyway,' said Dennis, not wanting the details that the glint in the demon's eye suggested were coming, 'how are you getting on? Have you found the other wizards, yet?'

'In a word... no.'

'Well, what are you doing?'

'I've got demons doin' 'ouse to 'ouse and pub to pub searches. Oh, and those uvver places where you wizards hang out.'

'What other places?' asked Dennis, his curiosity stirred.

'*You know.*' The demon grinned broadly, showing a set of mismatched, discoloured fangs. 'Those places where your hooman wimmin prance about, and take their vests off an' that.' He winked.

'What! I want those places closed down!' ordered Dennis. 'Immediately!'

'Let's not be too hasty, now. They 'ave a lot of harmful fun in them places,' said Hell, defensively.

'Who?'

'My fellow demons. Oh, and some of your wizards of course,' he added, chuckling.

'I don't think you're taking this campaign very seriously, Hell,' said Dennis. 'I think I need somebody higher up than you.'

The demon scratched its head with a very sharp claw, making itself bleed. 'Well, there isn't anybody higher. We don't do high and low.'

'Perhaps that was the wrong terminology,' Dennis conceded. 'Perhaps I need someone a bit more *sideways* than you – someone, or some*thing* with a bit more relevant experience, perhaps.'

'There's only one, shall we say... more parallel than me, and that's *Jamzamin*.' A deferential gush of violins would not have been out of place at this moment.

'And who is this *Jamzamin*?' Dennis sneered.

"E's our king, 'e is,' Hell replied, reverently bowing, as if the creature was present.

'Well, if he's the best you've got, he'll have to do,' said Dennis. 'Go and fetch him.'

'It'll cost you,' said the demon.

'I've told you before. When this is done, I'll have everything. So he can name his price – up to a point, that is,' he backtracked sharply, not wanting to commit to too much.

'You'll have to call 'im yourself.'

'And how do I do that?' asked Dennis, his exasperation growing.

'You take the staff and bang it three times in each corner of the room, while saying *Jamzamin* softly,' Hell explained. One corner would have worked, and there was no need to say the name. Hell just wanted to be more demonic, and enjoy making Dennis look stupid.

'Anything else?' said Dennis, coldly.

'Standin' well back would be a good idea.'

Dennis uncertainly held the staff ready. 'Stand well back from where, exactly?'

'From the first corner you strike,' the demon decided.

As soon as Dennis had banged the staff for the third time in the last corner, he sprang to the centre of the room.

Nothing happened. Then it continued to happen

'Well?' demanded Dennis. 'Where is he?'

'Be patient. He might be doin' something.' They waited some more.

'Not long now, I fink,' said Hell, nervously breaking the silence again. After far too long, a rumbling began beneath them. Hell looked fretfully at each wall in turn. Suddenly he shouted, 'Over 'ere! Quick!'

Dennis acted fast, and followed the demon's lead in covering his head with his hands, as the opposite wall exploded into the room.

'Not *again!*' the wizard complained, as his room filled with dust and rubble, and the acrid smell of sulphur fumes.

'Atchoo!' sneezed the newly arrived demon, seamlessly carrying on with, 'Cough, cough, cough,' and a string of curses, rounding it off with a long drawn-out sniff.

The thought of saying 'bless you,' crossed no one's mind.

Dennis and the demon king eyed one another through the smoke and dust, Dennis in disbelief and the demon, grinning hideously.

''E's 'ere!' Hell announced, taking the prize, hands down, for the most pointless remark of the day.

'Really?' said Dennis.

⸺◈⟨⟩◈⸺

84

Jamzamin stopped coughing long enough to complain. 'Why do I always have to arrive in a bloody explosion? All this bloody dirt and dust! And where does that awful *smell* come from?' He began coughing again, and dropped to his knees with the effort, and started banging the floor with his hands. In spite of this, the dust continued to clear, and the King of the Parallel Dimension began taking on a discernible form.

He wasn't by any means regal. But he was bigger, bulkier and louder than other demons, and those were his qualifications for the role.

Dennis was losing what little patience he had. 'Perhaps it would help if you took that cigar out of your mouth.' He shot a glance at the king-sized hole that Jamzamin had made in his wall, and as Hell went to help his master to his feet, the wizard laid into them. 'Are you idiots determined to wreck this place? First my floor, now my wall! Can't you enter a place like any normal person?'

Jamzamin snarled at him, and tapped his cigar into Hell's cupped hands, as if politely not wanting to let it drop on to the rubble-strewn floor. '*Person?*' We're not *Persons...*'

'Or normal,' Hell chimed in.

'...we're *demons*,' finished the creature, emphatically and proudly.

'Well, *demons*,' sneered Dennis, 'when I've tidied this place up *again*, I'll talk business, and you will listen.' He made a magical sign over the rubble, and muttered his rewind spell.

The demons watched, mouths ajar, as the wall rebuilt itself.

'I'm impressed, wizard,' said Jamzamin, admiring the repaired wall. 'Now, what did you call me for?'

Dennis turned to Hell. 'Tell him.'

'Well, your Royalness,' he began, with a cursory bow, 'This wizard is not 'appy wiv my attitude to the catching of his pals. And the fact that I ain't caught many, I suppose. So, 'e wants someone better, that's you, to 'elp 'im as well.'

'Where are these pals? – these other *wizards*, I assume,' asked Jamzamin.

'In the city hiding somewhere. An' they don't 'elp by keeping out of the way.'

The king looked at Dennis, 'What have they done?'

'Nothing,' Dennis snapped.

'They've done nothing, but you want them brought in. Why?'

'They've done nothing, *yet*. But as I'm going to be the sole ruler of life, the university and everything – and I don't want any of them plotting against me ...' said Dennis, underscoring almost every word to show how serious he was '...they need to know exactly how things are going to be.'

'Ha! Ha! Ha!' laughed the demon king, equally emphatically. 'So, that's it. And what's in it for me, then?'

'As I told your minion here, when I am master here, I will be able to afford you any favour – any *reasonable* favour.'

'Sounds good. Very good!' Jamzamin grinned, evilly. 'We could do with some sort of a foothold up here. Hell, go and call up more of the lads. I want this done in the next two hours!'

The smaller demon pinched his nose like a swimmer about to plunge in, and began to think Parallel thoughts. 'Wait!' shouted Dennis. 'Not in here!'

Jamzamin intervened and waved Hell from the room. Soon after he went out there was a distant explosion as the demon exited this world and re-entered his own. Dennis hoped he'd left a ragged hole in a wall somewhere on his own side.

***

Eavesdropping behind the stone slab, Wimlett had heard it all. He made his way back along the passage. The streets outside were remarkably quiet, in the circumstances, and he reached the city gates without incident.

'You weren't very long,' said Eydith, smiling but anxious.

'It's bad news,' said Wimlett, gravely. 'Worse than we thought. There are demons roaming the streets terrorizing everybody.'

'Why's that? How did they get up here? What's happening?'

'One thing at a time,' said Wimlett, marshalling his thoughts.

'Well?' said Eydith, not known for her patience. 'Don't just stand there with your hand flapping about. Tell us.'

He described all that he'd just seen and heard, and stared hard at Florence. 'Did you know about your mother's broomstick?'

She flushed. 'Yes. She did tell you – I'm sure she did.'

'Tell us what?' asked Eydith.

'There's a demon in it,' Florence whispered, glancing about, fearing someone, or something might overhear.

'Yes,' said Wimlett. 'And Dennis has summoned it!'

'It's not a very good demon,' said Florence, attempting to play down the severity of it.

'None of them are,' said Wimlett, unusually short with her. 'But Dennis has used this one to call up the King of the Parallel Dimension.'

'Oh, no!' Florence gasped. 'Can he really do that?'

Eydith sat back deflated. This was unforeseen. But, then, this was Dennis. 'Sprag, can we deal with this?'

'Yes, mistress. But not as easily as we first thought.'

'What about the Drum?'

'Its spells will help. And my presence helps not only to access them, but also to control and direct them. There is also a reciprocal boost to my own power, and to yours through me.'

On cue, the Drum glowed, and the runes on Sprag's polished exterior began to writhe. Eydith felt their connection, and her eyes glowed along with them.

'Right.' Eydith gave her head a few shakes, reconnecting with normality. 'Let's get going.'

Link picked up the Drum and hoisted it onto his chest, and in silence they walk into the city.

———◈◈◈———

85

Dennis paced his rooms, occasionally stopping to peer out of the windows. He could see the front gates of the university and the roofs of the nearer buildings. Great palls of smoke rose in several areas, darkening the sky prematurely. His attention swivelled towards an explosion – the latest of many. This time from the Piggin Wissall, it seemed. A grin creased his face, and he hoped this would finally lay to rest some memories he'd had trouble stifling.

A hush followed the explosion. The smoke from it hung in the air, and he imagined shapes in it. Then, louder in the eerie silence, the great gates began to creak open. There was a cracking of whips, and several shouts, as six wizards, their robes scorched and their faces smeared with soot, were shepherded into the quadrangle by some twenty demons. Dennis rubbed his hands together. 'At last, I have them all.'

NOT QUITE, said a voice darker than the inside of a cat.

Dennis turned from the window, and his face turned almost as white as the features that now gazed eyelessly back at him. '*Death*?' he whispered. 'So soon? And at such an inopportune moment.'

DO NOT FLATTER YOURSELF, WIZARD, YOU ARE NOT RIPE ENOUGH TO ENTER MY HOUSE JUST YET. BUT I HAVE A PLACE RESERVED FOR YOU. AND REST ASSURED, THE SANDS WILL RUN OUT FOR YOU ONE DAY. AND IF I COULD SHAKE THEM THROUGH, I WOULD.

'Then why are you here?' asked the wizard, his fear fast becoming irritability.

TO GLOAT, MAINLY. The Reaper grinned, blankly. AND TO ADVISE YOU THAT, EVEN NOW, YOU DON'T HAVE ALL THE WIZARDS LOCKED IN YOUR CELLARS.

'I know that,' said Dennis, curtly. 'Six of them are still in the quad, but it will only be a few minutes before they join the others.'

NO, said Death, waving a dismissive cloaked arm, THERE ARE STILL TWO, MAYBE THREE, THAT WILL STAND AGAINST YOU.

'And who would *they* be?' Dennis sneered, not believing that any of them would dare oppose him now. Though it was common knowledge that Death never lied. *But could He be wrong?* Dennis wondered. 'And why should you care?'

Death ignored that last question, because He wasn't absolutely certain Himself, and answered the first. I WAS ABOUT TO TELL YOU, said the Reaper, brusquely, IF I MAY? He waited a meaningful moment, and said, ONE CALLED LINKWOOD.

'Linkwood?' Dennis snorted. 'A Seventh Level? He's no match for me!'

PERHAPS NOT. IT REMAIMS TO BE SEEN. BUT THERE IS A GIRL...

'A girl?' said Dennis, stopping the Reaper mid-sentence, his tone drowning the very idea in scorn. 'What *girl*?'

IF YOU WILL JUST SHUT UP AND LISTEN, I WILL TELL YOU. He was tiring of the interruptions. He slid His hand inside His robe and gave Dennis's Life-Timer a swift tap. THE GIRL IS CALLED EYDITH. YOU WILL DO WELL TO TREAT HER WITH CIVILITY.

'Oh, I will,' Dennis countered, contemptuously. 'And then I shall crush her.'

I HAVE WARNED YOU! Death muttered, as He turned dramatically and stalked through the nearest wall. If He'd had breath, he would have known He'd been wasting it. The last Dennis heard of Him, for the moment, was the click, click, clicking of His unshod feet, and His sombre voice receding: WE SHALL SEE. WE SHALL SEE. WE SHALL SEE.

Dennis picked up the staff, and left the room. He padded down the stairs, and carried on down the stone steps to the cellars He arrived just as the demons were incarcerating the last six wizards, and stood at Jamzamin's side. When the door slammed shut, he looked in the cellar. There were so many in there, they were standing shoulder to shoulder.

'Why are they all in one cellar?' Dennis sighed.

'That's why they call 'im Jamzamin,' replied Hell, before the king could speak.

'There are a dozen cellars down here!' cried Dennis. 'Spread them out. Give them some room to breathe. I'm not totally without feelings, you know.'

'Where's my big hammer?' Jamzamin yelled to the cellar generally.

'What on Crett for?' asked Dennis, before anyone could get it.

'You want 'em spread out, I'll spread 'em out.'

'Just put some of them in the other cellars, man! Are you a complete idiot? – and not the wine cellars!' he thought he should add.'

Jamzamin didn't answer. He was wondering if he was complete, or had bits missing. It wasn't something he's been asked before. He waved a hand, telling the demons to do as Dennis asked.

'That's it, then. All locked up safe and sound.'

'Not quite. There are still two more out there somewhere,' he confided.

'Really?' said the king, glancing over his shoulder. Where?'

86

Eydith and the others were outside the university gates. 'I need to do something with this Drum,' said Link. 'I can't lug it around out here. If Dennis sees it, I'll be his number one target. And I can hardly defend myself, or even run, with this on my chest.' He looked around, hoping for suggestions.

'I know where we can leave it,' said Wimlett. 'Follow me.'

He followed the ghostly mage into the alleyway at the side of the building. Link realised where they were going. 'Good idea.'

The Drum was safely stowed in the room that Eydith used when Link first brought her into the university some months ago. 'Shall we go round the front and let them in?' said Link.

'No, you go back to the girls, and I'll open the gates. You might be seen going through the halls. And I can take a quick look around. See who's here. Give me ten minutes.'

Link made his way back to where Eydith and Florence were waiting.

'What's happening?' asked Eydith. 'Where's Father?'

'He's inside. He said to give him a few minutes to scout around, then he'd come and open up. We can't plan anything until we know what's going on in there.'

Eydith leaned on the staff. She was eager to get on with this, but she dreaded it. Nothing in her short life had prepared her for such a thing. Mixed feelings hardly described it.

Sprag picked up her thoughts. 'You are prepared, mistress,' he said, gently reminding her of all she'd done and learned lately. She smiled weakly, still in need of convincing.

Wimlett's head appeared through the gate. 'It's okay. Dennis is up in his room.'

'From where he can see us down here if he should look out of a window,' said Eydith, remembering the last time she was there.

'Has he got the staff?' asked Florence.

'Yes, and two demons are with him. One of them is bigger and nastier than any I've seen. It must be the king.'

'What's the plan?' asked Link of all of them.

'Attack,' said Wimlett. 'We have to overpower Dennis now before he gets any more powerful. Although he's sure to be expecting us, he doesn't know when, does he? I'll go ahead to watch and wait for when he's alone. It'll be better not to have a demon or two to contend with as well. Especially that big bast... that big one.'

But even as he spoke, Jamzamin and Hell emerged from the main building, and were loping across the quad towards the gates. Wimlett heard them. He turned to look, and poked his head back through the gates. 'Someone's coming,' he whispered. 'Demons. Two of them. The ones who were with Dennis just now.'

'Good. Maybe they'll open the gates,' said Eydith, wielding Sprag like a two-handed sword in readiness. Then, from the other side of the gates, Hell's voice echoed loudly and raspingly around the quadrangle.

'Oh, yuck! Look. It's that severed hand!'

Jamzamin was curious. 'What? Out Here?'

'Over there. By the gates!' The smaller demon pointed at Wimlett's hand bobbing up and down a few yards ahead of them.

Concealed nearby in the shadows of the cloistered walkway that ran from the main building to an annexe, were the even more shadowy figures of Death and Naphrat. They too saw the hand. Whereupon they exchanged glances: Death wearing an expressionless face that somehow conveyed 'HOW ON CRETT DID THAT HAPPEN?' and Naphrat answering with an osteopathic click of his shoulders, which translated roughly as, 'I don't have a bloody clue.'

The silent conversation over, the two figures resumed their roles as spectators.

'I've been spotted,' said Wimlett, urgently. Eydith reacted without a second thought. She brought Sprag round in a swinging arc and slammed him into the gates. The staff resonated with the impact, but the great weathered gates stood firm.

Nothing happened. Eydith implored Sprag to produce something. *Anything.*

'Give it a moment, mistress.'

On the other side of the gates, 'I think there's someone at the door,' said Hell.

'Then see who it is,' ordered Jamzamin.

'They haven't prop'ly knocked yet. Just a bit of a clanging noise.'

Jamzamin's eyes blazed more hotly demonic, and Hell decided to do as he was told. Though he didn't get the chance to execute the order.

The tall gates bowed and creaked. Their great wrought-iron hinges became over-wrought and finally snapped. They fell majestically back into the quadrangle, and would have landed with a crash that would have sent dust clouds flying in all directions, had their fall not been cushioned. The two demons took the full weight of the gates. Wimlett was also a casualty. His solid hand was trapped against the cobblestones next to the half-dazed demons.

Once the shock of it had passed, Hell and Jamzamin began to claw their way out. Wimlett had the same idea, and inadvertently placed his hand on one of them.

Hell stopped clawing for a moment. 'Is that you, your Royalness?' he asked.

'What?'

'You know... touching me.'

'I wouldn't touch you if you were the last demon in the Parallel Dimension!'

Flattered as he was, Hell ignored the insult. 'I don't think we're alone, your Royalness.'

'I don't see anyone else,' said the king.

Wimlett moved again. He had no wish to be this close to the demons any more than they did to him. Their movement had given him a little wriggle room. He moved his hand, spider-like, towards the top of the gates.

Hell saw something move out of the corner of his eye, and turned. 'Yuck!' he screamed. 'It's that 'orrible 'and again!' Seriously motivated now, he began frantically punching and scraping his way out.

Wimlett watched him. *There's no need for me to struggle*, he thought, *these stupid creatures will get me out quicker than I can do it myself.* Almost before he'd finished the thought, the demons had battered and scratched holes big enough for them to escape. He moved his hand into the gap and scrambled to his feet. They watched the hand rise from beneath the gates and fled back across the quadrangle to the main entrance.

Dennis opened a window to investigate. 'What's going on down there?' he called out.

Eydith, Florence and Link, stepped across the fallen gates into full view.

'Who are you?!' Dennis shouted.

'I am Eydith!' she shouted back at him. 'Remember me? You should. You had me thrown out last time I was here!'

'You!' yelled Dennis, in recognition. 'Hell! Get them out of here!'

Hell and Jamzamin emerged, and turned to see if there was any way they could do that. It was difficult because Wimlett had stepped forward and was holding up his hand, as though stopping traffic. He wiggled his fingers with the hope of increasing the 'yuck' factor. It had the desired effect, causing the demons to hesitate. But they stood their ground this time. They eyed the hand and looked at one another. The unspoken conversation was that the hand hadn't really hurt them so far, so perhaps it couldn't. But the fact that it was there, seemed to be enough to bring the bile creeping to their throats again, and they made no attempt to move.

'Get them!' screamed Dennis, waving the staff.

'Oh, no! E's got that bloody staff out again,' moaned Hell,

As a precaution, Eydith held Sprag angled to the ground in front of her. She didn't want to reveal she had it yet, or do anything that might compromise the staff's effectiveness before she could properly bring it into play.

As Wimlett hadn't moved, the demons decided reluctantly to shuffle past the hand on either side in an effort to get to Eydith. But Sprag twisted in Eydith's hand and the air crackled. An incandescent charge of destructive fire spat across the quadrangle, burning a great chunk of masonry from the wall above Hell's head. Eydith pulled the staff out of sight.

The two demons scurried back to the relative safety of the nearest doorway and disappeared. Dennis ducked back into his room. The ferocity of the blast had taken him off guard. *Where had that come from? Surely not the girl?* He hung back, a little shaken, and in case a second blast was headed his way. When the silence dragged, he stepped quickly back to the open window and sent a flash of blue lightning at Eydith. His aim was hurried, and he missed by yards, burning a hole in the perimeter wall, and demolishing a gate pier.

Sprag turned in Eydith's hands and returned Dennis's fire. A section of masonry under Dennis's window exploded, sending him reeling back into his room. He recovered quickly, and moved to another window, bursting it open, and throwing another fork of blue lightning down at Eydith, lighting the quadrangle.

She stood firmly behind Sprag, who deflected the blast – and wasting no time returning another red flame at Dennis – so powerful it took out a complete side of his room.

Dennis appeared at the hole, and furiously and hurriedly sent two more streaks of light down at them, before scrambling back out of the way. Link pointed his hands at the last place he'd seen Dennis and released his own magical fire at the spot. He ducked swiftly away, but Dennis didn't return fire. When he didn't show for a few minutes, they cautiously relaxed.

There was a deathly hush in the quadrangle after this first encounter. The air was tainted with the smell of burnt and melted matter – stone, metal and timber convulsed and fused by devastating magical potency. Florence was first to break the silence.

'Do you think he's still alive?' she whispered.

A door flew open, and a great lance of blue flame spat across the quad towards them.

'Yep!' replied Link, diving to the ground.

Dennis's aim was good this time. The blue fire charged hungrily at Eydith.

Link yelled in horror, 'Nooo...' and watched in stunned amazement.

It seemed to happen in slow motion. Her eyes glowed brilliantly when the flame reached her. She reached out a hand and plucked it from the air. In her hand, it became a jagged spear of solid fire, which she twirled and sent back as a spinning rotor that scythed through the wall above the main entrance, demolishing a statue of one of the university's founding wizards. Dennis disappeared hastily inside again. They saw him pass other windows heading away from the scene. He'd clearly had enough for now.

Eydith covered her mouth in disbelief at what she'd done.

Not wanting to lose the initiative, she led the others quickly to the door which led up to where Dennis had been. As they went in, two holes opened up in the cobblestones behind them, accompanied by minor explosions and the stench of sulphur, and the uncontrollable choking of two familiar demons arriving. One large, one small.

Link turned to face them while Eydith and Florence pressed on upstairs. The two demons grinned as they cleared their throats and started to creep forward. Wimlett was hiding his hand behind a piece of quadrangle statuary. It was a piece he'd always hated, and hoped it would get caught in the crossfire (though preferably not right now), *like that monstrosity over the entrance that Eydith had demolished, and he was glad to see the back of.* Seizing his opportunity, he snatched up a hefty remnant of broken window frame and got in step behind them.

Wimlett's chosen victim had to be Hell. He was the shortest of the pair, and the piece of wood would accelerate faster with the extra distance on its downward swing.

It smashed to splinters on the demon's scaly head. Almost painlessly. But it distracted the creature long enough for Link to release a flame that caught one of Jamzamin's horns. That had to hurt. The demon put some distance between them and sat down. He clutched his head, shuddered, and thought about what he was doing. Hell went to tend to, and commiserate with his Royalness.

When she and Florence couldn't find Dennis, Eydith returned to the quadrangle.

Link was doing his best to deal with more demons rising up through the cobblestones. He was firing off blasts, not sure if he actually wanted to hit a demon. Until today, he'd never used magic as a weapon, and was finding it both empowering and disturbing – something he could get used to, but wasn't sure he wanted to. And it was tiring using magic this much.

He was greatly relieved to see Eydith. Sprag sprayed a surge of red lightning across the quad. This seemed to be enough, and made the creatures pull back. But Hell and Jamzamin rallied. They roared their defiance and shifted their forms to resemble large ferocious dogs. Growling and slavering, they leapt at Eydith, as the other demons scurried down their holes.

Sprag spat venomous light again, sustained, and focused, forcing the shifters to sail harmlessly over Eydith's head and right through the open entrance door, from where they ran yelping, singed and smoking into the depths of the building.

87

Dennis had retreated to the cellars. He was issuing orders to the forty or so demons of various shapes and sizes that were guarding the wizards.

'You five! Go round to the left!' He pointed at a group of disinterested green things. 'You four! Round to the right!' he ordered another group, who were looking at their hands trying to work out which way was right – and perhaps, for all Dennis knew, who's turn was it to have the brain that week.

'You lot!' he called to a group that had become monumentally disinterested with the whole business, and were about to leave, 'You get upstairs and be ready to attack them from above. And you lot,' he went on, glaring at the large group milling around in front of him, 'Come with me!'

'Hold on a minute, mate,' said a defiant voice in the ranks.

'You have a question?'

'No, I have a statement!'

'Well?'

'It's our tea break, mate, so you'll have to wait.' He turned to a diminutive demon beside him. 'Put the kettle on, lad.'

'I can't believe you people!' screamed Dennis, ignoring the murmur that followed him calling them people. 'I'm about to take over the world. Starting here. Today. And you want to make bloody tea?'

'Don't *want* to, mate. Have to. You know... Union rules, see?'

'What the hell's a union?'

'You callin' me again?' At that moment, Hell and Jamzamin appeared at the door to the cellars, still scorched and smoking. 'That's it!' stormed Jamzamin. 'I've had it! They've bloody well upset me now!' He ranted on as he looked around the gathered creatures. Then he saw one he recognised. 'Kragli! Bring me that kettle before you put it on!'

The demon brought the kettle and handed it over. Testing its weight to be sure it was full, His Royalness took off the lid and upturned the contents over his own charred head, causing a great hiss of steam to mushroom into the air above him. When he'd cooled down, he surveyed the crowd, and solemnly announced... 'It begins.'

'Not yet, it doesn't,' Dennis smirked.

'What?' snapped Jamzamin.

'I said, not yet,' Dennis repeated.

'Why not?'

'It's their *tea* break,' Dennis explained, conveying his contempt with the unsubtle emphasis of a single word.

'Well,' said the demon king, crushing the kettle between his claws, 'it's just been cancelled. Any questions?' he asked, looking at the sea of faces.

None came.

'Good! Now... as I was saying... *It begins*.' He straightened up to his full imperial height and turned Dennis around to face the door. 'March!' he demanded. 'We're right behind you!'

'B... b... but,' Dennis stammered, thinking twice about using his depleted magic.

'I said, March!' Jamzamin repeated, and Dennis went slowly forward. The motley demon army fell in behind their king.

In the deep shadows of a nearby alcove, Death nudged Naphrat and whispered, I THINK THIS IS BEGINNING TO LOOK A LITTLE ONE SIDED, DON'T YOU?

Naphrat agreed. 'But what can we do, Master?'

WELL, THAT GHOST CHAPPY, WHAT'S HIS NAME...?

'Wimlett?' said Naphrat.

THAT'S THE FELLOW. WASN'T HE A GOOD WIZARD, AT ONE TIME?

'Yes, he was very good, I suppose.'

WHAT CAN WE DO TO HELP HIM?

Naphrat gave it some thought. 'A nice sword?'

MIGHT HELP, the Reaper agreed.

'Or what about loaning him some magic?'

YES, I LIKE THAT, mused Death. He slapped his bony hand against his skull with a hollow clonk! I'LL GIVE HIM BOTH. HE'LL BE MORE THAN A MATCH FOR THIS RABBLE. He grinned, straight-facedly. This was quite novel. He'd not been in the business of helping people before – discounting helping them to their ultimate destination – and all this excitement was far better than trying to run that dull tavern in the desert. He was glad He'd come back.

Shortly after, Wimlett felt a strange un-warmth flood over him, causing him to stop. He shrugged and continued along the passageway he was following.

'Where are we going?' asked Florence, in a whisper.

Wimlett paused again. 'We need to be systematic in our search, or we'll never find him. I thought we should start at the top of the Tower of Unknown Magic and work our way down.'

'What about the library, Father?' Eydith reminded him.

'What? Oh, we can't worry about that now. If Link still has that book, he'll have to pay the fine later.'

'No, I mean, don't you think we should protect it?' said Eydith. 'All that magic?'

'No. Dennis won't be thinking about that,' Wimlett reassured her.

Sprag glowed warmly in Eydith's hand. 'Mistress, there is no one above this level.'

She told Link and Florence what the staff had said. There was no need to go higher than the floor they were on.

'Good, then they're all down there,' said Wimlett.

As they crept forward, looking this way and that, they passed open doors and intersecting corridors. A sudden loud and metallic clattering caused them to stop.

'What was that?' said Eydith, on behalf of them all.

'I appear to have a sword before me,' Wimlett replied, unfazed. *A gift from an old friend, perhaps*, he thought to himself, wondering if his drinking buddy was nearby. 'It might come in useful,' he decided, picking it up. He had taken only a few steps when he realised he was carrying it in his invisible hand.

⸺⸻◆⸻⸺

88

Having assured themselves that non-one was in the upper levels, they made their way to the stone steps leading down to the university's subterranean vaults. Wimlett had seldom been down there in all his time at the university, as those that did rarely returned, until Death found them. It was down here that the original Archchancellors and creators of the Magic University were interred.

Subsequent Archchancellors were placed down there, too, alongside them, but were always mysteriously re-located elsewhere in the vaults. No-one ever knew who was responsible. In time, it was decided to leave well alone and lay to rest all other university heads in vaults away from the original crypt. The whole area was pretty creepy. Wimlett hoped they would need to go no further than the cellars. Even a ghost found it creepy.

The vaults were on the same level as the cellars, and were accessed through them. Wimlett doubted that Dennis would have the nerve to trespass that far – especially knowing how choosey the ancients were about the company they kept – which meant he must be in the cellars. Assuming he was still in the building.

Wimlett went first down the twisting stairway, and at each corner he peered round. If it was quiet, he beckoned the others to follow. But approaching the remaining turns in the stairway, he held back. He heard the sound of many feet coming up from below. All marching to different drums.

'I think we've found them,' whispered Eydith. She raised Sprag in readiness.

Dennis was first to appear around the corner, propelled forward up the narrow stairs by the crush of demons behind. Alarmingly for him, his way was barred by a large sword hovering in front of him. Hell and Jamzamin, at his shoulders, saw it next.

'Stop!' yelled the king, and his command was rapidly echoed by all those in his wake.

Dennis's reaction to the sword was to hit it with a bolt of lightning, which Wimlett deflected with the mirror-like flat of the blade, sending it ricocheting back down the stairway, singeing a few demons along the way.

A few of the cowardly creatures at the back decided enough was enough, and urgently clawed their way back to the Parallel Dimension.

Eydith came into view, and Dennis aimed a charge of blue flame at her, which was sucked away by Sprag. Wimlett had instinctively shot out a hand, as he would've done in his human days, and to his amazement, a burst of green fire erupted from his invisible fingers. The ghostly mage looked in disbelief, and wasted no time levelling it at Dennis. His aim was wild, missing his old enemy, but totally disarming two demons beyond him.

They shrugged their armless shoulders and wove their way back down the stairs. No point hanging about when they couldn't even put the kettle on.

Eydith backed up a couple of steps, and pointed Sprag over her father's head. A searing arc of crimson light snaked through the air, reducing eight demons to a mess that slithered down the steps. Eydith aimed again, and repeated the devastation, felling several more.

Dennis's face twisted and he snarled like a demon himself. He replied with a two-handed burst of energy, one blocked by Wimlett's hand, and the other deflected by a mystical wave from Link, who couldn't believe his luck. He didn't think he'd ever have strength enough to counter Dennis in a duel of magic. He had to remind himself to keep a cool head though. Overconfidence could be fatal.

The crowd of demons behind Jamzamin and Hell was in disarray, and the King of the Demons had to plough his way to the back, to stop them from retreating.

'Stop! You cowards!' he screamed, trying to shame them into action. 'There's only three of the buggers! What's the matter with you? Can't you destroy three humans?'

There was a general buzz of debate, as the demons considered what the king had said. 'Don't fink much of it, so far...' said one. 'Losing a few more...' said another.

Jamzamin was getting sorely vexed at the way his minions had seen fit to debate his words. 'Are you going to join in, or not!'

'No!' three of them chorused.

Jamzamin cut them down with a sudden lunge of his huge claws, and repeated the question.

'Well, being as you put it like that, your Kingness, we fink *now* would be a good time to join in.'

At the front line, Dennis had his work cut out deflecting a barrage of fire from Wimlett. And although he was holding his own, Wimlett's deflections were taking their toll on the demons behind him, whose contribution to the fight so far – apart from the occasional sortie, and some retreating and dying disgustingly – seemed to Dennis to have been little more than roaring angrily, and getting in one another's way.

Eydith kept Sprag aloft in a samurai pose and tried to concentrate amid the commotion. Her arms were beginning to ache. Florence, close behind her, sensed the problem and reached forward to support her elbows.

Link aimed both hands at what he could see of the demon horde through the swirling smoke and luminescence. A surge of power left his fingers at the same instant Wimlett released another formation of fireballs. Eydith, too, added her firepower.

All three wizards had unleashed their power at once. Dennis's defensive magic barely held. He summoned everything he had. The explosion of light and sound that ensued left everyone on the stairway, humans and demons alike, both deaf and blind for a full minute. The air in the confined space filled with acridity and wails of derision, and much coughing and cursing. Slowly regaining their senses, Dennis and the demons retreated down the stairs.

Link pushed his way to the front, spread his fingers and conjured a wind strong enough to clear the air. When the smoke had cleared, there was a gaping crater where the steps had been. The result of their combined assault.

'I think we might have overdone it a bit,' he said, grinning a little nervously.

'There's just room to squeeze by at the side,' said Florence.

'Well, come on, then,' urged Wimlett. 'It's not over yet. But mind how you tread.'

The four of them edged their way along the narrow ledge to the relative safety of the remaining steps, and continued down towards the cellars, where Wimlett guessed the other wizards were being held. There was no sign of Dennis or the demons. They approached the remaining turns near the bottom of the stairway with extreme caution. Wimlett took the lead, checking ahead as before. They were almost at the cellars, and the way looked clear, when, without warning, a troop of demons crashed through the wall ahead, Jamzamin and Hell leading the charge.

They were momentarily caught off guard by the ambush, but Wimlett rallied quickly and emerald fire flared from his fingertips. Jamzamin caught the full blast on his scaly chest and slumped to the floor. Three other demons dragged him to safety, while Hell waved the rest of the troop forward in a last desperate bid to overpower or kill the humans.

'Do you know how to use a sword?' Wimlett asked Florence.

She didn't answer, but held out a hand to take it anyway. It was lighter than she expected, and she held it nervously at the advancing demons. Sprag glowed for a moment in an effort to send more magic into the gleaming blade, only to realise there was no need. The sword took on a life of its own and began hacking and slashing while Florence held on, flinching.

Dennis arrived among the demons on the narrow stairs, furiously flinging spells and cursing as he was jostled off target each time.

Eydith and Link were inflicting severe casualties among Hell's troops – as was Florence, as the sword dragged her into the front line, eager for action. But, because of the fallen, it was becoming harder by the minute for any of them to engage in combat. And those demons that were still of a mind to do Dennis's bidding were having the same problems.

The number of dead and wounded littering the stairway between the two factions had grown so deep that neither side could go forwards until someone tidied up.

'Get back!' shouted Wimlett.

'Back?' Eydith questioned him.

'Yes! Retreat around the corner. Out of sight.'

Eydith reluctantly grabbed Florence and waved Link back. Wimlett backed up maintaining a rear guard.

When he joined them, Eydith wasn't happy. 'What are you doing, Father?' she rounded on him. 'We almost have them beaten.'

'We were losing momentum, Eydith. With that heap of dead and wounded building up I was soon going to be the only one who could get near them.'

'Yes, but...'

'We couldn't go forward and neither could they,' he insisted. 'Give them time to tire themselves out clearing the stairs and we'll go at them again.'

'Why don't we attack from both sides?' proposed Link.

'Because we can't,' replied Florence, a little breathless from tying to keep up with the sword, and happy for a breather.

'We could if Wimlett could go down and release the wizards from the cellars.'

'It's an idea,' agreed Wimlett. 'And we might just have time for that.'

89

Wimlett edged forwards down the steps. The smoke was clearing. The demons were too engrossed reclaiming their fallen comrades to notice his hand moving silently passed them against the wall. He passed a room with its door ajar. Dennis was inside arguing with Jamzamin, who was looking dazed and scorched after the vicious flame that Wimlett had dealt him.

The old wizard made his way down unhindered, and entered the door at the bottom. There were half a dozen cellars at this level. Which of them held the wizards was obvious by where the guards were posted. No other demons were visible. They were all helping with the dead and wounded, or had retired elsewhere to rest and recover. Or, they had deserted.

There were only two on sentry duty. They barred the way to a block of cellars on Wimlett's right. One of them had a jailor-size bunch of keys on a hefty ring fastened to a rope belt. Wimlett recognised the ring from the key-box in the Archchancellor's office. He was going to need those keys.

The sentries were sitting on the floor against the wall, one each side of the corridor entrance, and seemed bored and distracted. One was cleaning his ear out with the end of his tail, and admiring the lumps of gunk he wormed out. The one with the keys looked half asleep. *Maybe I can get him all the way there*, thought Wimlett, and went in search of something to hit him with.

He returned a few moments later with two chunks of broken masonry. He'd remembered his ability to pick up the sword with his invisible hand – and quietly cursed himself for leaving the sword with Florence. Though on second thoughts, it would have given his presence away too easily. He was relieved to find he could pick up things other than the sword with his other hand.

He had a plan. He knew he'd have to disable both guards at once. If he tried to deal with one, the other would be on him in seconds. The guards were seated at about the same distance apart as his two outstretched hands. Which meant that if he swooped at them with his arms wide, like a swan landing on a pond, and with a sizeable rock in each hand, he'd catch both of them square in the face. That would put both out of action long enough. Armed and ready, he backed up about twenty feet and rose to near the ceiling. Not easy with heavy rocks,

Silently, he screamed, 'Charge!' and launched himself down on the unsuspecting guards, just like a... well, exactly like an invisible maniac with a bloody great lump of rock in each hand. Suddenly he connected with a sickening double thud. The two demons never knew what hit them, and never would. Wimlett dropped the bloodied rocks and looked away from the damage he'd inflicted. *Well, there's a war on*, he reminded himself. This was not a time to be squeamish. He also reminded himself that these beings weren't human. It's a ploy in wartime to demonise the enemy to justify killing them, but in this case the opposition was already demonised, so no mind-games were required.

Wimlett unhooked the keys, and, with his insider's ex-Archchancellor's knowledge of them, he promptly applied key number 1 to cellar number 1. The first of the freed wizards stepped from the cell and looked around, bewildered, wondering how the door had opened itself. He was of Wimlett's own generation, and not unlike him in appearance. He saw the hand with the keys floating through the air from cell to cell unlocking the rest of the doors.

'Who's there?' he asked, softly, a little deferentially, thinking he might be dealing with an accomplished wizard who had perfected a cloak of invisibility.

Wimlett turned. 'Oh, it's you, Trinkel,' he said, and carried on unlocking doors.

Trinkel didn't hear, and repeated the question

'It's me – Wimlett. You haven't forgotten me already, have you?' replied Wimlett, still turning locks. Then something warm and old-cloth-like, passed through him. Looking down, he saw one of Trinkel's sleeved hands waving through him. His former colleague was trying to make sense of what he couldn't see.

Wimlett crouched on the floor, and with the sharpest key he scratched on the stone: '*It's me, Wimlett. A ghost. Follow me.*'

Trinkel rubbed his eyes and looked again. 'Wimlett... sir? Is it really you, sir?' He reread the message. 'Where to?' he asked the hand.

'*Up the stairs... deal with Dennis and demons,*' he scratched. It was long-winded way to communicate. And '*stop calling me sir*' was hard work, too, but needful.

'We can't face Dennis,' said Trinkel, alarmed at the prospect.

'?' was then scratched in the stone.

'We haven't got our staffs.'

Wimlett was appalled. Had standards dropped so low that hand magic had fallen out of use and they needed staffs? *Probably Dennis's way of keeping them weaker, so they wouldn't challenge him,* he thought, disgustedly. 'Hang on a minute,' he said, forgetting he couldn't be heard. 'If they were taken from you down here they can't be far.' A quick reconnoitre of the cellars located them. Getting back to Trinkel, he realised that he'd understood the question mark, and it dawned on him that he could use shorthand. He scratched a few arrows leading to the cellar where the staffs were stored. He even had the presence of mind to unlock it this time.

90

Along the block of cellars, wizards were emerging, stretching limbs and breathing deeply. Due to his contact with Wimlett, Trinkel, assumed command. He told them where to collect their staffs and where to assemble for a briefing. Wimlett hadn't seen so many wizards in one place, all working together towards the same end, since the time a brewery cart toppled over and shed its load on Main Street.

There were a few 'Yuks' when the assembled wizards saw the dead guards outside. Wimlett joined Trinkel and waved his hand in front of the wizard's face. Then again with his visible hand.

Trinkel quickly told them the little he knew: that their deceased and previous Archchancellor, Wimlett, was now a ghost, and was helping them against Dennis and the demons. Wimlett waved the key-ring in the air on cue to support this. A murmur spread through the crowd and they rallied. 'This recent demon episode was the last straw,' said one. There was another louder murmur of agreement. They were eager to do whatever it took.

Wimlett was about to explain about Eydith and the others, and about how they were going to co-ordinate an attack – and he was balking at the idea of scratching it all out on the floor or wall – when an unseen deathly hand delivered an unnaturally benevolent stream of dark magic towards him – more grey than black. Wimlett felt an icy, pricking sensation. It started from his newly-usable invisible hand and spread to every part of him. He began shivering violently, as if bucket after bucket of ice was being tipped over him. The assembled wizards watched in wonder as he shivered himself into visibility.

'Hello, Archchancellor,' said Trinkel, warmly taking his old friend's freezing hand.

'Phoar!' said Wimlett, audibly, hugging and rubbing himself, and jigging about, trying to get warm. 'What happened?' It was rhetorical. He looked down at himself. *Only Naphrat could have done this*, he thought, *or Death Himself*. Whichever it was, he was grateful. Not many people had Death on their side. He saw just the flicker of a shadow fading into the wall at his side. Death! Maybe the old Bonehead wasn't so incorrigibly grim after all.

Once Wimlett had thawed a little, he addressed the throng of caped and staffed wizards. It felt like old times. Like an oversized staff meeting – he smiled at his own pun. He hastily outlined what was happening and what he needed from them. Expected of them. Everyone nodded and raised a staff in solidarity. No-one doubted that Dennis had to be stopped. And the presence of the old Archchancellor brought home to all those who remembered him just how appalling Dennis truly was. Not one of them now believed the scurrilous tales that had been circulated about Wimlett.

There was no time to lose. Wimlett led the way to the stairs. They followed him up the first twenty-odd steps. Here Wimlett signalled them to stop. The door was around the next corner where Dennis and his chief demons were. There were probably more of them now. He whispered this to Trinkel who was at his shoulder, and who passed it back down the line. 'Once we start the attack, the noise will attract Eydith and the others.'

Trinkel nodded. He set his white-bearded chin at what he hoped was a determined angle and inched quietly forward. Wimlett peered round the corner, almost forgetting he was visible, and saw two guards at the door. Without hesitating, he summoned and threw a ball of phosphorescent green flame across the space between them. *Let battle commence.*

'They're back!' yelled a demon – the remaining one – and hordes of demons tried to pile out of the door at the same time. The tide halted briefly when two of the rotund ones got jammed side by side.

Wimlett continued throwing fireballs from where he stood, while Trinkel and the nearest wizards used their combined magical talents to deflect weapons and halt the flow of demons coming at them. Many surged up the stairs. From above, Eydith appeared and began using Sprag to devastating effect. Together with Link's battle-honed magical abilities and Florence's sword, they drove the demons back towards Wimlett and the other wizards.

More and more demons were being slain in a crossfire of angry magic, and many more were giving up or fleeing injured to the Parallel Dimension before they too became just grim battle statistics.

Dennis was shouting at Jamzamin, 'Get out there and help them!'

'Get out there and do something!' Jamzamin bellowed at Hell.

Hell went out, pressed himself against the wall, and watched the multi-coloured shafts of lethal magic criss-crossing the air outside. He heard the explosions, and the cries of those in the thick of it. Then he came back. 'No bloody fear, mate. You want it so bad, *you* go!'

'I told you!' yelled Dennis. 'When this is over, I'll give you anything you want! Anything!'

'So you did,' sneered Jamzamin. 'So you did.'

'Yes! Yes! Get on with it, then!' Dennis yelled.

'Right, follow me, you two!' ordered the king, remembering his royal prerogative. Not that he knew what that was. He thought he was just a bully.

Dennis and Hell marched into the passageway behind him, one on each side of his broad shoulders. Dennis could hardly believe the carnage that lay before them. Apart from a dozen or so demons that were helplessly pinned down in the crossfire, those that weren't dead or mutilated beyond recognition had fled.

Dennis ducked across to the outer wall of the corner, and saw Eydith above him. Eye contact was instant and hateful in both directions. He levelled his hands at Eydith, and two streams of orange flame licked up towards her. Sprag twisted in her grip and deflected them away in a shower of sparks, each leaving a smoking spot on the wall or staircase. Eydith advanced down a step. Dennis backed down towards the cellars, but the way was blocked by Wimlett and his wizards who were advancing slowly.

Knowing his power was stronger than the wizards on this front, Dennis turned and succeeded in injuring four of them before Wimlett could stop him.

Florence moved forward from below, sword in hand, and watched in mute wonder as it defended her formidably. The damage she inflicted, together with the damage being meted out by Eydith and Link, left only Jamzamin, Hell and Dennis, now standing in the haze of magical smoke. The rest of the demons had either fled or were dead.

It suddenly went quiet –the world seemed to hold its breath – as Dennis and the two arch- demons looked around and discovered they were the only ones left. Eydith menacingly levelled Sprag at the larger of the demons. Jamzamin backed away holding a hand, palm up, in front of him, fingers spread wide to indicate he had no intention to respond with any power of his own.

'That's enough!' called the demon king. 'There's no point to this anymore. We're leaving.'

'No! We're not!' screamed Dennis, summoning every ounce of baleful magic he could lay his mind to, and compressing it all into one vicious ball of crimson lightning that he hurled at Eydith with terrifying force and rage.

'No!' yelled Florence, wielding the sword and jumping in front of Eydith. She swung at the lightning, shattering the dense magic into a thousand shards of light, which engulfed her.

Nobody spoke for a moment. Dennis was depleted, and needed time to recover. Eydith, Link and Wimlett watched in open-mouthed disbelief as the swirling malevolent shards settled to the ground revealing Florence lying curled in a foetal position with her cloak pulled tightly over her face. One hand still clutching the sword.

Even the two demons looked on as if disconcerted.

Eydith stepped towards her and the sword hand twitched. She paused. A pang of hope. The hollow of despair in her gut was almost too much to bear.

A moment later, Florence uncurled herself and pulled the cloak back from her head. 'You alright?' she said to Eydith. Eydith hugged her and pulled her up in one swift movement.

Half a flight of stairs below them, Jamzamin and Hell grabbed Dennis by the arms and dragged him away. 'Wait!' called Florence.

The demons stopped. 'What is it now?' moaned Jamzamin.

'You can't take him!' she yelled, and Dennis shook his head in agreement.

'I can!' the demon persisted. 'He's mine, now! He owes me!'

'What do you mean?' said Dennis.

'You don't rule the surface world. Probably never will. You've cost the lives of a lot of my demons, and you're going to make amends.' Jamzamin's tone was as uncompromising as it was menacing. 'You're coming with me.'

'I'm not going down there!' Dennis countered, with dread and defiance.

The two demons started dragging him again. 'Oh, but you are,' said Hell, as a great hole appeared in the wall. Beyond it was a swirling blackness.

Eydith and Link watched unmoved as the demons dragged the protesting Dennis into the void. It was hard to take pity on such a man.

'I'll be back!' he screamed, as the wall started to rebuild itself behind him. And with great venom he added, 'And why could you never rebuild the bloody holes you made in my place!'

He was almost gone when an anguished voice cried: 'Father!'

Florence reached out towards the hole as the last stone found its place.

Eydith and Link stared incredulously at her and then at each other, and mouthed, '*Father?*'

'Yes,' said Florence, beginning to sob. 'Dennis is my father.'

'But...'

This was going to take them a while to process.

Eydith put a comforting arm around Florence's shoulder, which turned to a full hug. Florence sobbed and shook for a few moments, before dabbing her eyes with her sleeve and taking a few deep breaths.

As bad as Dennis was, Florence felt he didn't deserve the Parallel Dimension. She wanted to believe there was still a spark of goodness within him, somewhere.

Eydith wanted to believe it too, if only for Florence's sake.

The entire battle had lasted all through the night and most of the next day. They'd not notice the time pass, or how exhausted they were. But it caught up with them now, as they hauled themselves up the steps to the university grounds and some welcome fresh air and daylight, hardly believing they'd all survived.

91

With the disappearance of Dennis, the university used its own magic to restore itself to its former dilapidated homeliness. Trinkel called all the wizards to assemble in the Great Hall of Knowledge.

Eydith was standing nervously centre stage, flanked on either side by Link and Florence. Wimlett was in the wings talking to two shadowy figures that only he had noticed.

'It's over, then,' Wimlett remarked.

WHAT? said Death, who'd been absent-mindedly totting up the number of extremely ancient looking wizards in the audience.

YES. I SUPPOSE IT IS.

'I'm not really ready to pass over yet,' said Wimlett. And sighed.

JUST AS WELL, said Death. NAPHRAT GAVE YOU TWENTY YEARS, I MAKE IT YOU'VE STILL GOT A COUPLE LEFT. At this point, He paused for dramatic effect, and then finished, THOUGH YOU DON'T HAVE A LIFE-TIMER ANY MORE, SO WHO'S COUNTING? There seemed to be a twinkle in the Reaper's empty eye sockets.

Naphrat joined the conversation, 'And you can keep your visibility,' said Naphrat. 'Death has made it so you can switch it on and off to suit yourself. You'll work it out.'

'Thank you,' said Wimlett. 'Thanks to both of you.' They nodded graciously. 'Well, if no one needs me I'll be off. It's been a...' He faltered over the word 'pleasure', and almost shook Death's hand in gratitude, but one glance at the skeletal claw hanging from the Reaper's sleeve, and he thought better of it.

THERE IS ONE MORE THING, said Death.

'What's that?'

THEY NEED A NEW ARCHCHANCELLOR. ANY IDEAS?

Wimlett felt honoured that the Grim Reaper had asked his opinion. He thought for a moment, but apart from his own daughter, who was there? The wizards were not ready for her yet. And she was too young. He looked on in admiration at her addressing them all right now, telling them what had happened, and of the staff, and the power she had inherited. *One day*, he thought to himself. *One day*.

'Of course! Trinkel!'

GOOD CHOICE. Agreed Death. TRINKEL IT IS. GO AND MAKE IT HAPPEN.

Wimlett strolled from the wings to the centre of the stage, a place he hadn't occupied for many a long year. A murmur broke out in the audience upon seeing him. He acknowledged them with a slight bow of the head, and whispered in Eydith's ear, 'We need to call Trinkel up here. I want him to be the new Archchancellor.'

'Not Link?' she whispered back.

'Not yet. Too young and inexperienced. He wouldn't command their respect.'

She grudgingly saw the sense of that. She took a deep breath and stepped forward.

'Gentlemen wizards,' she began. This was met with a great deal of coughing and throat clearing.

Then the assembled wizards fell silent, and her voice echoed back at her from the vaulted ceiling of the Great Hall. 'I would like to announce your new Archchancellor – as proposed by, and seconded by my father, your former Archchancellor, Wimlett Tregrus.'

There were mutterings in the audience of 'most irregular,' but far more of 'oh, shut up!'

Link stuck his chest out, expectantly.

'Trinkel!' she called. 'Will you join me up here, please?!'

The embarrassed wizard stood up, and edged his way along the row, treading on some pointy-toed shoes and empty crisp packets as he went. Finally, he reached the stage, shook his old friend's hand to great applause, and began to recite a genuinely, and clearly unrehearsed acceptance speech.

While he was rambling on, outlining his plans to change as little as possible, and do everything pretty much as it had always been done, to many approving nods, Eydith, Wimlett and Link quietly left the stage, but Florence hung back.

'Well, there's nothing else I can do,' said Wimlett, as quietly as he could, in case anyone heard and thought there might be. 'I'll be off.'

He jumped when Death said, VERY WELL, grimly, from among the folds of the drawn curtains, where He lurked with His assistant. SEE YOU AGAIN SOON.

Wimlett didn't like the sound of that. He waited in the shadows while they clattered out to their horses. He even waved them off, and felt pretty stupid afterwards.

Eydith and Link had wandered out to the quadrangle to wait for Florence.

'Did father come out with us?' asked Eydith.

'No, mistress, said Sprag 'He's gone to find your mother, Triona. He communicated his fond farewells. He's not very good at goodbyes. He thought he'd slip away quietly. He'll probably be knocking on Death's door...'

The others went suddenly quiet.

'...in the hope that Naphrat might lend a hand.'

She was pleased that Wimlett was going to see Triona, and hoped it would go well, but sad that she wouldn't see him for a while.

Trinkel was scurrying across the quadrangle with Florence trotting in his wake. 'Wait!' he called. 'You can't leave now!'

Eydith had half a mind to try and outrun him to the gates.

'We haven't repaid you two for what you've done,' said Trinkel, between puffs.

'It isn't necessary,' Eydith assured him. Link agreed.

'There must be something?' insisted the new Archchancellor.

'Well, we don't have anywhere to stay,' said Link. 'Perhaps you could let us have a couple of rooms for the night.'

'Consider it done,' said Trinkel without hesitation. 'Now, will you come back inside? We're having a banquet... in your honour, I might add. You can hardly not be there!'

Link looked at Eydith with pleading eyes. This was a matter of food, after all. Lots of good food!

'Okay, come on. It'll be dark soon. We can leave in the morning.'

'Excellent!' snapped Trinkel. 'Though I should tell you that you are no longer a student here.'

Link was taken aback. That seemed a bit ungrateful.

'We're considering you to have graduated as a wizard in the last day or so,' he said, and cackled in a wizardly way as he put an arm on Link's shoulder.

'And what about me?' said Eydith, seizing the opportunity.

'I'd defy anybody to say *you're* not a wizard. Especially as *you* have the Archchancellor's staff, and not me! What that portends, who knows?! It won't come to me. Most irregular.'

Eydith gave him a resigned look. It wasn't of her doing. Moving on quickly, she said, 'So that big speech about keeping everything as it was…?'

He leaned towards her conspiratorially. 'I've researched the university archives thoroughly in my time here. I happen to have found that that's exactly how everything was once, if you dig back far enough.' He chuckled as he contemplated what he knew. 'Lady wizards, yes. And personally, I believe it's why the original Archchancellors won't let another Archchancellor in the old crypt. They're fed up with them all being men.' He chuckled again, more loudly.

'You could be right,' said Link, beginning to chortle himself.

The four of them filed back inside laughing together.

92

Early next morning, Eydith and Link were to be found standing by the newly repaired gates, waiting for Florence. She was late.

'Incredible to think she knew all along about her and Dennis,' said Link, broaching what hadn't been said between them.

'Though, in a way, I'm glad we never knew,' said Eydith.

'Me too. Absolutely.' Neither wanted to say more. But then...

Link said, 'It just struck me that if you're related to Florence, then you yourself must be related to...'

'I'm trying not to think about it,' she interrupted him. 'Only by marriage.'

They waited for what seemed an age before Florence appeared at one of the doors.

'Come on!' called Link. 'We've been waiting for you!'

'Where are you off to?' asked Florence.

'Link's going back to see Hector, and... where's your bag?' asked Eydith.

'Um... I'm not coming with you,' she replied, quietly, and a little self-consciously. 'Trinkel says I can stay and work here, and... and eventually become a proper wizard.'

'That's wonderful!' enthused Eydith. 'But are you sure that's what you want, Florence?'

'Yes. I've thought about it all night. I will become a wizard and then I will go and search for Dennis.'

'Is that wise?' Link warned.

'No, probably not. But he is my father. Sorry I kept that from you, but...' She didn't know how to finish, and they didn't press her. 'And I can't just leave him wherever he is,' she said, a little lump audible in her throat. 'Will you give my mother this letter, please, when you see her? It explains everything.'

Eydith took it. 'And we'll tell Esme you're safe, when we see her. Won't we, Link.'

'Hmm?' queried Link. His mind was on a much lower plain. Full of sewers. But he'd have to shelve that idea for now. Hector had other plans that would keep him busy for the next few years. And before that, there was Hector and Esme's wedding to attend. And, who knows, perhaps it would be a double wedding?

***

Another grey dawn edged over the ice-capped, green mountains of the Land of Kermells Tong. Just as it had yesterday, and in all probability, would again tomorrow.

END

Cast of Characters

Arfer	A garden gnome with a fishing rod. He lives in Esme's Garden with two others. One with a wheelbarrow and one with a rake
Basalt	A troll who was having a birthday celebration
Billy Turner	One of Dennis's guards
Cho kin	A student wizard from the Eastern Kingdoms on a student loan scheme
Chunk	A troll, and part-time bouncer at the Piggin Wissall tavern
Cut arm	A robber
Death	The Grim Reaper
Dennis	An evil wizard who becomes Archchancellor
Esmerelda Swampshott	A witch – Florence's mother
Eva	Herman the barbarian's youngest daughter
Eydith	A wizardess. Wimlett's daughter
Flint	A Troll in the Magic Finger who plays a sort-of piano
Gilbert the Giant	A barbarian robber.
Hannah	Herman the Barbarian's eldest daughter
Hassan	Dealer in second-hand magic carpets
Hector	Inventor and owner of the railway
Helga	Herman the Barbarian's wife
Hell	The demon of the staff
Herman the Barbarian	A tired barbarian, with a wife and three daughters
Hilda	Herman the barbarian's middle daughter
Jamzamin	The Demon King
Jook	A guard on loan to Dennis
Kragli	A demon
Linkwood (Link)	A wizard and good friend of Eydith.
Lofty	A short villain
Maddlin	A wizard who cannot sleep
Naphrat	Death's helper, and Wimlett's drinking buddy, who gets left in charge of the reaping.

Paske	University librarian
Pelgrum	A rotund wizard
Psoddoph	A guard on loan to Dennis
Red face	A robber
Rumpitt-cum-Slowly	An elderly wizard
Seamor the Stabber	A would-be hero, tired of getting robbed
Sprag	The Staff that belonged to Wimlett and was handed down to Eydith
Stan Twill	One of Dennis's guards
Stubbly	A tall villain
Traveller	Life-Timer salesman
Trinkel	An elderly wizard
Triona	Eydith's mother
Welt	Villain and landlord of the Magic Finger tavern
Wimlett Tregrus	A wizard and Archchancellor who died before his time and became a ghost. Eydith's father.

Milton Keynes UK
Ingram Content Group UK Ltd.
UKHW050731170424
441314UK00013B/310

9 781835 381410